THE BLACK WATERS

(BLACK WATERS SERIES BOOK2)

A E SPENCER

BLISS PUBLISHING

Text copyright ©2022 Shrimant Acharya

Bliss Publishing, the Bliss Publishing logo, are the trademarks of Bliss Publishing Pty Ltd.

ISBN: 978 0 645117134

Editor: Traci Finlay

Cover design by Nisha Dutta

i.nishadutta@gmail.com

Inspired by few women in Lucknow city of India who could defy the
social norms in the
19th Century,
And
Dedicated to all the women who are still rotting in the 21st Century
behind the Iron
curtain of Religious Practices and so-called moral standards of the
societies

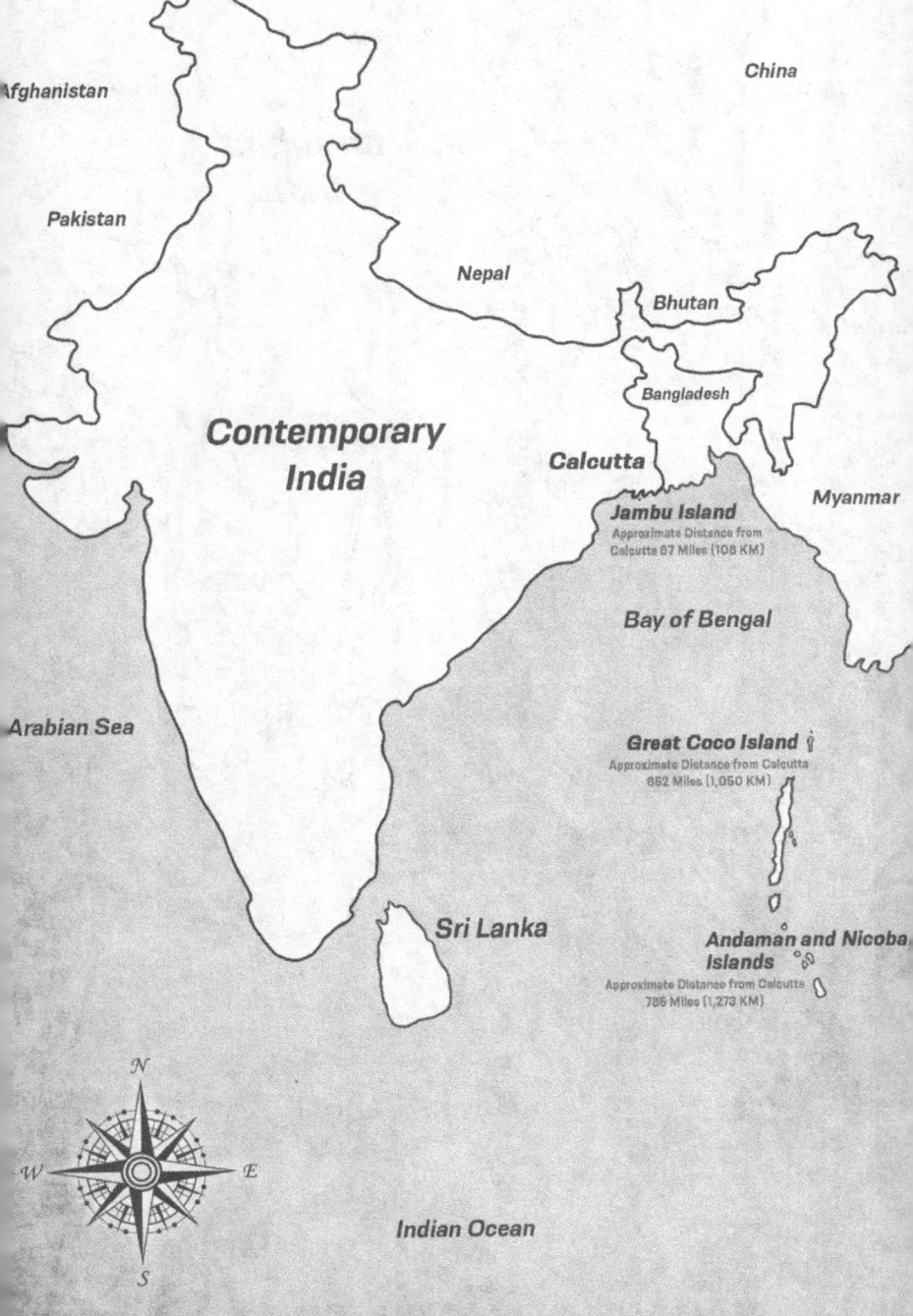

Afghanistan

China

Pakistan

Nepal

Bhutan

Bangladesh

Calcutta

Contemporary India

Jambu Island
Approximate Distance from
Calcutta 67 Miles (108 KM)

Myanmar

Bay of Bengal

Arabian Sea

Great Coco Island
Approximate Distance from Calcutta
652 Miles (1,050 KM)

Sri Lanka

Andaman and Nicobar Islands
Approximate Distance from Calcutta
786 Miles (1,273 KM)

N

W   E

S

Indian Ocean

INDIA INCLUDING ANDAMAN AND COCO ISLANDS

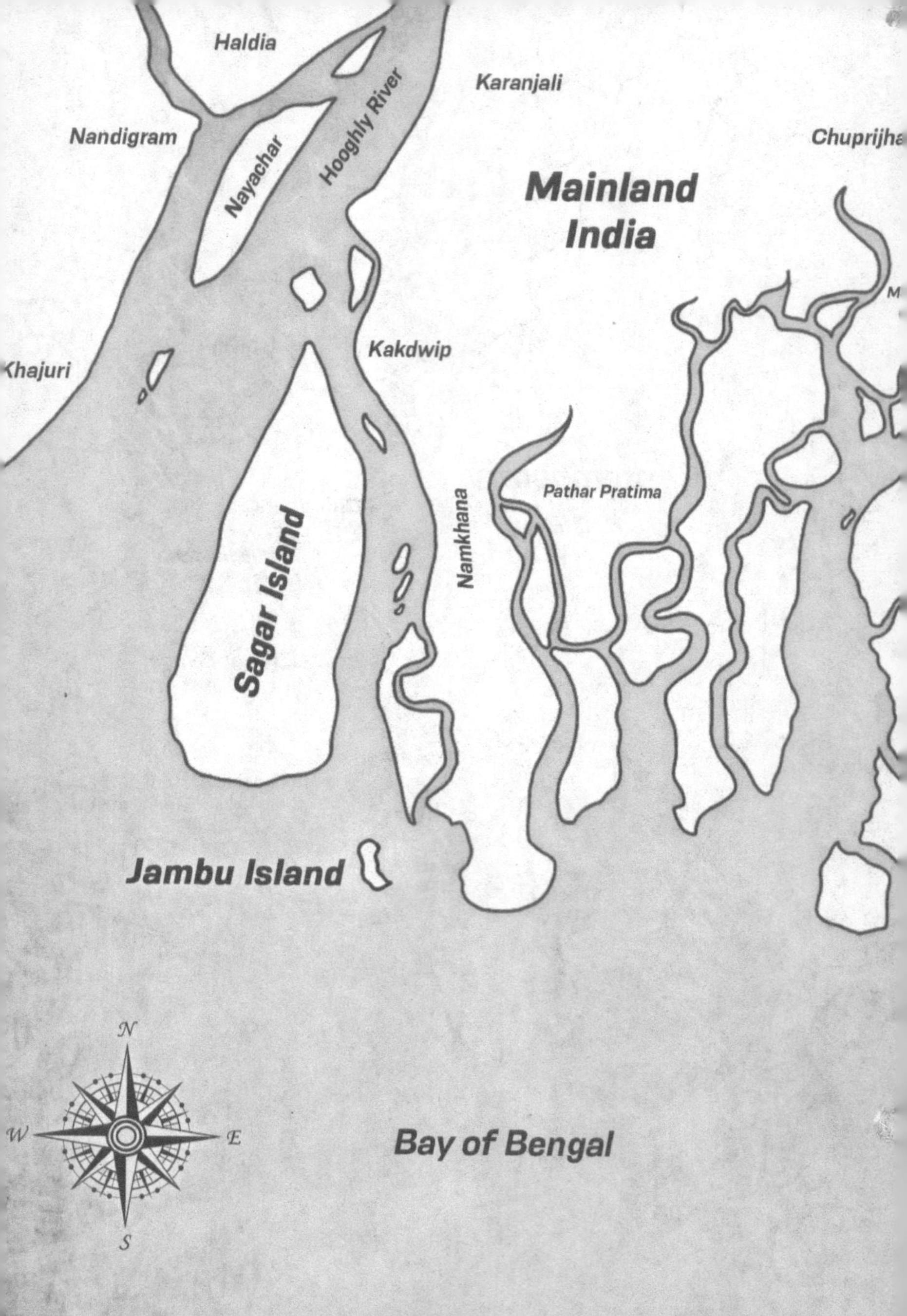

Haldia

Nandigram

Nayachar

Hooghly River

Karanjali

Chuprijha

Mainland
India

Khajuri

Kakdwip

Sagar Island

Namkhana

Pathar Pratima

M

Jambu Island

Bay of Bengal

SAGAR AND JAMBU ISLANDS

📍 Approximate Distance from Calcutta 67 Miles (108 KM)

Table Island

Andaman Sea

*Great
Coco Island*

Bay of Bengal

Jerry Island

N
W · E
S

GREAT COCO ISLANDS

📍 APPROXIMATE DISTANCE FROM CALCUTTA 652 MILES (1,050 KM

ANDAMAN ISLANDS

Coco Channel

Bay of Bengal

Land Fall Island   East Island

Peacock Island

North Andaman

Smith Island

North Reed Island

South Island

Mayabunder

Middle Andaman

Rangat

North Passage

Baratang Island

Havelock Island

South Andaman

Neil Island

Red Skin Island

Ross Island

North Sentinel Island

Port Blair

Rutland Island

Andaman Sea

North Cinque Island

South Cinque Island

Passage Island

The Sisters Island

South Sentinel Island

North Brother Island

South Brother Island

Little Andaman

Ten Degree Channel

N / W / E / S

📍 APPROXIMATE DISTANCE FROM CALCUTTA 785 MILES (1,273 KM)

CHAPTER ONE
AMELIA, 15 AUGUST 1862, 3 AM.
MONSOON RAIN DRIZZLING
CHOWRINGHEE AREA, CALCUTTA

Kala Pani, hundreds of miles from Calcutta, lies somewhere in the Indian Ocean—an island from where no one has ever returned. This is what everyone in India believes. At least, almost everyone I have met since 1857, when Rupen Naik got *life in prison* and was sent away on a ship, along with thousands of freedom fighters who fought against the British government of India.

Except for just two women—Sehnaz and me.

We are not the bravest women on the planet. Even now, I fear entering a dark room at night.

Sehnaz keeps her right arm on my shoulder and sits closer to me as I open the window of the horse cart. Icy winds along with drops of rain gush inside. I feel her heartbeat against my shoulders and mine against my ribs. Harry is sitting in front of me. I meet his gaze with an *I'm all right* smile. We are hoping the steady rhythm of the horses' hooves are covering up my and Sehnaz's collective heartbeats until we arrive at the Hooghly Port of Calcutta and board the ship.

"Andaman Islands, eight hundred miles away," Harry announces, "and you're just two women on a mission."

Oh, my! Can Harry still read my heartbeat even after five years? He was my fiancé then. Our wedding was only minutes away. It still hurts to think how he backed out in the last moment. Was it because I had police records of travelling with Sehnaz, the woman whom the British were looking for everywhere for that million-pound map?

Harry continues. "Amelia, you have Sehnaz with you, who stole the map of The Residency and escaped from Lucknow. The siege of The

Residency after that has made history. A woman's courage could shake the mighty British army."

Sehnaz giggles as I try to respond with another smile. But jealousy pinches me. What happened to my childhood dream in London—of becoming an enlightened woman and saving unfortunate women in India?

I should be proud of this woman, my closest friend. This is the woman who had saved me from the death trap my husband, Brigadier Colin, had laid. How can I forget Sehnaz's wit not only defeated his plans, but also forced the man to jump from the hills and take his own life?

I'm no longer that London girl seeking to be independent like men.

I peek out the window. The slow drizzle can't block the glow from the gas streetlights. I feel like we are driving on a street in London at night. Wide road, large mansions on both sides. But this is not London. This is the Chowringhee area of Calcutta. The British government has tried to replicate this like London. Only this locality, though—where the English have all their offices, where their families live. Apart from here, we have come almost ten plus miles across dirty roads with potholes and poverty screaming through the walls of the workers' hutments from both sides of the road.

A shrill scream slices through the calm night of Calcutta. Our cart surpasses a woman running, and then the cart comes to a complete halt.

I yank the door open and jump out to face the woman. Her fearful gaze begs me for help, and her dark skin competes with the darkness of the night. She is holding a tiny cloth against her groin, and bare breasts bounce up and down with her breathless ribs.

I scramble for something to cover her up; there're two men with us: Harry and the coachman.

The twenty-something-year-old woman is mumbling, folding her hands and tears running down her cheeks. I can't understand her a bit.

Sehnaz bursts from the cart with her scarf and covers the girl's bare breasts. She cradles her arm and guides her inside the cart. Harry, who had also got out of the cart, moves to sit by my side—Sehnaz and the girl in front of me. I twist the lantern for better flame, as if her dark skin would be lighter and I could find out more about her. She is sweating, unknown fear shimmering in her innocent eyes.

"She can't speak. I mean, we can't understand her language." I wish I could tell her she is safe with us.

"She looks like a negro," Harry says.

"Ne... Neg... Negro." This is the only word from the girl's mouth I understand.

Harry pokes his head out the window. "We will be late reaching the Hooghly Port. Don't stop again unless I ask you," he commands the coachman.

For a few moments, I had forgotten that we would board a ship to Andaman, and the delay means the ship could leave without us.

"This might be a slave girl," Harry says.

"Slave? Is it legal in India?"

"No, the British government has banned it both in England and here. But some sailors lead a double life."

I shoot a blank gaze at him.

"I know these sailors, as I have ships of my own. Many British sailors, while at sea, get involved in piracy or help the pirates in trading their loot. For quick bucks to be extra-rich. Some of them buy young African girls kidnapped from their land and use them as sex slaves. This girl might have been one of them. Escaped from her captor."

"Sex slave? What happens when the girls become pregnant?" My heart beats against my ribs.

"The captors kill and throw them into the water. I've seen pregnant dead negro women in Hooghly River, floating. The stories about the illegal slave trade circulate as soon as people see such bodies. This is the first time I saw a slave woman, alive."

This girl sitting in front of me might also meet the same fate, if not saved. Another urgency prickles through my blood.

I meet Harry's gaze. "This reminds me of the night of the twenty-sixth of May, 1857. I was fleeing my husband's home, The Residency in Lucknow, when the Sepoy Mutiny was burning the entire country."

"You remember the exact date?"

Sehnaz says, "Amelia writes everything in her diary."

"I know," Harry says.

"And Sehnaz has even given a name to my diary. The Pink Mutiny."

"Your diary has a name? You should publish it as a book."

"Are you sure?" I chuckle. "And the British government will throw me into the prison. For life. It has everything that could implicate Sehnaz and me for the war crime. So-called."

"It should come as a book decades after when we are there—" Sehnaz points at the sky— "in the heaven."

"Is it so sensitive?" Harry leans forward.

"Yes. It also includes everything from my childhood in London, my arrival in Lucknow through Calcutta, my days with Sehnaz when she was on the run with secret information of the British, and the day our wedding failed. Everything."

Harry's face falls. "I'm sorry. Apologies again."

I shouldn't have mentioned the wedding.

"No, Harry. I've forgiven you long ago. You're my friend. You're the only man I trust, after Sehnaz."

"Thanks." Harry nods then clears his throat. "You were saying how you fled that night."

"Yes. On the way, I saw a woman walking alone, holding a box on her head and a lantern in her hand. She had covered herself from head to toe in a burqa, like me. My soul said this was wrong. A woman walking alone at night didn't seem right to me. I gave her a lift, as she was going in the same direction as me."

Harry holds his gaze on me.

I glance at Sehnaz and continue. "And when I said I'm Mrs. Amelia Lawrence, the woman was about to jump from the cart and run away. I had to force her back. She was pleading, 'I haven't seen Rupen in ages.' I lied to her and said, 'I'm not the wife of Brigadier Colin Lawrence.' Can you believe this is that woman who is sitting with us?"

"Sehnaz?" Harry chuckles.

"Yes. And next morning I discovered she had the secret map that could make the British pack their baggage and leave India forever."

"You said nothing?"

"No. I was fleeing for my life, and nothing was more important to me. Next morning, the woman whom I had thought to be helpless only a night ago, took me with her boat in the river Gomti."

"Circumstances forced both of us to flee." Sehnaz giggles.

We hear the galloping sound of horses behind us. Harry looks through the side window. "Two men with guns."

My heart stops.

Sehnaz pulls a burqa from her bag and slips it over the girl's head, signalling her to remain silent. Then she lowers the lantern flame to a minimum.

The men come near our cart and ask the coachman to stop.

The cart screeches to a halt.

One of them brings the horse near and bends to bring his face to the window. An Indian soldier.

"*Kya hai?* What is the matter?" I say in broken Hindi and a perfect British accent. I know the man was not expecting a white woman travelling in the wee hours. Sehnaz has covered her head, as well. Only two faces can they see inside the cart—Harry's and mine, both white.

The man salutes me. "Sorry, memsahib. We were looking for a black woman. Have you seen any on the road? Running?"

My blood boils. "Was the woman a thief? Stole something?"

"No, memsahib. She... I mean... I..."

"Coachman, we're running late. Move on. Now." I jerk the window curtain closed on his face as the coachman gets the horses moving again.

"You managed so well, Amelia. This's already the first victory, and we just started for Andaman. A good omen," Sehnaz says.

A satisfactory feeling washes through me. I twist the lantern's knob for a better glow.

Sehnaz pulls the burqa from the girl's head and holds her hand. "Everything is all right now. You're safe. Don't worry."

Does a friendly touch communicate better than language? I want to say, *She didn't understand what you said.* But the girl twists her head to face Sehnaz and folds her hands. Her eyes are glinting with gratitude.

The cart moves on. We have lost little time and should be in the port well before the ship departs for Andaman. I open the window curtain again and peek outside. The gas streetlamps are now much brighter, as the rain has stopped.

A silence swells inside the cab. I twist toward Harry. He has fixed his gaze on the slave girl. An unknown tension has darkened his face.

"She is now safe, Harry."

"She is not. Only for some time. I am thinking I will hide her in my other house outside Calcutta."

"No, Mr. Harry," Sehnaz says. "One black woman among thousands of local Indians can never remain a secret. You can't stich the mouths of your servants and guards."

"I'm well known among the British authorities. I wouldn't have any issue because of this girl. But if people see her in the port, she will be a problem. Her captors must be some sailors who are leading the double life I was talking about. Sailor when they are in the harbor, and pirate when they're in the ocean. No government rules over the ocean. They're the rulers the moment their ships leave the port."

"I know you're influential. Who else other than you could have helped us in going to Andaman as schoolteachers? And you also convinced them I am a single woman and will have enough time to spread Christian values and education among the tribal people in Andaman. What a story, Harry!"

"That's Sehnaz's idea." Harry chuckles.

"Sehnaz, you, too!"

Sehnaz smiles at her praise. "We'll cover her in a burqa and take her with us as our maid. No one in the port will find out she is a negro girl. The tribal people of Andaman must be dark-skinned, too. Amelia will educate them and this girl together as part of their tribe."

Harry agrees. I realize we have just made an important decision about the girl's life without even consulting or communicating with her. Is this the life of a slave?

The girl lifts her veil and glances around. A childish innocence radiates from her eyes. I'm sure she is feeling safe with us.

"How much more time before we will be in the port?" I ask.

Before Harry can reply, the sound of another horse running behind us frightens me. *Oh, no. Not again!*

"Sahib, sahib. Please stop. Sahib, can you hear me?"

Sehnaz scrambles to put the burqas back on.

Harry asks the coachman to stop the cab. A man approaches and shows his face through the window. "Sorry, sahib. I was late. But I have brought this."

"I thought you couldn't arrange," Harry says excitedly.

"No, sahib, it took some time, but have I ever failed you? I went to your *haveli* and found you left for the Hooghly Port. Here is your item, sahib." The man gives a small box wrapped in paper through the window. "And sahib, the money..."

"We'll discuss the money tomorrow, not now."

10

"Right, sahib. Thank you." The man salutes Harry and goes back.

Harry gives the box to me.

I eye the tiny box and rotate it in my hand. *Is this a gift?* "What is this?"

"Open."

I remove the paper from the box.

The cab begins rolling, and Harry shouts, "Coachman, please stop."

I look at Harry. Why did he stop the coach?

A confident smile brightens his face. "We're almost near the port. So, don't worry. Please open the box."

I remove the item wrapped in white papers.

"A pistol?"

Sehnaz puts her finger on her lips. The slave girl's eyes widen, and she shifts closer to Sehnaz.

I whisper, "Harry, you are gifting me a pistol? Will I fight the English soldiers in Andaman and free Rupen? Do you think that's possible? Isn't it a wishful thought?" A shiver chases down my arms.

"You can't fight hundreds of soldiers there. But your and Sehnaz's brain will. This is for self-defence. Emergency only. Sehnaz has learnt how to handle it. She will teach you. And yes, the bottom part of the box has cartridges."

I place the pistol in its box and hand it to Sehnaz, who slips it inside the bag.

"Thanks, Mr. Harry." An appreciative smile curls on Sehnaz's lips.

I should've said *thank you* instead.

"Will you command the coachman now?" I ask.

"I've something else to say." Harry's eyebrows dip. "The ship you both will board is also carrying prisoners. Prisoners for *Kala Pani*, the Black Waters prison in Andaman."

Sehnaz and I exchange a look. "What, prisoners again? After the Sepoy Mutiny has been over for five years? The British have already sent those whom they thought were fighting against them. They must be ordinary criminals. Thieves and robbers."

"The British are in India for trade. They will not waste money on the criminals whom they can punish here. In fact, the British were consolidating the rule for the last five years after taking the reins over from the East India Company in 1857. Now they want to set the precedent."

I glace at him in desperation. Why is Harry saying all this when we're near the port and should board in less than an hour?

"I mean," Harry says again, "they're looking for old records and nabbing more and more people who had either betrayed them and joined the rebellion or those who have challenged the empire's might by any means."

"How is that going to affect us, Mr. Harry?" Sweat breaks out over Sehnaz's forehead.

"I have trusted men working in Calcutta cantonment. They are looking for a woman's name on the list. Even though only men can commit war crimes."

My hands begin shaking. "Which woman, Harry?"

He rubs his face and breathes deeply. "Sehnaz was a prime suspect, so be cautious."

I sense Sehnaz stiffen across from me. "You are joking with us, Harry."

"No, I'm not. The man never came back to me, and so I think Sehnaz's name is clear. So far, I've not heard of any woman going to Andaman as a prisoner. However, I have listed her name as Sez. In case..."

"And you're telling us now. I have been addressing her as Sehnaz." I clench my jaw but then control my anger. Harry doesn't owe us anything, and he's doing what he thinks is right, even though this information has just added an entirely new and terrifying obstacle in our attempt to go save Rupen.

"Sorry, I was waiting for the man to come back with some good news. I'm assuming there's no problem. But again, I am thinking. Should we wait for the next ship to go? It may be a matter of a month or two only. But we can be sure of Sehnaz's safety."

Fire glints in Sehnaz's eyes. "It's not that we will arrive in Andaman and Rupen will be a free bird. It might take months and even a year. You said prisoners are now living in open settlements as there's no real prison. And authorities are building a strong fort-like prison in Port Blair. Once Rupen is inside that prison building, his chances of getting out are zero. We have only few months. And I doubt the empire will run after an ex-courtesan for taking revenge."

"I think you are right. But just to be safe, remember, you are not Sehnaz." Harry says.

He orders the coachman to start the cab.

Within no time, we are in the port. The last time I saw Hooghly Port was when I arrived here in 1856 to marry Colin. Nothing has changed—one office building and several godowns. Three ships are resting in the river. But when a man standing on the deck shouts, "Remove the anchor!" we realize, to our horror, the ship is about to leave. Sehnaz is quick to cover the slave girl with the burqa, and we scramble out of the cab.

Harry calls out to two coolies, and they carry our suitcases to the ship.

"Bye, Harry. Thank you." I give him a quick hug.

"Once my ship receives orders to carry goods to Andaman, I will send a letter to you. Take care, Amelia. And Sez—you, too."

The moment we three are onboard, the ship starts. We stare at Harry's cab from the deck. But the sudden roar of people from the other side of the ship breaks the silence of the night. Everyone is running to the rear of the ship. The slogan, *Bharat Mata ki Jai—*Hail with Mother India," fills the air. We can't see the people who are chanting the slogan.

"I'm sure the patriots are travelling with us for the ultimate sacrifice in Andaman," Sehnaz says.

Harry was right. This ship is carrying war prisoners to Andaman prison.

My heart fills with sadness. I glance at Sehnaz, and her eyes are also pooling. "Cool down, Sehnaz—sorry, Sez. This time shall pass. The prisoners will one day get justice." I must remember to address her, Sez. She might escape life in the prison with this new identity. Harry is clever and has made a right decision to note her name as Sez.

"Allah is with me." Sehnaz gestures at the sky with her both her palms upwards.

I look away from Sehnaz and begin inspecting our surroundings. This must be the largest ship in the port. The steam from its boiler is touching the clouds. We have just begun looking for someone who could guide us to our cabin when a man comes to greet us. An Indian guard. "Are you Amelia memsahib?"

"Yes, I am."

"Sorry, memsahib, I am late."

"Late?"

He takes out a folded paper from his pocket. "A sahib gave this in the port. A letter for you."

The man runs toward the rear of the ship, from where the slogans are still being chanted.

Sehnaz's eyes go wide. "What's in the letter?"

Who else other than Harry knows we are sailing to Andaman? Why has he sent this to us? Is there something he couldn't have told us when he was with us a few minutes ago? I look at the port, which will vanish from our sight soon, and try to find his cab.

"Hurry Amelia, please see what he has written." Sehnaz's anxious voice chases me.

I open the letter. Harry had written in haste, and it's difficult to read in the darkness. We both move to a lamppost where the slave girl still stands, covered in a burqa.

Get off ship. Sehnaz blacklisted. Authorities know. Talk later.

Sehnaz runs to the side of the ship where we had come inside using the rope ladder. I follow her. As if we both would jump out and flee.

"The ship has already left the shore! There is no way we can get off now, unless we both jump into the water and swim back," Sehnaz says.

I look around. Everyone on the ship is at the rear end, either watching or trying to get control of the chaos.

I tuck the paper inside my bag. "How do authorities know you are in this ship? If they find out eventually, letter with arrest warrant might come in another ship , which might leave Hooghly Port after a month or two. You are safe until then. We have time to think," I say urgently, gazing toward the retreating land and planning our escape.

"Time to think? Look there," Sehnaz whispers.

A man is running along the shore and shouting, "Please stop the ship! Urgent message! Please stop the ship."

Sehnaz's time is over. And perhaps mine, too, as her aide. If we can hear what the men on the shore are shouting, others on the ship can hear, too.

Sehnaz squats down and opens the bag. The slave girl lifts her veil but drops it after a moment.

"Sez, what're you doing?"

"All others on the ship are with the prisoners now. If one of them comes here and hears this man, then I'm finished."

Before I can reply, Sehnaz gets up, holding the pistol.

"Sez, stop," I scream in a low voice. My heart is in my mouth now. The man is still running along the jetty, waving a paper. Is Sehnaz sure this is her arrest warrant?

Sehnaz is aiming at him. Has she gone mad? Another crime in her name? Anticipation of what might come blurs my vision. The pistol roars to life.

Her target is accurate. The man has succumbed to her bullet, lying in a red puddle. My blood freezes. Sehnaz simply stares at him. The slave girl lifts her veil in horror.

"What did you do, Sez? You killed..."

Sehnaz's angry glance seals my mouth. She throws the pistol in the bag. "Let's go inside. We are two innocent women—a teacher and her assistant, and our maid. We are looking for our cabin. And remember, women do not know how to fire a shot."

CHAPTER TWO

AMELIA, 15 AUGUST 1862, EVENING. MONSOON RAIN DRIZZLING HOOGHLY RIVER

For the first time, I notice tears in Sehnaz's eyes.

My heart sinks. "What happened, Sez? Why are you sobbing?" Sehnaz pulls the blanket off the bed and wraps it around herself.

I gaze at her, wondering if we could start a conversation to lighten her mood. But she buries her head between her knees.

Messy, dark clouds and drizzles of rain scorn at me through the glassed window of the tiny cabin we have been allotted in the ship. Energy drains from my body as I stare at the chipped wooden floor. "Sez, are you all right?" I touch her knees and ask again.

The slave girl silently watches both of us, slouching on the floor in the corner next to a chair and a dresser. She has removed the burqa from her face. My gaze goes to the heavy rain, which starts crashing against the glass window, and the ship shakes.

Sehnaz lifts her face and asks, "Where were you?"

"You were sleeping. I went to the deck, wondering when the ship will leave the Hooghly River and enter the Bay of Bengal. I came back when the rain started. So depressing everywhere, Sez. Let the rain stop, and we both will go to the deck. You will feel better. And don't worry." I bring my voice down to a whisper. "No one has doubted you. You're safe, and we will find a way to face this. We still have time, Sez."

"I'm not worried about my safety, Amelia." Sez raises her head and gazes into my eyes. "But what I saw on the other side of the ship shattered my resolve."

"You have been to the rear of the ship? When?"

16

"When you went out. I woke up when you closed the door and saw you sneaking out. You know I can't confine myself to a small room the whole day. I also went out, but in the other direction. After meeting some Indian guards there, I thought to gather some information."

"Information? Got something?"

"A load of it. So much I can't digest. The guards are treating the prisoners like animals and have no compassion. Some were hanging upside down with their legs tied, and some are screaming after getting lashes."

"You shouldn't have gone there. Not a place for us women. We can't tolerate such cruel scenes."

Sehnaz stares into my eyes. She is the woman who dared to shoot and kill a man this morning. Didn't she manage the spy network for Awadh kingdom? How can she cry like an ordinary woman?

"I saw... I..." Sehnaz says through a tight throat, "I saw Sheru, legs tied to a beam and foam coming out of his mouth."

I gasp. Sheru is such an energetic man. After leaving the British army, he had worked only as a guard for Sehnaz and sailed the boat from Lucknow to Varanasi. "What might have been the crime of Sheru?"

Sehnaz looks around and mutters, "You remember when we started sailing from Lucknow on the Gomti River? And the British ferry attacked us to get the stolen map from me?"

"Yes. How can I forget how that bastard English officer tore your blouse and grabbed your breasts? In front of his mates in the English boat? But the Indian soldiers came in time and ambushed all the British soldiers. So?"

"That's not all. Sheru twisted the head of the officer who had taken me hostage and killed him."

"I understand, Sez, but when each soldier in the scene died, who could've complained against Sheru?"

"Perhaps one of the Indian soldiers. After the war, the British were using some willing Indian soldiers as witnesses against their own, promising them amnesty."

Royal witness! Amnesty!

Colin's remarks drum inside my brain. *We, the British, have planted hundreds of thousands of moles among the stupid Indians. It is so easy to buy these poor natives. Throw a piece of stale bread at them, they will start licking your feet. Bloody dogs.*

Colin, my so-called husband Brigadier Colin, is long-since dead. But his words are true even now.

"That means someone might've testified against you. And you could've faced arrest had we not left Sultanpur to come to Andaman."

Sehnaz considers my sentence in silence. "I think you're right. I got some time because we came to Calcutta and devised the Andaman plan. God is with us, Amelia. We can win."

"No, we shall win, Sehnaz—sorry, Sez. We shall. We must."

She gets up. "Let's go outside. I am almost suffocating inside this room. Who else is living in the other cabins?"

"We've got one of the two cabins on the top floor, and Mrs. Morticia Hunt is our neighbour. She is the captain's wife. I had a bit of interaction with her. Not much. Maybe she was also sleeping the whole day like us. Everyone was awake last night, as the ship left early this morning." I pause to gaze out the window. "Rain is still pelting the windows. We can't go to the deck."

Sehnaz gets up. "Let's go downstairs. The kitchen must be there."

I'm glad to see the fearless Sehnaz again. "I also think so. I've seen an Indian woman walking along with Morticia. Might be a maid."

Sehnaz gestures for the slave girl to get up. "Let's give her a name. We can't address her as slave girl and expose her."

The girl aims her eyes at Sehnaz and then at me. Her lips wobble, but she stands and covers her face with the burqa. I'm sure she understands we are going out of the cabin.

"Name? But she might have some name already."

"But how do we know? She can't communicate. How is the name *Sadhna*? Means 'spiritual exercise to progress in life.' This girl will have to make lots of effort to become an ordinary woman, like others."

I smile with approval. "But she shouldn't come outside with us. How can we show we have a negro girl?"

"Why worry? The burqa is masking her from head to toe, and I have kept her hands outside the sleeves and inside the black robe, so that she can't stick them out and show her black arms."

Sehnaz knows the best way to move around with a concealed identity. Didn't she stay in the Hindu temple in Varanasi as Sheru's wife, identifying herself as Sanju? No Hindu priest even knew she was a Muslim. British have informers everywhere, and she has learnt how to evade them.

We step out of the cabin, with Sadhna covered in the black robe. The cabin to our right, the only other one on this floor, is locked. Morticia must be out. Stairs in front of our room lead us down to a hall. My attention goes to a room at the far end of it, including a hearth with a large vessel simmering above it.

Stifling her laughter, Sehnaz pinches my hand. "See that woman?" she whispers into my ear. "So tall, all muscles. Looks like a man wearing a dress."

"Stop giggling, Sez. You will spoil everything. She is Mrs. Morticia Hunt, I told you."

Morticia leaves the room and exits the hall without noticing us. Perhaps heading downstairs to the other floors beneath.

"Where's Sadhna?" Sehnaz asks.

We both turn around. She is standing on the first step of the timber stairs, other foot on the next, displaying her black ankle. Sehnaz trudges toward her and tugs her back. "This girl understands nothing."

"How will she, Sez? She knows neither English nor Hindi. Let's hold her hand when we're outside our cabin." With face covered and no words from her mouth, she is like a walking statue. We take turns holding her hand, and she moves along with us. Poor girl. Will she ever see what freedom means?

When we're about to walk inside the kitchen, Morticia comes back to the hall. "Hello, Amelia. Taking a round in our kitchen?"

I smile back.

"And who's this woman with you?"

"This is Se... Sez. My friend."

"Friend? Indian friend of a white lady? Strange. I thought she is your maid." Morticia throws a dirty glance at Sehnaz as if she is a zoo animal. *Even animals have feelings!*

"She used to help me in the school, teaching and managing small kids." I'm trying to give her a better impression of Sehnaz. How can I tolerate the insults of the woman who has worked in a senior rank of a kingdom, challenging so many men?

"Oh, really! And this one?" She looks at the slave girl.

"Our maid." Sehnaz answers.

Morticia nods curtly and goes inside the kitchen to instruct the cook.

The girl stands closer to me, like a child about to cling to her mother.

Within seconds Morticia is back with us. "You said Sez is your friend. What type of friend is she?"

I don't understand, but Sehnaz winks. "That type of friend." She lets out a mischievous smile.

Morticia also grins.

"You ladies must be bored," Morticia says. "There's nothing for women to do on a ship. Only men, and the maids are busy all the time. Why don't you join a ladies' party in the next room?"

"Ladies' party? When?" I ask.

"Now. Don't worry. You don't have to wear your best clothes here. This's informal, just to kill spare time. Come on. Follow me."

We follow Morticia. But where's Sadhna? I don't recollect when I let go of her hand. I look around. She has sneaked out through the door and is standing near the siderail. Is this girl going to jump into the sea? I drag her with me and follow Morticia to the adjacent room. This is another hall, almost empty-only one chair sitting on one side, and a bench on the other.

Morticia asks us to take seats and goes away. I mutter to Sehnaz, "What's *that type of friend,*' Sez?"

"I am sure that woman is homosexual or bisexual. She thinks we are also like her," Sehnaz mutters back. "Why is this girl always sneaking away from us?"

"Maybe she is not used to the burqa," I reply, "but both times she has tried to go away has been when *he* is talking to us."

"Who is *he?*"

"*She* is the new *he,*" I snicker, "and this girl must be thinking she is a man. Her voice is also rough, man-like. How do I convince her there'll be no men in this gathering? How do I communicate with her? She doesn't even know we have given her a new name."

We pull a wooden bench to a corner and sit together, keeping Sadhna between us—as if a mass gathering is going to happen and we need to take our seats. I notice there are three other women present, all Morticia's maids.

Morticia comes back and sits on a large chair. The three Indian maids come with wine bottles and glasses. My eyes brighten. *Oh, God, wine after so many days?* I glance at Sehnaz on my side. She also looks impressed. Even still, we are both full of tension. But then I remember Mata Radhe's teachings (when I was in the shakti ashram in 1857 for a month). She always said, *'Enjoy the present moment and don't worry about the future.'* Can Sehnaz and I both enjoy our first evening on the ship to Andaman?

Morticia's maid sets a stool in front of us and pours wine into glasses.

"No wine for this girl," Sehnaz says, gesturing at Sadhna.

My gaze lingers on Morticia. She is about six feet tall, and almost *chicken-breasted.* Without her long hair and female clothing, she would look like a man. So far, I haven't seen her husband, Captain Rave Hunt. Which man would marry such a woman?

"People don't enjoy working in Andaman Islands," Morticia says, "but you both chose the island for educating the children and also educating the tribals there. So, this evening is in your name, Amelia and Sez. Cheers." She lifts the wine glass.

"Cheers." I lift my glass with my left hand and feel a vibration. Seated closer to Sadhna, I feel she is shivering. The burqa is covering her from head to toe, and I can't see her face. Is she sick?

"Where's Malti?" Morticia asks one of the two maids.

"Memsahib, dressing up, next room. Come, now."

"You will see a fine dancer here," Morticia says with a loud, unwomanly laugh.

"If she knows I was a courtesan, and you were also a temporary courtesan for three months, she might ask us to dance, as well." Sehnaz whispers and lets out a suppressed giggle.

"Sez, don't utter that word here, please. We both are teachers, nothing else."

"Right. But what happened to this girl? Why is she shivering?"

A woman enters, wearing a colourful saree and bell-studded anklets. She must be Malti. I look around for the others, but she seems to be alone. When I was dancing in the *kotha* in Sultanpur, there would always be a singer and at least two men who would play instruments. How can there be a dance without a song?

"Veena, you sing," Morticia commands the other maid who is serving wine.

"But memsahib, I ... Me..."

"What, I? What, me? You said you can sing, and I gave you a job in the ship."

"Memsahib."

"No more memsahib. Understand? If you don't sing, I will make you stay on the ship naked, showing your tiny bubbies–to all the men." Morticia pinches Veena's breast.

Veena steps back a little and pulls the loose end of the saree to cover her chest. She moves her eyes around the room. "Song, not good, memsahib. But sing. Yes."

I swallow. This shy woman is struggling to preserve her honour.

"Good girl."

Veena clears her throat and starts singing, standing like a student punished by the teacher.

"Sounds like she is reciting from a poetry book," Sehnaz whispers to me and snickers.

I don't return the giggle; I don't wish to discourage this woman for her poor voice. She is a maid, anyway, and forced to sing. Instead, I clap. "Wonderful voice, Veena."

She stops and looks at me, then clearing her throat, she sings again.

Malti takes her first step. Looks like she is not a total novice. She is not that beautiful; otherwise, she could've joined a *kotha* as a courtesan.

"The dance and the song are not syncing." Sehnaz pinches my shoulder.

"That's okay. Enjoy your drink."

I glance at Sadhna. She is sitting still inside the black robes, and I can't see her reaction.

Every now and then, Malti adjusts her *pallu* on her chest. Morticia stops her after the fourth or fifth time. "Why are you covering up? This's a women-only audience. Remove your saree and dance."

"Remove?" Malti stares at her and wraps her arms around her chest.

"Am I killing you? Just remove it. The petticoat and the blouse are enough. Or do you want me to remove your blouse, too?"

Malti stands still as Morticia takes the saree from her torso and deposits it on a stool at her side. Her hands go automatically to cover her bulging chest, but she notices Morticia's angry stare, and she removes them.

"Now better. Start again."

Malti's steps become more and more awkward—she is quite conscious of her swinging bubbies.

"She should have worn a breastband underneath the blouse," I comment to Sehnaz. I recollect the way I had gotten dance training in Sultanpur. Bibi Khanum had always treated me well. No abuse, like what I am witnessing now.

"Look at Morticia's gaze. Dance steps are not syncing with the song, but her gaze is perfectly following each sway of Malti's breasts!"

"Ripe fruits."

"No, riper." Sehnaz laughs.

Malti stills and adjusts her breasts in the blouse when one unhooked button releases her left breast outside her top.

Morticia licks her lips. "Nice *diddies,* Malti. Why keep them inside?" Suddenly, she moves her gaze away from Malti's chest to Sadhna. "Why is this woman covering her head? Doesn't she know we are only women here?"

Before either Sehnaz or I can react, Morticia lurches from her seat and removes Sadhna's burqa with a jerk. Sadhna jumps with a squeal, as if a snake has bitten her. Morticia grabs Sadhna's arms.

"Where have you been, you whore? I told you not to step away from the ship. Do you know how much I paid to buy you? You couldn't earn that money in a hundred years." Morticia drags her and makes her stand before her.

Sehnaz and I get up. An unknown fear flashes through my veins as I stand closer to Sehnaz, who is shivering.

"Well done, ladies." Morticia hurls the words at us. "I'm relieved. She shouldn't have gone out. Never to a city in India. From now on, she'll spend her entire life inside this ship."

Sadhna is weeping and babbling, flailing around like a goat facing a butcher. But none of us can understand a single word from her.

"You've made a mistake, girl. No, no. A blunder. You disobeyed my command and fled. You deserve punishment. But today, we ladies are celebrating. So, your punishment will be mild. Happy?"

Sehnaz and I slump on the bench again and touch each other's hands, relieved that Morticia wouldn't punish Sadhna harshly.

"Who gave you this dress?"

Sadhna is wearing a frock of mine. I utter nothing.

Malti has stopped her dance and moved close to Veena, both looking at each other with confused smiles curling their lips. They are working with Morticia. Have they not seen this negro girl before?

"Don't say her name is Sadhna," Sehnaz mutters to me. "She might've a proper name."

"Do slaves have names?"

Morticia is wiping Sadhna's tears and ruffling her hair. Thank God, the girl is safe.

But then Morticia's fingers crawl to Sadhna's back. Is she unhooking her frock?

"You have nice little bubbies, girl." Her fingers are feeling every inch of Sadhna's tiny breasts while the other arm is busy unhooking her frock. Sadhna tries to hold her frock, but Morticia removes it from her body. The girl has no undergarment. She is now standing completely naked in the room.

"I should've given her a breastband," I whisper to Sehnaz.

"As if she doesn't know how to remove that."

"Thank God, there are no men in the room."

"There's one, grabbing her bubbies."

Morticia must have forgotten she is sitting with so many other women. Both Malti and Veena are huddling together as if their turn might be the next. Morticia is squeezing Sadhna's nipples with one hand and massaging her buttock with another. Shock slams into Sehnaz and me.

Morticia looks at Sehnaz. "Thanks again. I will share the stuff with you. Don't worry."

She stands, indicating the party is over. "You all can go to the dining room and have your dinner." Then she grabs Sadhna's arm and drags her out.

Before she exits, I pick up the frock and say, "Men will stare at her when she leaves this room. Let her wear this. This is mine, I had lent it to her."

"Not required. All the men here aren't with any females, and they're all starving. Let them at least satisfy their hungry eyes. She will not do the same blunder again. This is her punishment."

Flogging would've been a lesser punishment.

"She is beautiful." Sehnaz comes closer to Morticia and comments, "Where did you buy her?"

"Ocean market, Sez."

Sehnaz and I look at each other in surprise. *Ocean market! Where's that?*

CHAPTER THREE

SEHNAZ, 16 AUGUST 1862, EARLY MORNING INSIDE THE SHIP AND THEN ON JAMBU ISLAND, CLOSE TO THE HOOGHLY ESTUARY IN BAY OF BENGAL

Cockerels called to declare the dawn.

Sehnaz jumped from her bed. Was she dreaming? Was she still in the island mansion in the Gomti River, near Sultanpur? Are there cockerels in the ship?

Amelia was still in deep slumber. Perhaps she was enjoying some early morning dream. Sehnaz tiptoed to the window and slid the curtain open. Her heart leapt into the back of her throat. *Have we already reached Andaman Islands?*

She knew the ship would take at least two weeks to be there. But eight hundred miles in one day? Did the ship have wings and could fly?

She felt like she was in a dreaded dream where she was already inside the *Kala Pani*—Black Waters prison. Amelia's mild snores brought her back. *How many more days will we be together? Who knows if I will ever come out of that dreaded prison?*

Sehnaz had made up her mind to remain calm until now, assuming the ship would take longer to arrive and she had time to plan. How wrong she was! How much time did she have left?

She noticed the island, its forests, and a large old building. Sehnaz rubbed her eyes and glanced again. Yes, an island. Should she open her suitcase and recheck the map she had bought in Calcutta?

"Sez, what's up?" Amelia yawned. "Come back. We can still get some more sleep. Please, Sez."

"Time is up, Amelia."

"What time? Whose time?"

"Mine." She sensed her voice cracking. "We thought we had more than a month to plan."

"Yes. So?"

"We were wrong. The map is wrong. Andaman is so close to Calcutta. Last night when we went to sleep, the ship was still inside the Hooghly estuary. We were wondering when Bay of Bengal will come. Come and see, we are here. In Andaman."

"That's good, then! We worried if Rupen somehow escapes the prison, how he could come eight hundred miles across the ocean. If the island is near Calcutta, then we have a better chance to achieve what we want."

Sehnaz looked into Amelia's eyes. Wasn't this woman always more positive than she was? Slowly, she breathed in deep. Her heartbeat slowed down.

Both women came out of the cabin.

"Morticia has locked her cabin," Amelia said.

"She might have gone to the dining room."

Sehnaz and Amelia took the stairs and walked down to the dining hall. At this time in the morning, the teapot should have been simmering on the hearth. But the hall was empty. Amelia glanced at her.

"Let's go to the deck."

They came onto the deck and stood near the foremast, facing the rear of the ship.

"All the sails on the masts are down. Also, no smoke from the furnace," Amelia said.

Sehnaz didn't understand. They were new words for her, and she was also not interested. "What do you mean?"

"I mean, the ship has stopped."

"I can see that. Let's go to the rear."

As they began walking, the empty iron vessel mocked at Sehnaz like a ghost.

"Yesterday evening you had asked me to take you on a ship tour."

"Amelia, yes, I had. But this's not the time for that. Let's go and find somebody at least."

Amelia gave her a measured look as both walked past through a promenade deck.

"This is our cabin to the left," Amelia said. "You were standing behind this window a while ago."

Sehnaz stood on her toes and peeked inside—her and Amelia's suitcases, the bed they were sleeping in. "And the next one must be of Morticia. I should've locked our window from inside," she said.

"I think other than us women, hardly anyone comes to this side." Amelia led her past beyond toward the rear.

"Why? Don't the English soldiers stay in the cabins below this level?"

"You forgot Sehnaz, the floor beneath ours is the kitchen and dining. The level below that is the one for soldiers. I mean English soldiers."

"You know much more than I do about the ships, because you sailed all the way from England. But Amelia, do we have time to explore everything now? When we are in a hurry to find where all the men went?"

Amelia wrapped her arm around Sehnaz's shoulder and squeezed lightly. "Let's go past this."

They walked down the corridor of the ship with the sea to the right. Almost in the middle of the ship, Sehnaz noticed a cabin-like structure to the left but with no door. "Let's see if there's anyone here."

As the women stepped inside the enclosed space, they saw a ladder leading down to the darkness beneath. Sehnaz stood holding the siderail and shouted, "Hello, anyone there?"

A foul odour choked her throat. She pressed her scarf against her nose.

Amelia also tried. "Anyone inside? Please reply to us."

She waited a few moments. "None here. Usually, junior crew members of the ship are stationed here," Amelia said.

"Yesterday I had walked up to the stern but didn't care to see this. Might be the place for the Indian guards."

"Possibly. Smell the rotten curry? Let's go to the stern then, I'm sure we'll find someone there."

Sehnaz and Amelia came back to the corridor and walked to the rear again.

"Here is another cuddy," Sehnaz said. "Last evening I had seen an Indian guard here. He took me to the cargo area—to the prisoners. I'm sure some guards must be there to keep watch on the patriots. They can't leave them unguarded."

Amelia cast an appreciative glance at her. The cargo area wasn't far. Sehnaz remembered the place the guard had taken her where she could peep at the convicts who were being taken like cattle to Andaman. Neither any guard nor any prisoner was there.

"Seems like we have arrived at a haunted place." Sehnaz's voice cracked.

"Let's go back, Sez."

"No, we must check the stern, somebody must be there with the rudder."

"Are you insane? When the ship is not sailing, why would anybody be with the rudder? I don't feel comfortable here."

The murky and smelly cargo compartment below, the dark messy clouds above, and the gloomy coast of the island all chased them to the deck, which had the rope ladder connected to the jetty.

"How has everyone on the ship vanished while we were asleep?" Amelia asked.

"No, they might have gotten off the ship as we arrived in Andaman. And they have taken the prisoners to the settlements. Do you notice, there's another large island in that direction?" Sehnaz pointed west. "Didn't Harry say Andaman has five hundred or more islands? This must be one of them."

"That's all right, Sez. Let's get off, too, and walk to that house."

Only one night on the ship, and she had already begun to imagine it as a safe haven. Was she now stepping her way into a life behind bars on an island far away from the mainland India?

She dragged her feet and followed Amelia out of the ship, down the rope ladder, and onto a makeshift jetty.

"How does the island not even have a small port?" Amelia said as they walked up the shore toward the building.

Amelia has sailed from London to Calcutta and knows about ships and ports. Why does it matter whether the island has a port? It shouldn't have any prisons.

A narrow pathway through the bushes with nasty weeds on both sides derided Sehnaz. Something inside her was holding her feet still. "Do you see anyone in that house? I don't think we should go there. Let's go back to the ship and wait for the others to come back. And what if snakes come out from inside these bushes? Or other wild animals? Didn't you see the hills and dense mountains?"

Amelia stilled and cast a blank look at Sehnaz. "We'll die of hunger if we stay inside. Don't you realise all the others have left? Sounds weird, though. But let's see who is in that house."

"We should've brought that pistol with us."

They arrived at the entrance of the house—stone steps, wide but broken in places, almost a dozen or more. Steep. The large, wide doors appeared like an opening to a perpetual hell, where sinners get punished in boiling oil for the sins they've committed on the earth.

Sehnaz rubbed her arms briskly. "An old, shabby building. Might be a hundred years old. Think again before entering this house. Seems like a trap. Look at the thorny creepers around the veranda. Do you think anyone is living inside?"

"But this veranda looks like someone has just cleaned it with a broom, Sez."

Both peeked inside. There was a large hall. From the wall, a huge painting of a man wearing a turban mocked them. Sehnaz stepped inside with Amelia. Seemed like someone had cleaned only hours ago. A stone throne-like structure at the far end of the hall proudly but silently pronounced the century-old heritage.

"Some king must have built this long ago," Sehnaz whispered to Amelia. "Maybe this was part of his kingdom."

"Hmm, hm."

"But what are we doing here? There seems to be nobody. Where are all the crew?"

Sehnaz heard footsteps on the stone stairs. Someone was descending from the first floor. She turned to see that it was Malti. When Sehnaz and Amelia gazed at her, she covered her large bosom with the loose end of her saree.

"We came before dawn," Malti said. "Memsahib asked not to disturb you. Your sleep."

"Where are the others?" Amelia asked.

"Here."

"So many people, all in this house?"

"No, only memsahib, we three—me, Veena, and Chunni. And yes, that slave girl, too."

Nothing was adding up. Sehnaz felt a bit annoyed. "Where're all the others? I mean, the guards, the prisoners."

"We came, saw nobody."

Sehnaz and Amelia followed Malti to the first floor.

Broken handrails and peeling paints were proof that no one had touched them for decades. The walls had recesses with small, stone figurines that looked like fiery demons laughing at Sehnaz's fate, showing their ugly teeth. Unease danced through Sehnaz as she grabbed Amelia's arm and walked with her.

"Awake now, ladies?" A harsh voice startled them. Morticia was standing with a steaming teacup.

Sehnaz felt like a witch was standing before them. Would her next sentence be something like, "Welcome to the Andaman prison!"?

"Malti," Morticia commanded, "ask Veena to bring their luggage from the ship. And show them their room. Next to mine, okay?"

"Yes, memsahib." Malti bowed her head.

"Amelia, would you like some tea?"

"Yes, ma'am." Amelia smiled.

"A cup of tea for Amelia, Malti. Quick. Don't stand there looking at my face." She cast a fiery glance at the maid.

"Thanks, ma'am. And a tea for my friend, Sez, please."

"Yes, yes. One for Amelia ma'am's f...fr...friend." A mocking smile flashed on Morticia's lips. "Malti! Dumb woman! She left before listening to me. These Indians are so careless. Fit to remain slaves. It's too difficult to know who is a maid and who is a friend." Morticia stumped away toward her room.

Sehnaz couldn't bring herself to ask if this island was Andaman.

"Are we in Andaman?" Amelia asked instead. Sehnaz wondered why Amelia was in a hurry to know everything. She could have found out even without asking Morticia.

Morticia laughed. "How could we be? Eight hundred miles from Calcutta in one night? No, this is Jambu Island."

Amelia pinched Sehnaz. "See, you are wrong!"

"A storm damaged the ship last night, and we had to come here, Jambu Island. Will start again as soon as it's repaired."

Storm? How about the ship never even shook last night?

Eventually, Morticia left. Veena had brought their luggage from the ship and guided them to their room on the first floor.

They stepped inside a tiny and smelly room. The little sunshine that sneaked through the slits of the broken timber windowpanes highlighted the peeling paint of the walls and roof. The only thing in the room was a double bed—for them to share.

"I'm sorry, Sez," Amelia said as soon as they entered their room.

"For what?" Sehnaz turned back, tears pooling in Amelia's eyes.

She went and closed the door. "Nothing. This...this woman." Amelia's eyes softened.

"You're a tough woman, Amelia. I understand this type of insect. Now is their time. And we can't fight sharks in the ocean. Don't be sorry only because you're English, too."

"I know what these people think about Indians. My husband was always commenting, 'Black Lives don't matter. Black or brown, both are the same.'"

"Your husband? Colin?"

"How many times have I married, Sez?"

"And a brown woman like me made him jump from that hill. Sent his soul to hell. Ha, ha."

Sehnaz opened the window. A gush of wind along with splatters of rain sprayed water on her face. She slammed the window shut.

"Feels like we all are in a prison." Amelia said later that evening. "Other than going to that dirty bathroom, we haven't left the room. Even Malti served our food here, in the room."

Sehnaz got off the bed and ambled to the window, opened it slightly, and peeked out. "Still drizzling. Already dark. Almost. No way we can go out, even for a walk. Hey, hey, come and see this! So many people are coming here!"

Amelia jumped from the bed and came to her. "You mean the other people on the ship who had vanished?"

"No, come and see yourself."

Almost a hundred men and women, all tribal, lined up in front of the building. Women were naked above the waist, displaying their glorious breasts without shame. Four of them were holding a lighted torch and oil can, pouring oil on the flame from time to time.

"They're here to attack us!" Amelia whispered, putting her hand on Sehnaz's shoulder. "So many men with bows and arrows! Where are the ship's guards?"

"I don't think so. The women are holding flowers, fruits—and look at that man, holding an elephant tusk."

"Is something happening here?"

"Maybe they are here to see white people."

"Let's go down and see."

Both came out and saw that a lock was hanging on Morticia's room. They were about to step down onto the stairs when Sehnaz pulled in a tight breath and stopped to a complete halt. Veena was in front of them, and she clasped the bread and cakes she was holding against her bare breasts to cover up and stared at the floor.

"Veena, why are you only in a petticoat? Where's your blouse and saree?" Sehnaz asked in Hindi.

"Ma'am...ma'am said. Or...ordered." Veena's voice was made of ice, as if she had seen a ghost. "She said, women here, half naked. Show breasts. Custom. They feel bad. Malti and Chunni. Same. No blouse."

Surprise punched through Sehnaz. "What are these, then?"

"Ma'am. Gifts. For tribal."

"Gifts? Bread and cakes are gifts? And will she ask us also to remove our tops and show our chest?"

Veena was about to leave, but she stilled. "Balcony here, can see all. No one see, you."

Sehnaz looked toward the side to where Veena gestured. A small balcony with viewing holes facing the hall on the ground floor welcomed them. They could watch everything sitting on the stone bench. "Didn't I say a king has built this? Palaces have some private viewing locations from where queens and other female members could watch proceedings of the royal meetings."

"Royal meetings? Then who is the king here?" Amelia asked.

"Look there." Sehnaz squeezed Amelia's shoulder.

Morticia was sitting on the throne-like structure, her hair tucked inside a turban with a peacock's feather attached to it. Chunni was only in a petticoat and with no top. She was holding a hand fan and waving it near the throne.

One tribal man—he also had feathers on his head—came and bowed in front of her, offering the tusks.

"Only this man is wearing feathers," Amelia commented.

"He might be the tribal chief."

Morticia took a cake from Veena's hand and gave to the man. He bowed his head again and accepted his gift.

Women also approached her, one after another, and offered flowers.

Morticia said something Sehnaz didn't understand. "I think she knows their language, and she is behaving like a king."

"King or queen? She is still wearing a skirt."

Morticia asked Malti to dance and Veena to sing. All the men and women sat on the ground as if they were about to watch a theatre.

When Veena started singing, Malti and Sadhna began their dance steps. Sehnaz had never watched such a novice dance before. Malti, after taking a few steps, looked self-conscious about her plump, swaying breasts and covered them with both her palms.

Morticia jerked up. "No, Malti. No. Take off your hands. See how the black girl is dancing? Is she covering her breasts?"

Malti stilled. "Ma'am. Men here. Only women, good. Men looking."

"No one here will rape you. These people never touch other women. Better than people in India. Remove your palms or else..."

"Remove. Yes, ma'am. Sorry."

Within five minutes, the dance was over. Malti went behind the throne, covering her breasts again. Morticia stood up and said something in the tribal language. Everyone bowed their heads before leaving the hall. Malti, Veena, and Chunni all lifted their petticoats and wrapped them around their chests. Morticia left the hall and approached Sehnaz and Amelia on the stairs.

"You know their language so well, Mrs. Hunt," Amelia complimented as soon as Morticia came near them.

"Watching the show from the balcony, from the private space, you naughty girls!"

Sehnaz smiled at Morticia for the first time since yesterday morning.

Morticia looked at Amelia and asked, "Are you married?"

"Yes. But my husband died in the Sepoy Mutiny. In 1857."

"And you, Sez?"

"I'm a widow, too. Before that. He was an old man."

"Understand. You both like each other. Female to female. But marrying a man is better. Gives social security and respect. Do whatever, female to female, when the husband is not with you. Most of the time they're not at home, anyway."

"When will the ship arrive at Andaman?" Amelia asked.

"Four weeks. Give or take a few days. And yes, please don't move about on the island. These tribals are good. But there are cannibals on the other side. Not safe for you ladies."

Amelia nodded like an obedient girl, ready to follow all advice.

"One more thing. Tribals don't like same sex relationships. Never make love in their presence. They're more civilised than we think. Not the cannibals, though." She laughed and slipped into her room.

A sigh leaked through Sehnaz's mouth when she remembered they were on Jambu Island. She still had time to think about how to flee.

Sehnaz and Amelia walked downstairs. Flowers and fruits offered by the tribals were still lying next to the throne. Amelia took one flower bunch and fixed them into her hair. Sehnaz was about to do the same when Amelia said, "Don't Sez. You're the male partner here."

Sehnaz laughed. "She thinks we both are like her. And we should behave as if she is right. Know why?"

Amelia's gaze was that of ignorance.

"Women with same sex habits trust other women who are like them. Keep this in mind, Amelia. This woman might be our key to unlock Rupen's shackles."

"Also, she said that wedding a man is good for social security. Is this why she married Mr. Rave Hunt?"

Sehnaz laughed again. "Didn't she say men are always outside, anyway?"

"Yeah, so?"

"The ship is here, we're also here. Then where is Captain Rave Hunt? And where are the prisoners?"

CHAPTER FOUR

SEHNAZ, 18 AUGUST 1862, AFTERNOON
JAMBU ISLAND

"**M**a'am asked us not to allow anyone to go beyond this." Chunni was always comfortable with Sehnaz, as both spoke in Hindi.

Heavy monsoon rain made it impossible for Sehnaz and Amelia to go out in the last two days. The ship still swayed in the water on the makeshift jetty. When the rain stopped that afternoon, Sehnaz thought she could at least walk down the stairs to the terrace and look around the island. But Chunni was standing like a guard in front of the closed door.

Sehnaz took out some coins and gave them to her. Chunni gazed at her in surprise.

"Take this, Chunni. You've come here as a maid to earn some money for your family, and even willing to remove your blouse for that. Keep this extra cash. For your family."

Chunni took the coins and put them in her blouse. Emotion pooled in her eyes. "What should I do, ma'am? I am a poor woman. I was widowed when I was a child. No husband to feed me. Morticia memsahib said that tribal women are showing their breasts, and I have to show mine, too. Please, please, ma'am, do not tell anybody when you go back to Calcutta. I will lose my honour in my society. They've been mistreating me anyway, after my husband died. And my society will throw me out. The same will happen to Malti and Veena. They've husbands and children, too. Their reputations are in danger."

"I know, Chunni. Don't be afraid. I'm a woman, too, and I promise I will tell no one in Calcutta. But why you are standing like a security guard here?"

"Two tribal women have gone to meet Morticia ma'am on the terrace."

"Then what's the problem?"

"They're in a small room. Morticia... Morticia ma'am, is doing..."

"Doing what?"

"Shhh. She will hear."

"I wouldn't disclose anything, Chunni," Sehnaz whispered. "But you need to tell me everything."

"Ma'am took a long...long thing to do..."

"Long what?"

"Long, like men's thing inside their pyjamas. That one, men make women pregnant." Chunni tried to hide her smirk.

"Got it." A giggle escaped Sehnaz's mouth, but she turned to head back. As she was about to enter her room, the tribal women with Morticia came out and went down the stairs, both with smiling faces, as if they'd gotten something wonderful.

Amelia was standing near the door. "Why are those women so happy, Sez?"

"Come inside, you foolish girl." She pushed Amelia inside the room and closed the door.

"What happened?"

"Let's go out. The rain has stopped at last."

"Why did you close the door then, if we're going out?"

"Lower your voice, silly woman. She might come back from the roof."

Amelia stilled and looked into Sehnaz's eyes. Her gaze had questions.

Just before Sehnaz was able to pull Amelia out the door, another tribal woman came inside. Chunni was guiding her to the terrace when she met Sehnaz's gaze. She let out a silent giggle and walked past her.

They had only an hour or two for a brief walk outside the house before the evening. The afternoon sun was playing hide and seek with the clouds. Sehnaz needed to take a deep breath of the outdoor air as a free woman.

"Can you tell me now, what that was all about?" Amelia asked.

"People are the same everywhere, Amelia, be it the most developed country like England, or poor but cultured India, or even this uncivilised island. The same-sex love often brings a better bond than the relationship between a man and woman."

Amelia scrunched her brows. "Did that woman go to meet Morticia for that thing?"

"Yes. And you know what that manlike woman is keeping with her?"

Amelia said nothing, only stared at Sehnaz.

"She has sent her husband somewhere but has kept his *thing* with her."

Amelia bit her lips. "My God! How is it possible? That man would've died by now."

A chuckle blurted out of Sehnaz's mouth. "Just joking. They must be available in large markets in London. She is using a rubber-made penis to keep the island women happy. I'm sure some of them love female to female. And a woman like Morticia can very well recognise who is her type. Didn't you spot how those two women came out of the roof so happy?"

"What were they doing on the roof?"

"Morticia's secret spot is a small room on the terrace," Sehnaz confided as they walked toward the coast and then headed east alongside the seashore.

"Didn't she say to us that the tribal people don't like same-sex love?" Amelia asked.

"Right, they don't like their women to go to another man, either. And they don't know their women are coming to Morticia for this. The rubber penis. They think their women are meeting a white woman and in return, getting some gifts. All are happy."

"She knows this island better than anyone else. Didn't you notice how she has even learnt their language?"

Sehnaz stopped short. "Notice? Have you spotted how far we have come? We forgot about the cannibals! We should've brought our pistol with us, Amelia. Why did we forget?"

"Don't worry, Sehnaz. Let's walk a little longer. We can always come back before evening. Cannibals might be on the other side of the island. We'll not go far. Aren't you bored of staying indoors since the day we arrived here?"

They started walking again, the dark clouds having vanished from the sky. This was their first opportunity to walk through the tiny Jambu Island with the Bay of Bengal on one side and hillocks on the other, and Sehnaz and Amelia proceeded along the zigzagging pathway.

Amelia stopped. "Sez, see this narrow path? Human steps."

"Want to see? Let's go."

The winding pathways took them through the mangroves to the sea. A dinghy tied to a mangrove was swaying in the water.

"Wow, tribals know how to fish!" Amelia said.

"What else would they eat? Would they go to Calcutta and buy groceries?" Sehnaz laughed. "Let's go back."

"Why would they need a market here? Even in August there are so many mangoes in the trees. How is it possible?" Amelia said when they continued toward the west side of the island.

"Might be a different variety, Amelia. Not like the mangoes in your orchard in Sultanpur. And the coconut trees. I have heard they give fruits all year round. Just imagine, fish from the river, fruits and vegetables from the forest. Why *would* these people need a market? Even we wouldn't need one if we had this much in Sultanpur."

Amelia chuckled. "Yeah, unless you decide to cover only your groin and wander around displaying the assets on your chest."

Amelia's gaze went to a ripe mango on the grass. She picked it up and stared at it. "Nice smell, Sez. Like to taste?" She took a small bite. "Sez, yummy. So sweet! Did you find out where all the others are? Mr. Rave Hunt, guards, and prisoners?"

"Perhaps Mr. Hunt lets his wife spend her time here as a queen on his way to Andaman, and then takes her back on his way back. What would the wife of the captain do in Andaman?"

"No, Sez. Did you forget the training you had received? You're wrong."

"Which training?"

"You were once controlling the spy network for Awadh kingdom. You forgot everything? The ship is still floating here. How could they go to Andaman? Swimming in the ocean for hundreds of miles? And why did they leave us two? Are we not supposed to start work in the school in Andaman?"

Sehnaz stilled for a moment and gazed at Amelia before walking again. Frustration twisted through her. "I'm afraid, Amelia. My mind is not working sometimes. What was it your husband said? Needle in the haystack? They might have left us on purpose so that another ship could come and grab me for that map-stealing case. And they left you so that I wouldn't run away."

"Run away? Where? Into the ocean?"

A sudden noise drew them from their conversation. A pit opened in Sehnaz's stomach. Did they step into the cannibal's area? Her legs urged her to flee.

"Sez, let's go back. Maybe we have come too far."

Sehnaz stilled and tried to listen. Shouting of men sent flutters to her nerves. Human heads appearing through the bushes made her heart scream a warning. "Amelia, run, run."

They took off in the opposite direction. But people were coming from their front, too, so they darted onto another route, which led them to a narrow but roaring river. They stopped, and Sehnaz pulled Amelia behind a bush.

"Sit here and hold the branches to cover our face."

Sehnaz could hear Amelia's heart beating—her own, too. "Pray to God, they don't find us."

Surprise rippled through Sehnaz—a white man in only his underpants was sprinting. She lifted her head; almost a dozen men were chasing that man with bows loaded with arrows. When the English man jumped into the river and swam, one man loaded his bow, and an arrow flew like a bullet, hitting the man in his back. The river became pink, but within seconds, the swirling current made the man and his blood vanish. Loud laughter from the men tore into Sehnaz's heart.

"Cannibals. They were trying to capture the man and eat his flesh. He survived," Sehnaz whispered.

"How? He died. Poor man."

"You don't understand. This death is better than roasting alive in fire. Even cannibals don't eat raw meat or flesh."

"You will spoil everything, Sez. Be silent, please. They will catch us otherwise. You are talking too much."

"Me? Me talking? And you? Silent like a saint?"

A thumping sound from behind took them by surprise. Sehnaz swung back. A man stood near them, mouth wide, with an enormous smile displaying his dirty teeth.

Our time is over, Sehnaz thought. Death in Jambu Island is better than living in the prison for life. *But roasting alive in the fire? Oh, my God. And Amelia. Why should she die with me?*

Sehnaz couldn't say anything. She held Amelia's hand, who was sweating and shivering and taking small steps backwards. Sehnaz stepped back with her.

Someone clutched Sehnaz's arm from behind. She looked back. Another man was gazing at her with a gigantic smile on his face.

How happy he must be to have captured two delicious preys!

Amelia, 18 August 1862, Evening, Jambu Island

They are all around Sehnaz and me, herding us. Each one has bows and arrows hung on their shoulders. I can't understand their chattering, but I'm sure they are talking about us. Morticia was right. We should have taken her advice. There're two types of tribes in Jambu. Cannibal and non-cannibal. They all look alike—black skin, tall and strong, and wearing a tiny piece of tree bark covering the male organs only. And women? I glance around. Not a single woman. They might be waiting for their menfolk to bring prey so that they can cook dinner.

I steal a glance at Sehnaz as we walk along with our captors. Is she afraid, like I am? Or she is welcoming the guaranteed death? Didn't she say death is far better than life in Andaman prison?

I whisper to Sehnaz, "They haven't tied our hands. Look for an opportunity to run away."

"Run away? Where? Do you remember the path to the house?"

"We've got to run, either way. Once darkness comes, we should run and hide in the forest. Until morning. Where're the soldiers who came on the ship? They could have protected us." I am sure our voices are drowned out by the cacophony of the loud talking of our captors, who are walking leisurely through the zigzagging pathway—chatting, laughing.

"Amelia, did you notice that soldier who died?"

I cast a sideways glance at her.

Sehnaz holds my wrist, her voice shaky. "I think the soldier who just died was with us in the ship. They're all here. On another part of the island. The prisoners and even Captain Hunt also must be there."

"Why does it matter, Sez? If we don't run away, we will die." I try to peep through the smelly human wall moving around us. A hollowness balloons through me. My breath is now shallow.

"Will we survive if we run?"

"At least we can try. Scan around and try to find spots that can hide us. Be positive, Sez. See, they haven't secured our hands yet. My gut says we can still survive."

I gaze at her, agony written all over her face. But a burning smell of roasted meat sends another shiver through me. Both smoke and noise are filling the air.

"Amelia, are you smelling that?" Sehnaz asks, sniffing the air.

I point toward the billowing smoke. "Do you see what I see?"

"Smoke? The fire for roasting us?"

"Don't frighten me, Sez. Say, we are going to survive."

"Yes, Amelia. We will survive. God will help us."

Are we going to live to see tomorrow morning?

Almost half an hour walk, and no chance for us to run away. The group arrives at a village with their prey—two beautiful women. Hutments made of bamboo, clay, and straw surround a small, oval field. At last, we see women and children. Tiny pieces of bark cover their groin and bare breasts. Some of them have painted their face, breasts, and belly, with flowers fixed to the hair tied into buns. They all laugh and shout and clap when they notice us. Their dirty teeth frighten me. For the first time in my life, severe hatred for the tribals engulfs my mind.

A large, marinated pig is swinging from a stone pole over a flame. The smoke from the fire stabs my nose.

The men guide us to a large stone used as a bench. We are so tired, we sit at once—even before they make us. Sehnaz sits leaning against me. She is sweating, and it dampens my spirit.

Surprise hits me when I see a man beating a drum and another blowing an instrument looking like a trumpet but carved out of wood. This scene was normal to me among the tribals near Sultanpur. But here, in Jambu island? The women who have painted their bodies stand in a circular queue and dance to the tune of a man's singing, bending their waist forward and backward. Their naked, swaying breasts taunt us.

My gaze goes to the other side of the field. Two other elderly women are grinding something on a stone. Spices to marinate us?

A woman comes to us with two leaf bowls.

"I'm thirsty," Sehnaz says and gazes at the woman with desperation in her eyes.

The woman bends before us showing the bowls—some aromatic liquid, almost colourless with a whitish tint. I'm sure that it's not water, But before I can touch one, Sehnaz stops me.

"No, sorry, but thank you." She folds her hands at the woman.

The woman says something with a smile, but we can't understand her. Then she goes back toward the other dancing women.

"Sez, I am thirsty. My head is reeling."

"Mine, too. But do you know what was in that? Must be something to make us unconscious, so that we can't sense pain when they kill us. We must escape from here. They're having a pig feast tonight. Perhaps they will keep us for tomorrow. So, behave like a good girl so that they do not doubt our motive."

I inhale a deep breath. Isn't Sehnaz right most of the time?

The dance continues along with the beat of the drums and the tune of the song. I continue to focus on escaping, but chances are little. "Oh God," I say and look at the sky. Instead of God, I find a bright full moon. Is this a moon festival?

The drum plays, *Dha, dhin, dhin, dha. Again dha, tin, tin, tha.* Or Something like this.

Why didn't I notice before that the drumbeats, clapping, and dance steps are all in a sync? Wasn't I a dancer for some time in Sultanpur?

For a moment I believe Sehnaz and I both are safe and enjoying a cultural program.

The dance stops. My heart stops, too. What's next? Us?

A weeping young woman approaches an elderly man sitting on a mound. She has bruises on her face and body. I am stunned with the sudden turn of the events. Are they staging a drama?

I glance at Sehnaz. She has buried her head between her knees. Poor girl is going through so much tension in her life. If she gets away from these tribals, she will go to prison for life. But now, we both are in the same death boat, anyway.

"Sez." I nudge her with my shoulder and whisper in her ears, "Glance up."

"What?" she replies, her head still inside her knees.

"Are these people as uncivilised as we thought? Look what is happening here!"

When Sehnaz doesn't respond, I continue as if I'm running a commentary.

"The woman is showing some wounds on her body—and her breasts, too. Remember Colin had punished me with cigar marks beneath my breasts?"

"Who did this?" the voice from the buried head encourages.

"Must be a man, her husband. A young man is also standing and pleading something. I wish I understood their language. And the woman removed something like a necklace from her neck and handed it over to the man. The old man raised his hand like a sign of blessing, or approval, or... I don't know. And another young man is putting a similar stone necklace on the woman's neck."

Sehnaz raises her head, her eyes quickly finding the scene I've described. "That means she divorced one husband and married another."

My soul lightens to see Sehnaz glow up again amidst the dark clouds.

Two men begin dragging the woman's first husband after tying his hands. *Punishment for hurting the wife?*

"This's real quick justice, Amelia. You should've been in this community to get rid of Colin without drama. And you could've married Harry, too. See how cannibals can give better justice than the mightiest British?"

"Don't utter the word *'cannibal.'*"

"As if they understand English. Don't worry, Amelia. Think how to get out from here."

The thought of *being killed* carries me again to a dreary mood. "Sehnaz, do you think..."

"Yes, Amelia. Look, each one here is in a festive mood. I think the drink they had offered us is some kind of alcoholic one. My mistake, I thought otherwise. Keep your eyes and ears open and we can run away when they are least attentive towards us."

Least attentive? In fact, all their attention was on both of us.

Soon after that, some women begin to harvest the pig meat. They bring some food on two large leaves and place it before us. Sehnaz never eats pork as she is Muslim. I also fold my hands and shake my head, no. How can I eat when I'm going to be their food?

The women glance at each other, bow their heads to us, and step back. The entire congregation becomes silent for a while. Within minutes they all gather around the roasted pig to get their share of the feast. I have experienced in India people offering food first to the guests.

Whatever, I can't deny the fact that these people are still cannibals. All these gestures of goodwill are only until our time to be roasted. Don't people feed the animal well so that they can get more meat?

The feast is over in an hour. Two men approach us and gesture to stand. We stand up like obedient girls. When they ask us to follow, we do so. My heart pounds. Are they taking us to stay somewhere secured overnight?

"Sez!" I hold her wrist, tears pooling in my eyes. "I don't know if they will keep us together. I will admit something to you now."

Sehnaz doesn't answer but wraps her arm around my shoulder and squeezes gently. I cast a sideways glance at her. Her eyes are also pooling.

"Sez, you are the best friend I ever had. God forbid, if we die, we will go to the heaven at the same time."

A cold silence descends as we both follow the two tribal men.

After walking with them for almost a half hour, I ask, "Sez, why are we following them? They're not even looking at us. Shouldn't we flee?"

But Sehnaz gasps. "You foolish girl! Look ahead."

My eyebrows shoot up. "We're near the old palace!"

Once it's fully visible, both men bow their head to us, turn away, and return in the direction of their village.

We are alive! Wow!

Sehnaz grabs my shoulder and hugs me. She cries too, but silently. I hug her back and whisper, "We're still alive." My heart is still pounding like a madman's drum. Unable to grasp we have survived.

"Did you recognise them from that day when they came to meet Morticia?" I ask.

"How could I? You were with me, too. And remember, we were sitting on that balcony above and couldn't see their faces."

Sehnaz is right. She always is.

"Sez, do you still think these men are civilised? If these people aren't cannibals, why did they kill that English man?"

Sehnaz stills and eyes me, allowing a full minute of silence. "These people are very protective of their women. The guards of the ship are staying on another part of Jambu. And this English man might have tried to rape some tribal woman, as they don't cover their breasts. And see what happened? They didn't take his body for eating. His corpse must have floated to the sea."

I look at the old palace. It dazzles in the full moon and millions of stars in a clear sky. A tiny patch of white cloud floats in the distant horizon and smiles at me. "Sez, remember how we feared entering this building just days ago?"

Sehnaz lets out a giggle. "This is our lucky palace. If I ever marry, I would love to spend my first night inside this bungalow."

Sehnaz and marriage?

It's already late, around nine at night. Morticia must've known we went out on our own. She is not our boss or someone superior. But for some unknown reason, a discomfort envelops both Sehnaz and me. Will she be angry with us?

We tiptoe inside the old palace building. It is dark and calm. As we rub our eyes to get a better vision and find the stairs, a faint light approaches from the first floor. Veena comes, holding an oil lamp.

"Amelia, why don't you go to our room? I will talk to Veena and join you."

My heart beats rapidly—what news might Veena give to Sehnaz? And why am I so afraid of Morticia?

I don't wait long for Sehnaz. She comes to the room soon after and closes the door.

"The woman was not in a good mood this evening," she mutters, sitting near me on the bed.

"Is she angry at us? That we went out without permission? Are we her servant, like these three women?"

"Stop, Amelia. Veena has no idea why, either. She said Morticia was looking grumpy the whole evening. And you know what? We've got to keep someone as a friend."

"You mean Morticia?"

"Who else? Her three maids? She is the one with money and power. She is not only the captain's wife." She looks at me conspiratorially.

I need time to come to the conclusion that Sehnaz has in seconds. "What? She is not an officer in the government. Just a woman who can never be an officer."

"I don't know, Amelia, just guessing. Think how she is staying alone, without her husband, and enjoying the tribal girls. Didn't she say a woman should marry only for security? How many women can push the husbands away for days and enjoy tribade? Mr. Rave Hunt must be on this Jambu Island. The place the guards are staying."

"You think too much, Sez. Your brain is overactive after coming back from the islanders' feast. But I'm sleepy. Can we talk tomorrow morning, please?" I yawn and stretch, climbing into the bed.

But Sehnaz stays put. "Who has seen tomorrow, Amelia? If another ship comes here before we start for Andaman, it will bring a letter for my detention. Then I would sleep forever inside the Black Waters prison." Anxiety sprouts through her voice. The joy of survival vanishes from her eyes, and her lips tremble.

A sudden unease makes me jump, and I sit up straight on the bed. I had forgotten—being English, I'm safe. But the sword is hanging above Sehnaz's head.

"Do we knock at her room and say sorry? To keep her happy? Now?"

"No, Amelia. We've to do something different, which we have never done despite staying together."

I catch Sehnaz's eyes. I don't understand.

"Make love. I mean, pretend. But the sound should reach her room through these walls. This is the time to show we both are like her."

The daylong tiredness has withered me out, but my shoulders droop with comprehension. "I understand. No need to pretend. I have done that before."

Sehnaz freezes. "You have done—what? When?"

"Tribade."

"That means, you are...and I didn't know until..."

"No, Sez." I pull a pillow onto my lap. "Nothing like that. I am a traditional woman, not like—" I point toward Morticia's room— "but when you are hungry, you eat whatever you get."

Sehnaz stares at me with questions in her eyes.

"Madhuri had said this. In 1857, when I was a courtesan in Sultanpur and living in Bibi's *kotha,* she was my assistant. The *kotha* was closed to the patrons for the war, and I had nothing to do. The hilltop temple was my favourite view from my balcony. One evening, Madhuri took me through a tunnel, and we arrived..."

"At the Shakti Ashram? With the nude nuns?"

"Yes." I let out a mild laugh, keeping in mind Morticia sleeping in the next room. "I was there for weeks, practising nudism. Madhuri and I shared a room in the Ashram. One day Madhuri took me to the other side of the hill, a waterfall surrounded by rock walls. That day I came to realise women in Shakti Ashram do tribade. We did, too— Madhuri and I. For the first time, I got pleasure from a woman, though nothing like that from a man. She didn't have a penis, only fingers."

"And Morticia has a phallus."

"I know. But I have seen the replicas of Khajuraho temple in the basement of Bibi's *kotha*. Madhuri had taken me there, as well. Naked statues in erotic poses. Figurines of female to female using artificial penises. This was a custom in ancient India, I am sure."

A voice carries through the wall, startling us. Is Morticia not sleeping?

"Perfect timing, Amelia." Sehnaz's eyes brighten. "You have the experience! We can do it now. She should hear the sound. You need to moan, loudly."

I chuckle. "Why me and not you?"

"She thinks you're more feminine, and I'm like her, the male partner. You are the woman. I will do things, and you will shout, 'Oh, my, do me again, more please!'" Sehnaz giggles.

I clap my hand over my mouth to keep from laughing out loud. I am a novice in the field of acting. "How do I appear more feminine than you? You are—sorry, weren't you a real and famous courtesan in Lucknow? Patrons were queuing up to watch your performances!"

Dark clouds appear in Sehnaz's gaze. "That is past. Because I am taller and heavier than you. Whatever, we need to act. Now. We need Morticia's graces." Sehnaz opens the window. "This thick stone wall may block our drama, but her room's old timber windows have cracks in it. Your sexy dialogues and moans should reach her and wake her up."

"And she will be more angry with us."

"No, silly girl. No. This will arouse her, and she will call for Sadhna to satisfy her. Just do it."

I clear my throat, sitting on the bed, as if I'm going to sing. "Oh, my, oh, Sez..."

"No, Amelia," Sehnaz whispers and crouches nearer to me, "you like—I mean, you sound like you are reading a script from a piece of paper. No. You need to imagine what I am doing with you. And feel sexy."

I think for a moment. Closing my eyes, I imagine Sehnaz undressing me. But I feel nothing. My eyes open. "Sorry, Sez. I can't. I need a man for this. You are a woman, and again, I can only imagine. No, it's not happening."

Sehnaz deflates. "How did you it with Madhuri then?"

"She was, in fact, doing things. I didn't even realise she could satisfy me. I even had an orgasm that day. She started slow. Only touching in the beginning. When she proceeded further, I was so aroused that I couldn't stop her. But it was awkward, when I think about it. Woman to woman."

Sehnaz inches closer and places her palm on my shoulder. She lifts my face with her fingers and says, "You're a beautiful woman, Amelia."

I grin and roll my eyes. "As if you have never seen me before."

Sehnaz doesn't reply; she crawls her fingers into my hair. The tingle arouses me. Her finger slides over to my face, and then all the way down, tingling my neck. I feel my content smile. Her fingertips walk on my bubbies. Nipples. Both. Fingers snake in and squeeze my nipples. Has Sehnaz also done tribade before?

"Is this better, Amelia darling?" Sehnaz tries to thicken her voice to sound like a man, but her voice is not mannish.

I chuckle. "Don't pretend to be a man, Sez. You're still a woman. A beautiful woman any man would die for."

Silently, she unhooks my bodice. I try to moan again, sitting bare breasted in front of her.

Before I can attempt another, a deep, male voice surprises us. It comes through the window, perhaps from Morticia's room.

Someone is fighting with Morticia. She is shouting, too.

Sehnaz stills. We both sit at full attention.

"She thinks we are still out. And her windows must be open. Who might that man be?"

The voices become louder.

"I brought so much booty. Each time we are in the sea, I am amassing more. What for? What is my life?" the male voice shouts.

"Must be Mr. Rave Hunt. He has come tonight. Just listen," Sehnaz says.

"Life? You are alive because I have shut my mouth. The moment I tell everyone that you did sodomy, you will go to jail, you understand? You have done sodomy," Morticia screams.

"I don't understand what you're talking about. I am a normal man. You don't sleep with me, but that doesn't mean I sleep with men. Never. You like females and are always keeping me away from your bedroom. Why can't I be with you? Don't you have a vagina? Show me, and I will fuck you the entire night. Want to feel my penis? You might have forgotten when last you even touched that."

"Stop. I don't want to touch that mouse. That tiny one can't arouse me."

He makes a huffing sound. "I know you have *better* and *longer*. But that is not real, a rubber. And that's also to fuck other women. You're living like a queen on this island with money I am earning. No. Looting. So much risk I'm willing to take, only for you. My life is in danger the moment I go to Ocean Market."

"Queen? This old and broken palace. One heavy storm, this will fall to the ground. And what is that money worth if there's nothing here to spend it on? Didn't you promise me you'd rebuild this? Whe...e...e...n?"

A loud noise startles us, as if he's thrown or hit something, before he continues. "I need to bring materials on the ship. Didn't you see that the prisoners occupied all the space for cargo? Last time, same thing—authorities sent too many prisoners. Where was the capacity to bring building materials? And how do I bring workers to build? Wouldn't they go back and expose both of us? That we're building something on this island?"

"I have an idea."

"What?"

"Kill them all when they complete construction and throw them into the sea. Calcutta police will never find out."

He laughs mockingly. "Woman's brain. Huh. Only dirty minds. Wouldn't the police ask me when their family members report them missing? You're impossible to talk to, like always. I'm done."

Morticia's cabin door slams shut, and angry footsteps run down the stairs.

"Enough Sez, no more acting today." I get up and shut the window. "Time to sleep."

Sehnaz stretches on the bed and pulls down her sheets. "Amelia, did you hear?"

"What?"

"Ocean Market. Mr. Hunt said. And remember, Morticia had once said that was where she found Sadhna, Ocean Market. Where's that?"

I stare at the ceiling. Silence hangs for a few seconds.

"Wrong question. The correct one is, 'What is Ocean Market?'"

CHAPTER FIVE

SEHNAZ, 19 AUGUST 1862, EARLY MORNING, JAMBU ISLAND

Sehnaz woke up, sweating and panting. It must have been around three in the morning. Amelia was sleeping next to her in the same bed. Her soft snore aroused jealousy in Sehnaz. Amelia was English, so a first-class citizen of the country. She would never get punishment without a free and proper judicial trial. But for all brown-skin citizens, they were at the mercy of the English rulers.

A faint moonlight dazzled Amelia's white face. No, Sehnaz shouldn't have jealous thoughts about this honest woman, her best friend. Amelia had lost so much in her life, and she was coming to Andaman only to help her.

"Amelia, wake up." She shook her shoulder.

"Morning already? Good morning."

"No dear. It's still night. But..."

"But what?"

"Something struck me, and I couldn't sleep."

Amelia shifted into a sitting position and came closer.

Sehnaz said, "Last night when Morticia and her husband were fighting, she must have thought we hadn't returned. And she should never think that we are witness to some of her secrets. But in the morning when she finds us, that will be an awkward situation. I mean, we should pretend that we don't know about her murky life. That's the only way to use her secrets to our advantage."

"What should we do?"

"Go out and come back in at dawn."

"Are you mad? This is not a city like Sultanpur or even Calcutta. You will go out at night? You know, real cannibals prey at night."

"We'll not go far. When dawn arrives, we will make casual entry into the house. Morticia wakes up early. She will notice us. Remember —we had lost our way, but by the morning we found our way back. That will be our answer."

"And Veena? She had seen us last night."

"Leave that to me. I will put some tips on her mouth."

Sehnaz and Amelia changed into same clothes they wore last evening and sneaked out of the building. Moonlight led them through the narrow, winding path to the makeshift jetty. Sehnaz's gaze moved to millions of stars lighting up the sky, raising the hope of a sunny day ahead.

"No ship!" Amelia squealed.

"What? Where is the ship? Surprise. First the ship halted here and everyone other than we women vanished. I've been wondering which part of the island they are living on and why. And now the ship itself has vanished!"

"Don't worry, Sez. The captain's wife is with us. No way she is going to abandon us on this island. We will arrive in Andaman and get chance to free Rupen. We can take a stroll along the beach and go back in the morning. Maybe one hour more."

Sehnaz glanced at the jetty. The first morning she and Amelia had gotten off the ship, she had an obstructed view of the place. Faint rays of dawn illuminated the place now, And she realized the small bay was perfect to build the jetty.

"This is a natural small port," Amelia said.

"How?"

"You have never seen a harbour?"

"There is no port near Lucknow or Sultanpur, no sea there. Only one I saw is Hooghly in Calcutta. We came from there."

"Nah! That's a river port. Real ports are always on the shore of a sea or ocean. Look at how narrow stretches of hill on both sides are protruding into the sea, creating a natural breakwater and keeping the waves away. We can even take a bath here—no current."

"Not now. Not so early in the morning." Sehnaz's heart became heavy as the thought invaded in her consciousness. "I'll be going to prison soon." Her vision had been focussed on the shore.

"Nothing is going to happen, Sez. Ships don't ply every day between Calcutta and Andaman. The letter for your arrest might come in the next ship, weeks after. We've enough time to think and act. I feel it."

Sehnaz thought for a moment and glanced at Amelia. Her eyes beamed with confidence. Amelia used all her time in Calcutta in gathering as much information from Harry, since he was in shipping business and knew about the Hooghly port.

"Come on, Sez. Let's have a walk along this coast. Your mind will freshen up."

They walked along the sea, toward the direction from where sun was rising. The sky was clear, assuring a sunny day ahead. After walking for almost ten minutes, Amelia suddenly screamed, "Look, Sez! The ship. Our ship! It just left."

Sehnaz noticed the ship, but the Union Jack wasn't visible. "Where's the flag? And another ship is also going along with this one! No flag there either! Why has the ship left?"

"Something is wrong, Sez. Everything looks fishy. The other ship wasn't here last evening. When did it come? And where're they going? Andaman?"

"I don't think so. They might leave us. Not the captain's wife, though."

Sehnaz and Amelia hurried back to the old palace and saw that Malti was sweeping the floor.

"Memsahib is up, Malti?" Sehnaz asked in Hindi in a low voice.

"Nah, she's not here. I found out only this morning. She must have left with the slave girl and the big sahib early today. I heard the noise but didn't come out. I don't know where she has gone."

Sehnaz stood still and considered this for a few beats. She was sure the ship would come back. Morticia wouldn't leave her maids on Jambu Island forever. "Amelia, please go to the kitchen and make some tea for both of us. I will have a chat with these beautiful girls and join you."

Malti threw the broom on the floor and loped toward the kitchen. "Tea, ma'am, I come and make for you. You, are memsahib, no make tea, please."

Amelia put a hand on her arm. "I make a special tea, which Sez memsahib likes. So, please stay with her."

Malti stood dumbfounded, eyes moving from Sehnaz to Amelia. "Sez, memsahib?"

Oh, how can an Indian woman be memsahib? "Amelia, you are confusing her. Let them call me *didi*, older sister in Bengali." She smirked at her. "An Indian woman can't be a memsahib. Until her skin colour is white."

Amelia nodded and left silently to the kitchen. Sehnaz took Malti to a room. "Amelia ma'am is a gracious lady. See how polite she is with me? Come with me, and we'll have a small talk."

Malti looked back and forth between Sehnaz and a retreating Amelia.

"You may call me *didi,* Malti, all right?"

"Didi? Bengali, know?"

"No, but I can understand a little."

Malti narrowed her eyes. "Ma'am—sorry, *didi*—please do not tell anyone in Calcutta I was dancing without my blouse. I will be outcasted forever. No place in house, but on the streets only."

"You don't worry, Malti. I wouldn't say anything to anyone." Sehnaz laughed inside. She was a courtesan once, and she would dance wearing tiny blouses and skirts. But never had she bared her breasts in a dance.

Malti stood still, watching her face.

"You must come here often, Malti?"

"No, *didi,* only this time."

Sehnaz was sure she misunderstood her. She stepped closer. "You mean on the previous trips the ship didn't stop here? It went directly to Andaman?"

"No, *didi,* no previous trip. First one. All of us. Veena and Chunni both."

"Oh!" Sehnaz blinked, actively trying to hide her surprise.

"*Didi,* my cousin and her friends came once with Morticia ma'am. She said ma'am never takes the same maid the second time. Instruction from the government, she said."

Sehnaz eyed her, allowing a few moments of silence. Her reply sounded fishy. "Did Morticia ma'am say before she was planning to go somewhere?"

Malti scratched her head. "No. But Rave sahib was here. Last night. While going out, he was talking about some market."

"Market? This tiny island has some market?"

"I don't know, *didi*. I think he said Ocean Market."

The two words started swirling in Sehnaz's brain. On the ship, Morticia had said she had bought Sadhna from the *Ocean Market*. Last night also she and Amelia heard Rave and Morticia talking about it. What does that mean?

The aroma of steaming tea wafted from the kitchen, clouding Sehnaz's consciousness. She must go to Amelia and talk to her about this *Ocean Market*. And drink hot tea, too.

"You're an expert in extracting information, Sez," Amelia said when they took a stroll out again late morning.

"You can do it, too."

"No, Indian maids will not open up to me. I'm white."

"You will get plenty of opportunities in Andaman to dig for information, Amelia. You will interact with English guards and soldiers there. I don't know where I'll be. If I'm not with you, you will be alone. You should learn how to find information and where."

Amelia shot a blank glance at her.

"Don't overthink, Amelia. A bit of fresh air will lighten your head."

A young tribal man passed by, perhaps starting his day by collecting prey in the forest. Sehnaz shot a seductive glance at him. He stopped and turned back, then he came to Sehnaz and bowed his head.

"Namaste." Sehnaz folded her hands and bent her head a little, too.

"How do you know he's greeting you?" Amelia whispered from behind.

"Guessed. He looks like the man we met yesterday. He hasn't forgotten us. After all, we are two of the few women who don't have breasts." Sehnaz said over her shoulder, chuckling.

Amelia's hands went to her chest. "What do you mean?"

"I mean, we aren't *showing* our breasts. Like their women. Doesn't that distinguish us from them?"

Amelia giggled. "Can you ask him to take us to the hilltop? We shouldn't go there alone."

Sehnaz turned back to the man and requested him by pointing at the crest.

The man understood and took them to the crest. Sehnaz and Amelia stood, absorbing the amazing view thanks to this sunny morning. From there, the entire island was visible.

"Is this the river we saw yesterday?" Amelia asked, pointing at a small river passing through the middle.

"It's the only river, from what we can see. The poor English soldier's body must have drifted into the Bay of Bengal."

"He got the result of his karma," Amelia said, "so don't worry about him, and look at the village of the tribals. Small, thatched houses. Can't we go there and mingle with the women?"

"You sure?"

"Why not? Other than their scanty clothes, they all look cultured. That day when we witnessed their moon festival, did you notice how clean their village was?"

Sehnaz feigned anger at Amelia. "That evening? I was worried if we would survive, and you were checking out what their village looked like? Did you plan to enter it in your diary after arriving in the heaven? By the way, what did you notice?"

"They have flower plants in front of their huts. Frontages are so clean. Children playing on the road. Like any other village in India. Only they are impoverished, as per our perception. And look there. Another island! Looks much bigger."

Sehnaz's gaze followed Amelia's pointing finger. "I don't know the name of it. I've got a map in the room. Let's check it when we get back." Sehnaz panned her eyes eastward and yelled, "Amelia, look! Over there. Look at those thatched houses—and I can see soldiers there, both English and Indian. The prisoners must be there."

Amelia came closer to Sehnaz and wrapped her arm around her shoulder, staring in the direction she pointed out, mouth agape. "I can't understand why. Is this because Rave planned to take the ship for another mission?"

"Not sure. But yes, if these men are doing something fishy like Harry had said, it's good for our mission. From the British point of view, our plans are illegal, and dishonest people are the best resources for the job."

The August sun was warm, pinching their skin. They came down the hill, and Sehnaz gestured for the man to go.

Sitting beneath a mango tree, Sehnaz said, "Remember, Amelia—once Morticia is back, we probably can't talk this freely. Today is our Independence Day. You must be a wonderful actor and pretend to be something you're not if you want to get information. Use others to your advantage."

Amelia cocked her head. "Pretend? Isn't it wrong for honest people like us to behave artificially?"

Sehnaz turned to her friend solemnly. "I will tell you a story."

"Story?" Amelia sat up straight.

"Yes, like a story for the children. But listen to it."

Amelia smiled.

"Once, a snake became a saint's disciple. And the saint taught the snake never to hurt anyone. The snake agreed. Weeks later, when the saint was walking through the snake's living place, the disciple snake came and greeted him. The saint noticed it had injuries. When he enquired, the snake said children were playing when he was crossing the road. They hurled stones at him, injuring him. The saint asked why he did nothing. Snake replied, 'You have taught me never to harm anyone. Had I bitten the children, they would've died from my venomous biting.' The saint laughed and said, 'I said not to harm. That doesn't mean you shouldn't do anything in self-defence. You should've at least bared your fangs and protruded your angry tongue to scare them.'"

Amelia cocked her head. "This is the story?"

"Yes. And there's nothing wrong with pretending to be a person you are not."

"But Sez, I'm really worried about the behaviour of these people. Rave and Morticia Hunt. Why did they stop here? What are they doing now? Where have they taken the ship, and why have they removed the flag?

Sehnaz sighed. "I don't understand, either."

"I remember when Harry was organising our Andaman trip, he said many of these British officers who are sailing to Andaman—and those who are working there—are leading double lives. I didn't ask for details. Now I'm thinking I should have."

"Did he say anything about 'Ocean Market?'"

"Not the exact words. But their actions say a lot, though. Leaving the prisoners here and taking the ship out at night. You are right.

They are onto something illegal. And that might be good for our plan."

CHAPTER SIX

AMELIA, 25 AUGUST 1862, NIGHT, JAMBU ISLAND

It was such a sweet and sound sleep. I rub my eyes. It must be midnight. Sehnaz is sitting up straight on the bed, eagerly watching me. Moonlight through the narrow slits of the wooden windowpanes is not enough to see her face clearly. *Did something happen? Did she encounter a terrible dream?*

"Are you all right, Sehnaz?" I bite my lip. Should have called her Sez. Removing those three letters from her name could change her fate. Sehnaz's every moment is full of tension. The unknown letter carrying her *'lifetime in prison sentence'* is hanging above her head. Still, this awesome woman has guts to laugh and make jokes.

"Do you hear the commotion? Morticia is not here. Only we five women are in this house. But I can hear the voices of men!"

Anxiety makes me jump out of bed. I open the window's timber doors and peek through the steel railings. A cold breeze gushes through, and the moon is smiling from a clear sky. "A ship has anchored in the jetty. Men are coming out." *Did another ship come from Calcutta with a letter for Sehnaz's arrest?* I feel a sudden stab in my heart. Living in the same house as my dearest friend for the last five years has almost made her my soulmate. One soul with two bodies. How can I sleep in peace when danger is closing in on my mate?

Sehnaz leaves the cot and joins me. "Same ship. Maybe Morticia and Mr. Hunt are back. Did they come back from the *Ocean Market*?"

My shoulders deflate. "Don't get what that means. Or where that market is."

"These are the same people who were with us on the ship. But not all. But I don't see captain and his wife."

Sehnaz's observation is noteworthy; Rave and Morticia are nowhere to be found. "They will come. It's obvious. Just wait and watch." I think for a moment and then say, "Wait, why are we watching them? Don't we know Morticia will come here, and Mr. Rave Hunt will go to the other part of the island?"

But her eyes don't leave the scene before us. "I would love to see what people buy in the *Ocean Market.*"

Sehnaz and I stand like statues, leaning against two sides of the window until those on the ship have finished disembarking and the night is quiet once again.

Sehnaz murmurs, "Morticia might have already gone to her bedroom. Mr. Hunt must be with other sailors, we couldn't see them in the faint moonlight."

"You're right, Sez. Let's sleep." I yawn. We wouldn't be able to see what they bought from that market, anyway—unless Morticia has bought another slave girl like Sadhna. Why didn't she take us, or even the maids? Maybe she knows maids are Indian and could disclose what she did. Perhaps only Sadhna was fit to go with her, since she doesn't understand any language.

We are about to head back to the bed when Sehnaz grasps my arm. "They're here, Amelia. They're walking."

I follow her gaze. Both Rave and Morticia are walking along the shore, away from the house. Rave is holding a box on his head.

"We need to find where they are going." Sehnaz pinches my arm.

"Are you mad? If Rave shoots both of us and throws us into the sea, nobody in the world will know. Come back and sleep like a nice girl. What do we have to do with where they travelled or what they brought in that box?"

"Amelia, don't ask questions. Come with me. We need to catch them before they vanish." She turns and heads toward the door.

Sighing, I run after her. Malti and Veena both wake up when we scamper through the hall where they were sleeping. "Girls," Sehnaz says while still running, "don't tell anyone we've gone out. We're still sleeping in the room. Your blouse-less chest story is safe with me."

As we burst from the house, we trudge along quietly to keep pace with the couple. Tension rides in the air as we try to stay invisible.

"Here they are," Sehnaz whispers. "Maintain enough distance. They will never think someone is following them. But, just in case—" she picks up two bushy branches lying on the ground and hands me one— "hold this in front of you and walk on the side of the pathway. If they look back, freeze. They will think we are trees. Thank God, it is night-time."

I follow like an obedient student, and we creep after the couple like thieves.

Mr. Hunt—with the box on his head—follows Morticia, who flounces ahead of him. After all, she is the self-declared queen of Jambu Island. We wade through weeds and grass as silently as possible.

When the couple halts near a fork, Sehnaz nudges me with her elbow. We sneak behind a bush. Morticia glances around as we peep through the shrub with bated breath, then they take the path to the right. Sehnaz prods me and mutters, "Let's go back."

I nearly drop my branch. "Why? You don't wish to see where they deposit that box?"

Sehnaz simply strides back toward the house. Confused, I follow. As we arrive, she says, "The lion checks the surroundings just before entering his secured cave. They would have caught us had we followed any further. They were near their secret place. I will find a way during the daytime."

Who understands spying better than Sehnaz? We have to pretend to be asleep before Morticia comes back.

As we both climb onto the cot, I ask again— "What do we have to do with where they are going or what they are carrying in that box?"

"We should find their weaknesses. And strengths. That is the only light I can see at the end of the tunnel. She might be the medium we can manipulate for Rupen's and my freedom."

Footsteps dash on the stairs after a while. Morticia must be entering.

The next morning, Morticia's snoring jumps through her bedroom doors. The queen is taking a royal nap after many nights of exhaustion at sea.

"This is the best time to find out where they put the box last night," Sehnaz whispers as we tiptoe down the stairs. "Morticia will not wake up for at least another hour, and we will sip tea like well-behaved girls when she comes down from her room."

I send up a quick prayer— *God, please make Sehnaz's strategy successful.* But what is her strategy?

"I don't know yet," she answers when I ask, "but I learnt something while staying in disguise in the Hindu temple as Sheru's wife. I was often attending the sermons of the priests. The advice from Gita, the Hindu scriptures, still sounds inside me. 'You have right only over your karma, not its results. So, do not worry about the outcomes.'"

I glance at her in amazement.

Sehnaz nods. "I will never forget those lines. The day I started from Varanasi for Sultanpur, I doubted that I could save your life from your monster husband. I told Sheru, let's do our karma, whatever we think is right. Let's not think of the consequence. And you see what happened in the end."

I flash a smile. "Karma resulted in saving my life."

The slow breeze of the dawn blows our hair across our faces. The Bay of Bengal is unusually calm.

Soon we arrive at the fork where we had seen the couple last night, and then we turn right. After we walk for about three hundred gauges, a cave smiles at us at the edge of the road. Sehnaz's face brightens. "This must be the spot."

Freshly broken tree branches block its entrance, as if someone came here only hours ago. Four locked boxes wink at us through the branches and leaves. My eyes shoot open. Boxes with gold and diamonds!

"Let's go back." Sehnaz swings back and walks away briskly.

"Anyone can steal the boxes."

"Who? Tribals? They would prefer a dead pig instead. Golds and diamonds have no value to them. They don't use money."

"But we can." I jog to catch up to her.

"Of course. Only if the head on your shoulders looks less valuable. We know what is in the boxes now. That's all the information we need."

As we enter the building, the aroma of hot tea teases my tastebuds. Malti welcomes both of us with a magnificent smile.

"Is big ma'am awake yet?" Sehnaz asks her.

"Not yet. Tea is for you." She pulls the loose end of her *pallu* to cover her chest.

Sehnaz chuckles. "We are all women, Malti. We also have breasts like you. And I can bare them here, with no shame. As long as no man enters the building, I don't have a problem."

Malti's face blooms with a massive smile as she goes to the kitchen.

It seems we have achieved something with the discovery of Morticia's secret wealth. I must write this in my diary today. Sehnaz sits, facing me. Her glowing face makes me happy, confidence radiating through her eyes. As we sip tea, footsteps come down the stairs. Morticia is coming.

"Malti, please bring tea for ma'am," Sehnaz shouts.

"Good morning, ladies." Morticia approaches and slumps into a chair. "Good news."

We stop sipping our tea and gaze at her.

"The ship will start again tonight. Time to say goodbye to Jambu Island."

Morticia, 26 August 1862, Afternoon, Jambu Island

The hem of Amelia's frock blew with the wind as she took a stroll in front of the old palace. Alone. Morticia licked her lips while standing on the veranda, planning to join her. Amelia didn't care that her shapely legs were on display. Why should she? Only women were staying in this mansion. All of them, except one. Morticia herself. In fact, she was a man trapped in a woman's body. Desire pulled in her groin. *If only I could fix an artificial organ there and feel the sensation like any other man.*

"How are you, Amelia?" Morticia forced a broad smile as she descended onto the pathway.

Amelia turned back. An unease clouded her face when she saw Morticia.

"I'm fine, Mrs. Hunt."

"You may call me Mort. Morticia is a long name."

"Mort? It sounds... I mean, bit..."

"Sounds masculine? That's all right. My close female friends call me by this name. Not in public, though. You should call me Mrs. Hunt in public and Mort in private."

"I'll remember, Mrs. Hunt—sorry, Mort." Amelia chuckled.

"Now this's better. You look prettier when you smile. Are you bored on this island? In fact, coming from a city, nobody would like this islet."

"Not true, though. Sez and I can spend months together like this."

Sez? That Indian woman is my rival here.

"We still have time. The ship will start in the evening. I can take you on an island tour. Show you places."

"Places? Here?" A hesitation darkened Amelia's eye.

"Don't worry, dear. Your Indian friend wouldn't flee if you leave her alone for a little while. Please, come with me. The island is tiny. Wouldn't take much time."

Amelia flashed a smile that seemed too tight around the fringes.

As she came near, Morticia held her hand. Another tingling rippled hot through her.

After walking some distance, Amelia said, "I love to see that a woman is so respected here. Only males get such opportunities, and women become slaves to their husbands."

Morticia weighed Amelia's comment for a moment. "Are you also like me, who hates to see only men get lifelong careers? Something they can grow and be proud of?"

"Yes, very much. Since my childhood in London. I was the one daydreaming to be an officer in a government office. Positions reserved only for men."

Now I understand why this woman never remarried after becoming a widow and is seeking solace from another woman.

Amelia's clenched her fists. "Men not only make women their slaves. They sometimes treat them as lambs they can butcher whenever they want."

Morticia wanted Amelia to continue opening up to her. "How so?" she encouraged.

"I know a woman whose husband killed her and convinced the police it was a suicide. She was hanging from the ceiling when police came."

"That's so sad."

"And his second wife had to flee for her life when the civil war in 1857 kept the husband busy. The husband died in the war, and the wife was so happy to become a widow."

"Never seen a woman welcoming widowhood. But I understand." *Is the woman Amelia herself? She can't dupe me.* "Men are like this. My father was one of them. So much so that my mother committed suicide. I was a child then. Little."

"So you must hate your father."

"No, Amelia. In fact, I was very close with my father. He brought me up like a boy. He would often tell me I should've been born as a boy."

"A boy?"

"I mean, he taught me to ride horses, use guns, swim, and everything a man would learn. Even he supported me wearing boys' clothing, but at home only."

"Lovely, Mort. My father also allowed me to study maths at home, as it was a boys' subject. I also learnt horse riding. But I had no fancy for boys' clothing."

They walked along a narrow pathway going on a hill. "Have you ever come here?" Morticia asked.

"Yes—no, no. Not here. I saw this from a distance and was thinking about coming, but I didn't dare."

"I will show you the best view of the island."

After walking for almost ten to fifteen minutes, they settled in front of a small cave. Seated on the stone in the cave's facade, Morticia came closer and took her hand. Amelia's hand vibrated a little, as if an unknown man touched her.

"You are a beautiful woman, Amelia. I'm certain no man will understand your value. They just want an obedient wife."

Amelia smiled.

She likes what I say. Sure, she has never received genuine love from any man.

"Amelia, did your friend ever remarry?"

"I...she...I don't know." Confusion flashed in Amelia's eyes.

I'm sure that woman is you, Amelia.

"Did you think of a remarriage for yourself?" Morticia sat closer and pressed Amelia's palm lightly.

Amelia glanced around.

"Don't worry, Amelia. I'm acquainted with everything on this islet. This place is most secure. Gives lots of privacy. I spend some quiet time here every time we pass through this place."

Amelia flashed another smile.

"Your friend who fled from her husband should've known how to retaliate."

"Is that possible? A woman! The man is always stronger than the woman."

"Strong? Yes, but their brains often live in their penis. And ours—" she pointed toward her head— "are here. We are stronger. Only if we learn how to use it against men. Just because society thinks women are not equal to men doesn't mean they're weak."

Amelia gazed at her.

Morticia felt encouraged. Her plan seemed to be working. "My first husband. I could turn the table against him. Your friend could've done some such a thing instead of fleeing."

"How?"

"First, create a story and make it known to the public somehow. Men fear that more than a gun. And if possible, use the law."

"Law? Which law says women are equal?"

"No such law. But there is one law which is more favourable to women than men—a dreaded one. One which a woman can use as a sharp knife, that could slice through the strongest bones of a man."

Amelia's eyes widened. "Which law?"

"The law of homosexuality. You and I are sitting together, closely, with our hands on each other's shoulders. This is not an offence in England. But if two men were physically close like this and cuddling, it is a punishable offence. Did you realise this?"

"No. Really?"

"I used it against my spouse. I just wanted him to behave with me. But he was so terrified, he hung himself."

Amelia reeled back. "What did you do, Mort?"

Should I reveal everything to her? No. Too soon.

"I found an object to implicate him. To show he was making love with another man. That's all. Simple."

Morticia felt Amelia's smile of appreciation.

"Can I ask you something? If you don't mind?"

Amelia didn't reply. Her answer was in her gaze.

"Your friend. Sez. She looks so feminine, even though she is taller than you. Agreed, she has developed some muscles. But muscles only can't make you happy. How does she satisfy you?"

A pause. Amelia didn't respond. She was thinking.

"Like this?" Morticia touched Amelia's breasts.

Amelia smiled back. Suddenly, Morticia grabbed her face and started kissing her passionately.

"Your husband—" Amelia gently freed herself from Morticia— "Mr. Hunt." She swallowed. "Wouldn't he object?"

"Don't worry about him. I have secrets about him, too. He will never open his mouth." Morticia started unbuttoning Amelia's top.

"Not now. Please, Mort."

Morticia stilled. "I have an instrument which is not available to anyone. Sez can't even think of something other than using her hand to satiate you. But I've that in my bedroom. You will never think of a man's shaft once you taste that."

Amelia smiled. "Mort, you are so nice."

I see. And I will get you on my bed.

"You know, Mort, the woman I was talking about?"

"The woman who fled?"

"Yes. That was me."

Morticia smiled on the inside, but she controlled her emotions outwardly. *This woman will be my best companion. Finally, an English female.*

"I will invite you one night to my bedroom and surprise you with what I have."

The sun was dipping behind the hills. They both stood. Time to go back and board the ship.

CHAPTER SEVEN

AMELIA, 26 AUGUST 1862, EVENING, SHIP HAS LEFT FROM JAMBU ISLAND

W e start the second phase of our sail to Andaman when the ship leaves Jambu Island this evening. After having our dinner, Sehnaz and I both retreat to our cabin for the night.

"When I was in Bibi Khanum's *kotha*, Madhuri once showed me an ancient book called *Kamasutra*. It had dozens of sex positions. I should have visited the section for woman-to-woman sex, though."

"What else did Madhuri show you?" Sehnaz asks as she reaches above the bed and dims the oil lamp. She is almost ready for the first night's sleep on the ship after leaving Jambu.

"Replica statues of Khajuraho temple. And some figurines showing two men having sex together. Was it common in India?"

Sehnaz chuckles. "Possibly. If it is in a famous book and in engravings on temples. Are you worried about what you will do if Morticia invites you to her room?"

I consider it for a moment. "I don't think so. This afternoon, she tried to fondle me. But she has Sadhna, anyway."

"Sadhna is no match for you. You are beautiful, you have white skin—and also large bubbies."

I move closer to her on the mattress and pinch her. "But she doesn't have a shaft. I'm not interested in love with a woman. We both are sharing one bed since we boarded the ship. Have I ever touched you? I don't have such interest, Sez."

"Lo, didn't you just touch me? And I'm feeling hot. Oh, my, I will remove my clothes. Now." She removes her top and deposits on the bedside table.

I let out a supressed giggle. "Not that way, Sez. I didn't touch your private parts!"

"So what? I haven't slept with a man in years. And any touch, even if from another woman, is arousing me. Didn't Madhuri tell you—when you are hungry, you eat whatever is available!"

Sehnaz grabs my top and starts unbuttoning it. Her eyes dance along with the flicker of the lantern. Even though I understand this is just acting, I struggle to move past the awkwardness.

"Stop, Sez. Be serious. To be honest, I'm not interested in getting love from another woman."

"If you don't, start now."

"I can't do that."

"Listen Amelia, the work we both have undertaken will fail unless we both plan how to extract information and use people to our benefit. Didn't I tell you, the more acting you do, the better it is for our mission?"

"How?" I feel this is the same Sehnaz who was managing the spies of Awadh empire five years ago.

"Morticia and Rave seems to be influential among the British officials. They might be our medium to reach Rupen. You need to find out their weaknesses. If they are corrupt, we can think of bribing them. This is the way spying works the best."

I pause. The dimming oil lamp on the side table casts a lazy blink. Sehnaz is right. But how do I do perfect acting?

"We'll think about it later, Sez." Lying on the bed, I pull up the sheet. "You teach me how to act as a different persona to keep her happy."

As soon as Sehnaz bends to douse the oil lamp, a knock sounds on the door.

Malti is standing with an oil lamp facing me. A dark cloud hovers on her face.

"Ma'am," Malti whispers.

"Are you all right Malti?"

Her voice quivers. "Your honour, ma'am. Danger."

A naughty and suppressed smile dances inside my guts. Indian women fear losing the honour of sexual assaults or even having pre or extramarital affairs.

"What happened, Malti?"

"Ma'am, go, run..."

Is she thinking I will run away to preserve my honour? Where? Into the ocean?

"Malti, please tell me clearly." My voice is firm but low, like a whisper.

"Big memsahib, calling. In her cabin."

Why has Morticia sent Malti to call me when her cabin is next to ours?

"Okay, you go. Goodnight."

"Ma'am, not go, angry. Very angry. Me."

I plant my fist over my mouth. How long can I hide my giggle?

"Your blouse is safe on your bubbies, Malti." Sehnaz chuckles. "Go and sleep. Amelia memsahib will meet big memsahib. She is not worried about her blouse."

Malti retreats, and I shut the door and swing back to face Sehnaz. "Her bubbies are valuable, and mine are cheap!"

"This is an opportunity, Amelia. Go and grab. The best thing is she can't make you pregnant. But you can be closer to her and use it to your advantage. Remember, sex is the best bribe and so far she is our only known way to find Rupen."

It feels like walking into the butcher's house.

As Morticia opens the door with a seductive smile, stories of demonesses in various Hindu epics flash before my eyes. A perfumed candle on her side table blinks and mocks at me.

Is Morticia planning to make me her concubine?

"Sit down?" Her hoarse voice sounds like a man's.

She guides me to the bed. The cabin is around four times larger than ours. A sofa with a centre table adorns the room. The bed looks like a royal *palank* bed of some Indian king, and a set of fairies about to fly is designed in the headboard.

She pours some drink into two glasses and gives one to me. "Mahua."

The pleasant aroma of *mahua* tickles my nose with the first sip, and its floral taste leaves a fiery trail down my throat. "I never drink, sorry."

Morticia drinks almost half of her glass. "I love it. The men of Jambu make it. You can get this in Calcutta, too. Tribals of Bengal and Orissa also extract this drink." She gazes at my glass idling on the table.

I realize then—the tribals of Jambu had offered this drink to Sehnaz and me when we thought they had abducted us.

Morticia sits near me. She holds my face with one hand and kisses my lips. Disgusting. But what do I do? Sehnaz has trained me never to show my feelings to her.

"I love you, Amelia."

"L... lo... love you, too." I slap a smile on my face.

She removes my blouse. Is this what Malti feared? But I'm sitting in a closed room where a woman is looking at my breasts. What would she do other than fondle me?

My bubbies are now in Morticia's palms. But she is gentle with them.

Amelia, force a smile and be proactive.

I put my nipples in her mouth, like a mother pushing hers into the mouth of a newborn. She displays her appreciation with a chuckle.

"Oh, Morticia, you...you are so good." A forced moan jumps out of my lips.

Can Sehnaz hear me moaning?

Morticia gets off the bed and starts undressing. This is the chance to pour more *mahua* into her empty glass. Her half naked body is on display for me now. She is wearing a breastband over her nearly flat chest, making it flatter. A noticeable bulge has tented her underpants.

A terrified surprise punches through me. Is this a man dressed like a woman?

Sehnaz's jokes flashes in my mind—*You'll never be pregnant*—and I shiver. Escape from the lion's den looks impossible. Morticia's ugly chest frightens me. She even has some chest hair. Looks like she has shaved them.

My hand creeps onto her bulge when she hugs me. It must be a rolled-up cotton sheet to give a manly look to her groin. Thank God there's no real man inside.

But what next?

Now it's my turn to remove my clothes. Should I also be in my drawers, like Morticia?

"No," she mutters. She removes my clothes, making me stand before her stark naked. Why do I feel awkward? Didn't I stay unclothed in Shakti Ashram, among the nude nuns?

But Morticia is no nun. She is very much a man in a woman's body. I take this chance and pour her another drink. She finishes the glass in one gulp and smiles at me.

"My...my s...sweet darling."

Is *mahua* a powerful drink? Can I make her reveal her secrets?

Thank God I took only one sip.

"Mort, darling," my dramatic action starts, "people of that island are uncivilised. But they respect you."

"I kn...know. I will make a small city for them."

"City? Where?"

"Jambu. They will wear clothes, and the children will go to the school."

"How will you do it, Mort? You need lots of money for that. Will Mr. Hunt give you so much to spend for the tribal people?"

She takes another drink from me. Will she tell me about the booty she and Mr. Hunt have hidden in Jambu?

Morticia opens her cupboard and takes out a packet.

"You will get the best experience tonight, Amelia. Don't tell anyone I've this. Got it after spending lots of money."

An unknown fear stops my breath for a while. What's in the pack?

Morticia smiles and removes a penis like object from the packet.

A jerk shakes the ship, and the package falls on the ground. As she bends to pick it up, an excruciating pain arises between my thighs. Is this because I'm getting too nervous?

I jump off the bed. Morticia gazes at me. "Don't worry about the money, darling. I know where I'll get the funds to build Jambu kingdom."

I hug her. "Mort darling, I love you so much. But this *mahua* is too strong. My head is reeling. It is killing me. Right now, at this moment."

Morticia's gaze goes blank. I'm sure *mahua* is riding over her. As she grabs the bedframe, I help her onto it and lay her down.

"I've...l...lots of money, Amelia. Don't worry."

"Thanks, Mort."

I put on my clothes and gaze at her before running to my cabin. "Goodnight, Mort darling."

She doesn't respond. Did *mahua* show its colour?

It's almost midnight. Shock fills me when I find Sehnaz is not inside the room. Where can she be at this hour of the night? Is she in danger?

I take out the pistol from my suitcase. As I trudge onto the deck, the drizzle and darkness blur my vision.

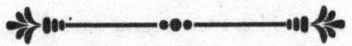

Sehnaz, 26 August 1862, 10 PM, Ship in Bay of Bengal

Sehnaz couldn't sleep. How could she? Amelia had gone to Morticia's cabin. She might take at least two hours. Would Amelia exploit every potential situation to find out a way to save Sehnaz from life in prison and also help Rupen's escape?

So far, she had no clue how they both would achieve all this. Seemed like an impossible dream.

She stepped out of the bed and opened the window. A gust of chilly breeze ruffled both her hair and patience. She glanced at the sky. Moonlight blended with the clouds and had taken the same scarlet red colour as the uniform of the merciless British occupiers.

The ship was mid-sea. Guards must have been sleeping, as the risk of any prisoner escaping was impossible. An idea flashed inside her brain. This was the right time to explore the ship and also to connect with the convicts. She took out some money from her suitcase, got to her feet, and walked out of the cabin. The deck was empty.

A passage took her to the rear side of the ship, and Sehnaz noticed that no guards were there, either. *What a perfect time!*

She was about to reach the cargo area when a guard appeared and saluted.

Sehnaz gazed at him. An Indian. Would her plan work tonight?

"What is your name, sepoy?" she asked.

"Bilal, ma'am."

"Bilal, are you the only guard tonight?"

"Yes, ma'am. Although it's not necessary. Who will run away from a ship in the middle of the ocean at night? But what to do? Rave sahib's order."

She didn't wish to waste time.

"That's good, Bilal. Can I ask for some favour?"

"Favour?"

"There's no risk to you, Bilal. And..." She glanced around to make sure no one was listening and brought her voice to a whisper. "I will reward you."

Bilal's eyes glowed in the faint light of the lamp he was holding.

"I would love to look at the prisoners."

"But, ma'am, they're all sleeping."

"I can hear the noise. That means some are still awake."

Bilal came closer. "Right, ma'am. We are transporting the prisoners the same way people move cattle. Inhuman conditions. I pity them."

Sehnaz gazed at Bilal. He must have been one of the many soldiers who had never joined the rebels during 1857's mutiny. And now he's enjoying freedom and a job.

"Sheru!"

"Sorry, ma'am?"

"No, nothing. Some name slipped out of my mouth." *Poor Sheru. How is he now?* Sehnaz removed money from the tiny bag she had hidden inside her clothes.

"No need, ma'am. I will ask for it when the work finishes. In a safe place."

Safe place?

Sehnaz followed Bilal. Within minutes, they arrived at a locked door. He fished out a key from his pocket and opened the door of a tiny cabin. A metal ladder led to the cargo area below.

"It is difficult to climb down the ladder, ma'am. I mean, for ladies. Risky." He opened a tiny window and peeked down.

"Here," he muttered again, "some lamps are still on. You can see something. Please come."

Bilal gave space to Sehnaz. She peeked at the cargo area below, leaning against the metal window. A foul smell pinched her nose. Bilal was right. British authorities hadn't differentiated between cattle and prisoners of war.

All the prisoners were sleeping on the dirty floor. Only two oil lamps in different corners were blinking. Her gaze went to the backside of a man who was sitting near the lamp reading something. He had broad shoulders and appeared tall, head buried in a book. Dark thoughts passed through Sehnaz as she stood there for almost ten minutes, covering her mouth with her scarf, trying not to cry.

Bilal hinted from behind her—time to go back. The man earned his bribe for today. She would ask him about his night duty so that she might come again.

Sehnaz straightened her body. She was about to go back, but a coughing sound below stopped her. She swung back and peeked again. The man she was watching just doused the lamp.

Sheru!

She stilled. He must be Sheru. Even though her gaze fell on him for only a fraction of a second, how could she forget the man who had helped her sail through Gomti and Ganga River? This was the man who had faced many hardships to keep her safe.

Bilal's whisper brought her to her senses, and she came out of the tiny, hot cabin.

"Thanks, Bilal." She took out the money from her bag.

"Not here. Let's go to a secure place. I don't want to rot in prison, too." An upbeat tempo sounded in his voice. Who doesn't like extra money?

Sehnaz walked with Bilal. Just after about twenty feet, he unlocked a tiny cabin and said, "Please come inside."

Sehnaz stepped in. She must negotiate with this man for more visits. She was sure Sheru might have noticed her, as Bilal's lamp was throwing some light on her face, too.

"How are you, Sehnaz?"

A shock passed over Sehnaz's body. How did this man know her actual name?

She stared again into Bilal's face. A cruel smile curving his lips frightened Sehnaz.

"I am Sez. Who is this Sehnaz? You must be mistaken."

Bilal snickered. "I don't know who this Sez is. However, I recognise you, Sehnaz. I was in Lucknow. Rupen sahib was your patron, and you were a famous courtesan."

Another shock passed through Sehnaz's veins. *Famous courtesan?* Yes, she was at one time famous in Lucknow. Did that mean she could never hide her identity? *The sepoy mutiny was already over five years ago. What does this man know?*

"I was there when you left the *kotha* after obtaining the confidential map of The Residency."

Sehnaz swallowed. Her heart thumped inside her ribs. *Calm down, Sehnaz! Don't show you are afraid.* "Wrong. Who told you?"

"Someone. Another courtesan who was on English payroll? That map was important, and because of that Rupen sahib besieged The Residency, the prestigious fort of the British."

"You must have me mistaken for someone else. Yes, I know about The Residency siege. Everyone in the country knows. So what? The English won and captured Rupen. Betraying his trust. After chopping off the heads of his wife and two daughters. That also everyone knows. Then what I've to do with that? Can't you see I am a friend of a white woman? Do you think a white woman would be friends with a courtesan who had helped the rebels?"

"Amelia ma'am?"

"Yes." Sehnaz's breath became normal. *Am I now winning the argument?*

Bilal lifted his chin. The defiant glint in his eyes pierced Sehnaz's confidence. "You, Amelia ma'am, and Sheru got into a boat in Gomti River, outskirts of Lucknow. I even remember the date. May 1857."

Everything around Sehnaz seemed like it was revolving. She glanced around for something to hold on to, as if a furious cyclone was about to blow her away.

Nothing to hold in sight.

She stepped back a little and leaned against the wall. It was time to be strong and pretend ignorance. There was no other way to save herself from the dreaded Andaman prison.

Sehnaz inhaled deeply. "You must have seen someone else. Did you see them early in the morning? Just before dawn?"

"Yes."

She forced a laugh out. *Another point to counter this man!* "Darkness might have blurred your vision, Bilal. You saw everything wrong, and you're bluffing now. You need this bribe, take your bribe, and go away."

His eyes glinted as he inched closer. "Bribe? Where is the bribe?"

Bilal's foul smell made Sehnaz scramble to go away. She composed herself and opened her purse string.

"Wait Sehnaz, I haven't finished."

"What else?"

"That morning my vision was all right. My eyes saw everything, even in the dark. How else would I know that the boat with a dozen British soldiers stopped you mid-river? Didn't the officer who jumped onto your ferry ask for that map?"

How could this man see? All the soldiers in that boat were white, and another rebel ferry ambushed all of them. She was sure this man was not there.

"What are you thinking, Sehnaz? I was in another boat, following yours. I had a strong binocular with me."

"What did you notice?"

"I witnessed the rebel ferry ambushing the soldiers. Although not all of them."

Sehnaz paused. Arguing with this man wouldn't work. She needed another way to get rid of him. To save her life from the prison.

"What I got before that, when the officer jumped into your boat, that is important." Bilal licked his lips.

A tent in his groin mocked at Sehnaz. A whispering chill sunk into her chest. Her hope to avoid the prison was shattering into pieces.

Bilal touched his middle leg. "The scenery I saw that day, oh my."

He paused for a moment and started again. "Didn't the officer take away your saree?"

She flinched and couldn't argue further.

"And then he tore your blouse, too." He licked his lips again. "And your...your *ripe fruits?*"

"You must have noticed what happened after that?" Sehnaz's eyes were radiating fire.

"Sheru killed him. Oh, what a sweet death! I am also ready to die once I touch your bubbies." His eyes sparkled.

Didn't Sehnaz advise Amelia only hours ago to surrender to Morticia?

This was her turn. Then what if she became pregnant?

Bilal latched the door from the inside and took out his knife.

Sehnaz forced a seductive smile on her lips. "You don't have to blackmail me about this, Bilal. I was a courtesan and have slept with so many men that I've lost count."

"Nice girl. Then I will take again and again."

Bilal stepped forward to grab Sehnaz and started kissing her.

She had a sharp inhalation. Either she would swallow her pride or surrender her freedom to the British.

Her soul cried for freedom.

"Please call me Sez, if you want to, again and again. Okay?"

"Done." He removed Sehnaz's blouse and grabbed her bubbies. "Your nipples are lovely, Sez." He moaned.

The man seems to be in a hurry. Isn't this the best time to defeat him in his own game?

"Remove your pants, Bilal. I haven't touched a man's shaft for ages. And I'm hungry."

"Lower your voice, Sez. You will spoil everything."

What is this man afraid of?

"All right." As Sehnaz tugged his shirt with force, some buttons broke and came away.

Bilal's hands slipped from Sehnaz's breasts as he grabbed his shirt. "You will get me caught, Sez. Am I going to fuck you, or you to me?"

This is your medicine, Bilal. Right now, you get to see what a former courtesan can do.

Sehnaz grabbed his face and kissed him passionately, pulling his palms over her breasts. As Bilal's face was in her control, she unlatched the cabin door.

Bilal moved his lips away and started sucking Sehnaz's nipple.

"I love you, Bilal," Sehnaz moaned.

"Calm down, Sez. Lower your voice." Bilal released her nipples when Sehnaz grabbed the tented portion of his pants.

"What is this, Bilal? Your shaft is so weak! How would you do it with me?"

She felt a shock vibrating through Bilal. He left Sehnaz and unbuttoned his pants.

"No, it's all right."

"Show me." Sehnaz held his love-handle as if she were examining it. "Not at all. It is sleeping." She felt his penis softening after her comments.

Sehnaz had recollected the old trick of how to play with a man's mind.

Suddenly, the door of the cabin jerked open. A shocked Bilal stood up straight and scrambled for his shirt and pants.

"So, here you are!" Amelia stood there with her pistol.

Bilal stood, shivering, folding his hands. "Sorry, ma'am. I will never do this again. Please forgive me."

Sehnaz and Amelia both chuckled as Sehnaz put on her blouse. When both were about to leave, suddenly Bilal took out his gun and shoved Amelia. She fell on the floor, her pistol landing at a distance. Throwing himself on her, Bilal grabbed Amelia, his own pistol still in his grasp.

Rain began to spatter against the windows.

Horror and anger both engulfed Sehnaz, blood rushing to her brain. This man knew her secret. Even if he let them go tonight, he could ruin her life the next day. As Amelia struggled to free herself, Sehnaz lifted her pistol and hit Bilal's ear.

Bilal's grip over Amelia slackened, and she stood up. Bilal fell unconscious on the floor.

"We need some water to sprinkle on him," Amelia said, staring at him.

"He is a poisonous snake, and he will bite as soon as he gets up. He knows my name and also what I did with the map of The Residency. He was blackmailing me."

"What do we do, then?"

"Finish him." Sehnaz's grip on the pistol tightened.

"Are you going to shoot him?" Amelia's eyes widened.

"No. Blood. People will know from the sound and blood on the floor." She glanced around. Rain continued bombing down against the windows. "This is the perfect time, Amelia. No one is around. You hold his head and I, his legs. Either we push him into the sea and kill him, or he will finish me tomorrow. No one will know where he has gone."

It was just a splash in the Bay of Bengal.

CHAPTER EIGHT

RUPEN, 27 AUGUST 1862, MIDNIGHT, ANDAMAN PRISONERS' ENCAMPMENT

T he gun sound tore through Rupen's slumber. He woke up and glanced out the tiny window of his cottage on the east side of the prison encampment of Andaman Islands. A half-moon mocked at him through the slits of the monsoon cloud. Blank fires were not new to him. Occasionally, night guards shot at the air. The only way to frighten the inmates against escape attempts in the open-air prison in the jungle.

He got off the bed and poured a glass of water from the earthen water pot kept on the floor. The faint moonlight reflected and dazzled on the copper glass in his hand. A chuckle escaped from his mouth. The days in Lucknow where he was living in his palatial mansion surrounded by the servants were gone since 1857, when he lost the war to the British and was taken into custody.

This is his fifth year in Andaman prison; he counted.

"We are proud of you, *pitaji.*" His slain daughters' chorus voice sounded in his ears.

Rupen held the glass with one hand and walked to the window, glancing at the sky. The dark clouds at places had cleared up, showing patches of blue sky. Three stars from the eastern sky smiled at him. "Oh, there you are, you naughty girls! Were you waiting for the clouds to clear away before you would talk to me? It's midnight, go and sleep."

"We are in heaven, dear," a lovely voice echoed inside his heart as a mild gush of wind touched his skin and a gentle fragrance tingled his nose. A memory bubbled in his heart. This was the same perfume he had bought from a Persian trader for his wife. She was wearing the same even after becoming a star!

"So, you are also with the girls! Not getting sleep? How did you find me?" he gazed at the third star and muttered.

"We don't need sleep like the mortals on the earth, dear." His wife's soft voice sounded inside his soul. "We were trying to look for you in the prisons of India for the last five years. Then we came to know the British have sent many war prisoners to Andaman. It's so nice to see you after so many years."

A patch of dark cloud came over the stars and covered the view, sending a shock wave through Rupen's heart. He raised the glass and drank the water in three large gulps. The air was humid and pinching his skin. He remained standing there for a while, hoping to see his family again in the stars. The cloud was moving slowly, raising Rupen's hope.

His wife and daughters smiled at him again after a few minutes.

"*Pitaji*," his youngest said, "We saw other senior rebel leaders imprisoned in India. Why did you come all the way to Andaman?"

"He didn't come by choice, you silly girl," the eldest corrected her, "*Pitaji* is the bravest of the rebel leaders and the British is afraid he might attack them again and send them back to England with their baggage for ever."

Rupen chuckled and nodded his head in appreciation.

"But dear," the largest of the three stars asked, "I saw Nawab Wajid Ali is in a new palace in Calcutta, but under house arrest. Many royals and senior generals of other kingdoms who had revolted against the British are in prisons, but they are calling them *political prisoners*. Means they are living in luxury but can't go outside. Then why are you languishing here?"

Rupen chuckled. "Didn't you hear what our eldest daughter said? They're afraid of me. But don't worry. Here also I am living as a political prisoner. I'm not living the terrible life like ordinary prisoners. The authorities have provided me this cottage, and a servant comes to cook and wash for me. I don't do physical labour like others."

"Still, this is a prison for you," his wife lamented from inside the star. "The man who had lived in a luxurious mansion all his life is now happy to live in a one-room cottage? And no one to talk with?"

"This is the best I can get here. I've a friend who sometimes comes and talks to me."

"Who?"

"Dr. James Pattison Walker, the governor of Andaman. He was in Lucknow before the war in 1857 and knew me. I have even convinced him and specially arranged for my fifteen soldiers of Awadh kingdom."

"You mean those fifteen soldiers are not suffering like any other prisoners?"

Rupen closed his eyes. How would admit to his wife in heaven that the arrangement was in exchange for Dr. Walker sending the soldiers with Captain Hunt to help him in piracy? The governor is a corrupt person and didn't trust any other inmates for the job. They could open the lid of his illegal work and authorities would find out how a senior official was amassing wealth partnering in piracy with the notorious Captain Hunt.

"Dear, I've something to..." He lifted his eyes, but alas, a gigantic cloud had already blocked his view. Rupen let out a sigh. A gush of chilly wind blew inside the cottage along with drops of water. Thunder boomed outside.

Rupen's heart broke into pieces when he closed the window. Authorities were regularly torturing thousands of prisoners in the encampment. How could Dr. Walker make him agree to persuade his loyal soldiers for his own nefarious use? He had thought this was only a temporary arrangement, but that immoral work was still continuing. *God, I will rather rot like those thousands of prisoners, but show me the way out of this dreaded sin.*

Thunder boomed, and lightning streaked through the crevices of the wooden windowpane. Rupen climbed on his cot. There was no chance to view the stars again.

Somewhere in the distance, he heard the gun sound again. First one and then several in a row. Surprise rippled through him. The rain smashed against the windows, and he pulled the sheet over him in an attempt to sleep. But the faces of his slain wife and two daughters appeared in his mind again.

A knock sounded on the door. A man with a British accent shouted, "Rupen sir, please get up."

He sprang up and sat straight on the bed.

"Sir, please open the door. Dr. Walker has sent me. Emergency."

Rupen jumped from the bed and opened the door.

There was an English soldier standing on the veranda, drenched in the rain. A few feet away, another soldier was securing two horses against a tree.

"Sir," the man breathed hard, "Dr. Walker sent us with this letter."

Rupen took the letter, walked inside and lighted the oil lamp.

Dear Mr. Naik,

I am writing this in a hurry. Prisoners have revolted and killed one guard. They have also taken around fifty guards as hostage and threatened to kill them. Our men have tried to frighten them with blank fires, but you know all the prisoners are ex-soldiers and they know how to fight. I'm afraid they will kill those innocent guards, most of whom are Indians. And you will appreciate I can't fulfill their demands and make them free. Impossible. The soldiers in my command are not attacking, as they don't want their colleagues to die. But if the rebels ambush the besieged guards, I have no other option but to order a shootout and you know that means at least a few hundred inmates will die.

I'm sure you, with your reputation and leadership skill, can bring a quick solution to this.

Yours sincerely,

Dr. James Pattison Walker

A chill crackled down Rupen's skin. This was madness. Even if the rebels somehow fled, where would they go? Perhaps they didn't know Andaman Islands were eight hundred miles from Calcutta.

He stomped out of the room and said to one of the soldiers, "Give me one of your horses and then guide me to the spot. Immediately. Now."

"Yes, sir," the man responded.

Rupen jumped onto the saddle of one horse and the soldiers on another, and all of them ran through the whipping rain. Rupen could see only the silhouette of the horse ahead of him in the darkness. He lifted his head and looked at the sky, the cloud above the encampment slowly clearing away. The horses waded through the mud and weeds inside the wood. Choruses of a thousand or more people, "Hail with Mother India," alerted him he was near the rebel spot. In about twenty minutes, he arrived at the large open area and halted around a hundred yards away from the location.

Dark clouds had cleared away, allowing the moon to spread some light. Rupen at first didn't make out what he could do. He was less concerned about the worries of Dr. Walker and more about what could be the consequences of such a revolt for the inmates.

He could see the backs of thousands of men who had surrounded the hostages.

"Friends!" He got off the horse and tried to draw attention. None heeded. His voice drowned in the cacophony.

"Hail with Mother India." Another chorus shook the jungle.

He looked around; the two British soldiers who had escorted him were standing behind him, shivering, helpless guns hung on their shoulders.

"We want..." a man in the crown started a slogan.

"Freedom from Andaman." All inmates completed the sentence.

Rupen thought of wading through the crowd to walk inside, but that didn't seem to be practical. He remembered the prisoners were from different parts of India. Other than Awadh kingdom, he was not a known figure to rebels in other Indian kingdoms.

"Do you have a lamp?" he asked the English soldier behind him.

"Yes, sir."

"Then light it now and give it to me."

The soldier immediately lighted the oil lamp and handed it over to Rupen. He sighted a hillock nearby and climbed on it, holding the lamp.

"Friends," he screamed with all his might, lifting the lamp against his face.

The commotion calmed down in an instant, and thousands of faces swung around to face him. A current passed through Rupen's nerves. It wasn't possible to see the reaction of so many people in the faint moonlight. He also had the risk of mistrust of being a British agent.

"Friends," Rupen said again, using all his strength to make the loudest voice possible, "I am Rupen Naik, I was the army chief of Awadh kingdom."

The crowd burst into another chorus of slogan which Rupen hadn't expected.

"Our leader..." one rebel who stood on a tree branch screamed.

"Rupen Naik." The crowd responded.

"Long live..."

"Rupen Naik."

Rupen had never dreamed in the past five years that so many prisoners knew his name.

He raised both of his hands to pacify the crowd.

"Friends," he spoke again in Hindi, "the guards who are under the siege are all Indians. I mean, most of them are Indians. They are our brothers. They have come here at the instruction of the British, leaving their families far away. The authorities here are the least bit bothered about their lives. They can bring another five hundred Indian guards to replace them, either from Calcutta or Madras. That too in a matter of a month. So, please do not kill them. Can you all hear me? DO. NOT. KILL. THEM."

A wave of murmuring spread through the crowd of rebel prisoners.

Rupen waited for a minute to see the outcome of his speech.

"What about our freedom?" a man in the front row shouted.

Rupen had no answer. He could at best talk to Dr. Walker. But Dr. Walker was the governor of Andaman, not of India. He had no authority to take such a decision about the inmates. The authorities in Calcutta were at least bothered about either the prisoners or the Indian guards. Their lives had no value to them.

He must pacify the prisoners, or his failures could see the Indian guards dead before the dawn.

"Friends, this is not the time to discuss this point. I will talk to Andaman's governor and ask that none of you gets any punishment for this rebellion. But only the viceroy of India can make a decision about freedom. So please leave the guards now. They don't deserve to die because of a foreign government's injustice to us. We can't kill our own blood."

Another wave of murmuring and the ring of inmates surrounding the hostages loosened.

His speech was showing its effect.

"I promise you people," Rupen spoke again, "that I will do my best for you. Whatever is possible for me. But my humble request—please leave the guards. Let them go."

The army of the inmates parted, and the hostages were out. Except about five, they all were Indians. They stood before Rupen and saluted him. "Thank you, sir. We're grateful for our lives."

The soldier who had accompanied Rupen came forward and said to the guards, "Please go back to your barracks."

"Thank you—" Rupen folded his hands to the prisoners— "now it is too late at night. Please go back to your designated huts and get some sleep." He came down from the hillock and watched in silence as the prisoners dispersed. Then he gazed at the English soldiers who had accompanied him. "Now please take me to my cottage. And one more thing, please tell Dr. Walker not to take action against the inmates who had started the revolt."

Amelia, 27 August 1862, Afternoon, Ship sailing in Bay of Bengal

Sehnaz's fate scares me. She is also spooked since last night's events, after the second murder she has committed. We both had dragged Bilal to the edge of the ship, but she gave him the last push into the ocean. I didn't have that courage.

Self-defence is not a sin. Right?

But in the eyes of the law, self-defence for avoiding prison is a grave crime. Unfortunately, this is the truth.

What would happen if others were to find out we killed Bilal?

Sleep dodged both of us the whole of last night.

Sehnaz hasn't come out of the cabin all morning. She is sick and needs rest. Except for going to the dining hall for breakfast and lunch,

I also haven't dared to go out. With even a slight noise outside, my nerves are making everything inside me pulsate.

"If anyone had seen us make Bilal disappear last night, we would be in handcuffs by now," Sehnaz says. "Amelia, this's the time to be strong. Your eyes are saying we both are the culprit. Please control your mood and go out for a walk. We didn't kill that man. He must have drunk too much and fallen into the water. But you know nothing, Amelia. No one should ask you. Please go out pretending you are taking a stroll and gather what is happening."

"You had been to the cargo area, and others might have seen." Unease feathers through me at the thought of going out.

"So what? I went to explore the freight the ship is carrying. And that was the night I was not getting sleep. How does that relate to someone's disappearance? And remember, you don't know that a man named Bilal even existed."

I have never been to other parts of this large vessel before. With no rain all day today, Sehnaz's advice sinks in.

You will be all right, Amelia. Pretend you are just out for a leisurely walk. Control your nerves.

Our cabin has a window, which opens to the corridor on the right side of the ship. If a man walks from the deck to another part of the vessel, he can easily peep through our window and see us. This is the reason we often keep this window closed.

The level beneath ours is the kitchen and a hall. The bottommost part is for five British soldiers. I guess Captain Hunt also stays there. How does he avoid embarrassment from sleeping alone when his wife is on the ship?

I've seen these areas before—on the same day we had boarded the ship at Calcutta. But I still stroll around as if this is part of my *leisurely walk.* Then I step out to visit other parts of the ship I have never been.

I arrive at the middle of the ship. I stand there silently and watch. Last night I had passed through this and didn't notice the staircase leading to somewhere I don't know.

He is a poisonous snake, and he will bite as soon as he gets up. Sehnaz's anxious but angry voice last night still sounds inside my brain.

My feet drag me to the siderail, and I bend over to watch the water. Is Bilal's body still floating in the water?

"Good afternoon, ma'am."

I flinch and stand straight.

An Indian soldier salutes me.

"*Kaise ho?* How are you?" Hindi words slip out of my mouth.

A familiar smile forms on his face. "You are the first English lady who has come to our side," the guard says to me in Hindi.

I silently thank Sehnaz for teaching me the language.

"Where do you people stay?"

He flashes a smile, still standing straight, as if responding to a senior officer. "Memsahib, through this stairway. One level down."

I nod and respond with a smile. "And prisoners?"

Suddenly his smile vanishes. He turns left and stands facing the rear of the ship. "Memsahib, you see that small cabin?"

How can I forget that until even my death? I cast a quick glance at the tiny cabin where Bilal was assaulting Sehnaz last night. And the open space in front of it where both we women fought and killed that bastard. It's roughly fifty feet away from me.

He continues, without waiting for my reply. "Hardly twenty feet from there, there is the cargo compartment. They all stay there."

I picture a brief layout of the ship. First the deck and the rooms for us and Morticia. One level down, there is the kitchen and dining hall. The bottom most part is for the British soldiers.

The soldier is still standing there, probably awaiting for me to ask him more.

"Can I go inside and see how you people are living?"

"Memsahib, you?" He throws me a measuring glance.

I should have thought before asking. Bilal must be one of them. Am I going see how his mates are looking for him?

This is the perfect time to politely go away. I inhale a deep breath. No, I must see their reactions to Bilal's disappearance. Didn't Sehnaz teach me, *information is the best weapon to fight against the enemy*?

I slap on a smile and say, "Just curiosity, if you don't mind..."

"No, memsahib. We will be fortunate if you visit our living area. Even Captain Hunt has never visited inside. But..." He glances down.

"But what?"

"You wouldn't like it, memsahib. It's messy."

"That's all right."

I step onto the stairs, and the soldier follows me to the level down, leading us to a stinking hall.

The discrimination between white and brown blows on my face once I am inside. English guards living on our side have wider bunk beds, and they eat from the same kitchen as we do. Indian guards have one makeshift kitchen near their narrow beds—congested and dirty. The smell of stale food swamps my nose, but I'm determined not to show my reaction.

"I love Indian food. My maid in India always cooks for me." I force a smile while another guard is busy frying dried fish.

"We hardly get anything proper to eat, ma'am. Rice, chapati, dal and dried fish are our staple foods. Vegetarians have to be content with three items. With our depleting provisions, we all go half-stomach these days. Until we arrive at Great Coco Islands."

Guilt washes over me. English soldiers on our side never starve. Bread, cheese, meat, everything is in plenty in our kitchen.

"Why didn't you guys bring enough groceries? You knew how many days the ship would take to reach Andaman, right?"

"Yes, ma'am, but we didn't know we would stay so many days on Jambu. No market there. I don't understand why Rave sahib ordered the crew to make a stopover."

Another guard coughs and draws the man's attention, signalling him through his eyes. Is he asking his friend to be careful while talking to me? After all, I am English.

Or are they talking about Bilal? Another wave of discomfort shakes my nerves. *Breathe Amelia, breathe.*

"Why the Great Coco Islands? Aren't we going to Andaman directly? Or is there another stopover?"

"We must, memsahib. We will buy supplies from there for the people working in Andaman. That island is under Burma, even though the same British are ruling over there. They are the supplier of all groceries and even clothes to Andaman. We can buy something for us, too. Until then, we will get half or even less food for us."

Except showing my sympathy, I can never solve their problem. This discrimination must get a place in my diary. I still dream that one day, the contents of my diary will serve as a history of British rule in India, its bigotry against the natives, the iron stick it used to suppress the dissension.

Other guards watch me in silence, a fearful respect to the only English woman visiting their place with a sympathetic ear. Is anyone worried about Bilal, who vanished last night?

The thought of killing Bilal makes me sweat again. Am I not Sehnaz's accomplice in his murder?

"This place is stuffy, ma'am. And hot, too," the guard says.

Did he notice I'm in fact perspiring?

It is time to say goodbye to him and leave. What if someone comes and starts talking about the missing Bilal?

As soon as I am in the corridor, my gaze goes to a man I believe is in a captain's uniform. He must be Mr. Rave Hunt.

"Good afternoon, Mrs. Spencer." Captain Hunt stops, displaying a wide smile. "Are you wanting to inspect the ship? How are we managing things here?"

I take a brief pause. How did he know me? Is it because I'm the only white woman other than his wife? Or has Morticia told him about Sehnaz and me? "No, Mr. Hunt. Only curiosity and boredom brought me to this side."

Is my forced smile enough to hide my anxiety?

"I can take you on a tour of this large ship, if you wish."

My outfit is hardly provocative. But Mr. Hunt's eyes rotate around my body, consuming me.

Poor man. He is married to a woman, who is no less than a man. Is he not hungry to enjoy the closeness of a *real* female?

"I would love to see the ship, Mr. Hunt, with you." I fake a seductive smile and watch the reflection in his eyes. Sehnaz and I both heard the fight between the couple when Morticia accused him of being a homosexual. Is this true, or is his wife just playing games with him?

Didn't Morticia tell me how I should've manipulated my husband?

Mr. Hunt shows me where the Indian guards live but without taking me inside their dirty, cave-like cabin. I pretend to have never been inside and show no interest in peeking in.

Then we move to the next section of the ship.

"From here onwards is the cargo section," Mr. Hunt says. "We bring some provisions from Calcutta for those who work in Andaman, and also for the prisoners. But most supplies we pick up from the Great Coco Islands." He casts a sideways glance at me.

Even though the Indian guard had already educated me about the Coco only moments ago, I feign ignorance and allow him to repeat the same information. I'm determined to develop a friendship with both

Mr. and Mrs. Hunt (separately) and see whom we can use to find a path of freedom for Rupen—and also Sehnaz.

"Where do the prisoners live, Mr. Hunt?"

He gives me a measuring look. "You may address me by my first name, Rave."

"Thanks, you also—please address me as Amelia. Not Mrs. Spencer."

How would I convince this men's world why I have forsaken my dead husband's last name?

"You were asking about the prisoners' section, Amelia."

"Yes."

"I would advise you never to go to that side. Because you're a woman."

Thank goodness. We both are women, so who would assume that Bilal is missing because of us?

"It is dangerous for you to visit them. They are all unhappy because the British government is sending them to Andaman jail, the most feared prison in the country—named *Kala Pani*, which means Black Waters."

An Indian guard approaches and salutes him. "Sir, I tried everywhere. But didn't find."

Rave clenches his fists. "You are not searching a city, man. Only this vessel. I didn't ask you to look for him. I know he is not here. But did anyone see him? He must have fallen in the sea."

"Sir, I don't think he is so mad that he would jump into the water at night."

"I don't think so, either. But it is possible he fought with someone. Someone might have pushed him out."

I feel as if my head is reeling. I can't stand here anymore. "Rave, may I now go back to my cabin, please?"

"Yes, Mrs.—sorry, Amelia. It was a nice meeting you. See you again, soon."

My legs urge me to flee. I need to lie on my bed before I fall unconscious right here.

CHAPTER NINE

RUPEN, 31 AUGUST 1862, MORNING ROSS ISLAND (PART OF ANDAMAN ISLAND GROUP IN THE BAY OF BENGAL, 800 MILES FROM CALCUTTA) PRISONERS' SETTLEMENT

"**Y**ou guys want my blood? All right. I am here. You all have axes, and I've nothing. Come." Raising both his hands, Rupen stepped forward, but with caution. Axes in the hands of fifty plus prisoners used to chop trees could slash his head at any moment.

Rupen cast a quick glance around—many trees were lying on the ground in the thick Andaman rain forest housing the prison encampment. Even during the daytime, mosquitoes and other insects would have a party day sucking the blood of the unfortunate men who had been cursed to spend their entire life here.

The arguments and the accusations suddenly fell silent. "Come... on. And kill me."

The men stood still with axes in their hands. Others who were chopping wood stopped working and wandered over. He stared at them, confidence building in his veins.

Most of them were frail and stinking. Overgrown beards, prematurely grey hair, dirty and torn clothing, but eyes still dazzling with the courage they once had while fighting against the British.

"I came to talk to you people while the English guards are attending the Sunday church service and the Indian guards are watching the outer circle of the encampment."

He expected some reply. Some sort of acknowledgement from the inmates. But none came. He wondered, was this the calm before a storm?

"Come on, friends. Please say something. I am one amongst you." His confidence was withering away slowly.

He was alone, surrounded by the angry inmates and trees. The hutments where they lived were on another side of the encampment.

People in the detention centre envied him. Everyone there was a prisoner, irrespective of whether he was a general in the army or an ordinary sepoy.

Everyone? No. Except just one man. Rupen himself.

He lived in a distant corner of the Ross Island prisoners' encampment—near the gate that led to the residence of Dr. James Pattison Walker, first superintendent of the British government after they set up prison in this remote, God-forsaken location. Other prisoners respected him as he was the Chief General of Awadh army, who fought against the British and lost in 1857.

Rupen's muscles relaxed when the axes no longer looked intimidating. Waves of sympathy rolled out from his heart as he looked at the prisoners whose only crime was that they had battled against the British.

"Sir, forgive me for opening up my mind. I am an ordinary sepoy, the junior most in the rank. And you are the army chief," one frail looking man said, squeezing the handle at his side.

"I was. Now I'm a prisoner like you. No difference."

"Right sir, but in our eyes, you still are the same *bahadur* army chief. We were expecting you would guide us when we revolted here. You could have become our leader here again, in these prison camps."

"Leader? Again?" Rupen's voice boiled with anger. "Did anyone ask me before you all decided on an uprising? And to be frank, what you people did was not a rebellion at all. It was like a child's tantrum, too immature. You all attacked the only soldier you saw in front of you. Was that a plan? Or a moment's outburst?"

"Either way, sir," a frail looking tall man joined, "it was still a rebellion against the British."

"Not at all." Rupen clenched his fists. "This type of fighting brings nothing. Have you ever thought that the place we are now is over eight hundred miles from Calcutta? It's only ocean. Vast and dark deep-sea. Where would you go? Swim to Calcutta? Build a boat by joining logs and sail?"

"No, sir. But..."

"But what?"

"We could have gone to other islands."

"Other islands?" Rupen shifted and sat on a fallen log which was lying between him and the inmates. This made him feel like he was closer to them, more inside with them, and maybe they would trust them. "Andaman has over five hundred seventy islands. All full of tropical forests—dense and dangerous. Uncivilised tribal people. Most of them don't like outsiders in their area. For them British and Indians are all the same. They attack any outsiders they notice."

"But, sir, some islands have no inhabitants. We could have settled there." The man said folding his hands, his axe leaning against a tree on his side.

"For how long? Until the government brings more battalions from Calcutta to hound you from there?"

"Then what do we do, sir?" Another inmate with a long beard said, and then slumped on the ground.

Frustration stabbed Rupen's guts. He darted his eyes at the men, and then at the sky, for an answer. A sigh escaped his mouth. "To be honest, I also have no clue. I have some plans. Not sure if they will work."

The man with shaved head came forward, pushing others to the side and stood before Rupen, his axe hanging at his waist. "Sir, some of us have been here the last four years, and had accepted our fate. Now that the British are sending more and more soldiers who had taken part in 1857 mutiny, our numbers have increased and so has our hope of freedom."

Rupen looked up at the man and let out a friendly smile. "I wanted the rebellion to stop so that none of you would die of the firing. Remember, we are all humans. We survive on hope until our last breath."

"Sir, hope will not take us to our home."

"I understand. But the more revolting you do, the sooner the British will build the fort-like prison in Port Blair. A prison where each inmate will get a tiny cell. A tiny, dark unit with no window. You will stay their alone. Not enough space to stretch. How will you stay there, sitting on the floor? People will die sooner than anyone can even think."

"Sir, you know about Port Blair?" The tall one asked.

"Why do you think I am trying to please Andaman's governor, Dr. Walker? He is going slow in building that one. It may take years. This place is a prison, but you guys live in open space, inside hutments. At least at nights you all can talk to each other. You can even sing religious songs to keep your mind occupied. Pacify the mind. That's the only way to keep you healthy, too."

"Sir, will we ever see our families again?" the soldier who has lost one leg asked. "This is a prison for life. Will the British ever release us?"

Rupen scrambled for an answer. "They may. None of you are criminals. Only freedom fighters. The British realise that after living here for a few more years, most of you will be weak. Weak from having insufficient amounts of food, and from sickness. Not an enormous threat to the British Raj. They are spending lots of money on Andaman. When the government realises releasing you guys is no longer a risk to the Raj, then your dream of seeing your families will be a reality."

He glanced around at their reactions. Was his answer convincing?

Before he was able to gauge their responses, an old man came forward from among the men. "You will live a hundred years, sir. I may not live to see that day. But that is okay with me. I have no family. I am a hermit."

Hermit? Surprise slammed into Rupen. He always thought the inmates were only the rebel sepoys. *What is a hermit is doing in a prison?* He felt he should have come to meet the soldiers before.

An Indian guard came, brandishing a gun and a whip. "Everyone, go back to work. Now."

Within minutes, the place became empty. He was there alone with the old man and the guard. Now it was beyond Rupen's doubt why the inmates fear the guards so much.

Rupen asked the guard, "I saw scars on these people. How can you people beat the prisoners who are sick? Don't you have morality?"

"Sir." The man stood up and glanced around. Then he gave a quick salute. "Each prisoner gets a target per day. If they don't finish, the English soldiers will give us the same treatment." The man's features were guarded, as if he feared any English soldier noticing his actions.

Rupen was still commanding respect from the Indian sepoys on the British payroll! He felt his lips relaxing with his own faint smile. But guilt moved inside his guts. Thousands of prisoners were doing hard work every day without a break. And he, another prisoner, still enjoyed a comfortable stay and friendship with Dr. Walker. Seemed unfair to all those who deserted the British army to join the rebel forces.

The guard left, leaving Rupen alone to indulge in his own thoughts.

He was the only high-profile inmate whom the authorities in Calcutta had granted the political prisoner status, the same one they had granted to the rebel Indian kings who had lost the war in 1857 and were in various Indian prisons or under house arrest in their own palaces, like Nawab Wajid Ali. Rupen, however, was the only political prisoner who was sent to Andaman. Did the authorities consider him too dangerous even in a prison in the mainland India? He was getting similar privileges—a comfortable living and salutes from the guards. A silent chuckle came out of Rupen's mouth in praise of the diplomacy skills of the British government. They knew how to satisfy the ego of the rebel royals and generals like him.

Rupen glanced at the men busy chopping trees. Reduced to skeletons of daunting work. Blood and dried wounds mocked him through their torn and dirty clothes.

He swung back to go to his cottage, but his gaze went to the old man. "You are still here? I thought you went with the other prisoners."

"Sir—" the man folded his hands again— "I am too old to work. The officials are kind to me and have exempted me from the hard work."

"That's good to see." He walked away.

"Sir," the old man continued, walking alongside Rupen. "If you permit, can I say a few things? Before the English come back from the church? I may not get this chance another time."

Oh God, I have to listen to this man's story now! "All right, but be quick."

"I got punishment for sheltering two women in my ashram."

Rupen stilled. "Two women? You mean they were rebels?"

"Don't know, sir. But they allegedly stole the horse of an English soldier. I still don't believe they did. But who would have convinced the soldier?"

This man must be hallucinating. He stood gazing at the hermit.

"I can never forget that day, sir. It was May in 1857. When the rebellion was in full swing. One afternoon a ferry came to the Gomti's bank. Near the temple where I lived those days. A man and two women requested shelter. One woman was white. A *firangi*."

Rupen felt as if he were in a dream. "You remember their names?"

"Yes. They told me the names. The man's name was Sheru Pandey. He was the boatman. I had never seen a brahmin rowing a boat."

"And the women?"

"Amelia. The *firangi*."

A lightning bolt of a thought struck Rupen. How could he forget the day when the British army captured him and transported him in the Gomti River with Brigadier Colin? And Colin had even suspected Rupen's hand in his wife Amelia's disappearance.

"And the other woman?"

"Sehnaz."

Rupen's thoughts flew back to the days when he was leading Awadh army against the English. It was Sehnaz who had sent the map to him. A soft corner for the woman whom he once loved made him wait and listen to the old hermit.

Rupen connected the dots in his mind. Colin was trying to contact Sehnaz so that he could find Amelia. Was this the reason he volunteered to take Rupen's last letter to Sehnaz?

The hermit gazed at him without a sound. Rupen forced a smile. *Can this man read my mind?*

"They said they were going to Varanasi and need some days' rest. You know sir, we treat guests like gods. The temple had a spare bedroom. The two women got the room, and Sheru slept on the veranda. They anchored the vessel in the river, near the temple."

"They stayed there for some time?"

"Only a night, sir. Sheru had told me they might stay for a week. But the next day something happened…"

"What?" Rupen felt his eyes widening.

"In the morning, one English officer came riding a horse. Sheru and Sehnaz had been to the market. Amelia ma'am was there, but not in the temple. She might have been on the riverbank or the orchard surrounding the temple."

Sehnaz was carrying the map of The Residency. The piece of paper he had relied on to give the death blow to the British in Lucknow. Did this old man know this?

"The officer asked me if I knew a woman who was carrying important information against the British. A map. I swore I had no knowledge. But he pointed at the anchored boat and asked if the occupants were in the temple premises."

Rupen's gaze penetrated the hermit. Terrible thoughts crossed his mind. He let the hermit continue.

"Something was wrong. A *firangi,* white woman, a Muslim woman and a brahmin boatman. Something was fishy. Sheru had the muscles of a soldier. I told him they had left. But then I remembered—if the officer searched the rooms, he would find their luggage, women's clothes."

"What did the officer do?-Did he search the temple?"

"Yes. And I almost froze. I closed my eyes and mumbled a prayer to Lord Shiva when he started examining the rooms. And Lord Shiva listened to my prayer."

Rupen was a devotee of Lord Shiva and Goddess Kali. He muttered a quick prayer and then asked, "Lord Shiva listened? How?"

The hermit raised both his hands at the sky as if pointing at the God in heaven. "Lord Shiva made their belongings vanish. Everything disappeared."

Rupen couldn't believe what the man was saying. Amelia's and Sehnaz's belongings vanished? He glanced sideways.

"Sir, I think you do not believe me. I am a devotee of Lord Shiva. Worshipped him all my life. And he showed his appreciation. Saved the ladies."

"So, the soldier didn't find them?" Rupen stroked his imaginary beard.

"No. When he came out, he didn't find his horse, either. The ferry had vanished. When he ran to the riverbank, it was sailing in the mid-river. He accused the women of taking his horse. Sir, how can the women take a warhorse? Impossible. I understood Sheru might have seen the horse and fled in his boat. The women must have been with Sheru. I believe that's also an act of Lord Shiva. The soldier could have ridden on his horse to the cantonment and gotten a powerful vessel to catch Sheru's boat and capture the girls. The soldier was furious about losing his horse. I said that it might have slipped off its harness—it must be around, grazing."

"Sounds logical."

"Yes. We searched inside the orchard. It was not there. We looked outside. The horse had vanished. Gone."

The hermit's story was amazing. His face didn't show any sorrow or pain, which he had seen on other prisoners.

"*Swamiji*—" he remembered that so far he hadn't addressed him properly and had not even asked his name for the sake of courtesy— "then how did you come to this prison? And I'm sorry I have not shown proper respect to a monk. Apologies." He bent in a namaste pose.

"God bless you, my son. Let Him give victory to you."

A sigh moved through his soul. Would he ever get out of this prison in this life? Even the so-called friendship with Andaman's governor Dr. Walker was of no use.

"*Swamiji*, how did you arrive here?"

The monk smiled. "The ignorant soldier didn't realise that for me, any place is like a temple. He was furious—enraged over the lost horse and the women. I understood he was after some valuable information, which could have brought him ample reward. And the thought of punishment from his superiors frightened him. He arrested me for helping the ladies. I said nothing. Didn't even resist. For some time, I was in a prison in Sultanpur. And one day they transported me to Andaman Islands."

"I will walk you to your camp, *Swamiji*." Rupen and the monk walked side by side.

The church service would end soon, meaning the English guards would arrive in a while. Rupen didn't wish them to know he was enquiring about the wellbeing of the prisoners.

"My tiny cottage is my temple," the monk said. "It was Lord Shiva's wish to bring me here. I give solace to the prisoners. They feel they are getting the Lord's blessings through me. I had no family when I got arrested. Here I have a large, extended family. And I would love to die with them around."

They arrived at the monk's cottage—a thatched house with bamboo walls around. There were enough slits for free entry and exit of mosquitoes, mice, and other insects. The roof was so low that it was difficult for a man to stand properly inside.

Rupen threw a helpless and guilty glance at the sky, thinking of the plight of other prisoners. The last four years he'd been aloof to the unfortunate situation of the soldiers. He'd been concerned with only the fifteen soldiers who were from Awadh army, helping them in getting slightly better living conditions in the prison in exchange for helping in illegal activities of Dr. Walker and Captain Hunt.

Am I doing the right thing?

The monk coughed. "Are you all right, sir?"

Rupen realised he was lost in his thoughts. He let out a sad smile. "Yes, I am. Please continue."

Sir, if you allow, I will give you some advice."

"Yes, *Swamiji,* I will be happy to receive advice from a wise man like you. Please."

"There's no point in waiting for an indefinite period, dreaming that one day the British will release the prisoners. That day might never come."

"I understand. But what can I do?"

"My suggestion is, you try to escape from here. Whatever way you find. By deceit, if required. And arrive in India. You can force the government to release the prisoners. You should live in a secret location and send letters to all the kings who have surrendered to the British. Not only the kings, but to all rebel leaders like you who were fighting against the English. And make them aware of the brutal conditions the ex-soldiers are suffering here, the agony and torture they face daily. That might force the English to change their mind."

Rupen noticed the English soldiers taking their position in the encampment. He shouldn't arouse their suspicion.

"*Swamiji,* I will take leave of you for today. I will remember your advice and work on it. Namaste."

Rupen trudged to his cottage, but the yell of an officer made him stop. He stilled by a large mango tree.

His gaze travelled around a hundred gauges, one out of two English soldiers shouting at three Indian guards, "You worthless natives, making friendship with these bloody prisoners!"

"No, sir. We were carrying out your order, sir," one guard said, folding his hands. The other two guards were silently standing, their hands also folded, and their gaze down.

Rupen could only see the officers from the back through the woods, but he noticed the guards clearly—although he wasn't sure if they saw him.

"Carrying out an order? Look at those two trees. What did those lazy men do the whole day?" the officer shouted again, pointing at two felled mango trees.

"Sir, you had ordered to knock down those two trees."

"Knock down! Who would chop off the branches? Can't you apply your own stupid dirty brain? Do I have to explain in detail? Why?"

The guard stood silently.

"Answer me!" The I soldier charged forward.

"My mistake, sir."

"Punishment. No off today. You will work twenty-four hours. Both. Understood?"

"Sir, the prisoners are still working with other trees. They are—" he moved to his left and pointed— "they are in that other orchard. I will call them and ask to clean off the branches."

Rupen was about to walk away, but the other soldier charged forward and grabbed the collar of the guard. "Sir said you are getting punishment. Don't you understand? How dare you argue with him?"

The other guard, who had been quiet up until now, came closer with folded hands. "Sir, please forgive me. Aslam has been sick for the last two days. He was coming for duty, as his leave application was not sanctioned. Please spare him the extra duty, sir. I will do it in his place."

The first officer laughed loudly. "You stupid people don't understand me, huh? When I said twenty-four-hour duty as punishment, it was for all of you. Not for that. What is his name? Aslam? Yes, not only for Aslam. Understood? Now, don't look at my face. Go to that other orchard and call those buggers here."

The guards saluted and walked away.

Rupen approached the soldiers, who stopped and gazed at him.

"I'm Rupen."

"We know, sir. You were the head of Awadh army. But, sir, you are also a prisoner and shouldn't interfere with our job."

Their voices told Rupen that regardless of his prisoner status, the men still had some respect for him.

He decided a diplomatic approach might get a better result. ""You are right, but I am a political prisoner, as I was a general. Not like these inmates." He knew other than him, all other political prisoners were in Indian prisons; Dr. Walker had told him. "And don't forget I was the one who helped Dr. Walker in containing the rebellion. Thousands of unarmed prisoners, when they decide, could throw you all in the Bay of Bengal. Your guns can kill most of them, but as they outnumber you, there won't be any British solder left at the end."

The soldiers glanced at each other, and then one of them said, "And then you realise, sir, what will happen. A shipload of English soldiers will arrive here from Calcutta and Madras. They could eliminate all the prisoners. Then what?"

Rupen wanted to snatch the man's gun and blow away his skull. "Your ghosts will witness that from there." He pointed his finger to the sky. "And you people like that? Do you know how many British soldiers died when that uprising happened? Fifteen. All right? What did you do? You people didn't even find out who killed them in the dense woods. Whom would you eliminate? And how many? All the prisoners?" He swung around and left without awaiting an answer.

CHAPTER TEN

AMELIA, 7 SEPTEMBER 1862, MORNING THROUGH MIDNIGHT, SHIP NEAR GREAT COCO ISLANDS (664 MILES FROM CALCUTTA AND 170 MILES FROM ANDAMAN)

Sehnaz's sobbing wakes me up. She is standing near the window. I jump out of the bed and approach her. How can I console a woman who seldomly cries?

She points at the shore. "We're in Andaman, and my days of freedom are ending, Amelia. At any time, another ship will come with the letter."

My heart drops to my feet.

The word *letter* sounds like a bullet to both of us. Neither of us wants to discuss that. The life of the only woman prisoner would be worse than a hell for Sehnaz, and I don't want to even imagine it. But there is one thing she doesn't know.

"No, Sez. This is not Andaman. I forgot to tell you last evening. This is, in fact, Great Coco Islands. Something like Jambu or even bigger. Captain Rave told me yesterday. The ship will take provisions from here for Andaman. How did you think we would arrive at Andaman overnight?"

Sehnaz doesn't pay any heed to me.

The drizzling sound of the rain tenses my muscles. Another island like Jambu? Maybe the buildings are inside, not visible from the ship because of the tall trees.

"Sez, we still have time. This is not Andaman."

She wipes her tears and hugs me. "Amelia," she mutters as if someone outside will hear, "I was checking. Not one, but several islands are here. I think I shouldn't wait until we arrive at Andaman.

It's better to escape here where no one knows I'm a criminal. How can I rescue Rupen if I'm confined in jail for life?"

"Are you mad, Sez? How will you live on those islands? Live among wild animals? And what about the tribal people?"

"Death here is better than spending life in a prison. And if the tribals are like those of Jambu Island, what's wrong with them? They're not cannibals. Uncivilised by our standard, but better than the English."

"No, Sez, Burma controls this island. I mean, the British rules over Burma. Don't think of running away from here."

The ship drifts into a small jetty where a narrow bay has created a natural but small port. There's nothing to uplift my or Sehnaz's spirits. The rope ladder from the ship is touching the stone floor of the coast, and an uneven path full of large stones leads to the island. Tall tropical trees are blocking the view of the place, and beyond those are many hills, large and small. How could Sehnaz live here if she escapes from the ship?

We walk out of the cabin and arrive at the deck.

Rave is shouting, "Hurry up, men. Hurry up. We have only a few hours to finish loading all the provisions." Then he turned to a man. "Henry, run to Coco market and ask Jacob to open the godowns. If he is not there, run to his home and bring him. He is a lazy fellow."

Rave is clearly in a hurry; he wasted lots of time in Jambu. But the monsoon rain is not cooperating with him. A sigh comes out of my mouth. The longer the delay, the better for Sehnaz.

"The place is so hostile. How do you think workers will load heavy bags of provisions into the ship?" I ask an English soldier.

"They have to," he replies as another Indian guard glances at him with what looks like fearful amazement. "These dark-skinned prisoners must finish the work on time, come rain, storm, or whatever. The lash will do the magic." He flashes a smile, expecting appreciation from me—another English.

How can I admire such inhuman treatment of the prisoners? These soldiers should realise that they're not convicts, rather prisoners of a civil war. England has several wars against France. How would we react if France were to put the English prisoners to similar treatment?

The guards herd the prisoners in a line onto the island by way of the rope ladder. Sehnaz and I stand on the deck and watch. Sadness has clouded her beautiful face. She stands near me and watches each prisoner getting off the ship, as if her term would also come.

As Sheru climbs down, Sehnaz's features tense. I pull her toward me. "Calm down, Sez. Don't show you know him."

She doesn't listen. Sheru touches the ground and meets my gaze above, but I try to hide my reaction. I exchange a sidelong glance with Sehnaz. She has also met his gaze.

As soldiers force prisoners to hurry down the ladder, the weight of the men becomes too much, and the ladder breaks off, throwing half a dozen men onto the rocky ground beneath, one on top of another. The Indian guards on the ground run toward them, helping the men up while the English soldiers standing on the safety of the deck hurl abuses at them. The slightest delay irritates them.

"These two men can't get up, sir." One guard helping the injured prisoners glances up. "Heads bleeding, gone unconscious."

"Don't waste time on them," Captain Rave yells. "We've lost enough time in Jambu. Drag them to the side and connect another ladder."

"Sir, what do we do with them? Please sir, they will die." The Indian guard looks up, his gaze asking for sympathy.

"Didn't I command you not to waste time? Carry them to the side and make way for the others. We will push them into the ocean while leaving. Two prisoners less wouldn't matter to the authorities."

My blood boils at the cruel treatment. Is mine an Indian mind trapped inside white skin?

I steal a sideways glance. Sehnaz is sweating, anger radiating from her eyes.

I grab her arm and guide her to the cabin.

"I am anxious, too. But this's not the time to show our feelings."

"Aren't you sad and angry, Amelia?"

"I am. Didn't you teach me to become an actor? Didn't I visit Morticia's bedroom that night and offer my body to her tribadism desire? Do you think my soul permitted me? Did I enjoy her company?" My gaze goes straight into her eyes. "This man is transporting prisoners all the time. This might be his usual behaviour."

Sehnaz stares at me. Her brain must have stopped working.

I gaze at her, wrapping my arm around her shoulder. "Sez, I'll think of a way."

"Way?"

"A way out for Sheru."

"I don't understand, Amelia." Sehnaz walks to the window and watches the shore.

I join her. "I think this is a big chance for Sheru. His freedom."

She gives me a blank look.

"Didn't you hear? 'A few prisoners less' means nothing to the authorities. Every time they transport men to Andaman, some prisoners must be dying. In accidents like what happened today, or sickness. I've seen the unhygienic conditions they live in inside the cargo chamber."

Taking out a piece of paper from my purse, I ask her to write something in Hindi.

The British don't care if there are a few less prisoners when the ship arrives in Andaman, because some deaths are inevitable en route.

"What do we do with this?" Sehnaz asks.

"Sheru is intelligent. I am sure he will understand."

She chuckles. "Today your mind is running so fast, Amelia."

I pinch her arm playfully. "Why do you think you will always be one step ahead of me? We need to prepare for any adverse situation, where we might have to stay alone and won't be able to get each other's opinion."

Sehnaz's eyes grow dark. "You will live on Ross Island of Andaman. And I—I don't know where."

As I fold the paper and slip it in my skirt pocket, my mind spirals into a dark corner. How many days can we—two close friends—stay together? Will I ever be able to see her?

"Andaman has over five hundred islands. You should hide in one of them where the tribals live. Better than no-man's island. If I'm successful in freeing Rupen, we will arrive over there and get you."

"Not as easy as you think, Amelia. On which of the five hundred plus islands will you look for me?"

Deciding to address that problem when it arrives, we head out to the deck and duck beneath the extended roof of a cuddy. Our action could help Sheru get his freedom today. Rave is holding an umbrella and supervising the loading of the ship. Prisoners are holding packed, heavy jute bags on their backs and climbing the rope ladder one after another. Rave shouts, "Only one man at a time. If this ladder breaks, we don't have another."

The class division based on skin colour is loud. English guards avoid the rain with umbrellas while their Indian counterparts are standing on the shore, soaked, along with the prisoner-workers. Some of them are helping the men holding the heavy bags to climb the swinging rope ladder.

When Sheru meets my gaze again as he climbs down the ladder the second time, he smiles. An English guard on the ship notices and comments, "You thought of some joke? Looks like the loads are nothing for this man. He is stronger than others. Give him heavier loads."

My shoulders slump. A second's worth of a smile costs Sheru so much! Sheru drops his gaze and continues down the ladder.

We wait until rain stops and approach an English guard. "Hello, can you please help us in going down? We are bored to death here and would like to walk around on the shore."

He cast a curious glance at both of us. "Sorry, ma'am. Rainy day, and the conditions on the shore are not good for ladies."

When I notice Rave watching us, I flash a seductive smile. My so-called woman lover is somewhere enjoying the warmth of the indoors, so it would be no problem if I flirt a bit with her husband.

Rave lifts his hand and gestures for the guards to take us down. For the first time, two English men leave the safety of the ship to escort us, one holding my hand and the other, Sehnaz's.

I assure them we are only going for a short stroll and will be within the sight of the guards.

It turns out that Coco Islands is not what we had thought while resting up on the ship. Behind those small hills and tall trees, we find a small town boasting of its shops, unpaved roads, and brick houses.

As we wind our way through the high and low curves along the narrow pathway, we come to a small market. Most people are of Burmese appearance, but we also notice some English men and women.

The unpaved roads in the market are muddy. People have placed rocks along the path as steppingstones.

I look at the sky. The rain might pour again at any time, and we should go back before that. I wonder if we'll be able to.

We wait near a bush. Sheru crosses our path with another heavy load. His head bends with the weight, and we can't meet his eyes.

"Did he see us?" I ask Sehnaz.

"I don't think. Poor man."

"Call him anything, but poor. He is a brave man, and that's his asset."

Sehnaz smiles. How many more days will I see her smile?

We don't have to wait for long.

Sehnaz whispers. "Amelia, Sheru is coming this way. Quick."

I glance around. The letter wrapped around a pebble is ready inside my fist.

"There is no one, no guard even." She pinches me.

Just as Sheru is about to cross us, I let out a low coughing noise, and throw the paper-wrapped stone at him. I look at the sky to check the cloud, stealing a quick glance at Sheru.

He bends down and pretends to scratch his ankle, pocketing the letter.

Quick Sheru, quick. The eager words stop inside my mouth as my heart races. He pockets the letter and trudges ahead.

We scurry back to the ship. Sehnaz comes close to me and squeezes my arm. I steal a sideways glance at her. She replies with a quick grin. Will Sheru find his freedom today?

As the day passes and darkness arrives, Captain Rave Hunt's impatient mood throws everyone into a tizzy. At one point, three workers collapse from exhaustion, and the English guards begin whipping them.

"Don't worry about them. I need the ship to sail before evening. Three more prisoners won't matter. Throw them into the sea and let them flow away with the waves. Focus on the others."

Sheru stills for a moment and looks at the injured mates, but one English guard rushes to him, swinging his whip. Panic wrenches in my gut. He is about to hit Sheru, but his colleague stops him and whispers something. The guard lets Sheru go. I shut my eyes and sigh with relief.

The men must be hungry. I haven't seen them getting any food breaks.

Captain Hunt realises by the evening that the work wouldn't finish and he wouldn't be able to sail that night.

"Listen, boys," he shouts standing on the deck, "we will start early in the morning. But finish the loading tonight. At any cost."

The rain has stopped completely, and the moon is spreading some light through slits of the clouds. A mild cold breeze waves away the humidity from the air.

I slap another flirting smile and shoot a sugar-coated dialogue. "That's a wise decision, Rave! You have so much experience."

Rave glances back at me with a salacious smile.

"If you can relieve the weak workers from working, that would be so nice of you, Rave

Rave puffs out his chest and smiles at me again. "Guards, ask only the strongest to continue work."

Wow, my smile is working on him!

Only a dozen men continue working—Sheru being one of them. A large oil torch above the ship and another on the jetty spread some light. As the evening progresses, I see only one Indian guard on the jetty and only Sheru carrying the last few loads. I frown.

Everyone is tired. All the English guards and all but one Indian guard go to their cabins. Captain Rave also retreats.

Impatience boils in me as I continue commuting from the cabin to the deck from time to time. My gaze follows Sheru's movements. He must be starving. He must be thirsty. Is his brain able to think?

After some time, the last guard on the jetty also climbs onto the ship, ordering Sheru, "Only ten more bags. Finish them and come back."

As the guard advances onto the ship, he meets my gaze and smiles. "He can't run away, ma'am. The ship is safer than the island at night."

I plaster a smile on my face and nod my head. He vanishes from my sight, but before I can drop my fake smile, Sehnaz breezes up next to me.

"Can you see that light, Amelia?" She elbows me and points toward the sea on the east.

Another ship is approaching the island. Its light blinks inside the sea.

"The ship is not far and may be here within an hour." Panic drowns Sehnaz's voice. "And if it's from Calcutta, I'm sure the letter for my arrest..."

"It might be from Rangoon, as well," I try to assure her.

Sehnaz is wringing her hands. "What if it is from Calcutta?"

Panic builds in my chest, too.

"Keep an eye on Sheru." She runs inside.

Sheru is climbing the ladder with another heavy bag on his back. Our gazes meet. He flashes a faint smile, then pats his pant pocket twice. And then, before climbing again, another smile, which looks meaningful to me. The letter must be in his pocket. Does he have a plan? I stride into the cabin.

It was a tiring day for all. Morticia's cabin door is closed. None of the maids are around. Tomorrow morning, the ship will sail for Andaman. I step inside our cabin. Sehnaz has already packed her bag.

"I would rather be the food of a wild animal, but I must die outside a prison." She stands up and hugs me.

Has the time come for our separation?

I keep her in my embrace and squeeze her with all my strength, trying to hold back my tears. "I promise, Sez, I will do everything to free Rupen. If required, I will become a whore to whoever can help me out."

She releases me, and I glance at her packed bag. "Do I run to the kitchen and bring some food for Sheru? He must be starving."

"Already did."

We stare at each other for a few beats. Five years of deep friendship is now entering its toughest testing phase. Sehnaz opens the window and drops her suitcase on the corridor outside. Before she jumps out the window, she casts a last glance at me, "If God allows, we'll meet again."

I run down the corridor through the deck. Sehnaz is already near the rope ladder. There's no one else around. I mutter a prayer. "Ma Kali, you are the Infinite Energy. Please give enough strength to my friend. Let her survive."

I open my eyes, and my gaze falls on Sheru. He is also about to get off. Maybe he has a few more loads to bring. Sheru carries Sehnaz's bag on his head and helps her climb down.

My heart is in my throat. This is the moment. This is the decisive moment for both Sehnaz and Sheru.

A small boat comes to the shore. The torch in the boat shows me the face of a Burmese man. Sheru runs to the vessel, still holding the suitcase on his head. Sehnaz follows him. Within minutes, the boat vanishes. I am appalled by Sheru's preparedness. How did he make a quick friendship with a local Burmese man who lent him his boat? I had imagined he would hide in Coco Islands.

A dark feeling hits me as I wander back inside the cabin and lie on the bed. If the letter comes in the next ship, will Captain Hunt send his soldiers to find Sehnaz?

Sleep is a hard commodity tonight. I know questions will come in the morning about Sehnaz. Her absence from the ship. This is not the night to sleep, but the time for action. But what action can I take? Sehnaz's mantra rings in my ears. "The more drama you can do, the more success will be at your doorstep."

A flutter of nerves ripples through me. Can I keep my promise to Sehnaz?

A sleepy Morticia opens the door after I knock a few times.

"I can't sleep," I mutter in a seductive tone, "and Sez's snore is loud. Can I spend some time with you, Mort darling?"

She is still not out of her sweet sleep.

"It's all right if you want to sleep, Mort darling."

"No, no, please come." She holds my arm and drags me inside.

I hold my breath and plant a kiss on her filthy mouth. "Love you, Mort darling."

I remove my top and let Morticia fondle my nipples.

Sehnaz, 7 September 1862, Midnight to 8 September morning, Great Coco Islands and then Jerry Island

A pleasant surprise moved through Sehnaz when she found Sheru speaking Burmese with the man who rescued them in his boat.

"British army transfers trained Indian soldiers to Burma. I was there just before I ran away and joined the Sepoy Mutiny," Sheru explained, sitting on the boat's floor and leaning against its wall.

Poor man must be starving. All Sehnaz could find in a hurry was two pieces of breads and some pickle. She should have brought something more for him to eat. But did she get time for that? Her decision to flee was at the very last moment. God helped her through Sheru.

She stretched her tired legs, sitting near Sheru. His scent was so familiar, and it softened her panic. A memory of proximity sliced through her fears. He was a man she had depended on for her security five years ago, and now, they were travelling together again. The only difference was that they were now in the Bay of Bengal instead of the Gomti River.

Sheru was sitting straight, as if to fight back any attack from his captors. Was he not exhausted from lifting heavy loads for almost fifteen hours? And what about the mental stress after fleeing from the prison? But this was much better than the torture he was enduring before. Sehnaz recollected that breath-stealing scene when the ship left Hooghly Port—the foam coming out of an unconscious Sheru's mouth. Her nerves tightened.

A yearning to massage Sheru's tired muscles stirred in her. But should she even touch him? No. Never. Sheru was faithful to his wife. Or has he changed through the years? "You must be tired, Sheru."

Sheru let out a mild laugh and gazed at her. A sea of pain was striving to hide inside his eyes. "What to do? This was the only chance to escape."

Sehnaz chuckled at the memories of when she was hiding with him in Varanasi's temple lodge for over a month, pretending to be a couple. English spies were after her life. She remembered how Sheru had always maintained a physical distance from her, sleeping on the floor, leaving the bed to her.

"Do you still remember, Sheru, when we fled from Lucknow and arrived in Varanasi?"

"Lord Shiva had helped last time." Sheru gazed at the sky and folded his hands. "And I am sure, will help now."

How could Sehnaz forget that evening?

That was the evening when she was sitting shoulder-to-shoulder with him, and desire had overpowered both Sheru and Sehnaz. The sweet memory was still raw and caressing her soul—his touch on her back, Sheru's fingers crawling over her blouse and unbuttoning it, caressing her nipple.

That was a loving moment for her, but was it the same for Sheru?

Sheru had run out of the temple and did penance. Penance for touching a woman inappropriately other than his wife. How many women were lucky enough to find such loyal husbands?

She glanced up at the dark clouds that had cleared away, allowing the moonlight to help the Burmese man steer the boat. Would Captain Rave with his soldiers and binoculars come running after them?

Relief washed over Sehnaz when the Burmese man turned the vessel toward the south and sailed along the coast. Sehnaz thanked God, as no one from Rave's ship would find them now. Right?

The man spoke to Sheru in Burmese.

"Great Coco is a group of five islands," Sheru translated for Sehnaz, "and we are going to Jerry, a smaller island seven miles to the south. No English man lives in Jerry, so it's safe for us."

Sehnaz smiled and nodded. What else could she give to Sheru?

"His name is Aung." Sheru said. "We became friends."

"Hello, Aung!" Sehnaz shot a smile at the man. She was sure he didn't know English. Hopefully the gesture was enough for him.

It was almost dawn when they arrived at Jerry Island. A thatched house, tiny and hidden behind a dark tree, welcomed them. That was Aung's village.

"He has offered me a room until we build another for ourselves," Sheru said as they entered the empty room.

Sehnaz placed her suitcase near the wall and let out a giggle. "God has helped us through Aung. You might have told him my name. What? Sanju?"

Sheru smiled. "Not yet. How can I say before asking you? I didn't even know until the last moment that you were coming with me."

A few minutes of delay from Sehnaz would have been catastrophic. She could've never come with Sheru. God was great!

"Should we not identify ourselves as a couple? You, Sheru Pandey, and me, Mrs. Sanju Pandey. Like we did in Varanasi?"

Sheru stilled and gazed at her. "All right ma'am."

A chuckle slipped out of Sehnaz's lips. "Ma'am? No. Sanju."

"Okay, Sanju." Sheru nodded.

Sheru had seen a pond on the way to the village, so he borrowed a cloth from Aung and went out for a bath. When he came back, Sehnaz told him, "At daybreak, people will know one prisoner and one woman have vanished. Remember, you aren't just another prisoner out of thousands. Everyone has seen how you worked without a break when others couldn't. They must notice. We have to think of a way, Sheru."

Sheru sat cross-legged on the floor to start his morning prayer. "I couldn't bring my clothes, as I was afraid the guards would notice. But I didn't forget to bring the holy Gita hidden in my pocket." He then opened a page of the Gita and read out loud for Sehnaz, "I have right over karma, not on the result. I will do what I believe is right, but leave the result to God."

A smile slipped through Sehnaz's soul. "Okay, Sheru. Now please show me where I can also take a bath?"

Sheru closed the book and got up. "Let's go. I will take you to the pond."

"What about your prayer?"

"Don't worry, I can still pray sitting on the grass near the pond."

He took her the short distance to the pond.

"This's an open place. I need to make some enclosure for you. Maybe within a few days. For now, I will move over there, give you privacy." Sheru walked up to a tree and perched on the grass cross-legged, keeping his back to the pond. Time for his morning prayer.

As Sehnaz entered the cold water of the pond, her mind wandered. The other ship which was approaching the Coco must have brought a letter for her arrest. With Sheru by her side, would she survive?

CHAPTER ELEVEN

AMELIA, 8 SEPTEMBER 1862, MORNING AT AROUND 10, SHIP HAS LEFT GREAT COCO ISLANDS

I didn't sleep the entire night. Sehnaz and I have been living in the same house for the past five years. I've always felt like she was my sister in a previous life. Otherwise, how would a London woman like me and a courtesan of India who met at night in Lucknow become inseparable?

It is around ten in the morning. The ship left Coco Islands at five and has already sailed farther into the ocean. There's no danger of going back and finding Sheru and Sehnaz. I know Captain Hunt wouldn't worry much about Sheru. He is just another number. He has thrown four prisoners into the sea, alive or dead, I don't know. Four will become five. How does it matter?

What if the other ship has already brought a letter against Sehnaz?

I must tell Morticia before others find out and ask me.

My tired eyes wink at me from the mirror. The tears flow the moment I think of losing Sehnaz. This is perfect time to meet Morticia.

I trudge out, ignoring the stunned look of Malti and Chunni. "Memsahib, crying?"

A sob starts in my stomach and soars out of my mouth as I meet Morticia on the deck.

"What happened to you, Amelia?"

"C...can you p...please come to your cabin? U...urgent."

Morticia hurries, and I shut the door as soon as we are inside.

"I was sleeping, Mort darling. I was in a deep sleep."

"That's all right. Are you not supposed to relax at night?"

"No, she was with me when I returned from your room last night. Sez. I slept on the bed. And now, when I woke up, she was not there. I looked for her throughout the entire ship. She is nowhere."

I realize now that I should've gone to the other part of the vessel looking for Sehnaz before coming to her.

Morticia is clever and better than me at acting. She might see through me and discover my motive. I should have been extra careful and thought of a masterplan. Have I already ruined it?

A content smile on Morticia's face stuns me. Has she noticed the anomaly in my statements?

"Please, Mort, please. Tell Mr. Hunt to take the ship back and locate her."

"Are you insane, Amelia? Rave will never agree to go backward. We have already delayed the ship in Jambu, and he is afraid of the questions that will come from the authorities in Andaman. Don't think about that woman, Sez. Am I not enough for you?"

Thank God. Sheru is also safe now.

I inch closer and wrap my arms around her shoulder. "How long? How long you will be with me?"

Morticia squeezes my shoulders. "Look at me, Amelia. Please stop crying."

I wipe my tears and gaze at her.

"You will stay with me in our house in Ross."

"Your house?" A cold, sick sensation drops through my stomach.

Morticia pulls the chair nearby. "Sit here." She asks and stands near me "Then you have another option, the school. Teach during the day and sleep alone at night, in the classroom. That's the only alternative for you."

Is this woman trying to scare me?

"Ross Island has a severe housing shortage. Authorities do not want to construct more houses, as the plan is to move the entire prison to Port Blair."

The thought of staying as a permanent whore for this woman makes my heart pound in the back of my throat. But this's not the time to cry over that. Didn't Sehnaz and I plan to give some misinformation?

I pretend to weep again, but Sehnaz's absence brings real tears from my eyes. "Mort, Sez was not a common woman. How do you think

116

an English woman has been so friendly with an Indian? But this is confidential. Please promise me you'll never say this to anyone."

Morticia's eyebrows shoot up, and she scoots closer to me. Bringing her voice to a whisper, she says, "I promise."

Sehnaz has made me memorise the dialogues.

"She is—no, *was* a princess. A real princess. A Muslim ruler. Nawab Wajid Ali of Awadh."

Wajid Ali had several queens, and he must have had many children. Who keeps count of them, anyway?

"A Nawab's daughter?"

"Yes. But she had one problem. She had to flee from the palace when her parents found she was sleeping with other women. You know, Mort, how conservative Muslims are."

"I understand. Even advanced countries like England don't permit this."

"Right, Mort. She was hiding in an ashram where only Hindu nuns lived. In Sultanpur. She later came to live with me as my assistant. That was when the rebellion finished. Her father, Nawab Wajid Ali, surrendered and accepted the offer from the British. At last, he retired in Calcutta."

Am I making it too long?

Morticia is listening, mouth agape with incredulity.

"One of her stepbrothers had taken out lots of gold and diamonds before they fell to the British and had hidden them on one island of Andaman. A no-man's island. And he had a detailed map of the place with the booty. Sehnaz is lucky. That stepbrother also died in the war. She somehow had found the map and was coming to Andaman for the treasure. I don't understand why in the last moment she changed her mind and vanished."

A smile touches her mouth. "You should appreciate that the friendship between a white woman and a brown Indian woman can never last. What is she? A princess? I know the royals of India. They consider them to be on par with our queen. She must have thought you are an ordinary woman."

"I am an ordinary woman, not a queen," I correct Morticia.

"But you are my queen." Morticia smiles at me.

I exhale and run my palms down her thighs. "Mort, every lover says this to the beloved. What's new in this?"

"No, Amelia. Trust me. You will be queen of Jambu Island, and I, the k—no, the senior queen. I mean, I'm the husband queen and you, the wife queen."

I laugh. "Come on, Mort. Jambu is a state?"

"The British don't care about thousands of tiny islands around the country. Also, they don't like to mess with tribals. Why would they want to rule over a tiny place like Jambu? Even if it ever becomes civilised, how much tax they can collect? Not enough even to send a tax collector there. I will set up an island kingdom, make them civilised, and rule over them. Next time I go back to Calcutta, I will bring materials and workers to build a proper house and also some roads."

"You are so good to the islanders, Mort. They would adore you and even worship you. But, but Mort..."

"But what?"

"I was the wife of a brigadier. I know how much income the captain of a ship earns. That, too, from a private ship. Captain Hunt is not even a government employee. How much money he could provide that you would be able to build a kingdom in Jambu?"

"Don't worry about money, Amelia. You will find out when time comes. Your Mort is sitting on top of millions. You will forget your Sez, the princess. And you will be the real princess. Only you need to cooperate with me. Help me when the occasion comes."

Scepticism is probably reflected on my face. This is not enough information for me.

A knock sounds on the door, and Malti's voice on the other side spoils my plans. I could have extracted more out of this woman.

"Memsahib. What do we cook for lunch?"

Morticia shoots a smile at me and gets up. "Money is plenty in the Ocean Market. You are my woman. Leave it to me."

I return to my cabin and stand near the window. My gaze goes to the clear, blue sky. A small patch of white cloud in the distant horizon grins at me. A rare scene during a monsoon—that, too, in a tropical area. *Sehnaz, your plans are working. We will free Rupen. And you, too, will enjoy your freedom at last. Divide and rule.*

Morticia's statement hits me again. Money is available in plenty...

Where is this Ocean Market?

CHAPTER TWELVE

RUPEN NAIK, 9 SEPTEMBER 1862, ROSS ISLAND, DR. WALKER'S HOUSE

"The authorities in Calcutta will be happy for you when they receive my letter, Mr. Naik." Dr. James Pattison Walker poured some *mahua* in a wine glass. "This is fantastic. English wine is nothing compared to this tribal variety."

Rupen lifted his glass.

"Cheers to the man who helped the British contain the uprising," Dr. Walker said.

Rupen gave a measuring smile. He needed to coin each word with utmost caution, even though he'd known Dr. Walker since before he was a doctor in Agra's government hospital. Walker had even come to Nawab Wajid Ali's palace s few times to treat one of his queens.

Times have changed. Army Chief Rupen became a prisoner in Andaman. Walker invited a prisoner as a guest. Did this surprise Rupen?

Mrs. Walker called for her husband from the kitchen.

"Excuse me a moment," Dr. Walker said as he moved from the drawing room to the kitchen, leaving Rupen alone in the parlor.

Rupen twirled his wine glass while he waited for Dr. Walker to return. He had failed to understand why the authorities chose a doctor for the Governor role in Andaman. Whatever the reason, he should never underestimate the capacity of this man.

Walker had chosen a perfect place for his residence. The ocean was a stone's throw away, and the encampment started within two furlongs—far enough to ensure his security in case of a prisoner uprising, but also close enough to monitor them. He still required Rupen's help to contain the prisoners' unrest.

That Rupen lived in a cottage close to the fence of the encampment might also have been another strategy by Walker. With some amenities, his life in the prison was much more comfortable than the ordinary prisoners'. As a political prisoner, he deserved all the amenities, anyway. Didn't all other imprisoned rebel kings and ministers enjoy the same benefits in Indian prisons? He was the only one who was sent to Andaman.

The British were not stupid enough to provide amenities to senior ranking inmates like Rupen. Divide and rule. He understood it very well. Didn't he also play to their tune when some convicts destroyed the barricades and tried to escape?

I am not stupid, either. Rupen smiled from inside. *Wasn't that childish? How could the rebel prisoners escape to India? Wouldn't the English capture them there and award severe punishment for breaking out of jail?*

Dr. Walker came back. "Sunday afternoon is a right time to spend time with friends, Mr. Naik. On the record, you are an inmate. But in practice you are an out-mate, ha, ha, ha. In fact, until a proper prison building comes, each prisoner is an out-mate. All are living outside, in hutments."

Rupen laughed, too.

"I am curious to know more about the war you fought, Mr. Naik. You were a great general. You had tremendous success besieging The Residency in Lucknow. We in Agra thought the English would lose the war. We even planned to pack our bags for a final return trip to England. How did everything change?"

Rupen's smile faltered, and a dizziness hit him in his bones. "The great Major General Sir James Outram betrayed me. I could have created havoc like at the Bibighar Massacre. A genocide in The Residency would have been much more severe."

"You are right, Mr. Naik. We all panicked then. People were even betting in Agra. Some said Rupen would kill everyone inside the fort. Others said Rupen is an ideal man. He would never slaughter women and children."

"That is correct, Dr. Walker. Those who are weak kill women and children. I never targeted them. But the English didn't play fair game.

They bribed some of my security people and kidnapped my family. My wife and two adolescent daughters."

"That made you surrender?"

Rupen's fingers clenched into a fist. "No way. A genuine patriot never surrenders for his personal gains. I never surrendered—I became prey."

Dr. Walker leaned forward. "How so?"

"I had a friend. Brigadier Colin Lawrence. He was my close friend before the rebel war. He sent me a letter requesting me to release one hundred women and children in exchange for my family. Believe me, I had no plans to harm the women, but had kept them for negotiation only. All I had wanted was non-interference in the matters of Awadh kingdom. Sovereignty of Nawab Wajid Ali Shah. That's all. I never asked the British to go back to England."

"So, Brigadier Colin betrayed you?"

"I don't think so. But the Major General James Outram used him against me as he was my friend. I released fifty women in exchange. Collin had promised to bring my family. That was the first of August in 1857. How can I forget that day?" Rupen swallowed back his tears.

"Colin came in a horse cart. And my family—" Rupen took a pause — "in another. But when Colin opened the door of that other carriage, I saw a large plate." He closed his eyes. That scene was still fresh in his mind, the wound still raw and painful.

"A large plate, with...with three chopped heads. My family was staring at me. I could have finished Colin at that very moment, but I didn't. Within hours Major Outram attacked, both from the side of the Gomti River and also from inside The Residency. I fought but lost the battle."

"I'm sorry for your loss, Mr. Naik. Terribly sorry. That was not the way to win a war. I apologise for the deeds of that coward British general."

"Why would you apologise for the misdeeds of another man? I believe in karma, and he must meet his destiny. I am sure. One day."

Dr. Walker refilled the glass with more *mahua* as a servant brought some fresh snacks for them.

"I'm just curious, Mr. Naik." Dr. Walker took another sip from the glass. "You are such a patriotic person. You sacrificed even your family to save the kingdom. How did your conscience allow you to help the authorities contain the uprising in this jail? You even acted against the very Indian soldiers who once were with you against the British."

Rupen took another sip and thought. *How do I say to this man that the whole idea of the uprising was baseless? For no benefit of anyone at all?*

"Dr. Walker—" Rupen cleared his throat— "I gave my life for the Awadh kingdom, but the ruler Nawab Wajid Ali cooperated with the English by signing a treaty, giving everything to them. And in exchange, what did he get? Freedom, a nice small palace in Calcutta, and a lifelong pension even the prime minister of England would envy! And me? I am rotting here in the Andaman prison. Did he ever think about the sacrifices I made working as a general for him?"

"You're absolutely right, Mr. Naik. And I must admit you were an absolute capable general. If the British army had people like you, they could conquer the world."

Rupen forced a smile and set the empty glass on the table.

"Another glass, Mr. Naik?"

"No, please. This is too strong."

Walker poured another glass for himself. "I have another question, Mr. Naik."

"Another?"

"I had heard a courtesan had helped to source The Residency map. She was even managing your information network. What is her name? Is she still in Lucknow?"

This man is trying to extract more than I can give. Sehnaz might still be in Lucknow. I don't want any trouble for her. She should never perish in a prison like me.

"We don't take the help of any women in war. Battle is for males only. I always keep women out of it. Men should always protect them. Maybe some courtesan might have provided some information to our spies, but that's all."

Walker remained silent.

Rupen glanced up. "And Mr. Walker, if you have finished, I have some requests."

"Please. I will fulfill whatever is within my capacity."

"Prisoners need better medical facilities, Dr. Walker. So many of them are dying of malaria, diarrhea, and other diseases."

"You are right. I have written a letter for more doctors and more medicines from Calcutta. Our bureaucracy sitting in Calcutta doesn't understand how we are pulling on here."

"And one more point."

"Please."

"Inhuman level of workloads is distressing for the inmates. Your guards don't even spare the sick, and they harass them to achieve impractical targets from them. You must consider this."

Walker paused for a while. His gaze flicked for a moment toward Rupen, then he looked away. "You know, Mr. Naik, I have met some officials who came from Australia. You should have seen how they treated the convicts in Sydney. They have similar settlements. Like here, in Ross Island. Convicts were building roads, houses, all the while living in the open encampments. Never think that we are giving different treatment. They were all white people."

"But you must understand, the prisoners here are not convicts. They were all soldiers. Prisoners of war. They deserve better treatments."

Walker arranged himself in the chair. "My hands are tied, unfortunately." He averted his gaze away from Rupen. "The orders are coming all the way from Calcutta."

This man is adamant. Rupen recollected the advice of the monk just over a week ago. He must get out of the prison at any cost and arrive in India. The time has come to implement his advice.

"Dr. Walker," Rupen said diplomatically, "I understand your position. I have another proposal."

"What?"

"Did you know, the tribal men had attacked Ross Island once?"

"Yes."

"No one has ever tried to make a friendship with them. With my abundant time, I can help the British amend the relationship."

Dr. Walker placed his wine glass on the table and stared into Rupen's eyes. "How?"

"To make a better relationship, you need to talk to them. Isn't that true?"

"Yes." Walker gazed at him intently.

"And for that you need to know their language."

"That is the problem, Mr. Naik. No one knows that. This is unfortunate."

"Now you understand the problem. But you have the solution."

Walker didn't respond.

"If you allow me to go to the other islands and stay with them to learn their language, then it would be easy for the British authorities to develop a better relationship with them."

This was an unusual proposal, Rupen knew that. A few moments of pause hung in the air. Dr. Walker's eyes narrowed. "I agree. I will try. Just keep in mind, there's strict instruction from the higher authorities not to antagonise the tribal people. You must take care of that."

"I know. And thanks a lot. I'm sure I will be of more use to the authorities. Dr. Walker, I will now beg your leave. Goodnight."

Rupen got up to leave.

Dusk was ambling into Ross Island. The monsoon cloud had cleared away. A beautiful rainbow smiled back at Rupen.

That day is not far. I will earn my freedom again.

CHAPTER THIRTEEN

SEHNAZ, 10 OCTOBER 1862, MORNING, JERRY ISLAND (SOUTH OF GREAT COCO ISLANDS)

Sehnaz glanced around, sitting near the pond. No one. All the men of Jerry Island would go to Great Coco early in the morning and return in the evening.

Jerry had around thirty people—including Sheru, herself, and Aung. This pond was like her private bathroom. With the Bay of Bengal thumping against-the shore one furlong to her left and large trees and bushes on the other three sides, a sense of security washed over her. Dangerous wild animals never visited this tiny island floating to the south of Coco.

Confidence bloomed in Sehnaz. She removed her dress and sat on a stone near the pond, in only her underwear. She had plenty of time to enjoy the mild heat of the autumn sun.

Waves of the Bay of Bengal chuckled and slapped at the shore. Nowadays Sheru had a boat to transport workers to and from Coco every day. By around nine in the morning, Sehnaz always came for her daily bathing ritual. Until Sheru came back in the evening, the entire island was lonely for her. No one to talk to.

Jhumru purred and crawled along her leg.

"Mew."

"What Jhumru, don't you like this place?"

"Mew."

"You like it, no? I didn't like it, until yesterday when I met you and brought you home. You see, Jhumru, until yesterday I was the sole woman on this entire island. Aung said the British brought only male workers from Burma. But now there are two. Do you know who that other woman is?" She chuckled. "You, silly. You, the beautiful Princess Jhumru."

Jhumru came to lie in her lap, burying her head into Sehnaz's bare belly.

"Are you angry with me, Jhumru? Not talking to me? What did I do?"

Sehnaz thought for a while. For the first time she had somebody who would listen to whatever she said.

"Any idea, Jhumru, how you became a cat? Me. I had to make the beautiful woman in you into a cat. Believe me, this is for your own safety. There is not a single woman on this island. What if they cast dirty eyes on you? I need to save your modesty. And one day, when a handsome prince comes asking for your hand, I will chant the verses again. You will again stand here as the most beautiful young woman. Like a fairy. Happy now?" She chuckled while ruffling her white fur.

Jhumru jumped down from Sehnaz's lap.

"Come back, Jhumru. Tonight, I will introduce you to Sheru. Last night he came so late, I was already in bed. He slept on the veranda and didn't wake me up. Tonight, for sure. He is a nice man. But he will not be your prince charming. You know why? Because I have my eyes on him.

"He is a Hindu brahmin and I am a Muslim, and even if he had lost his whole family, he still would never marry a woman outside his community. Where would he get a brahmin girl here? When Aung gave us the only spare room of his hutment, he started sleeping on the veranda. I told him, being a woman I've no problem sharing my room with him. But look at him! He didn't agree. But one day, he had to break his promise. Did he sleep with me?"

Jhumru, who had been watching Sehnaz from a distance, began slinking toward her again.

"You are eager to know, Jhumru, if he slept with me? You naughty cat!"

Jhumru licked her paw arrogantly.

"No, that night it was raining. The whole veranda became wet. I asked him to come inside. You will laugh when I say what he did. He kept a pebble in between us and chanted prayer until he slept to avoid the temptation of touching me."

Jhumru lay near her feet.

"So, would you like to hear more about Sheru?"

"Mew. Mew, mew."

"Don't be so happy, Jhumru. You saw him in the morning. Did he talk to you? No? Ha, ha, ha. He keeps his distance from beautiful women. You are also not a brahmin. Otherwise Sheru is a perfect match for you. He is tall, muscular...and also handsome. You've not seen how weak he looked when we both escaped into Jerry Island. Now that he is eating regularly, he has recovered a lot, even looking much better than he did five years ago."

Sehnaz paused. This was the first time she had someone to talk to after almost a month on Jerry Island. Sheru started going to work in Coco the very next day after they arrived in Jerry. Aung said no worker from Burma wanted to work in this remote and far-off location. And those who had come here because of false assurances of better wages than they were getting in the mainland Burma—they had no way to go back. She had made the right decision when escaping the ship. The British living in Coco all came from Burma, and they had no interest in the rebels of India. Sheru was also safe here.

A sigh escaped from her mouth. Would she ever go back to India?

Sehnaz didn't realise Jhumru had vanished. She jumped up and glanced around. It seemed she was a pet cat already—and missing, too. Is she trying to find her owner?

Sehnaz finally found Jhumru lying near a small tree. She ran and scooped her up, clinging to her bare belly.

Sehnaz's life would be hell if Jhumru left her.

Sehnaz sat back on the stone. "Never leave me, Jhumru. How would I live without a friend? My only friend? I stopped talking for a while and you got bored? Okay, okay. I will continue chattering with you."

She let her thoughts wander, thinking of what to say.

"Yes, Jhumru. I will tell you how Sheru saved my life one day. It's not a story, remember. This is true life. You will see how Sheru is a genuine hero. You want to listen?"

"Mew." Jhumru purred and glided along her leg.

"You love hearing about Sheru. You're also a young woman, and you love to see handsome men.

"I was escaping in River Gomti with Sheru and Amelia after stealing a sensitive map to help Rupen in the mutiny. But an entire group of British soldiers attacked us in the mid-river. Their chief jumped to our boat and assaulted me in full view of his soldiers—tore down my blouse and even grabbed my breasts. But his bad luck, a rebel boat arrived from nowhere and ambushed all the British mercenaries except that officer."

Sehnaz paused as Jhumru walked onto her lap and placed both paws above her breasts, gazing into her eyes.

"Sounds interesting? You promise you won't tell anybody? A woman's respect, Jhumru."

"Mew."

"Grabbing my neck, he pointed a sharp knife at me and ordered all rebel soldiers to drop their guns. You know, Jhumru, like the speed of lightning, Sheru grabbed the officer's neck and twisted until blood streaked down the man's face."

The autumn sun was slowly heating up the air. Time for Sehnaz to enter the cool water of the pond.

"You want to know what Amelia was doing with me in the boat? Yes, she is an English woman who had fled her husband's home. Otherwise, that man would have killed her."

Sehnaz removed her undergarments and stood in knee-deep water, completely naked. Laziness was still holding her feet back. Her skin was hot. Jhumru came and sat near the edge of the water.

"You are also a female, Jhumru. Why should I be ashamed to stand naked in front of you?" She giggled.

Sehnaz lifted her breasts and squeezed the nipples. "What do I do, Jhumru—when the man who stays with me is controlling his mind so much that he would never even look at my things? I have to do something. I am now enjoying my own bubbies? Are you jealous of my large breasts? I was showing them off to my patrons when I was dancing in Lucknow's *kotha*. You should have seen their reaction. They were going mad. But I have never revealed them whole like I am doing now. I was wearing tiny blouses, showing only the upper half to the public. And the moment I chant the verse and turn you back into a woman, you will also have beautiful breasts like mine."

She took another step inside the pond. Suddenly, a feeling of being watched engulfed her. She turned around, carefully scanning her surroundings. She noticed when a crow flew above her. Nothing new. A fish jumped and slapped on the water. Everything looked normal. But still...

Once more, she scanned the trees and the bushes. There was something in those trees, maybe a creature, and it was watching her.

Sehnaz felt it in her gut. She glanced at the stick she had deposited on the bank. Sheru had given the pole to her. The only weapon Sehnaz carried with her.

A pair of eyes moved around in the bush. A bolt of recognition passed through Sehnaz. It was Aung. Why was he staring at her?

A funny smile crackled in her mouth. She didn't care. Aung was single. It was possible he wanted a woman's company. Let him watch. What could he do, anyway? Aung was short and weak. If he attempted anything, Sehnaz knew how to get him under control. She was never an *abala aurat,* a helpless woman. She had the courage to protect herself. Didn't she kill Bilal on the ship when he was attempting to rape her?

Instead of advancing into neck-deep water, Sehnaz stood there in a position that would give the best view to Aung. She lifted her boobies again and again as if she were showing trophies to an audience. Then she moved her palm inside her thighs, massaging her labia at a slow pace. The absence of a man in her life hit her bones. But she couldn't sleep with anyone. And never with Aung. He was no match with either Rupen or Sheru.

"Mew." Jhumru called for attention.

"Sorry, Jhumru. I forgot about you. This man is thinking I haven't seen him because he is hiding. But I don't care. He must be starving for a female companion. Let him get an eyeful. I'm also getting aroused. Aren't you? The weather is so pleasant."

Sehnaz gave another sideways glance. Aung had slipped away. She chuckled.

"Enough, Jhumru. Time to go home and cook. I'm starving. Aren't you? I will cook rice and fish. You know, Sheru was a strict vegetarian. But after arriving in Jerry, he is eating both fish and meat. Poor fellow. His vegetarian food is not available here. Who would do all the farming for him?"

Sehnaz covered herself with clean clothes and went home, carrying Jhumru in one hand and her clothes with the other. Aung was sitting on the veranda, burying his head in his knees. He looked pale and weak. Compassion washed through Sehnaz, and she decided not to inquire of him hiding by the pond.

"Didn't you go to work today, Aung?" Sehnaz flashed a seductive smile.

Aung lifted his face and smiled, showing his broken and yellow teeth.

He still doesn't realise I know he was watching me naked.

"No. No work. Contractor said."

"Aung, I will ask you something if you don't mind."

She was not sure if he understood.

"Question? Yes. Ask."

"Why haven't you married?"

"Me? Marry? Yes. Marry. Married."

It was difficult to understand what he wanted to say.

"Are you married?"

Aung nodded.

"Yes or no?"

"Yes. Yes."

"Then where's your wife?"

A dark cloud covered his face.

"My wife. Had. She had. Was."

Sehnaz struggled to comprehend. Did his wife pass away?

"Where's your wife? Here or above?" Sehnaz pointed at the sky.

"No, there." Aung's finger was pointed parallel to the ground.

"Where?"

Aung pointed to his right. Sehnaz figured it out. "You mean north? Coco island?"

"Yes. Took away."

Something was seriously wrong.

"No woman here. Less. Everywhere." Pain shimmered in Aung's voice. "I go. One day. Went. Market. Coco. Contractor gun. Showed me. Took away. Now, his wife. I, no wife."

Anger and anxiety swirled in Sehnaz's consciousness, and she couldn't move. She had anticipated that one day Sheru would get a day off and take her to Coco Island. But now she realized that was a dangerous plan.

"No woman in Coco?" she asked.

"No woman. Less woman. Ship coming. Burma. From Burma. With women. Lots. Workers get a wife. Not alone."

"That's good, Aung. You will also get another woman."

"No. No." His voice cracked. "No other. My wife. Love her. Contractor gets another. I pray. Him. I get my. Wife back. Here. Love her."

Sehnaz struggled to control her tears.

"You are a nice man, Aung. I'm sure you will get your wife back. Today, I will cook for you. Eat together. All right?"

Aung chuckled. "Thank. You wonderful cook. Will eat."

CHAPTER FOURTEEN
AMELIA, 11 OCTOBER 1862, ROSS ISLAND

I stand like a guilty but obedient wife in front of Morticia.

"Never give this girl anything to wear."

Morticia had just jerked away Sadhna's frock, which I had given her to cover herself.

"I had allowed her clothing only on the ship, since she couldn't have run away in the ocean. Don't you remember how she vanished in Calcutta? Thank God you got her back. Otherwise, you can't imagine how much it costs to get a slave like this after slavery became illegal."

I've been staying in Morticia's house since arriving at Ross Island of Andaman almost three weeks ago. She was right. Getting accommodations in Ross is not only difficult, but impossible. New constructions would begin soon in Port Blair. Rave—who is almost always in Port Blair—also confirmed the same. I would have to stay in the school, which is not safe. It doesn't have a proper fence and is far away from the locality. I didn't have any other choice.

I glance at the maids. Malti, Veena, and Chunni—all three smirk at Sadhna as she stands without clothes again.

"Mew." Rumi purrs and walks around me. The cat had occupied the empty house while Morticia had been in Calcutta. Now Rumi is my friend. A friend I can spend time with when this large bungalow would be empty again in a few days.

"Oh! This cat is always spoiling my mood. Veena, Malti, take her away. Now. Quick."

I am about to bend and pick her up. Something forces my waist back to a straight position, like a spring.

Malti carries out the command. "Come, Rumi." Lifting the cat with a smile, she cuddles her and begins to walk away.

"Stop, Malti!" Morticia screams.

What else? I wonder.

"So you're the one who is spoiling this animal? Who gave it a name? *Rumi!* What nonsense! Now it's thinking we're all outsiders, and this bloody cat is the owner of the house?"

A dark cloud covers Malti's face, and she shivers. None of the three maids are good at English. They don't understand when we talk with a fluent British accent.

"Take her away, Malti," I intervene. At least she knows Rumi has feelings.

Once Morticia and I are alone, she turns to me with a smile. "Don't feel bad, Amelia. If that girl goes out of the boundaries of the residence, everyone will know we have a slave. Malti, Veena, and Chunni will go back with me when Rave and I return to Calcutta. Who will be with you? You can't find a maid here in Andaman. This is for your own benefit. I will leave her for you. She is your maid now. You know how much I love you."

It's a fact that I am pretending to be her female lover. But I'm in no mood to obey everything like a dumb woman. Don't wives fight with their husbands?

I don't know how I can convince her. All I want is for Sadhna to live like a civilised human and remain clothed. I force a smile to my face. "I know about America. Where slavery is legal, yet none of the slaves live naked. She is a young woman. How can she remain unclothed day in and day out?"

"The police would catch the slaves if they tried to flee in America. But if this girl flees here or in Calcutta, I can't even complain to the police."

This response is ridiculous, but no reply comes to my mind.

A smile curves across her lips and her eyeballs move. "I will make a law to make slavery legal."

I hold back the laugh bubbling at the back of my throat. "Law? Where? Andaman?"

"No, Jambu. When I set up my kingdom there."

"You will keep the tribal women as slaves?" I blink rapidly with astonishment. This woman really believes she can set up an independent kingdom. And with slaves, no less.

Morticia turns toward me still seated on the sofa. Her eyes brighten as if she is already the ruler of a kingdom. "No. No...no. The tribal men will rip my bones into pieces. I can't even bring Indian women as slaves. If the news arrives in Calcutta, the British government will crush my tiny kingdom. They have already tasted what happens if you disrespect Indian traditions in the 1857 Sepoy Mutiny. I would rather import slaves from Africa."

I know Morticia won't stay in Ross forever. She will go back with Rave to Calcutta. Maybe within a week, but God knows when. And I will allow Sadhna to wear clothes again. A defiant smile slips through my soul. I sneak away to hide my feelings and thoughts from Morticia.

Dusk is creeping in, and I mosey out to the backyard for a quiet moment before evening. The Bay of Bengal is a stone's throw away from Morticia's garden. I seek to kill my depressing mood by sitting on the lawn.

After arriving at Ross, I joined the local school—the only one in Andaman. None of the Indian employees here can bring their families. Only English, with their wives and children. I'm also the only female teacher here. I had expected to meet the superintendent of the prison, Dr. Walker—who is also the official head of Andaman—by now, but he has been busy.

Many burning pyres had welcomed my arrival at Ross Island three weeks ago, when I accompanied Morticia and Captain Rave from the port to her house. The awful, acrid odour engulfed my soul.

"Welcome to the island of malaria," Morticia snickered, "but don't worry, mostly Indian workers and prisoners are its prey. Whites get adequate medical care. But one need to be extra careful."

Depression swallowed me so much I didn't get sleep that night. Sehnaz should have been by my side.

Now again Sehnaz's absence is punching holes in my heart. She had become family to me. More than a blood sister. I am sure Sheru is with Sehnaz and is taking care of her. Didn't he save her when the British soldier tried to molest her in the Gomti River?

Will I ever see Sehnaz again?

When I come back inside, I see Malti waiting for me, fear burning in her eyes. "Memsahib is looking for you upstairs." Did I do something wrong?

Morticia is sitting on the balcony waiting for me, and Chunni is serving *mahua* in a glass.

"Come, Amelia. We'll have a drink."

Even though my blood boils inside me I plaster on a smile. It's still not evening yet, and this woman wants to drink! Whatever. I must cooperate with her. This is part of my strategy I had agreed to with Sehnaz. She has contacts here, and she is also corrupt. And I don't know if anyone else can help me out. At the moment, this is the only way I can figure out how to help Rupen flee from here. Not an overnight task, and I must stay focussed.

Chunni retreats from the balcony, and I clink my glass with Morticia's and take a little sip. Morticia drinks a large gulp.

"Oh, I love this *mahua*."

This drink gives kick sooner than wine.

Morticia is about to take her second gulp when Rumi comes to me and climbs on my lap.

"Chunni!" she screams.

No one responds. "Chunni," Morticia shouts louder, "come here. Now!"

Chunni comes running up the stairs.

"Take her and leave her in the jungle. I can't tolerate it anymore."

I don't understand how a lovely cat can irritate this woman. Rumi has done nothing to disturb her. Is she jealous of the affection I show to the cat?

"Memsahib," Chunni pleads, "Cat away. Outside, gate. Many. Many times. Not good. Come back."

"Take her out. Far away. And leave her in the jungle. Not just outside the gate, you dumb woman."

"Yes, memsahib." Chunni lifts Rumi again and walks away.

"Chunni," I call her back, "it's already dark outside. Don't go out now. Tomorrow. Understood? Day time. Not now." I can also speak in broken English.

I glance at Morticia. She says nothing. Am I winning her over? Or annoying her?

A plan comes into my mind. There is a small shed not far from the bungalow. I will keep her there. Someone will feed her. It's a matter of days only. Once Morticia is on her return sail, I'll bring Rumi back. I'm sure I'll find another accommodation before Morticia comes back. But Rumi's company is important to satisfy my loneliness here.

Morticia remains silent and continues drinking.

Chunni would never allow Rumi to come back upstairs. There are enough rooms below to lock her up. And no other maid will come until dinner is ready.

So far Morticia is my only known contact who I can think of using to reach Rupen. She must trust me enough for my goal.

I move my chair a bit and sit closer to her. Darkness from the cloudy evening has blocked all view of the outside world. But the roar of the ocean sounds like music to me.

Morticia's glass is now empty. I pour another drink for her.

"You, too?"

"I don't drink a lot. I still have some to finish." Can I extract some information tonight from her?

I move my hand down Morticia's shoulder to her arm. "You have muscles even a man would envy, Mort darling." My voice is low, seductive.

She winks. "I should've been a man. God made a mistake and gave me the wrong body. But that's good, anyway. I'm getting benefits of both the worlds."

Confused, I just gaze at her.

"You don't see how? I would have to work for money. I mean, had I been a man. Rave is earning for me, as I made him my husband. And again, I'm not taking care of him like any ordinary woman. Any woman would cook, bear children, and obey the husband's commands. Didn't you do that when your husband was alive? And sleeping with the man at night so that he can fuck your hole."

My eyes are wide open. No woman on the earth could have thought of a life like this.

"And see, I'm doing nothing for him. He is so scared of me, as if I'm the husband." She laughs so loud with her hoarse voice that a bat on a nearby branch flies away.

"You are lucky, Mort darling."

"Yes, I am." She pulls me closer and plants a kiss on my cheek. Morticia's foul mouth no longer makes me feel like throwing up. Have I got used to living in the gutter?

Morticia touches my bubbies. "I love your assets, Amelia." She tries to feel my nipple through my clothing.

"Not now, please. Maids might come."

"No maid will come unless I command. They understand how upset I can get."

"True." I touch her thighs, pressing the muscle.

"You love to sleep with me, Amelia?"

"I always have. From the beginning."

"Then why do you go back to your bed after I make love to you?"

"Oh, that! I ... I have a nasty habit of sleeping alone. Even when I was with my husband, I would often rush to another room after getting the daily dose of love."

"All right. Same with me; I love having the bed to myself. I never allow Rave to sleep in the same bed the whole night."

Has Rave ever slept with her, even once since her wedding? I have never seen her husband coming to her bedroom. He always sleeps in a room on the ground floor, taking Sadhna to his room. Morticia and Rave actually share Sadhna.

Morticia tries to remove my top.

"Mort darling, not now, please."

"Why are you afraid of getting nude? There's nothing to be ashamed of. And you have an impressive body, anyway."

I say nothing while pouring another glass of *mahua* for Morticia.

"You know, Amelia, there is an ashram in Sultanpur. Hindu nuns stay nude all the time there. No shame, nothing. People have even seen and reported them."

I was also there for a month. She is lying—people haven't seen them nude and reported them. Wrong. They don't allow any males inside. The temple cum ashram is above a hill outside the locality and cordoned. Guards stay outside the barricade round the clock to stop any intruder.

"Where're you lost, Amelia?"

"Oh! Nowhere. Just thinking if Mr. Hunt might come back and see me here with you."

"Don't worry about him. He goes to so many islands, including Port Blair. You know a new prison is coming up there?"

"Yeh..." I'm not interested. I need some other information. Is she not yet drunk?

"Mort, life will be dull when you go back. I'll have to make friends around here. How would I spend my time otherwise?"

"Yeh, Amelia." Morticia gazes at me through the rim of the glass. "But be careful. People here aren't the same as on the mainland."

"How?"

"There, in India, the British have a proper administration. They can control everyone. Punish the wrongdoers. The situation here is quite different. Administration is slack outside the mainland. Government's grip is loose. Some of these people have friendships with pirates who are doing free trade at sea and earn lots of dirty money. People like Rave and I are giving proper service to the queen. We work hard sailing between Calcutta and Andaman, as you know."

For the first time, I hear Rave's praise from Morticia's mouth— however little it may be.

"You should be beware, Amelia. You don't know who is leading a double life."

I see. You're also one of them. I've seen the plunder you have hidden in Jambu.

"Mew."

Oh! my God. Rumi again! Now Morticia will get furious with Chunni. Poor woman!

I stand and shout, "Chunni, please take away Rumi. Hurry!"

I look back and am surprised to see that Morticia has taken Rumi in her hands. Has she changed her mind?

"I told you so many times, you cat, this is my house. Understood? My house." She points one finger at her own chest.

Is Morticia becoming fond of this pet? It's possible. She might even start playing with Rumi today or tomorrow. Like I do. And enjoy it, too. Rumi is so cute!

"The stupid maids, they don't know how to keep you under control."

Her harsh and derisive laugh shakes my bones.

She lifts the glass from the table and guzzles all the *mahua*. Then she gets up, holding Rumi, and saunters to the edge of the balcony.

"Foolish cat, so many times the maid has dropped you outside this gate, and you have always come back. What do you think? The house remaining empty when I go back to Calcutta means you own it? No, no, no. Do not underestimate me. My name is Morticia. I am the boss. Anywhere I go."

I don't know if she is playing with Rumi, or if she's furious with her. I rush up behind her. "Mort darling, I'm feeling aroused."

She looks at me. Her eyes spit fire. I need to do something now.

"I am. Believe me." My mind goes blank as I remove my top and the breastband and hold my bubbies. "Please come. I can't wait."

"You idiot cat! I told Chunni to leave you in the jungle tomorrow —"

"Sure, I will also see that she drops the cat in the forest. Tomorrow morning, sure. Promise."

"You don't have to promise anything, Amelia. This's not your job. So many times I've told these stupid maids, take her to the forest. They don't understand. Since the day I came here I've been suffering."

What does she want now? To take her and leave her in the forest? Now?

"Mort, the night is not a safe time to go out into the woods. You see?"

"The forest? It starts right there. Right outside this fence. You want to see?"

My eyes flutter. I give her a weak smile, but something wobbles in my chest. I try to talk to her, but my lips tremble. "I...I love..."

Morticia doesn't pay heed, but lifts Rumi over her head.

"No, no! Mort, please! Nooooo!" I grab her arm, but Rumi has already left her hands, flying through the air like a stone being thrown at something. Her soft little body hits the teak tree outside the fence and splatters.

I close my eyes. "No! Mort, no!" I run down the stairs, tears gush down my cheeks.

Maids come running. "Memsahib. What? Memsahib."

"I, me, Rumi..." My throat chokes. Am I so weak I can't even save a cat? How would then rescue Rupen?

Captain Rave Hunt is standing in front of me when I step on the ground floor. Embarrassment floods my senses. I am wearing only a skirt, having left my top and breastband on the balcony. Topless. Bare breasts. Covering them with my palms, I swing around to face the wall.

To my horror, Sadhna is already standing there. Naked.

I continue standing face-to-face with Sadhna. Sobbing and shivering. As if it were my turn after Rumi.

Rave's steps sound closer, and I brace myself.

Someone drapes a saree over my shoulder. Malti's loving touch cools me down.

Rave continues closing in. My heartbeat shoots up again. The feeling of being trapped in a ghost house overwhelms me. But he grabs Sadhna's breasts and drags her to the nearby bedroom. Is Sadhna also another voiceless animal?

Malti helps me turn around and drapes the saree properly over me.

Veena brings a chair and helps me down into it.

Chunni gives me a glass of water. I gulp it down my dry throat.

I hear noise from the bedroom Rave had taken Sadhna into.

I can't think further. "Malti, please help me to my room."

CHAPTER FIFTEEN

AMELIA, 12 OCTOBER 1862, ROSS ISLAND, MORTICIA'S HOUSE

I struggled to sleep all last night. Rumi's bloody, her torn limbs, hounded me whenever my eyelids drooped a little. My body was hot. Burning from a high fever.

Malti sat beside me, wrapping a wet cloth on my forehead. She stayed for hours—until she felt the fever come down.

Around the early morning, I drifted into a deep slumber. When I wake up late in the morning, Malti smiles at me and whispers, "How today? Memsahib?"

"Better. Thanks for last night. Did you also get some time to sleep?"

"Morning, little. Yes."

I leave the bed and sit on a chair in the same room. Going out of the bedroom means I have to face either Rave or Morticia or even both. I may need more time to come to terms with life without Rumi.

Veena gives me a cup of steaming tea. The vapour from the cup warms me up a little. Last night was like a painful, dreaded dream. I try not to think about Rumi. Bur her image, her 'mew' and the way she was slithering around me constantly churns in my memory.

"Memsahib—" Chunni stands close to me— "not think. Gone. Past. Forget."

"I will try, Chunni, but it may take some time. Where is Sadhna?"

"Here. Kitchen. No clothes."

Pause. We call her *Sadhna* only when Morticia is not around.

Footsteps sound behind me. Nervousness hits me again, and I jump from the chair.

Morticia enters the room. *What is she here for now?*

"Good morning, Amelia." She smiles. She doesn't look drunk, like last night.

"Good morning, Mort da..." The words struggle to come out of my mouth. I again sit on the chair.

I inhale a deep breath. It's true, I'm missing Rumi. But my aim to move to Andaman was to rescue Rupen. The strategy to befriend Morticia was to use her for my motive. So far, I have met no one else who could help me. Had Sehnaz been here, she could have probably found the right person. She was a spy and learnt the tricks of the trade. But I know nothing, except the fact that I have given words to her.

I muster strength to bring a smile on my face and gaze at Morticia.

"*Sadhna* is a nice name," she says, "what does it mean? I think this is an Indian name."

"Sadhna means... I mean... It's just a nice name. Nothing else. We used to call her a slave girl. Shouldn't we hide the fact that we have a slave with us?" *God, I can talk diplomatically!*

Morticia chuckles. "You are my well-wisher, Amelia. I will also use and address her in the new name. You are right—slave-girl word is not safe to use."

I take the last sip of tea and give the empty cup to Malti.

"Malti, bring one tea for me, please."

Please! Morticia's voice sounds unbelievably polite.

Malti stands there looking at me. *What is she waiting for?*

"Another tea, memsahib? Fever. Good."

My smile gives her the answer, and she goes back to the kitchen.

"Amelia, can we go for a stroll in the backyard?"

Stroll in the garden? The memory of Rumi's severed limbs tightens my nerves. I'm sure Morticia notices my hesitancy.

"The body of the dead cat was lying on the north side of the house. This morning, I called for a worker to clean it up. We will go to the backyard, east. I think the view of the ocean will lighten you up."

Malti brings tea for us. Morticia and I head outside, with our teacups in hand. The autumn sun gently caresses my skin, taking away much of last night's pain. An old bamboo gate opens the backyard toward the sea, which is only a furlong away. I step out of the fence, forgetting the plan of a *chat* with her.

She coughs—maybe warning me she is still with me.

"You should've built this house facing the sea and nearer to the beach." I try to begin a neutral topic which would take my mind away from Rumi.

"I didn't build this. The government has built everything you see here. There's no private house, either on Ross Island or any other part of Andaman. Of course, tribal people live in their own hutments. The front of this house opens to the street."

"Sounds logical."

After taking a few steps, I stop.

"I understand you are still upset about last night..." Morticia forces her voice to sound feminine. "But you don't know, how sensitive I am to the cats. It makes me sick. I sneeze and my eyes become watery when I come in contact with any cat. But I shouldn't have killed her last night. I was drunk and out of control."

Is she asking for my forgiveness? Or another plan to continue using me? But I also need to use her.

"I understand," I say and continue walking. The waves of the Andaman Sea cool down my nerves. I don't wish to continue Rumi's topic. May her soul live in peace in the heavens.

She stops and looks at me. I don't understand how to bring Rupen's topic to the conversation. "Where is Captain Rave? Did he go to the church?"

"No, he went back to Port Blair. He rarely stays here. He is looking for new business opportunities there."

We arrive at the beach and continue our stroll.

"Amelia, can I ask you something?"

I still. A faint smile has brightened her face. For the first moment, I notice a different version of Morticia.

"No employee from the mainland comes here willingly. Why did you choose to be a teacher here? I don't believe the government would ever force a woman to come to Andaman."

If I don't use Morticia's better mood to my advantage, all my sacrifices like providing sexual pleasure to her so far will go down the drain.

"My husband was an army officer," I recollect, even though I had already admitted I had fled from my husband. How do I bring that topic up again?

"He died in the war?"

"Yes. But I believe in karma."

"Karma? What does that mean?"

"It means, whatever sin you do in this life won't leave you, even after death. I have some unfinished job for salvation of my husband's soul."

Morticia halts and stares at me. *Can I hide my nervousness and tell a white lie?*

"I was in Lucknow—The Residency?" I continue.

"Yes. I know. There was a siege. A courtesan had stolen a sensitive map and given it to the rebels."

My God, this woman knows it all! Does she know that woman was Sehnaz?

"My husband was Rupen's friend. Rupen, the Chief of Army of Awadh kingdom."

"You mean before the rebellion?"

"Yes. But he used that friendship to con him. English soldiers abducted Rupen's wife and daughters. And when Rupen agreed to release a hundred women from the besieged fort, my husband took his family back to him. But he took their chopped-off heads instead. That's when he surrendered, and The Residency came out of his clutch. My husband captured him and sent him here, life in prison in Black Waters."

I gaze at her. Does she perceive I'm about to trick her?

"I didn't realise your family made such a contribution to the victory of the British. And sorry your husband is no more. He deserves all my respect."

The woman is slowly coming to the track. But I am also entering a dangerous phase of my plans. Can I convince her?

"My husband had promised something to Rupen. The man lost everything. And chopping off the heads of his wife and two innocent girls was too much. He had given his word to find his wife's wedding ring and send it to Andaman, as a memento. But he died and couldn't fulfil his promise. But he had found the ring."

Let the white lies start! From here on out, my God!

"You're an admirable wife, Amelia. Even after whatever he did against you to make you flee home."

How do I say I was the reason for Colin's death, and I was the happiest person when he jumped from the hill in Shakti Ashram?

"So, you have brought that ring to complete your husband's unfulfilled promise? I'm sure his soul is watching you from above with pride." Morticia points at the sky.

A crow caws from a tree, as if it is listening to what I am saying. Has Colin been re-birthed as a crow for all the sins he had done? I try to hold back a laugh, thinking Colin has become a crow. Result of karma? I'm sure no western person knows what *karma* means. An important element of Hindu religion.

Sehnaz and I never planned this scene. I should have bought a ring from Sultanpur or Calcutta. I wonder if there is any shop in Andaman which sells gold ornaments.

We come under a mango tree, and Morticia stops. "I know about Rupen. Who doesn't? The British government has put all the top-grade rebels like ex-kings and ex-ministers as a special class called 'political prisoners.' They enjoy almost all the amenities of a normal person on their social level, even though they are in prison. But I believe all those political prisoners are in the jails of India. Government feared a man like Rupen could start another bloody war, so brought him here."

"Political prisoner?" This is a new term for me. "So, he also could have been a *political prisoner* because he was the army chief of Awadh?"

"He is, even here. He is not like the average Indian prisoner here. Rupen has been kept inside the prison encampment but in a separate cottage with amenities suitable to his status."

If I could convey Sehnaz her Rupen is not suffering like the ordinary prisoners.

"Can I see him? I want to say sorry on behalf of my husband and deliver the ring personally." I cross my fingers behind my back, praying she doesn't ask to see the ring.

Morticia hesitates. I don't understand what is going on in her mind. Did I expect too much too soon? Or did I expose my real motive? If Rupen is the only prisoner having a special status here, will my plan to rescue him be easier or more difficult?

Morticia gets up. "I will try. But not any time soon. We will go back to Calcutta within a week or two. Wait until I come back."

As I follow her back to her home, I press one hand to my heart, otherwise it would leap out in joy. For the first time, I have progressed in my plans to make Rupen free.

CHAPTER SIXTEEN

SEHNAZ, 20 OCTOBER 1862, MORNING AROUND 8, JERRY ISLAND

"The day looks sunny, Jhumru. I must dry this wood. Do you know, Jhumru, that dried wood gives better flames in the hearth?"

Sitting on the veranda of the hutment, Sehnaz looked at the makeshift kitchen Sheru had built. Bamboo panels covered three sides of the kitchen, and the fourth side opened up to the veranda. Sheru was so intelligent! He had even used dried coconut leaves inside two layers of bamboo to make the roof. Sehnaz's favourite place was the hearth—which sat right in the middle with a load of chopped wood on the side.

"What are you thinking, Jhumru? When I chant to make you a young woman again, you can also help with cooking. I will teach you. Until then, just watch me—how I'm cooking."

"Mew. Mew, mew."

"Lower your voice, Jhumru. Aung has gone to work, but Sheru is sleeping."

Sheru was always out working in Coco by this time every day. He didn't get regular weekly time off. No work meant a holiday. Did his contractor tell him there was no work for him today? Good, let him get some rest.

Jhumru returned after a short stroll. Sehnaz took her in her arms and walked a few steps from the cottage, lest her conversation would disturb Sheru's sleep.

Monotony was killing her. What could she do? Amelia couldn't be with her, and Sheru wouldn't take her to Coco until the men there weren't hungry enough to grab any non-English woman they saw.

Something about Sheru was eating her from the inside.

"You see, Jhumru, Sheru returns so tired every night, he can't even talk to me. But what would he chat about with me? I am neither his wife nor a girlfriend. Then why, for the second time, has God pushed us to live in the same bedroom? Who on this earth would believe a man and a woman are spending nights in the same room and not even touching each other?"

"Mew."

"You also don't believe it? I see. You are a young and intelligent girl. So what if I made you a cat? Your mind is still human."

Jhumru licked Sehnaz's feet. "Hi, hi, you are happy now that I praised you, huh? I will tell you something confidential. But promise me first you will tell no one. It's a secret. Promise?"

"Mew."

"Got it. Do you know what happened after Sheru saved me in the boat? We planned to rest for a few days and got shelter in a riverside temple. Amelia, Sheru, and I—all three. We stayed there. Only for a night. The next day, when Sheru and I came back from the market, we saw an English soldier on a horse at the temple. I got scared that he had come to enquire about me. As soon as Amelia saw the soldier, she looked around and gestured for me to stay back. You know who saved me?"

"Mew, mew."

"Sheru? No. Wrong. You are wrong, Jhumru. Amelia had learnt horse riding. We both escaped, stealing the soldier's horse, and Sheru sailed in the river. Know why? The soldier would have run to bring a speed boat and gotten us. Isn't Amelia a hero, too, like Sheru?"

Jhumru jumped on her lap and tried to touch her face.

"We fled to another place on the outskirts of Sultanpur. All three of us. And there... I made the biggest blunder of my life." A sob gathered in the back of Sehnaz's throat and shook through her whole body.

Jhumru may have sensed that her friend was feeling low and started rubbing her face against Sehnaz's cheeks.

"I betrayed Amelia, Jhumru. The next morning when we took shelter in Sultanpur, Sheru noticed she was talking to a local man. He wasn't comfortable knowing that Amelia was English and her husband was a brigadier. We suspected she was playing a game and might be helping the British capture us. We...we abandoned her there, alone, and ran away. Why didn't we think that only a day ago, she had helped me run away on a horse?"

Amelia's absence still chased Sehnaz. She glanced at the sky. A clear sky. A white cloud in the distant horizon winked at her.

"You know, Jhumru? This cloud is on the south side. And Andaman is also to the south of Jerry Island. Amelia thinks a dark cloud in a clear sky brings bad luck, and white, the opposite. Will she be noticing this cloud from wherever she is living?"

Jhumru hopped down and ran to the room.

"Jhumru, no, Jhumru. Don't go there. Sheru is sleeping."

Sehnaz ran inside. Sheru was snoring, facing the ceiling. But his morning erection made Sehnaz chuckle, and she covered her face. Sheru's toned biceps aroused her. Then her gaze fell on Jhumru, who was sitting near a bag she hadn't noticed before. A colourful cloth poking out of the bag surprised Sehnaz. She picked it up and pulled it out.

She tiptoed out of the room and said, "Let's see, Jhumru—what has Sheru brought?"

Sheru has brought a skirt! Sehnaz chortled. This must be for her. She peeked again inside the bag. A blouse and a breastband.

"Jhumru, come and see what Sheru has brought for me. First time in my life. Even when we were living together in Varanasi, he had bought nothing for me, except food. I don't understand this man, Jhumru."

She took off her top and wore the breastband. Perfect fit! And the blouse? It was hugging her skin.

"See Jhumru. So beautiful. And he brought nothing for you. Poor girl! Since I'm keeping you as a cat, you don't even need a blouse, as you don't have breasts."

"Mew. Mew, mew." Jhumru ran away.

"I was not sure whether it would be a perfect size for you."

Sehnaz spun back and noticed Sheru standing with a smile on his lips. "You rascal, how did you find my size?"

"You will find nothing in Coco Islands market, other than some food items. Two days ago, a ship came from Rangoon with some women's clothes and some proper women. When I arrived there, I found only a few pieces."

"Clothes or women?"

His face fell. "You are joking with me. What will I do with women? Don't you understand me?"

"Unfortunately, yes," she whispered.

He cocked his head. "What?"

"Um, and you got nothing for yourself?"

"I'm a man and can manage with torn clothes. How long you will manage with the same old dresses? And luckily, out of those few pieces, I found something I thought would be your size."

Sehnaz felt she was gazing at an unfamiliar man. Sheru wanted her happy.

In fact, Sheru deserved a big hug. But she knew him. She shouldn't make him feel awkward.

"Thank God, you got an off-day after so long. Where do you take baths daily, Sheru? You leave so early."

"Coco."

"Okay. But today, please go to the pond here and bathe. Then I will show you something, and you will remember me for life."

"What?" He flashed a toothy smile.

"Have patience, dear. You brought me lovely clothes. Is it not my turn to gift you with something? What do you think? That I am a woman and do not earn money, so I can't give you anything? Come, let's go."

They walked to the pond and Jhumru followed them. As he entered the water, Sheru said, "Sorry, I couldn't make an enclosed space for you. You are bathing in the open."

"That's not a problem, Sheru. We are only two women here. One is naked all the time. Who would notice me when all the men go to Coco for work?"

Sheru was giving her a puzzled look. "Which woman stays here?"

Sehnaz giggled. "Why are you interested in seeing the naked woman? Okay. You want to know? See here. She is with me." She picked up Jhumru.

"Jhumru? Jhumru is a woman?" Sheru chuckled. "Were you talking to *her* all morning? I thought there was another woman on this island."

"Sorry I disturbed your sleep."

Sheru finished bathing, and Sehnaz guided him into a forest and then to a hillock. Pointing at a piece of stone, Sehnaz asked, "Do you understand what this is?"

"What?"

"This is oval-shaped with a hole in the middle, correct? And now come to the other side."

Sheru followed Sehnaz.

"And now look at this piece of stone. Cylindrical, isn't it?"

He stared at her.

Sehnaz giggled. "You stupid, don't you understand? Can you lift this and come with me to the other side?"

Sheru lifted the cylindrical stone, and they arrived near the oval one.

"Now see if the cylindrical stone fits in the hole in the oval one. It fits? Perfect. Now you got your Shiva *Linga*. Penis inside the vagina. You worship him. Sorry Sheru, no disrespect."

Sheru gazed at her with a blend of disbelief, confusion, and gratefulness reflected in his eyes. She pinched his arm. "This is not a dream, Sheru. But a dream come true. I was living with you in the temple lodge in Varanasi, and I know these stones put together symbolise Lord Shiva."

Sheru stood in silence, tears rolling down his cheeks. He knelt on the ground and kissed the stone.

"I had stopped praying to you after what happened to me. You took away my family. You didn't even help me when I got life in jail. But now I have understood your plans. Oh Shiva, my God. You are the one who guided me on how to escape, and now you are here. With me."

Sheru got up and gazed at Sehnaz, gratefulness dazzling in his tears. He stepped forward, opening his arms. Sehnaz stepped forward as well, anticipating his hug—she even felt the warmth of his body on her nerve endings. But Sheru stopped. His open arms had gone back to a hanging position.

Disappointment stung Sehnaz, but not surprise. Sheru couldn't touch a woman who was not his wife nor even a lover.

Sehnaz feared Sheru might sleep again on the veranda. His life would be in danger of poisonous snakes that moved around the house at night.

Sheru sat on the rock, and Sehnaz sat near him.

"God is with us, Sheru. He has saved us before, as well."

"Maybe. But I still do not understand why he punished me. I might have committed a sin."

"Sheru, what had happened in the temple lodge was my fault. Fire was burning inside both of us. Only a temporary urge controlled you. And you went to live in a different place for the penance. Lord Shiva is not that cruel that he would punish you for that. In fact, I have learnt from the Hindu nuns of the Shakti Ashram that ancient Hinduism never looked down upon sex. That's the reason Lord Shiva, instead of a human-looking statue, expresses HIMSELF as the symbol of sexual copulation."

Sheru glanced at the sky with folded hands and then at Sehnaz. "This knowledge is too much for my mind at the moment, Sehnaz. If you knew what has happened to me, your opinion would change."

Sehnaz shifted closer. "I don't know. You have never told me. Am I not your closest friend, Sheru? Why else has God brought us together so many times?"

Sheru lifted his face and gazed at Sehnaz. He needed her sympathy. "Remember the day when you met Amelia ma'am again in Sultanpur?"

"Yes, at the Shakti Ashram. Her husband was all prepared to get her arrested for the *map stealing accusation*. But in the end, he had to jump to his death from the hill. God came through me to save, Amelia." She smiled.

"And the next day I returned to my village in Bihar. I hadn't been in touch with my family for more than a year. When I arrived home, I found both my parents had been dead for months."

"Oh! Very sad news, Sheru."

"There was more bad news for me in store." Sheru paused and glanced at the Shiva Linga stone. Complaint against his God was dazzling in his moistened eyes. "There was a rumour that I had died in the war. The most shocking incident was that my wife had remarried. That, too, to my close friend."

"You mean your wife had married your friend?"

"Yes."

"And you still loved her?"

"Yes, very much."

"I know, Sheru. You were so faithful to your wife that when we lived together pretending to be a couple in Varanasi, you slept on the floor. I've never seen a man with such a strong character other than you. Why didn't you approach her and ask her to come back?"

"I tried. But she was already seven months pregnant by her second husband. And my cousins had occupied my parents' properties. I didn't have a place of my own to stay."

A fierce craving to hold Sheru's hand and comfort him bubbled in her heart but didn't dare to come out. "You didn't fight to get your property back?"

"I did. Told the village elders that I was fighting against the British and even killed an English officer when he attacked our boat in the Gomti River, hoping they would help a patriot. But that went against me. My cousins informed the British authorities."

Sehnaz needed a moment to register this horror. "Sheru, you mean you got arrested in 1857 and the authorities sent you to Andaman now, in 1862?"

"No, Sehnaz. No. I'm not that cowardly that I would have sat awaiting the police to come and pick me up. I escaped. I was hiding. Only three months ago, the police nabbed me. That's a long story." Sheru rubbed his eyes as if he was erasing a memory. "But you...tell me about you."

Sehnaz told Sheru everything about how she and Amelia came to Andaman to rescue Rupen. "I don't know if Rupen can ever be free. But I am thinking about something that could make both of us wealthy, Sheru. I have the means. A reserve of gold. Only need your help."

Sheru turned to her and raised his brows. "You mean, you have found gold hidden somewhere? Some place I need to dig with a shovel? Where is that?"

"Not here. Far."

"How far? Jerry is such a small island, walking from one end to another will take less than an hour. How far is that?"

She shakes her head. "Another island."

His eyes widened. "Another? You mean Coco. You have gone to Coco when I am not here?"

She shook her head and smiled. "No, Sheru. It's in Jambu. The island where our ship stopped for more than a week."

Sheru stared at Sehnaz. He looked lost.

"Jambu is close to Calcutta."

"But where is the treasure?"

"Rave and his wife Morticia have hidden booty in Jambu island. Amelia and I both suspect they do illegal trade in the high sea for gold and diamonds, which they have concealed in a cave. Tribal people in Jambu don't understand the value of stones or the yellow metal. Therefore, his loot is safe. Until people like you and me arrive there."

"Nice dream, Sehnaz. How far is this Jambu from here?"

"I have checked my map. Almost six hundred miles. Give or take a few."

"And how do I get there? Swim in the Bay of Bengal?"

"We need to hire a boat, Sheru. You are sailing a boat daily from Jerry to Coco."

"And you think the owner of the boat will allow me to take it six hundred miles away?"

"No, just steal it."

"Sehnaz, that's a small vessel. Sailing from Jerry to Coco alongside the coast is different than sailing in the sea six hundred miles. We need a bigger one. Something like a ship. Who will rent us a ship? To a man who is wearing dirty and torn clothes? That, too, in a remote island like Great Coco? Even if, suppose, an Englishman believes us, he will use us to find the money for himself."

Sehnaz didn't know the answer. But she also didn't want to throw away her dream. That was the only way they both could get another life.

"Time to cook lunch, Sheru." Sehnaz got up with Jhumru. "Let's go. Maybe afterwards, we can come back and set up the deity in a small cave. A makeshift temple. If we will be here forever, you need a permanent temple. And think of building a house for us. How long will we share Aung's half collapsed hutment?"

Sheru smiled at her and started walking.

Sehnaz's heart swelled at the rate she had never felt before. She cast a sideways glance at Sheru while striding along with him. Sheru's face had brightened up, making her spirits soar. And for the moment, all her worries fell away.

CHAPTER SEVENTEEN

AMELIA, 20 OCTOBER 1862, AFTERNOON, ROSS ISLAND

The sky is still clear when I return home from the school at around two in the afternoon. My mood has been upbeat since the morning for no particular reason—or a reason which has no logic.

This morning when I left for school, I scanned the sky. My old habit. Noticing a patch of white cloud in a clean blue sky, my mind thrilled. The cloud was toward the northern end of Ross Island.

Great Coco Island is in Andaman's north. Has Sehnaz seen it, too? After living together for almost five years, she knew my relationship with dark and white clouds in a clear sky.

As I arrive home, a large horse cart blocks my way. Morticia has her own cart parked inside the gate, so what is this one? Is someone visiting her? The luxurious look of it signals my brain. The Ross Island population, if we don't count the prisoners, is only a few hundred. Who else other than the governor of the island can afford such a cart?

I tiptoe inside the house. The coaches of both the carts are standing on the veranda. Where are Malti, Veena, and Chunni?

Malti comes from the first floor in a saree she would only wear on special occasions. I try to say something to her, but Veena comes down the stairs and says, "Memsahib, big memsahib is looking for you."

Rave is in his room on the ground floor when I walk past it toward the stairs. Did something happen when I was in the school?

Upon entering her room, I see that Morticia is wearing a nice dress, as if she is about to go to a party. She steps forward with an enormous smile and hugs me. "You are my genuine love, Amelia."

I expect a kiss from her foul mouth and hold my breath to control my reaction. Fortunately, Morticia kisses my cheek instead. These last few days she has been sleeping with Sadhna. Thank God, she is not using me as her sex partner now.

"Had I been a man, I would have already married you," she says.

Married me? Am I just a body who doesn't need to give consent? Isn't that what most men think about women?

"Where're you lost, Amelia?"

My brain alerts me—act wisely. How can I forget Sehnaz's guru mantra? *Wake up the actor in you, Amelia. Quickly! This is the only way to ensure she arranges a meeting with Rupen when she comes back from Calcutta.*

"I adore you as if you were my husband, Mort darling." *Does this sound natural?* "Are you going somewhere? A party?"

Morticia laughs. "This is Ross Island, Amelia. Not Calcutta. Maybe when Port Blair comes up and more people from the mainland arrive, you can expect parties."

Suspense still hounds me.

"I trust you, dear. More than anyone else on this earth." She begins locking some large tin and wooden boxes. "I am not carrying all this with me. They will be in your custody. And Sadhna, too."

"What?" My heart swells so much in joy that I find it hard to hide my smile.

She swings around and faces me, still holding the keys. "I'm leaving. Today. Now. Rave said we need to start at once. Quite the short notice for me. This man wouldn't amend his plans. He can't."

An artificial complaint flashes on her features. She doesn't sound angry with Rave. A rare behaviour on her part. She is happily complying with Rave's decision and still pretending to be unhappy. Is she also acting like me?

At this time, I am forcing myself to look sad that Morticia is leaving.

We both have our own secrets we are trying to cover up with artificial smiles.

"Remember Amelia, never allow the slave girl... I mean Sadhna, never allow her to wear anything. Other than when she gets her period. She can cover her groin with a small cloth. She is a wicked girl. She'll run away."

I nod. Who cares about her instructions from the moment she leaves Ross for Calcutta?

I step forward and kiss her cheeks, again holding my breath. "Can I come to the port with you?"

"Yes, why not?"

Am I forgetting something? I scratch my head. "Mort darling, can I also keep your horse cart?"

"Sure, I was going to ask you. Rave would have deposited that with a friend."

I steal a glance at the mirror and check my reflection. Am I looking sad enough?

When the face cannot pretend, the tongue should fill the void. "I will miss you, Mort darling." A mild sob feigns through my throat.

"I will miss you too, Amelia. But don't worry, I will come back soon. And I will help you to meet Rupen." The genuineness in her voice caused me to actually burst into tears.

They are in a hurry—urgency sounds from every action of both Mr. Rave Hunt and Mrs. Morticia Hunt. For the first time, I find the couple are in harmony and working together. Is the mutual hatred between them real or something else?

As Morticia climbs into the luxury horse cart along with the three maids, she hands me a bunch of keys and asks me to lock the main door. Rave has already gone in the other carriage.

Sadhna is inside the house. I lock the main door and gaze at the keys. Everything is happening in a whirlwind this afternoon. I can't believe that Morticia is leaving me in charge of all this. I'm happy— she trusts me and will help me contact Rupen when she comes back. *Sehnaz, I am now confident I will succeed in the words I have given to you.*

We arrive at the so-called port in less than an hour. Nothing compared to the Hooghly Port of Calcutta. It's just a few jetties to secure the ships inside a natural bay. A small house with a tin roof provides some space for the visitors.

A tall gentleman is talking to Rave. Morticia climbs out of the cart and greets him.

"Dr. Walker. Please meet Amelia, she is the only woman schoolteacher in Andaman."

Rave and Dr. Walker stop their conversation and glance at me with admiration.

So, this is Dr. James Pattison Walker? He must be a close friend with both Rave and Morticia.

Dr. Walker steps forward and extends his hand. "How do you cope with life here, Mrs...?"

"Amelia Elliott Spencer," I finish for him.

"Yes, Mrs. Spencer."

Spencer is not Colin's last name—rather, my mother's maiden name and Elliott, my maiden name. What would be my reply if Dr. Walker asks me about my husband?

"I am sure you are repenting for coming to Andaman, Mrs. Spencer," Dr. Walker says.

A smile escapes through my lips. "You may just call me Amelia, Dr. Walker. And yes, I understand no one is interested in coming to this place. But don't the English children here whose fathers are busy in the royal duty need proper education? Their future shouldn't be in the dark because of the loyalty of their fathers."

"You are such a far-thinking woman, Amelia. You deserve all the praise for your decision. I must give you an appreciation letter." His eyes flash with admiration.

This should be another milestone in my acting. Without the favour of the top administrator, how can I even imagine reaching Rupen? Isn't that my sole purpose for coming eight hundred miles into the ocean? Although teaching these children has been especially rewarding, the truth is they would be getting a perfectly good education whether I was here or not.

"Thank you, Dr. Walker." Should I have addressed him as *Sir* instead?

Morticia says a quick goodbye to me and climbs the ladder to enter the ship. I was expecting a friendly hug from her, but she doesn't even look sad. Is this because there are other people with us?

Surprise strikes me when Rave and Dr. Walker move to a corner and talk in a low voice. Does this man share secrets with Rave? But then Malti, Veena, and Chunni all wish me *namaste* before following Morticia. I'm sure Morticia will replace them with new maids on her next trip to Andaman. Malti's beautiful smile, Chunni's affectionate care, and Veena's friendly chatter will be only a distant memory. There will be no one to talk to me. Sadhna doesn't know English. Morticia, besides keeping her nude, has never taught her. Could I teach her?

When the ship leaves at last, and the Indian coach drives me back to the bungalow, my mood turns sour. Shouldn't I rejoice instead, as Morticia has gone?

Sadhna's innocent eyes welcome me when I unlock the main door of the bungalow. I swing back and gaze at the coachman, who is still waiting for my instruction. His eyes are dancing with joy at the sight of the naked black woman standing in full view.

Here is another pervert!

I slam the door and gape into the man's eyes, the fire burning in my bloodstream. His gaze drops to his feet.

"Ma... Ma'am, I... I will feed the horse now. Any work after that?"

I would have ordered him to get lost had I not thought about the horse and its supper.

"Yes, feed the horse and go back home." Anger seeps into my voice. I understand no Indian can bring his family to Andaman, and they must starve for women's company. So what? Am I not single?

Why can't men amend themselves?

I open the door again and look for Sadhna. She has gone inside. Guilt washes over me as my negligence has exposed her to the coachman.

I open my suitcase and find the dress I had given to her earlier.

"Sadhna, where are you Sadhna?" I call.

She appears before me with a smile.

"Sorry dear, I should've been more careful."

Her eyes talk to me. Of course, she understood what I just said. Isn't it right that communication between two souls doesn't need a language?

Sadhna's eager gaze reminds me that the dress is still in my hands.

"Wear this, Sadhna. I will give you more. No more naked."

She steps forward and hugs me. Kissing her cheeks, I hold her face. She must be around eighteen. A child, almost. My heart sinks.

Tears fill her eyes.

"No, my baby. Don't cry. I will take care of you and make you a proper woman. Educated and independent."

Did I promise too much to her, which I might never fulfil?

As Sadhna puts on the frock, I decide to take her out to the seashore through the narrow gate in the backyard. It's almost dusk, and no one should be around. I don't want people finding out a negro girl is living with me. Why should I give people a chance to think I bought a girl and am using her as a slave?

A knock sounds on the door. The coachman might have come to take my permission to leave.

My blood boils.

"Okay, please go home." Didn't I already ask him to go back after feeding the horse?

Another knock.

Doesn't this man understand plain English? I flounce to the door and throw it open.

A woman is standing in front of me with a measured smile on her face.

"Hello, I am Eliza. Mrs. Eliza Wilson. Wife of Dr. Nick Wilson. Your neighbour."

"Oh, Mrs. Wilson. I am Amelia. Glad to meet you." I extend my hand and realise I omitted the *Mrs.* from my name. That word always brings a painful memory to me. "Please come inside."

I should've asked Sadhna to hide in a room. It doesn't matter now because she has already seen her.

Eliza passes a quick glance at Sadhna. She also returns a smile. Has Eliza seen Sadhna before?

I eye her as she moves to the table. She is slender, blonde hair tied into a bun, and she has a sweet voice which almost cools down my nerves.

Amelia, don't trust anyone before knowing them. Better start a safe topic for discussion.

"I am so happy you came to meet me, Mrs. Wilson. May I call you Eliza? Just Eliza?"

"Sure. We must be of the same age. I have a son, Luke. He turned seven this week."

I force a smile, thinking about how to proceed with the conversation.

Before that Eliza asks me, "You have no children?"

I don't understand if this is a question, or if she's just confirming what she already knows. Seriously, I am in no inclination to give details of my brief married life. "No child. I am a widow. And no plans to marry again. I am at the service of Jesus. That's why I came all the way here to teach children, as I learnt teachers never come here on their own will."

Did I create enough of a barrier to protect my secrets?

I want to ask her why she never came when Morticia was here, but that would be too much too soon. On second thought, she might have come when I was in school. Has Morticia asked her to keep an eye on me and report back?

"You must have met Morticia before."

Eliza doesn't answer but asks if we can walk to the beach.

I guide her to the backyard, and we walk to the shore through the narrow bamboo gate.

I must be careful with this woman.

"This girl doesn't know English. I don't know how to communicate with her. Morticia shouldn't have left her with me." Is this enough to explain that I have no hand in buying a slave?

Eliza glances around and whispers, "This is sensitive. A secret. I don't know if I should tell you."

My eyebrows shoot up. "I promise complete confidentiality, Eliza. I am not that type of woman who would fill up other's ears."

"The girl is a slave."

I already know this. But decide to pretend this is new to me. "Oh! Is that so!"

"I feel embarrassed to see the naked girl, hence I never came to visit before."

We settle on the sandy beach. The Bay of Bengal slaps its waves on the shore in a rhythm. I don't know if I should be sad about the misfortune of this innocent young girl.

"This place is not safe, Amelia. My husband has already applied for a transfer to the mainland. Unless a replacement arrives from the mainland, we can't go back. I'm surprised you chose to work here." Frustration clouds her eyes.

I nod at her. "I understand. I'm also afraid of malaria."

"No, it's not malaria. Do you know there was a prisoner uprising here?

I cock my head. "Uprising? When?"

"Two months ago. In fact, there is no prison here. It is all an open encampment, on the north side of Ross."

I glance at the large brick building of Morticia's. I have noticed the hutments from the school, which are just to its north. The school is the dividing line between Indians' housing and the posh English colony where we live.

My mind is now with the uprising and what happened thereafter.

"I'm sure the sepoys lost again, like the 1857 mutiny?"

Eliza sneers. "The Indians lost the 1857 rebellion as they have no unity. Here it was the same story, repeated. But what happened was a dangerous trend. Five thousand plus ex-soldiers imprisoned in an open encampment. And a few hundred armed guards."

"But the prisoners must be unarmed. How could they even fight?"

"Fight? Soldiers can use anything as weapons when they are in a mood to attack. Inmates cut trees with axes, clean the jungle to make roads. All the instruments they use at work, they used to attack the guards and snatch away guns from them. Nick and I were so scared we thought they would kill the armed soldiers and attack the white civilians."

What if Rupen has already escaped during that brief uprising? My promise to Sehnaz would be complete without even trying. I gaze at Eliza. Is this too good to be true?

"Walker was, in fact, unable to control thousands of inmates. They're all trained soldiers who have fought in the war. One Indian inmate, he was a senior rebel leader once, helped Walker. Rupen."

"Rupen?" I feel like someone shot me with a bullet. "He helped Walker repress the uprising? Against his own men?"

"You know Rupen?"

"Who doesn't know him? Rupen was the chief of the army of Awadh kingdom. He had besieged The Residency in Lucknow. This man could have ended the British rule had he succeeded. Luck favoured us, the English."

I am in no mood to stay here on Ross Island a single day after this. The only reason I came here no longer exists. Sehnaz and I were so happy at our island mansion in Sultanpur.

Why did you do this, Rupen? What happened to you? You were such a patriot!

I would scream at the top of my voice if Eliza weren't with me. All the drama I have endured for the release of this one man, Rupen. Why did I sleep with Morticia against my conscience? Become her whore? Why?

"In fact," Eliza continues, "Ross Island is too small to accommodate all these. Port Blair will be the right and safe place for everybody. Prisoners will all stay inside the large secure jail there. No more revolt." Eliza chuckles.

I want this conversation to be over and to go back home. Had I known this a day before, I could even have gone to Calcutta with Morticia.

Desperation creeps inside me.

Holding the binocular, I gaze into the sea as if I can find Sehnaz on some island and tell her—no, shout at her, *"Sehnaz, your Rupen has changed! Your Rupen is a traitor!"*

The binocular shows me a ship anchored in the sea. Recognition bolts through me. It is Rave's ship. Two boats are floating near it, and more than a dozen men—all Indians in prisoner's uniform—are climbing on the ship from the boats through a rope ladder. Rifles are hanging on their shoulders.

Another shock slams me. Dr. Walker was having a confidential conversation with Rave just before the ship left Ross Island.

My vision blurs. "Eliza, please, can we go back home? I am getting a severe headache."

CHAPTER EIGHTEEN

MORTICIA, 8 NOVEMBER 1862, EVENING, BAY OF BENGAL, RAVE'S SHIP

M orticia noticed the heavy box on the head of one of the prisoners as he disembarked from the other ship anchored nearby. She'd left Ross Island on 20 October, which was a long time to stay inside an anchored ship in the Andaman Sea while Rave hired another vessel and went out for his other business—risky, but rewarding. But she was sure Rupen's twelve men were enough to capture and loot any merchant ship Rave chose.

"You're a lucky person, Morticia." She wished she could pat her own back; instead, she sipped *mahua* while sitting on the deck of her ship. "At this rate you will set up the Jambu Kingdom soon."

When she saw Rave getting off the other ship holding a tin box, she was sure the operation was a hundred percent successful. Nothing was more profitable than a high-sea looting business. And when the chief of Andaman, Dr. Walker, blessed them by providing the prisoners for the operation, her work became even easier.

Even after sharing her booty with Dr. Walker for giving her the ex-soldiers, she could keep a handsome amount for herself.

Now she must count how many of those prisoners came back. She must send the exact number back to Andaman prison, along with Walker's share.

Rave approached with a victorious smile on his face. "It was a simple operation. The victim ship surrendered without a fight."

Morticia wanted to smile back and congratulate him for all the boxes of plunder he had looted. But two weeks sitting inside the vessel and waiting? Wasn't it too much? She let out a frown instead.

"And that took you more than two weeks to come back from? Did the victim choose an auspicious time to surrender?"

Rave's grin morphed into a scowl. "Why didn't you join me? Because you wanted to stay safe. You don't want any bullets fired when you are in the ship, huh? Why? I shouldn't have hired another vessel for the expedition and pay for that."

Morticia didn't wish to express her happiness for Rave's success so soon. The best way to control a man was to underestimate his best achievement. "Why did you take so long? I thought you all died fighting. I was so worried about you."

"Me or the loot I am bringing in?" Rave cast a sardonic glance at her. "Do you think the victims were waiting to welcome us? We have to wait and find the right ship. If we encounter any vessels carrying soldiers, we could be the victims instead. Do you know that? Also, we need to be sure the ship has something we can steal. Something valuable. Did we go to rob the clothes coming from Manchester?"

Morticia stopped arguing as Rave left, and she continued counting the soldiers. Twelve ex-soldiers cum prisoners had gone with Rave. Only ten of them returned. Two less?

A worried Morticia hurried to find Rave. *Where did this man run off to already? So irresponsible!*

She found an Indian prisoner and asked him, "Sepoy, did you see what happened to two of your mates? I am worried about their wellbeing."

The man watched her for a second and walked away without answering. His eyes were burning with hatred.

Dark thoughts snaked through Morticia. Something was seriously wrong. She had committed to Dr. Walker to give him back the same number of prisoners she had hired from him. He wouldn't let her use the inmates again.

Who knows, he might even ask a lion's share from the booty for the reduced headcount.

She trudged forward and reached for the man again. "Soldier, please listen."

The man stopped. "Don't call me a soldier. I was a sepoy before. I am a prisoner now. And the work you got us to do is that of a robber."

Morticia must think of a novel way to handle the man. She must find out why two men didn't come back. Didn't Rave just say the victims surrendered with no fight?

"They...they sh...shot themselves," the man said, his voice faltering. "And I should've done the same. I have committed a sin. All of us. All twelve. I should have also committed suicide. This should have been the last moment for me. No more piracy. You English people have snatched away our lives from us. And now you have stolen our souls, too. I will go to the dreaded hell. The Death God will deep-fry me in boiling oil for the sin I have done." The man began weeping.

Morticia stood in silence. She had no sympathy for the man's emotions. But this wasn't the last time she would hire inmates from Dr. Walker, and most likely, the same men would join the operation.

Morticia managed a compassionate grin and looked into his eyes. "I will reward you, soldier. It wasn't me who is keeping you in prison. This ship will be here a few more nights before going back to Ross Island. And I will give you plenty to drink. You can enjoy partying here tonight and tomorrow night."

The sepoy folded his hands, eyes still moistened. "I don't need your party, ma'am. Can you make us free? Tell Dr. Walker that we all died while fighting. Our bodies have drowned in the sea. And drop us off somewhere outside Calcutta. We will live in India with changed identities. At least we can lead free lives."

Morticia's heart pounded inside her ribs. For a moment she felt she was weak, like any other ordinary woman on this earth. She needed the same men again to continue her and Rave's piracy activity. What else other than freedom could appease these men? "Not possible, sepoy."

Rave had come up from behind and heard the conversation. "We will come back from Calcutta within months. If you people give me your addresses—I mean, your family's addresses, I can bring their letters in next trip."

The sepoy turned toward Rave and folded his hands, tighter this time, a glimmer of hope radiating from his eyes.

This is such an impractical man! "Soldier, please go back to your cabin. I will come to you when I am ready with the reward. You will be forever grateful to me for this."

The soldier left, wearing a displeased look on his face.

She spun toward Rave. "Why did you promise something you can't fulfil?" Her mood morphed from concern to anger in a second. "You're planning to take these exact same men next time, aren't you?"

"Of course." Rave looked away.

"Shame on you, Rave. Each time I bring different maids from Calcutta. Know why?"

Rave didn't answer. Of course he understood, Morticia had told him each time she changed her maids.

"And so many times I have said, bring new people. Haven't I? All the prisoners in Ross are ex-soldiers. Thousands of them are sitting idle. Doesn't Walker know this?"

Rave cast a careful glance around and came closer. "The soldiers will listen, Morticia," he muttered. "Try to understand. These soldiers are all Rupen's loyal men. He couldn't send anyone else. Most of them are from other states and never accepted Rupen as their rebel leader. They are boiling in anger. You realise what will happen when you give loaded guns to a bunch of angry prisoners who hate everything English?"

"What?"

"You don't know? You dumb woman!"

Anger tightened Morticia's nerves.

"The first thing they will do is shoot down both of us. Because we are the only two English in this ship."

"You mean those twelve soldiers are special?"

"They all are Rupen's men. I don't know what the equation is between him and Dr. Walker. Whatever, I'm not concerned. And now their number is down to ten. Thank God they shot themselves, not you or me. They are too loyal to Rupen."

"I will do something so that the other soldiers remain loyal to me. Not kill themselves."

"What will you do?"

"Leave that to me. I'm not a dumb man like you. Do not, I repeat, do not distract me. We have only tonight and tomorrow. We'll drop them in Ross the day after tomorrow. Do you understand?"

Fuming, Rave stomped off.

Morticia trudged to the ship's kitchen. All three maids were cooking dinner. She stood there in silence and watched. *Veena's is not worth it. Chunni? Just okay.* She focussed her gaze on Malti.

Malti returned a smile. "Hungry, memsahib? Cook fast, for you." She bent to lift a spatula from the floor.

Malti's blouse is not big enough to hide her large bubbies.

"Come with me, Malti. Now." Morticia swung back and started climbing the stairs, listening to make sure Malti's footsteps were following her.

She arrived at the door of her cabin. "Wait here." Entering her cabin, she fished a key out of her cupboard and came back.

"Enter with me." Morticia opened the door to the stairs that led to the top floor.

Malti remained standing there, balking, arms crossed.

"What happened? Malti? Come, quick!" Morticia slapped on a smile.

Malti climbed the stairs, her eyes clouded with fear.

Morticia knew that to achieve anything, carrots must always precede the stick.

She walked inside the only tiny cabin on the terrace of the ship. Only she had access to this place. Malti nearly dragged herself in. Morticia arranged the bedsheet on the cot, then swung toward her and gazed into her eyes.

"Malti, within a few days we will arrive at Calcutta, and you will go back to your home. Your family. Are you looking forward to it?"

Malti flashed a reluctant smile. Morticia could even hear her loud heartbeats.

"Who else is in your family, Malti?"

"Husband, mother-in-law, three daughters, and a son. The eldest daughter, marry, year next."

"Marry? You don't look like the mother of a girl of marriageable age! And you must need lots of money for that? A dowry? And you have other daughters, too."

"Yes, memsahib. I came, maid, so. From a good family. Husband, said no. Said, no maid. I said, work, for money. Morticia memsahib. Good. He allowed."

A sardonic grin escaped from Morticia's face. "You are an understanding woman, Malti. And you need money, don't you?"

Malti didn't reply. Her eyes were weighing everything, and Morticia could read them like an open book.

"You need loads of money, Malti?"

"Ye—yes, memsahib."

"I will give you enough to spend on the marriages for all your daughters. And no more maid job after this. Good?"

She nodded.

"Okay, now, remove your saree."

Malti stepped back, hesitation burning in her eyes.

"Why worry? Didn't you remove your blouse and dance while coming from Calcutta? All women. And now, only me. A woman."

Malti clutched her saree's *pallu* tightly above her beating chest.

Morticia grabbed her hands and forced them down. "Don't worry. I wouldn't do what I do with the slave girl."

"Memsahib, word?"

"Yeh, I am giving my word. Now remove that saree." Impatience was bubbling in her blood.

Malti removed her saree and stashed it on the bed. Morticia took it and deposited it on the wooden stool nearby.

"Next, blouse."

Malti stilled.

"Didn't you hear, Malti? I have promised to give you so much, and you are still hesitating? Do you not trust me?"

"Trust, memsahib. To you, trust."

"Then remove."

Malti's large bubbies sprang out as she unhooked her blouse.

"Nice fruits, Malti. You know why you are poor? Because you are not selling these fruits. Veena and Chunni can't sell. Theirs are tiny."

Morticia noticed a light of pleading in Malti's dark eyes. Her muscles tightened—the carrot has been taken, time to apply the stick.

"Petticoat. Remove."

She had no courage to say no, but her head shook side to side.

Morticia was losing patience. She knew this woman would never cooperate, so she went out and within a minute came back with a rope. Malti began sweating and trying to control her sobs, her palm going over her mouth.

Impatience swelled Morticia's anger. Unless she carried out her plans, the piracy business would be over forever. She gave a forceful push, and Malti fell onto the bed. She stuffed the cotton sheet in her mouth and tied her hands to the head rail of the heavy bed so quickly that Malti didn't have time to react or resist.

"Malti, for the last time I am telling you—your life is not in danger. Did you hear? Your life is safe with me. Just do what I say." Morticia yanked off her petticoat. Then, locking the door from the outside, she went to the border of the terrace where Rave was loitering.

"Rave, send that man."

He cocked his head. "Who?"

"You forgot already? That soldier. Ask him to come to the terrace. Now."

She waited, but within a second, she came to the edge of the roof and asked, "Have they all deposited their guns?"

"Yes," Rave called.

The soldier came running and panting within minutes and stood before her. Morticia slapped an artificial smile on her face. "Didn't I say you I will throw you a reward?"

The soldier stood still, his gaze hovering over Morticia. "Will I see my family again? No more prison in Andaman? Ma'am, please take us with you to Calcutta. Tell Walker sahib, all of us died fighting the enemy ship. Just ten of us among five thousand wouldn't matter to him."

Morticia tried to contain her sneer. "And Dr. Walker will shoot me and Rave sahib after that. No, sepoy. I am not that brave to fight against the mighty British. Even though I'm an English myself."

The sepoy stood still; misery streamed across his face.

"I can do what is in my control, sepoy. And Rave will also try to contact your family and bring a letter. But today, I have something special for you."

"I am not interested in any party, ma'am. And I don't drink."

"You wouldn't drink alcohol. But something else every man on the earth would love to eat and drink..."

"What?"

"Do you remember your wife? How long were you married when you came to the prison?"

"Just after the rebel war. Yes, I love her very much."

"Don't you feel the absence of a woman in your life?"

The sepoy's eyes pooled with tears.

"I know, sepoy. And I have already arranged it."

The teary eyes of the man switched into a beam. "My wife? She is here? How was that possible?"

Morticia laughed inside at his eagerness. "Your wife is a woman, isn't she? All you need is the love of a young woman. But you must snatch the love."

"Snatch?"

"Don't waste time, sepoy. Other sepoys need it, as well. Come with me."

She opened the cabin door and stood near it. Malti had accepted her fate and was lying still on the bed.

"Go inside the cabin and close the door. I will be here, on the terrace. Finish as soon as possible."

The sepoy looked amused.

This man doesn't yet know what I have arranged for him.

As soon as he stepped inside, Morticia shut the door and walked to the other side of the terrace. A warmth of satisfaction washed over her skin. Tonight, she would organise entertainment to three soldiers. The remaining nine, she could spread throughout tomorrow morning and into the night. Malti had a wonderful body to quench the male thirst.

A howl sounded behind her. She swung back and saw naked Malti running toward her. Urgency prickled Morticia. The sepoy was a fool. He should have done it without untying her. Didn't she tie Malti in the proper position? Hands tied, mouth stuffed and thighs open, inviting the hungry shafts of the sepoys?

Morticia couldn't decide what to do. "Sepoy, hold her. Quick!"

But the sepoy didn't budge, and Malti was loping toward her. She would have to handle the woman herself.

It was too late. Malti jumped into the sea. Morticia ran to the side and saw a swirl swallowing Malti inside the ocean.

Morticia felt her own blood swirling and sucking down her heart. Her breath stopped for a moment, but she drew in enough air, and her sharp brain bounced back again with ideas.

She decided not to call people to rescue her.

She still had two women onboard. Her game was still on.

"Why did you untie her? Wasn't her position proper to fuck her?"

"Fuck her?" he growled, eyes spitting fire. "She is a married woman. Do you realise what would happen to her had she become pregnant? Would her family accept her back? Ma'am, death is a hundred times better than this. How many other sepoys had already done that with her? Tell me their names. I will see they all get punishment."

Morticia cast a quick glance around. Frustration flooded in her blood. "Quiet, sepoy. Silent. Don't shout if your shaft has no energy left."

The sepoy accosted her, his tall and muscular body swelled in anger. "What, you are saying, I'm not a man? Open your thighs and I will show you what sort of man I am. A real man never plays with the honour of a woman."

Morticia glanced around. She was alone on the terrace with him, and he looked like an outraged demon who could twist her neck and throw her into Andaman Sea. She repented for her own taunting comment. "You unnecessarily worried for her family. She would have served all ten of you, and I would've pushed her into the water. I don't want her to spread the news in Calcutta. I only wished you people to remain happy."

"Happy? Like this?"

The angry soldier trudged to the door leading to the stairs. Morticia glanced around. If all ten sepoys got together, Rave and she wouldn't have a chance.

The latch of the exit door was tight, and the sepoy was struggling to open it. When someone pushed the door from outside, the sepoy stepped back. There was no time to waste—Morticia grabbed an iron rod and hit the man's head. His unconscious body fell over Rave, who was just entering the terrace. Rave tried to hold him, but he had to bend with the body until it came down on the floor.

"What did you do?" An anxious Rave slumped near the sepoy and tried to feel his pulse. "He is no more."

Morticia slammed the exit door shut and latched it. "Was anybody coming with you?"

"No, but this is foolish. We have already lost two soldiers. And now one more. What reply will I give to Dr. Walker?"

"Don't cry like a stupid, spineless man. Is he giving the men for free? Is he also not getting commission from us? And who is counting prisoners? Aren't they dying of malaria and cholera? This man would have run to the backside of the ship and informed his mates. And remember, my life is precious. I mean—mine, and of course, yours."

"Only your life, Morticia." Rave's knees buckled when he stood up, a look of extreme anger in his eyes. "If one day someone will offer a bag of gold in exchange for my head, you will kill me, too."

Morticia stood still, anger spurting from her heart. "One day? I don't know. But if you behave like an idiot, I will finish you today. Now."

Frustration crinkled in Rave's eyes. "What do I do now?"

"I have to tell you that, too? Use your brain."

A long silence hung between them.

"Leave the body here. You can come back at night and push it into the water. No one should see you."

Rave nodded.

"And remember, as long as this ship is in the middle of the ocean, I am the queen."

CHAPTER NINETEEN

SEHNAZ, 17 NOVEMBER 1862, MORNING, JERRY ISLAND AND SOUTH OF COCO ISLANDS

A smile escaped Sehnaz's mouth while she was still in bed. Thank God, with winter coming, the sunrays had delayed invading the hutment through slits of its thatched roof. She could sleep longer.

She changed sides, and her eyes opened for a moment. Did Sheru get an off day today? By this time, he should have left the bed and gone to work, leaving her alone for the day!

The warm sunrays didn't allow Sehnaz to enjoy any more slumber. Is Jhumru still sleeping? Jhumru always slept on the veranda on a bed Sehnaz had made using jute bags. She loved her bed and never disturbed Sehnaz the entire night. But she should have come inside and begun licking her feet by now. She got up and manoeuvred her way alongside Sheru to move out of the room, making no noise. Gently shutting the door behind her, she peered at Jhumru's warm bed. She was not there.

"Naughty girl!" Sehnaz muttered under her breath before walking some distance from the house. "Jhumru. Jhumru, my baby! Where're you?"

Panic flickered through her stomach. No wild animals roam Jerry Island, only snakes. Did a snake swallow Jhumru?

Unlikely. The snakes she had seen on the island were not large enough to pose danger to a cat.

Her heart jumped inside her ribs, apprehending some unknown fear. "Jhumru, didn't I tell you? Never go out without me. Where do I find you now?"

Sehnaz ran to the east, scanning around. Walking around two hundred yards, she stopped at the Andaman Sea. Then she ran south along the coast, the sea to the east, and Jerry with all its coconut and mango trees to the west. "Jhumru, come back," she yelled, looking at each bush she met on the way. The hutments of the village she crossed leered at her like ghost-houses. Workers must have gone to Coco for the day.

It was a short walk of fifteen to twenty minutes only. She wondered why she had never come and explored the island before? An angry Andaman Sea stopped her on the south of Jerry. The waves looked aggressive to Sehnaz. She inhaled a deep breath and swung back, keeping the sea to her back. Such a tiny island! A tremendous storm could wash the entire island into the water. Did it make sense to live here for long?

She noticed water on all three sides, the Bay of Bengal to her left, the Andaman Sea to south and right. All within walking distance.

There was no trace of Jhumru. The last direction she needed to explore was north. She couldn't lose her only companion when Sheru went to Coco for work. "Jhumru, my baby. Are you angry with me?" A sob gathered at the back of her throat, but she swallowed it and continued walking along the coast toward the north, keeping the Bay of Bengal to her left.

She continued walking until she had no idea how far she had come or how long she had been in the forest.

Her gaze fell on a boy—holding Jhumru close to his chest and kissing her.

Sehnaz stilled, body rigid. The dark-skinned boy was wearing only a bark to cover his groin and must have been around fourteen. The way he was talking with the cat and the way Jhumru was reacting made her feel that the boy owned her.

Dark thoughts smoked into her mind. Would she lose Jhumru forever? Who would she spend time with during these long days when she had no one around?

Sehnaz never thought a sweet dream would be over so soon. It seemed like yesterday when she had found Jhumru in the forest. The way the cat came to her and licked her feet, she should have known she was already familiar with humans.

Sehnaz glanced around, finding no other tribals. She stepped forward, drawing nearer to the lad.

He met her gaze, a warm smile on his face.

Sehnaz failed to understand whether the smile was at her or for getting Jhumru back.

She couldn't talk to the lad, but used the little sign language she knew and asked him to give back Jhumru. The boy also said something to her, but the words were meaningless to Sehnaz. Why didn't God just make one language for the entire world?

The boy pointed toward the north, still holding the cat with one hand, and said something. Meaningless words. Had he intended to return Jhumru to her, he would have already done so.

She glanced at the sky and noted that the sun was rising at a slow pace. Sheru must have woken up by now, and he would worry about her. Could she fight or even persuade the lad to spare the cat? No, Jhumru was back with her actual owner and probably loved it.

Tears rolled down her cheeks. "Jhumru, I am going. Love you." She spun back and left in a hurry. The sooner she could get out of Jhumru's sight, the better.

"Mew."

Sehnaz slowed down. Did she hear something? No. It was just a delusion. She walked again, this time with longer strides.

"Mew."

Sehnaz stilled and swung around. The boy was following her, holding the cat. As she gazed at him, he bent and placed Jhumru on the grass. She came running to Sehnaz and jumped into her arms. Clasping Jhumru close to her breast, Sehnaz looked at the boy and said, "*Dhanyabad,* thanks."

He would never understand Hindi or English. Sehnaz hoped that her grateful glance was enough to show she was thanking him.

She had never been so thrilled since she left Calcutta with Amelia.

"I will show you something today." Sheru beamed as Sehnaz arrived home holding Jhumru.

"You look so cheerful today. Did you meet somebody?"

"First, go to the pond and take a bath. I already finished mine. We will go there now."

On their way back from the pond, Sehnaz plucked some fresh flowers. "Today is Monday, Sheru. Did you choose today as your off day, as this is the most auspicious day of Lord Shiva?"

Sheru nodded. "Supervisor's mood. Every day is good for praying to your deity. Is this flower for Lord Shiva?"

They went to the cave, which was the makeshift temple for the Lord, and offered the flowers. When they were finished, Sheru led the way through the woods.

Sehnaz could remember the place she had met the tribal boy a while ago. Where did he go?

It wasn't far, and they arrived at the northernmost tip of the island. Sehnaz saw a submerged sandbar.

"The other side is Great Coco Islands. I sail to it every morning. We can walk to Coco through this sandbar when there's a low tide."

It was the second surprise for Sehnaz that day.

"We have to wait until the low tide clears off the sandbar."

"How did you know about this, Sheru? You have never come here."

"Do you know why I always prefer to work on Sundays? Because the English sahibs go to the church, and I get some free time. After sailing to Coco, I use a horse to commute between places.-Yesterday I reached the south end riding on the horse and saw this. There's a clear pathway. But walking all the way to the northward part of Coco in the forest might not be a good idea."

After waiting for an hour, they noticed the water was just a little above the sandbar. They walked almost two hundred yards through the knee-deep water and arrived at Coco Islands. It was a sort of freedom feeling for Sehnaz. She was no more imprisoned on the tiny Jerry Island.

"Sheru, look there. Turtles." She placed Jhumru on the ground and ran after one of them.

"Hold on, Sehnaz. You might run over their nests."

Sehnaz captured a small turtle and massaged its shell. A chuckle escaped from her throat. "No Sheru, don't worry. I'm careful."

"They are green turtles. Our English sahibs are fond of their meat."

Sehnaz stopped grinning. "They're so cute. How could one kill them?"

She placed the turtle on the ground and scooped Jhumru to her hip. The sandbar had come up above the water. Dense trees didn't make it possible to peer far into Coco Islands. A strong desire to walk farther north and explore the island erupted in her.

"How far is the place you work from here?"

Sheru's eyes narrowed. "Hm, maybe, around seven miles. This is much bigger than our Jerry. There are two more islands to the north of Coco, Table Island and the tiny Slipper Island."

"This morning I walked across all sides of Jerry, it's so tiny a strong cyclonic tide can wash all of us away."

Sheru chortled. "As long as God decides to keep us alive, no power in the world can kill us. Lord Shiva wanted to make me free from the British prison, see how I could escape. It was HE who organised a timely friendship with Aung."

A feel-good moment engulfed Sehnaz's conscious. She was dreaming of leaving Jerry and living somewhere livelier. "Sheru, how big is the Table Island?"

"Bigger than Jerry. Why?"

"Can't we move there?" She glanced at him with lots of expectations.

Sheru laughed. "It is a no-man's-land." Then he stopped.

"What happened?"

"We will not go far," Sheru said.

"Why?"

"Yesterday I came riding a horse. I could have run away had any tribals attacked me. But today..."

"Sheru, look!" Sehnaz shouted. "A tribal village, there."

Smoke was coming from the direction she pointed. Someone was cooking lunch for the family.

Sheru froze. "Lower your voice, Sehnaz. They are dangerous. I heard they have even killed an Englishman before."

Sehnaz's heart was not ready to believe Sheru. "You already know the officers in Coco take women from Indian and Burmese workers. Have you ever seen an Englishman with any tribal woman?"

"No, never."

"When we had halted in Jambu, I saw the tribal men chase and kill an English soldier. Both Amelia and I were witnesses. Know why?"

Sheru gave a blank look.

"The Englishman thought tribal women were easy and tried to molest them. They never tolerate insult to their females. In fact, to me, they are more civilised than us."

Sehnaz insisted they at least walk to the tribal village. She could spare some time and come to teach them. Make them literate.

Sheru made a namaste sign. "Lord Shiva, protect us, please."

As soon as he finished his quick prayer, a thumping sound jolted them. Four men with loaded bows jumped from a tree and stood before them.

CHAPTER TWENTY

RUPEN, 22 NOVEMBER 1862, NORTH BAY ISLAND (PART OF ANDAMAN AND NEAR ROSS ISLAND)

Rupen got off the boat and walked along with two English guards.

"Sir, this is North Bay Island," one guard said. "We have information that the tribal chief lives on this island. But he also commands over the people of a few other Andaman Islands."

"Thank you, gentlemen." Rupen managed a grin. "And you all would appreciate that I'm a political prisoner. A friend of Andaman's governor, too. Please do not treat me like a prisoner in the presence of the islanders. I am here to accomplish a special task for Dr. Walker. Try to learn the language and become a bridge between the British and tribals."

"We know, sir," the second guard said while walking alongside Rupen, "but we know little about this place and can't even identify who is the chief."

"That shouldn't be a problem. I will manage that." A confidence brewed inside Rupen. This was his first step toward the planned permanent freedom, and he already smelled that in the pre-winter air of North Bay Island.

It took around fifteen minutes through the narrow pathway in the woods. They met a few men. One of them was wearing a leather cap with a peacock feather on the top. He must have been the *sardar,* the tribal chief. Rupen bowed his head with a namaste pose. Without knowing their language, that was the only way to convey his respect. Then he cast a sideways glance at both the English guards, who were standing straight at his side.

"He is the tribal leader. Please show your respect like I did."

"Why us? We are English."

Rupen didn't reply. He had already prepared his mind to swallow the British pride he hated and fought against.

The chief hinted for him to follow. A narrow, snaky pathway covered by tall trees on both sides took them only about ten minutes to arrive at the *sardar's* place. Pointing for Rupen to sit on a stone bench, the chief vanished inside a cottage.

"Please, do not hold guns like you are ready to fire," he insisted to the English soldiers. "The man is the head tribal here and understands the difference between a friendly and hostile gesture."

The guards lowered their guns.

Rupen glanced around the expanse of the large banyan tree beneath which he was sitting. The area was clean and paved with stones. Almost a dozen timber logs made a circle, which provided nature-made sitting spaces. *What type of island is this? I don't see anybody other than this man.*

The *sardar* came out with three women. *One must be his wife and the other two his daughters,* Rupen guessed from their age and appearance.

Appearance?

He glanced at the two soldiers through the corner of his eyes. Both were ogling at the two young girls, their large breasts only partly covered with flowers. He stood up to greet the women and pretended to rearrange his belt, elbowing both Englishmen at his sides. "Don't stare, if you guys wish to go back alive," he muttered.

The *sardar* said something while pointing at the women, and all three of them bowed their heads to Rupen.

Something rang a bell inside Rupen's mind. Did he say *raja*, king?

When the *sardar* continued repeating the same word in some of his sentences, it was clear to Rupen—yes, he was saying *raja.*

"You call me *raja*?" Rupen asked him in Hindi. Who knew if he might have known other words, too? And wouldn't it be easier for Rupen to learn the tribal language if the man already knew some Hindi?

"Raja. Came ago. Here. Marry," the man replied in broken Hindi—all in one syllable words. Pointing at his wife, he said, "Daughter. His. Dead."

Rupen struggled to interpret. The wife had a different skin tone than her husband. He reconstructed the man's broken Hindi inside his mind. *A king came and married here. He is dead and his daughter is this man's wife.*

The man again asked him, "Raja. You?"

Is he thinking I am also a king? He was sure none of the two English guards would understand what the man said when he, too, had difficulty interpreting. *Yes, it appears like I am a king, and these two men are my bodyguards!*

He tried to suppress his snicker. *Is it so wrong if he thinks I am?*

When the women went back inside their cottage, the man also followed them, leaving Rupen to ponder what he just learned.

A man came from outside and married a tribal woman, identifying himself as a king... Rupen was sure he must be from India. How else did this man know Hindi, even if very little? Could he also do the same? Marry a girl and settle here? No. That would be a daydream. Whenever he would come to this island, English guards must come with him. Was there a way he could run away and hide?

Rupen glanced at the soldiers. They were exchanging sidelong glances. *Can't they just leave me alone with these people? Who knows, could they also catch few Hindi words, because maybe they were working in India before coming to Andaman?*

"Gentlemen, are you not tired of standing? Why don't you sit on that stone for a while? I will be here for a few hours at least, as per my discussion with Dr. Walker." The distance from the second stone bench was enough to give him some privacy.

The women came back with food bowls, and the man came holding banana leaves. When he spread a leaf on the ground, his wife served steaming rice on it. The daughters also followed by serving vegetables and half burnt fish.

Rupen wanted to ask why there were no other men and women. But the *sardar's* limited Hindi stopped him.

Halfway through his meal, he noticed the two Englishmen also siting cross-legged and eating from the banana leaves with their fingers. A smile escaped his mouth.

He wanted to lift his head and gaze at the *sardar's* beautiful daughters. He had even forgotten that he had come to master the local language, and instead he started dreaming. *How well will it be if*

I settle here, and these girls become my wives? Can I persuade Dr. Walker to send me alone without the guards?

With a renewed hope for freedom and a newfound familiarity with the *sardar* and his beautiful daughters, the hours flew like minutes for Rupen. His first lesson was more than wonderful. He didn't even realise how quickly the time came to return to the Ross Island.

While on his way to the boat, Rupen noticed another ferry by the seashore, but at a distance. Almost a hundred tribal men and women were following just two individuals—a man and a woman. A hill between made it difficult to reach them.

Rupen recognised the Englishman, Dr. Nick Wilson. He might be there to provide medical treatment to the island's patients. Now he understood why he didn't see anyone other than the *sardar's* family.

His gaze fell on the woman accompanying Dr. Wilson. But he was sure that woman was not his wife, as Rupen had seen Mrs. Wilson before. He could only see the woman from her side. Memory of a known gait swirled inside him. Who could that woman be?

The guards were in a hurry to take him back to the prison. But Rupen stilled, focussing his gaze on that woman.

It didn't take long for him to recognise her.

Amelia? What is she doing here?

Amelia, 22 November 1862, North Bay Island (Part of Andaman Island group and near Ross)

I wave my hands at the men and women while entering the boat.

"For the first time, so many women came to my camp," Dr. Nick said, "even with no sickness."

"Why so?"

"Because a woman has come with me—that, too, a white one."

A smile comes out of my mouth. This man is so generous, he is using each bit of his time to serve patients. Eliza must be proud of him. It is almost dusk, and the sea is rough because of the wind. I ask the Indian boatman, "How soon we will be on Ross?"

"Ma'am. Not long. But if you permit me, can I pick up my catch?"

"Catch?"

"Yes, ma'am. While you both were with the islanders, I sailed almost a mile to the south, along the coast. There is a small bay-like place, where large prawns are available. I have set a fishing net. It will only be a few minutes. I will bring the catch to the ship. Sahib knows. That is my routine whenever sahib comes here."

Dr. Nick smiles. "Let him! I, too, get a share. Eliza and Luke love them. I'm sure they are planning for a prawn dinner tonight."

"And your maid Shanti will cook prawn curry?" I chuckle. "I will ask her to teach me the curry recipe."

"You have almost become her friend," Nick mutters with a chuckle, "the British society doesn't appreciate friendship with a maid, especially India. Though Eliza and I have no issue with that."

I weigh Nick's comment for a while. "I can connect well because I respect her, and I also know some Hindi. She is from a respected family, but circumstances made her family poor. That can happen to anyone, even to an English. Believe me Nick, if the British start respecting local people, there won't be another Sepoy Mutiny."

Nick just smiles.

My thought floats to Eliza. My first and so far only female friend I have on the Ross Island after meeting her two weeks ago, the day Morticia left Andaman. Not only her, but I have also become a friend to her kid, Luke. It was Eliza's suggestion I accompany her doctor husband and teach some English to the islanders when he came here on Sundays to provide medical help as a goodwill gesture from the British government.

"Ma'am see, we have arrived. Only fifteen minutes." The boatman beams as he secures the chain locker to a tree on the shore and jumps out. "That place is close to here, ma'am. Sahib knows. Only ten minutes, will be back."

I bring a smile to my face. I might also get a portion, and it would be a wonderful dinner tonight.

A faint wailing pierces my ears.

"Dr. Wilson."

He is busy watching something.

"Dr. Wilson, can you hear something? Something like a woman's..."

"Weeping? Yes. I do." His eyebrows bump together. "We don't have much time, Amelia. It's dangerous to stay here in the evening— that, and it's too windy here."

"What do we do?"

"We can't wait until the boatman comes back. Might be unsafe for you. Let me check. Myself."

He is about to jump to the shore when I decide to come with him.

We follow the sound. Within minutes, the wailing becomes louder.

I am about to howl when Nick grabs me and covers my mouth with his palm.

A pregnant woman tied to a tree stops crying and looks at us.

"Loud talk will alert islanders. This is sensitive. We have to be careful."

"What's this?" I whisper.

"This is a punishment. For some crime, we don't know. Maybe a death punishment. They have left her here so that she'll die of starvation, or some wild animal will kill her. She can't even defend herself. She is so well secured against the tree trunk."

"But why?"

"No time to ponder over that."

Nick takes a knife from his pocket—which he always carries while on the island—and releases the woman. She gets up and stands in silence.

"We must take her with us. But no one here can find out. And this is the perfect time. Almost evening."

"With us? To Ross?"

"Yes. But if these men learn I have done this, the next time I come here, they will send me to my grave."

"How would they find out?"

"These men sometimes come to Ross to find herbs that aren't available here. And you know, being a doctor, many people come to my home, even during odd times."

"Then I will hide her with me."

CHAPTER TWENTY-ONE

SEHNAZ, 24 NOVEMBER 1862, SOUTHERN PART OF COCO ISLANDS TRIBAL VILLAGE

"Thank you, Agatha ma'am. Had you not been present that day, these men could have killed us. You came right on time."

It was the first day for Sehnaz and Sheru after moving to the southern part of Coco Islands, to the tribal village. Sheru had taken a few days off and built the cottage with the help of the villagers. Sehnaz was thrilled to learn this one English woman from Coco volunteered to teach tribal villagers. The three of them were gathered in the newly built cottage.

Agatha smiled. "You can't blame these men. They are simple. But in the past our men had tried to get the benefit of their innocence and tried to molest their women. But I'm sure you will love the stay here. And for your children, I am here, to teach."

Children? Sehnaz and Sheru exchanged a sideways glance.

"That's all right. I understand. I too have no child. But I am a volunteer teacher here."

"Do you commute every day to the Coco town, ma'am?"

"No. During the daytime I teach the children, and in the afternoon when men and women are free from their daily chores, I teach some of them, too. Sometimes, I stay here in the evening. Can you see the cottage over there? These villagers made it for me. But my husband stays in the Coco town."

"You can stay in a hutment?" Sehnaz asked.

Agatha smiled. "I didn't fall from the heaven."

A relaxed smile escaped from Sehnaz's mouth. "And ma'am, if you don't mind, can I also help you with teaching? I was working for a school, too."

"Where?"

Sehnaz weighed the answer for a moment. Should she say she was in Sultanpur? With Amelia? No. So many secrets would spill out. How could she trust a woman she'd known for only a short period of time?

"I was in Calcutta."

A massive smile widened Agatha's mouth. "Lovely. I had been in Calcutta for a while, too. We will have a delightful time together. I am wondering why you people came all the way from India to work on such a remote island?"

Is this woman trying to get all the information from us? Sehnaz couldn't think of a quick answer and pinched Sheru's arm.

"Ma'am...the truth is—" Sheru swallowed— "We didn't get any work after the Sepoy Mutiny, and our villagers threw us out, as she was from a lower caste. Someone said wages here are better. And ships are commuting between Coco and the mainland, anyway. We can go back anytime."

"I know. The caste system in India is horrible. No one here will mind what your religion and caste are. You both can live a peaceful life."

Agatha lifted her small trunk in preparation to go back to Coco. "You both take your time to settle in. I will go back to my husband. It's dangerous to leave men alone for so many days. And yes, your cat is lovely, Sanju."

Sehnaz and Sheru both stood in namaste pose.

"We will eagerly wait for you here, ma'am." Sehnaz said.

The horse cart carrying Agatha vanished in the jungle as Sehnaz and Sheru stood there, watching.

"How did you say so many lies, Sheru? And caste? When did I become a low caste woman? You could've said I am a Muslim." Sehnaz made a face and looked at Sheru. "Don't know. I didn't have time to think. I was against moving here. That day I saw this English woman, and—didn't we stay in Jerry to avoid the British scrutiny?"

Sehnaz reeled back, arms crossed. "I see. But I had thought all English in Coco are from Burma. How would I know she was from Calcutta?"

Sheru burst into a laughter. "Now who said all the lies? Why did you say you are from Calcutta? You know nothing about that city. Don't you think she would find out everything in just one day?"

"I didn't know what to do, Sheru. I thought I shouldn't say anything about Sultanpur and even Amelia."

Sheru let out an assuring grin. "Either way, this woman doesn't look dangerous. God will protect us."

"Yes, and please don't call me Sehnaz. I am Sanju. Your wife."

"Wife? The same drama here again?"

"Didn't you say your village people threw us away as you married a low caste girl, me?"

Sheru chuckled.

"We will have fun in our new place, Sheru."

Amelia at home, 24 November 1862, 10 in the morning, Ross Island

"I gave her a name—Vanaja." I giggle at Eliza. "Do you know its meaning?"

"Sounds like a Hindi name." Eliza settles on the sofa and casts a curious glance at the pregnant tribal woman Dr. Nick and I rescued yesterday. Today is Monday, but I decided to miss school. I need some time to take care of this new woman who might need lots of attention. Eliza is also curious to see and learn about her.

"Yes, Vanaja means 'born in a forest.' She might have a name already. But we have to shield her forever. So, a different name is always the first step to cover up the past."

Leaning against a wall, Vanaja keeps staring at both of us, and even Luke who is snuggled next to his mother. Her baby bump pokes through the dress Sadhna, and I have made her wear.

"Morticia's large house and the vast compound surrounded by trees are good enough to keep these two women secretly. And see how clever is her husband, Mr. Rave Hunt, is? She chose a house which was at the end of the road. No one will come up here unless there is a need," Eliza says.

"Mr. Hunt? His idea?" I am about to say it was Morticia's brain, but stop.

"Amelia, I have brought a few of my worn clothes. Nick said my size would fit well on this girl." Eliza takes out the clothes from a bag she had set on the floor and shows them to me. "Nick said I should come here and help you with her."

What a wonderful man, that Dr. Nick!

"And look at this boy. He is so attached to you, he didn't go to school because you took a day off."

"Luke, my boy." I hug him. He returns a smile.

My heart fills with gratitude. I can't imagine how depressing my life would have been at Ross Island without Nick, Eliza, and Luke. I pick one dress and approach Vanaja. "You will look like a fairy in this beautiful dress, girl."

Vanaja lets out a mild chuckle. I'm not sure if it's because she likes me talking to her or she loves her new dress. But I have been talking to her since yesterday, irrespective of the fact that she understands nothing.

"Amelia, is this how you taught language to Sadhna?"

I gaze at the curious eyes of Eliza. "Yes. And it worked!"

"You are a wonderful teacher, Amelia. How did you learn this technique?"

Even I didn't know this was a *technique*. "Don't know. But this worked on her so well. It might work on Vanaja, too."

Sadhna enters with two cups of steaming tea and a massive smile on her face, but stands still. We await thinking she would serve them to us.

Eliza leaves the sofa. Taking a cup from Sadhna, she places it on the tea table, then hugs her. "I am so happy, Amelia, you taught her how to make tea? But she doesn't know how to offer them to the guests."

I burst into a laughter. "Me? No. This is courtesy of your very own Shanti."

Eliza also laughs at me.

"Aunt Amelia, I will also drink tea." Luke calls me aunt even though I am a teacher in his school.

Before Eliza reprimands him, I say, "No, my child. Tea is for adults only. I will give you milk with sugar."

"I don't like milk." Luke makes a face.

"All right, I have something different for you. Tastier." I wink.

"What?"

"Rice pudding. Do you love it?"

"Yea!" Luke jumps off the sofa and runs to me. "I love rice pudding."

"I knew it," I say with a chuckle, and Eliza joins in. Sehnaz had taught me how to make this pudding.

Before we finish laughing, the aroma of curry fills my nose. I swing back to find Shanti—Eliza's maid and my dear friend—entering the house with a bowl. "Prawn curry," she announces, her face beaming.

My mouth salivates. "Hello, Shanti! I thought you cooked prawn curry last night and forgot about me." "No, memsahib. No forget. You. No cook curry last night."

"Thanks, Shanti." I take the bowl from her and give it to Sadhna. "Sadhna, keep this in the kitchen and also take Vanaja to the room. Let her lie down on the bed. She needs to rest. And yes, bring a bowl of the rice pudding I had made yesterday."

Sadhna smiles. Even if she can't speak English well, she can understand most of what I say. So much development within just five weeks since Morticia left!

"Shanti, sit down." I point at a chair.

She cast a quick glance at Eliza, hesitation blurs her eyes, and I notice that Eliza's face had tightened.

"No, memsahib. I go kitchen. Your kitchen. Talk with Sadhna."

Eliza's face brightens up again, and she takes another sip of tea. "Good, Shanti. Amelia memsahib is teaching English to Sadhna. You also teach her how to speak Hindi."

Shanti stops for a moment to listen to her employer but doesn't respond and leaves the drawing room.

I sip tea and begin a conversation. "Yesterday I travelled off Ross Island for the first time. It's not as huge as I had expected."

Eliza doesn't reply; she is lost in some thought. Her gaze goes to the hallway leading to the kitchen where Shanti just walked.

I try again to start the conversation. "Shanti is such an amiable woman."

"Woman?" Eliza's eyes widen. "Oh, yes, she is an excellent maid. Never steals. Works hard and cooks delicious curries."

I rarely use the word maid. And I feel Eliza's discomfort because I referred to Shanti as a woman, not a maid. I sigh quietly. This is not Eliza's fault. She is a gentlewoman otherwise. But she goes with the trend. With the flows. Why should I expect all nice ladies to think like me?

But I'm sure Nick would never think such things of the maids and Indians as Eliza has expressed.

"You never considered of hiring a maid while coming here?" Eliza asks.

I hesitate while trying to come up with a good reason. It was Sehnaz's idea not to bring our maids from Sultanpur. They are good and simple. But what if some unwanted information leaks out of them?

"I should have, Eliza. But I had no time. And I also hoped maids would be available locally here."

Eliza lets out a light laugh and set the teacup on the table. "Nothing is available here in Andaman. I had to think twice before giving my old clothes to Vanaja. Because you can't just go to the market and buy stuff as we did in Calcutta. Ships come here with merchandise. But with negligible quantity."

Shanti comes in with the bowl of pudding and gives it to Luke.

"Thank you, Aunt Amelia." He literally snatches the bowl from Shanti.

I revert back to my talk with Eliza. "Yesterday, I went to North Bay Island and saw Ross Island for the first time from a distance. It's not as big as I had assumed."

"You found out now?" Eliza leans forward. "It's all in my fingertips. North side is the prison encampment, inside the jungle. Then comes the Indian guards' quarters, just to its south. Then your school and the small market. And next, officers' quarters, on this side. This house is the last one."

"Did the government plan to make the Indian guards' quarters as a buffer?"

"Yes, in case prisoners break the barrier and try to attack us. Such a clever plan, huh! That's why the British are ruling the planet."

Even Sehnaz can make this much plan. What is great in this?

"You are smiling, Amelia."

Am I? "Oh no, I am only admiring the intelligence of our people. But the dorms of the Indian guards are so tiny and... I mean, you can tell the difference between their and our accommodations."

Shanti comes over and collects the empty cups from the table. Luke also gives his empty bowl to her.

"I made Vanaja to sleep. She was weeping. Sadhna said she hadn't slept last night," Shanti says.

"Thanks, Shanti. Last night she woke up a few times screaming. I had to run to her each time and pacify her." The agony of being tied up and waiting to die has given a colossal blow to her innocent mind. What crime could she have committed? No woman deserves such harsh punishment. So much stress is not good for her pregnancy.

"Nick said she had received punishment by the tribal chief. Death punishment. How barbaric! Who gives death punishment to a pregnant woman? When will they be civilised?" Eliza's eyes are full of concern for this girl.

"Who said only uncivilised people are barbaric? Even children as young as seven go to the gallows in England if they commit felony."

Shanti leaves the room, and Luke follows her to the kitchen.

I turn back to Eliza and a bit apprehensive she would reprimand Luke. But surprisingly, she does nothing.

"Their numbers are more than the English," Eliza reasons, "and they are all here without families. The government planned this to cut costs. They all live together like staying in hostels."

We both jerk up to a scream from the back of the house. Before we both could react, Vanaja comes running from the hallway, Shanti following her.

"Shanti, quick, grab her," I yell.

Shanti grabs her from behind and drags her back. "No Vanaja, good girl, come back."

Vanaja slumps on the floor and weeps uncontrollably, blabbering in her language. I kneel near her and pat her back with another hand on her shoulder.

"She should never go out of the main gate. Men from North Bay Island come here sometimes to collect herbs that aren't available there. They might report to their chief." Eliza is standing next to us, concern in her eyes.

"I know. Nick has already warned me. But how do I explain this to her? I can't take leave from school every day. Who else will look after her when I am in the school?"

Eliza gazes into my eyes. "I think you can take a few more days' leave. Mrs. Dunhill was saying you are the additional teacher as you have come here voluntarily. If you stay at home, I will also join you when Luke goes to school."

Who is Mrs. Dunhill, and how does she know so much about me? I don't dare ask who she is or what else she knows. It is true that the teachership work in Andaman is only a pretence to come here for Rupen. But I must make all efforts to help Sadhna and Vanaja survive and have successful lives. That is who I am.

Vanaja has stopped weeping. A smile of confidence comes out of my lips. "I will apply for more leave."

CHAPTER TWENTY-TWO

AMELIA, 24 DECEMBER 1862, ROSS ISLAND

Seated inside the horse cart, I say to Eliza, "This will be my first Christmas Eve party in Andaman." She has been eagerly awaiting this for a month. But I've not been very interested.

After lots of self-arguments, I have decided not to judge Rupen for his role in suppressing the rebellion in the prison. I have given my word to Sehnaz, and my word is important to me, as is Sehnaz. Rupen's freedom is my sole purpose of coming to Andaman. And the Christmas Eve celebration will be the perfect occasion for me to create new contacts.

Arriving at the party hall, I feel like I'm in another world, maybe in London. Everyone here is white. Authorities haven't invited a single Indian. Didn't the English learn anything from the mistakes which caused the Sepoy Mutiny to break out in 1857?

I walk up to Dr. Walker. After my first introduction to him while farewelling Morticia, I didn't get a chance to meet him again. I'm not sure if he will listen to my suggestion. Still, I muster the courage and let out a grin. "Sir, I have a request, if you could kindly listen to me."

Walker lifts his gaze from his wineglass and looks at me.

"Sir, I was in Lucknow before the Sepoy Insurrection in 1857. So many times, I had been a guest in the palace of Nawab Wajid Ali, along with my husband. They always treated the Britishers with honour, even though an undercurrent of tension was there. Shouldn't we invite the Indian employees here, too? After all, they have also been away from their families for so long."

Walker narrows his eyes. "We can't leave the prisoners unguarded. You know this is an open encampment. As all English soldiers are here at the celebration, Indian guards are all on duty."

I tilt my head in what I hope is an innocent gesture. "All?"

"Yes. And even if—suppose I invite a few, they are all low-grade staff. Can you believe none of them can hold a fork and knife? The basic etiquettes of an English party."

My forehead puckers, cracking my innocent façade. "Is properly holding a fork and knife a symbol of civilisation? I know Indians treat the guests as if they are only second to a god." Disappointment crawls over my skin, and anyone could notice.

Everybody glares at me. Did I offend the senior-most officer of Andaman?

He displays a patronising smile. "I understand your point, madam Amelia. I can invite only one man. But he is a prisoner."

"Who?"

"Rupen. The ex-army chief of Awadh."

A happiness floods my mind, and it overflows. I'd come simply to make contacts to help Rupen, but here he is being presented to me on a silver platter! "That would be so nice of you, sir. He has even helped you to contain the prisoner uprising. He deserves a reward."

Did I say more than required?

Dr. Walker immediately sends a server to get Rupen for the party.

After all this time, I will see Rupen again—and after he's been imprisoned. I frantically prepare myself to face him, to figure out how to somehow convey my intention of coming here with Sehnaz—and the sacrifices Sehnaz made for all this. A ruckus from across the room intrudes my thoughts. My gaze goes to the main door of the hall. Half a dozen women are shouting at a saree-wearing woman, as if a wild animal has trespassed into the party. She is Shanti, Eliza's maid.

I run to her rescue. "Wait, ladies. Please wait." I wrestle through the women.

"Memsahib!" Shanti grabs my hand. "She is sick. Quick. Vanaja."

Vanaja? Ice forms in my veins. *She is a non-existent woman. None other than Dr. Wilson's family knows I have kept her hidden at home.*

Grabbing Shanti's hand, I take her out, past the wide veranda of the hall, to the lawn. Eliza jogs up behind me. I swing back and whisper, "Something has happened to Vanaja. Maybe labour pain. Or something. Please call Dr. Wilson. Eliza, it's urgent. Please."

Eliza turns to run inside, but I stop her. "Eliza! Please say nothing. Confidential. Just call him outside."

Within minutes, Shanti, Eliza, and I get into Nick's carriage and rush back home.

Eliza places a hand on my knee. "No one except my family knows you have kept two women hiding in your house, Amelia. And hiding Vanaja is more serious. A seed of dispute among the tribals, which my husband never wants."

"Her life is at stake. Shanti says she is vomiting blood."

Nick perks up. "Blood?"

I see the reflection of the death warrant in Nick's eyes.

As we arrive home, Nick says this is a miscarriage.

Sadhna, in her broken English, tells me Vanaja was out last night and had brought some herbs. She had then boiled them and drank the medicinal water without my knowledge.

"This woman knows how to end the pregnancy. Herbal treatment. But it's dangerous in advanced pregnancy. I have to bring some medicine." Nick quickly runs next door to his home to brings some tablets. Shanti grinds the medicine to a powder, and after mixing it with water, she forces it down Vanaja's throat.

"This might help. But we need to wait and watch."

Tension ticks through my jaws. Will Vanaja survive?

Another thought pounds through my heart. Will I miss the only chance I've gotten to meet Rupen tonight? I drop my head into my hands.

We wait almost two hours before Vanaja's vomiting stops and she falls into a slumber. Nick checks her pulse from time to time. Finally, Nick says Vanaja should be all right, but someone should be with her.

Who else other than me? There's no chance I could meet Rupen tonight. Sadhna can't leave, and Shanti might not be able to handle it again if Vanaja becomes unwell at night.

Eliza says she is not in the mood to go back to the celebration, and through a miraculous twist of fate, she offers to wait on Vanaja.

I lope forward, engulfing Eliza in a hug. "Thanks, Eliza! So much." I don't want to miss my only chance to meet Rupen.

Nick and I both jump into his cart.

As we arrive at the hall, we notice men and women are slowly leaving. My heart drops.

"Looks like we missed the event altogether. Let me see if some leftover food is available for us. I am famished." Nick jumps off the cart.

My eyes dart around. I don't need any food, but I must meet Rupen. That, and not attracting too much attention.

Hoisting myself off the carriage, I glance around. Is Rupen still inside the celebration hall, or has he already left?

And then I see—he is there, hardly fifty yards away. Just about to vanish inside a carriage. Most of his hair has turned grey, and crinkles have appeared on his forehead—five years of stress from the war and the prison. But his broad and powerful shoulders still span almost the width of the cart's doorway. The tall, dark and handsome Rupen, the ex-army head of Awadh. He meets my gaze and stills. The faint light of the lantern on the carriages is enough to show the eagerness in his eyes.

The three guards surrounding him stare at me. I dip my gaze down as Rupen enters the carriage and the guards shut the door.

Rupen, 24 December 1862, Night , Ross Island

Lonesomeness haunted Rupen as he stepped inside the horse cart. He didn't even appreciate that he was the only prisoner who attended the Christmas party, a reward from Dr. Walker for his help in controlling the uprising.

For the first time after so many years, Sehnaz's absence stirred his soul.

"I will never be your wife but will remain your best friend." These were Sehnaz's words when they had hatched plans together—how she would use her information network to provide sensitive secrets of the British camp in Lucknow.

The softness of her chest when she hugged him for the last time was still raw in him. "We will meet after the war, Sehnaz. I love you."

The war was over five years ago, and Rupen failed to digest the fact that the *life in prison* sentence meant he could never meet her again.

And after meeting Amelia's gaze tonight, his soul was looking for his best friend Sehnaz, who was also his adviser.

Did Amelia want to say anything about Sehnaz? Why did she come only when the Christmas party was over?

He would have been more than happy if, instead of appreciating his help by making him a guest at the party, Dr. Walker would have rewarded him with freedom. He was like a fish out of water in an all-white Christian gathering. Rather, his eyes were darting around to find Amelia. And he didn't see her until it was too late.

After almost a half hour, the cart left the road and entered the prison encampment area inside the forest. Rupen now felt like he was, in fact, an inmate like the others. Why else didn't he dare to stay and talk to Amelia? What stopped him?

He thought to ask Dr. Walker about Sehnaz's whereabouts. But that might be counterproductive. It was difficult to study that man. Would he ever be able to taste freedom one day, or would he spend his life in this hell?

"Your cottage, Sir."

"Thanks." He smiled. He was the only inmate whom Indian as well as English guards addressed as *Sir*. What irony! The man who commanded Awadh's mighty army appreciates only one word, *Sir*.

Rupen was so immersed in his deep thoughts he forgot to say goodnight to the guards who escorted him back to the prison. Entering his one-room cottage, he shut the door and lit the oil lamp.

Time for some meditation.

Rupen sat in lotus pose on the floor and closed his eyes. He focussed on his breaths and slowed them down. In a matter of a few minutes, Rupen would feel his nerves slowing down, and head to toe relaxed. His breathing continued, but his focus wandered around, and instead of slowing down, his nerves began racing. Even during the height of the war with the British, he had always controlled his mind.

Was it Amelia? Was Sehnaz somewhere nearby and remembering him?

He tried meditating for another five minutes but still failed to focus. It was close to midnight, and he understood he couldn't get the sleep, so he got up and opened the door. With his shoulders wrapped in a shawl, he stepped out. He ambled along the narrow pathway with tall mango and coconut trees on both the sides, blocking the moonlight. Gulmohar, the Royal Poinciana trees, teased him at places. This was not the season for their flowering, but Rupen still could smell the scent of the full-bloomed flowers.

A memory stirred his sense. Sehnaz loved to fix bunches of Gulmohar flowers in her bun. Was she somewhere near here? Did the authorities punish her for the stealing of the map?

His gaze went to the large hutment partly hidden behind the trees to his right. Rupen stilled for a moment and watched it. His ten loyal men lodged in this special hut, a benefit he had negotiated with Dr. Walker. Negotiation? No, it was a bribe. These ex-soldiers worked as mercenaries for Rave Hunt's piracy, in full collaboration with Dr. Walker. And the benefit? Better food and no inhuman work like thousands of other prisoners. And cost? Last time two men didn't return from Rave's expedition - twelve became ten. Rupen's heart sank whenever he thought of the two lost friends.

"Oh, Lord Shiva..." He folded his arms, head tilted to the sky, and eyes moistened. 'Forgive me. I, the ex-army chief of Awadh, do not intend to do this sin just for better accommodations or food. I have the physical ability to toil like thousands of other unfortunate inmates. But my intention is freedom. Including my ten loyal men. Unless I go out from here, how can I fight against the foreign power that has occupied my country? But I don't know how I would escape from here. Certainly Dr. Walker will not help me. But you can, and I am sure when the time comes, you will show me the light.'

He sucked in a deep breath and sauntered ahead. His nerve cooled down a little after the prayer, but not enough to get him back to sleep.

"Namaste, sir." A voice alarmed Rupen. He didn't realise that he was already inside the general prisoners' encampment. Rupen stopped. A tall and athletic man with curly hair stood on the side of the path.

"Namaste," Rupen replied with no interest in talking to him and swung back to return to his cottage.

"Sir, I think you didn't recognise me," the man said from behind.

Rupen stilled. Being a famous man, almost all inmates knew who he was. But why did this man expect he must recognise him?

He turned to face the man. A known smile on the man's face awakened his memory. "You... I mean... No."

"Sir, I am Mithun. I was in Sultanpur as a police inspector."

"Mithun? Police?" Rupen remembered he had seen him, but still couldn't recollect when and where. So many people working for the British knew him when he was the army chief. Why did that matter now?

"How did British police come to this prison as a convict? Did you join the rebel camp in 1857?"

A smirk on Mithun's face dazzled in the moonlight. He glanced around and edged closer. "Sir, I was with the police until two months ago. Came to this prison only last week," he said, bringing his voice to a whisper, even though the nearest encampment hut was about two hundred gauges away and there were no guards nearby.

"Sir, I was Sehnaz's informer all throughout the war. She advised me never to leave the British and fight against them while pretending to be their trusted employee. But sir, we have met in 1955, well before the rebellion. I was in Lucknow then."

Rupen closed his eyes and muttered a quick prayer to Lord Shiva. "God, is this the reason you disturbed my meditation and pushed me out of the cottage?"

"Sir, you said something?"

Rupen opened his eyes. Mithun's eyes were overflowing with unspoken words. "I said something? No. Nothing. Please continue."

"I saw the way Colin cheated and captured you. You were a hero, Sir. You didn't harm a single English civilian in The Residency. And the British side should have never killed your wife and—"

Rupen raised a hand. "Please, do... don't. I am sorry, Mithun. But please don't remind me." A sob gathered in the back of his throat.

Mithun bowed his head. "I am sorry, Sir. I didn't come here to rub salt into your wound."

What other news does this man have for me?

"Sir, I saw when Mr. Colin took you into custody. But I was also there when he died."

"Died? You mean Colin is dead? How? During the war?"

Mithun smirked. "War?" He paused. "Of course. But a different war. A personal one involving his wife."

He realised they both were standing on the pathway, and guards might notice them during night patrolling. "Mithun, let's get into the woods, a place where no one could listen to our discussion."

Both tiptoed inside the forest and stood behind a bush of bamboos.

"This place is good. You said something about Colin."

"Yes, Sir. Colin had made all the plans to kill Amelia, his wife. He had even arranged false evidence that Amelia was the woman who stole the map of The Residency and passed it on to you. Many soldiers, including me, surrounded the Shakti Ashram where Amelia was planning to marry another man. You know about Shakti Ashram, Sir?"

"Who doesn't? Above the hill, in Sultanpur. Near the Gomti River. Amelia was marrying another man?"

"That is another long story, Sir. I will tell you everything."

"Did Colin get Amelia? I mean, did he come there after getting information that his wife was about to marry another man?"

"Not sure, Sir. But he had taken a letter from Sehnaz that said Amelia was the one who helped her in stealing the map. But, in fact, he had forged the letter."

"How?"

"I didn't ask Sehnaz that much. But she got the information about Colin's plans. Sir, no doubt, she was an intelligent woman."

Rupen's heart skipped a beat. "Was? What do you mean?"

"Sorry, Sir. I don't know where she is now. But Sehnaz had gotten a letter from Colin's ex-wife which she had addressed to the Viceroy Lord Dalhousie, asking for help as she suspected Colin would kill her. But nobody knows how that letter ended up with Sehnaz."

Rupen let out a silent chuckle. Mithun's eyes also danced along with the exciting information he was delivering, one after another.

"Sehnaz brought the letter on the day Colin had besieged Shakti Ashram with other soldiers. I was with him. He was about to capture Amelia. She ran away to a hillock, probably to jump and take her life. In the nick of time, a magistrate arrived with an arrest warrant for Colin."

Rupen frowned. "You said Colin died."

"That's true. Colin jumped from the hill. Suicide. And even after his death, he became a laughingstock in Sultanpur cantonment. He was using the government machinery to settle his own domestic battle, but in the end, had to give up his own life. A brigadier bested by two women."

Rupen nodded at Sehnaz's praise, but his chest squeezed too tight. "You were working for the British, but an Indian's heart will always be with his blood. Not with the whites."

Mithun stilled for a moment. Rupen noticed a dark cloud hovering over his eyes. The fellow gave him so much information, but he had yet to ask him about himself.

"Please tell me, Mithun, you were on the British payroll. Did they come to know you were an informer? How did you get this punishment?"

Mithun's face fell. "No sir. But the rebellion is not yet over. Another group is secretly trying to start a war again. I was at a loss when you lost the war and sentenced to Andaman prison. I planned to join the group. A batch of arms were coming from Calcutta by boat. I, along with another man, went to snatch the guns and run away. But it was a last-minute action and failed. My friend died in the firing. They caught me and I got punishment. Andaman prison."

Rupen placed his arm on Mithun's shoulder. "This is sad. You are a hero. But your expertise was in digging the information for the rebels, not to join the rebel openly. Believe me, even though you were getting a salary from the British each month, you were still a patriot. And you should have continued there."

Mithun looked up. "You are right, sir."

"But unfortunately, you don't know Sehnaz's whereabouts."

"She was living in Sultanpur after Colin died. After the war, Amelia bought an island mansion on the banks of the River Gomti. She became a schoolteacher. Sehnaz lived in the same bungalow and also taught Sultanpur girls and older women. Outside the school, of course. But..."

A shock passed through Rupen. "But what, Mithun?"

"A few months ago, we got instruction to nab Sehnaz. She was finally being accused of stealing the map of The Residency. I still don't understand why the government woke up after five long years."

Distant memories, unbidden, curled like smoke in Rupen's mind.

Mithun continued, "One of my English colleagues was in charge of the task. He was a regular visitor to the *kothas* of Sultanpur and knew many more courtesans with the name 'Sehnaz.' It is a popular Muslim name, anyway. He gave a report that out of a half dozen Sehnaz's he knew, none were the woman who had stolen the map. Sehnaz survived because of her name. But I didn't want to take a chance. My daughter was studying in Amelia's school, and, taking advantage of that, I went to warn her. It was last August. But she wasn't there. Servants told me Amelia had just left for London for a year."

"But Amelia is here!"

Mithun's brows raised. "Amelia? Here?"

"I saw her this evening. I had the fortune of visiting the Christmas party, courtesy of Dr. Walker."

The whistle of a guard alerted them both.

"You must go back to your hutment, Mithun. But you can still fight the battle even here. In your own way," Rupen murmured.

Mithun gave a blank look. "How, Sir?"

"You can befriend some of the Indian guards here. And that would be useful. I have some plans. If that materialises, I will help you escape from here. But that is confidential. I have never met you. And now, you go back through the trees. Don't come near the pathway. I'm sure the guard will never go inside the dense trees at night."

Mithun's eyes beamed with gratefulness. "You are great, Sir. I am leaving. But what about you?"

"I will stay here for a moment and go back. Sometimes I walk on the pathway at night, so they are used to this."

Mithun left. Rupen sat on the grass. Could he request Dr. Walker to allow him to meet Amelia? But what if he would trick him and nab Sehnaz?

CHAPTER TWENTY-THREE

AMELIA, 26 DECEMBER 1862, ROSS ISLAND MARKET, AROUND 11 IN THE MORNING

This morning when Eliza said a ship has arrived from Burma, I planned to visit the one and only market of Andaman, Ross Island Market. Since arriving here, I have yet to visit the marketplace. After Morticia and Rave went back to Calcutta, Shanti, Eliza's maid, has been bringing groceries and vegetables for me—whatever is available. It's true—to find a maid here is almost impossible. And I can't send Sadhna or Vanaja to the shop, because according to the people of Ross Island, they don't exist.

How many secrets will I keep on holding?

Within a day or two, all the women's clothes will sell out, and I need some dresses for both the girls.

There are four or five small hutments selling goods in the market. After buying clothes for both my girls, I keep them in the bag and roam around. I find nothing interesting for myself. Eventually, I leave the market and sit on a large, dead tree branch. The sunny day has attracted many women, but I have never taken interest in befriending anyone.

My mind whirls around Rupen after missing a golden opportunity two nights ago to meet him. I don't know if or when I will get another chance. Did Walker invite him to the Christmas party because he now supports the British instead of the patriotic Indians?

Conflict arises in my mind again. Am I doing the right thing if I help Rupen out of this prison? Should I risk my life and reputation in helping the man whom I had known as a patriot before and is now a traitor?

A mild laugh escapes my mouth. I am thinking like a patriotic Indian, forgetting that I am a British on the opposition side. And if I help a prisoner escape, I might end up in jail.

Am I sane?

Sehnaz's face floats in my imagination. She is my best friend, and I still hope one day we will meet again. All I am going to do is honour the promise I have given to her. It really doesn't matter to me whether Rupen is a patriot. My sole aim is to see a smile on Sehnaz's lips. I am alive today because she risked her life in crushing Colin's evil plan against me. Didn't I promise myself to risk anything for her?

A woman comes to me wearing a massive smile. "Hello, Amelia. How are you? I am Sophia."

"Hello, Sophia." I slap on a smile. *How did she know my name? Oh, I am the only female teacher in Andaman.*

I hesitate to engage in conversation with her. Will this woman make me spill my secrets? Then I think, what is wrong with participating in some light chitchat?

I commit myself to judge each word before it shoots out of my mouth.

"The weather is good, isn't it?" Can there be a safer talk than this?

Sophia sits on the log next to me. "Your house is just opposite the sea. Did you come here for the nice weather?"

This woman knows so much, even where I live. Does she know I have kept two women hidden in my house? Could she find out I am planning to help a high-profile prisoner flee?

I need to say something and get rid of this woman. "This market is so small, the clothes I bought are not up to my taste."

"Yeh, you are right. There was nothing that attracted me. To be honest, I never buy dresses here. I always get them from Calcutta. What did you buy? Show me?" Her gaze falls on the bag in my hand.

I grab the cotton shopping bag tightly at its top helm. *Oh, my. Why did I say I bought clothing? They are for Sadhna and Vanaja. This woman will fish out everything from me.*

"Oh, no. I had bought some but returned them to the shopkeeper and told him to hold on to the money, so that when the next shipment comes, he will keep some nice ones for me. Then I bought some vegetables."

I hope my bag—and the secret—are safe in my hands now.

Sophia sits straight. "Yes, Amelia. We have to bear this until a large market comes in Port Blair."

I infuse some curiosity into my voice. "There's a grand market in Port Blair?"

Sophia giggles. "Not now. I expect that there will be one when construction of the new prison finishes. It will take time. That's why authorities are not developing this market. The prison here is an open encampment. Guards can't even sleep at night as they have to keep an eye on the prisoners. Poor guards. But I am lucky. My spouse is a senior officer. He comes back home each evening."

I understand. She wants to say, *her husband is an official.*

"You see, Amelia, why some junior staff can never be officers?" She chuckles.

"Why?"

"My husband was saying, the guards who are watching the inmates the whole night are dumb. Even if the prisoners break out and flee, where would they go? The British are not fools to have made the prison in Andaman—eight hundred miles away from India."

She is right.

Sophia gets up, ready to leave. "Come to our home, Amelia. Whenever you feel like. I have two servants, both from Calcutta. They will cook for you."

I glance at her from behind. Did she talk to me simply to inform me that her husband is an officer, and she has two maids? Can I say to her I have two women with me at home, and they are both humans and not maids?

I watch Sophia as she walks away. As I am about to get up, another woman approaches. She looks to be in her mid-forties. She is a little chubby but attractive. Her hair is pulled back and she is wearing a long dress with a belt. *Oh, no. Another woman?* Flashing an artificial smile at her, I ask her to sit, planning to have a quick courtesy conversation and go back home. "Hello, I am Amelia. And you?"

"I know, you are the schoolteacher. I am Anita."

"Anita? Nice name. Are you also from Calcutta?"

"No, my spouse was in Madras before coming here. Did you get some nice dresses?"

Has she seen me buying clothes? I try to remember if any woman was in the shop when I stuffed the cheap clothes into my bag. "No,

Anita. I would have to go back to Calcutta on holiday for any good shopping. It's not possible here."

"You're right. Nice dresses never reach people like us." Anita scans her eyes around as she talks to me. "Only to show that we are inferior to them."

"Inferior. To whom?"

"The woman who was talking to you."

So this woman was watching me when I was speaking to Sophia? Is Sophia also keeping watch on me?

Anita continues without waiting for my reply. "You would appreciate knowing, Amelia, that ships come with so many different items, but little in quantity. But the senior officers get the first opportunity to grab the best, leaving the cheap items for families like us. I am still using the dresses I got two years back from Madras. It's only a matter of months, though; he will complete his three years, and we will go back."

She pauses to catch her breath. "And malaria. So many people here die of malaria. Mostly without medicine. You live in the far south. From my place I can see smoke from cremating dead bodies of Indian guards almost every other day. There's always a shortage of medicine, and those poor people suffer for the inefficiency of the senior officers here. Even English people die, even though they always get preference in getting treatment. The sooner you leave Andaman, the better."

"Malaria?" A shiver chases my bones.

Discontent burns in her eyes. So far, I've been thinking only the Indian guards are unhappy here. Class discrimination is dividing the English, as well.

"I understand, Anita. The market is tiny. An enormous market is coming up in Port Blair, though. Once the prison building is complete, all these will close, and hopefully you will find everything like you do in Madras."

A sad smile crosses Anita's features. "I'll be back in Madras by then. Port Blair will take years to finish."

I nod. I would love if the prison took years to complete. The moment prisoners move inside the fort like structure, Rupen will have no chance to flee.

"The government would like the prison to come up as soon as possible. But the senior officials like that woman's husband do not.

Know why? Because they use the prisoner-soldiers to fish in the ocean where they can't." She lets out a snicker.

"You mean, catching fish?"

This time, Anita laughs at me. "You are too simple, Amelia. You are fit to be only a teacher. What I meant is that senior English officers use the Indian prisoners in piracy and share the loot."

Piracy? Ocean Fishing? I remember the words 'Ocean Market' Morticia had used when Sehnaz and I had boarded the ship in Calcutta. And the same term Rave had used when he was with Morticia in Jambu. The scene of Rave's ship anchored in the sea the afternoon he and Morticia left Andaman for Calcutta, Indian prisoners climbing the ship from a boat. I can now join all the dots.

Sophia appears from a shop and startles me. "Don't give in to that woman, Amelia. She is here to fill up your ears."

I am at a loss for what to say, but Anita steps forward with her hands on her hips. "Who said I filled up Amelia's ears?"

Sophia scans her up and down haughtily. "I know what you are up to, Anita. And don't lecture me like that. Remember, my husband is a senior official. And yours, a junior guard. Behave with me."

Anita clenches her fingers. "I know what a woman like you is up to. Everyone knows what you have done."

Sophia cowers slightly, her eyes darting to the ground. "Don't talk rubbish."

"I am not. Only telling the truth. Your first husband was a worker in the gun factory. You poisoned him to marry this officer. Didn't you?"

That's enough for me—I stand up and scurry away from there. These gossips are ruining my peace. Don't I have too many worries already?

Amelia, 26 December 1862, Ross Island, Afternoon

I trudge back home.

Since Christmas Eve, everything has been going wrong. It began with Vanaja's miscarriage and my missing out on meeting with Rupen, and today the depressing talks with the women in the market.

My only consolation for the day—I got some clothing for the two girls. Sadhna is too slim, and my own dresses have been a total misfit for her. And Shanti has wrapped Vanaja with her old saree. At least from now on, both can have some proper clothes.

Tension continues to build. Even though I don't know many people here, being the only female schoolteacher, everyone on this island knows me. Almost everyone. Did the shopkeeper notice I bought two different size dresses, and neither would fit me? Will he know I have two more women at home?

As I enter the house, a sense of foreboding rattles me. Do I have more surprises in store?

Sadhna always greets me with a smile. But today she stands before me, horror radiating from her eyes.

"What happened, Sadhna?" I flash a smile to lighten her mood. "Take this. A dress for you."

She takes the bag and sets it on the table. *Doesn't she want to see what I brought for her? I am sure she understands this much English.*

"Shanti," Sadhna says, "there, Vanaja. Looking."

"Good, Shanti is here and looking after Vanaja." I proceed to my room.

Sadhna follows me. "No, memsahib. No. Shanti..." she whispers and touches her head.

"Sadhna, what happened to Shanti? Is she all right?"

"No, memsahib." Sadhna places her finger across her lips, trying to quiet me. Anxiety snaps through her eyes.

I follow Sadhna to the next room where Vanaja is sleeping on the bed. Shanti is sweeping dirt from beneath the cot with her hands. But to my surprise, I find they are roots, herbs, and dried flowers—the ones Vanaja used to end her pregnancy.

Why does Shanti need them?

When Shanti realises I am there watching her, she jumps to her feet and stands in front of me. Some herbs fall from her hand. "Mem... memsahib, I am. I am here..." She tries to avoid my gaze.

"Were you cleaning the room?" I ask lightly to save her from embarrassment. She might be looking for these herbs to use as an alternative medicine. But then why is she behaving as if I have caught her doing something wrong? I point to her fist closed around the herbs. "You want to keep them? All right, Shanti. Keep them." I force a reassuring smile.

She opens the top loose end of her saree and bags the herbs into a knot. *Are these herbs so valuable?*

She rushes out of the room with wobbly feet.

"*Suno,* Shanti—listen,"I say in Hindi and step toward to her. *Since when do I apply the Hindi Sehnaz had taught me?*

A surprise bubbles in her eyes. She is in some kind of distress, and I must pacify her. She has always taken care of me whenever I have visited Eliza's home. Have I ever asked her about her family in India? Guilt washes over me. I wrap my arm around her shoulder and guide her to my bedroom. "*Baitho,* please sit down."

She squats on the floor. "No, Shanti. Chair. Here, please."

Her hesitation is visible when she gets up and gently sits on the chair after dusting off her buttock. *Is the wooden chair more valuable than a person's self-confidence?* We, the English, are responsible for creating a culture of hatred and discrimination against the poor section of the native Indians. I have never seen her sitting on a chair in Eliza's home.

Sweat drips from her forehead. I see her heart beating through her blouse. Am I troubling her more?

I go to the kitchen to bring a glass of water. Sadhna is standing there, watching me. "Don't worry, Sadhna. I am taking care of her. Maybe she is unwell."

"Memsahib. She unwell."

"Yes. I understand. She is not well."

"No, memsahib." She places her palm on her belly. "Here. Here, memsahib."

"She has an upset stomach?" I also place my palm on my belly and go into teaching mode— "Upset. Bad. Pain."

"No, memsahib." She places her palm again on her tummy and swells it.

"Pregnant?" I almost shriek, and then levelling my voice I repeat, "Pregnant? Baby?"

"Baby. Here, memsahib."

A clear picture sparks inside my brain. Shanti is a widow and is on her way to give birth to a bastard child. Also, the island's men are starving for women's company, especially Indian soldiers who haven't gotten permission to bring their families here. Has someone raped Shanti?

Shanti should never take a similar risk like Vanaja. She could have died, and she is lucky to remain alive today.

I walk back to the bedroom and give her the glass of water. She gets up, gratitude and respect dazzling in her teary eyes.

"Don't stand, Shanti. *Baitho*. You need rest. Drink this." I say in Hindi mixed with English.

She gulps the water in seconds and gazes at me. "Thank, memsahib. Thirsty. Good. Thank."

"You remember your family? Back in India? Children? Any? *Kaun hai?*"

"Children? No." She steals a glance at her tummy. It has yet to grow with the baby inside. "Husband. Dead. Widow." Guilt struggles to hide inside her eyes.

"Father? How? Hindi. Tell. I understand. Very little. Tell me."

Born in a middle class brahmin family, Shanti had gone to a Hindi primary school. Her father, who was in prison for a year for supporting the rebels during the Sepoy Mutiny in 1857, had to sell his farmlands for a pittance to repay the loans to the village moneylender. He had to get Shanti married into a poor family, as he didn't have money for a dowry. But her husband died within months of the marriage of some unknown disease. Remarriage was not an option for her as it was against the community's custom.

A sad smile crosses Shanti's face while narrating her story in pure Hindi.

"What about your in-laws? Didn't they support you when you became a widow?"

She gazes at me. Raw pain winks at me from her eyes.

Her in-laws harassed her for the property, and her parents could not help. She left her village in Bihar and came to Calcutta with a villager. The man introduced her to some English family there, and she became a maid.

This story is not unusual with many young widows in India.

I should find the person responsible for this. Is it a rape, or has she slept with a man on her own accord?

"Trust me Shanti, I will help you." I touch her tummy. "No child. Promise."

Shanti smiles. She trusts me.

"Father? Who?"

Her gaze drops to her feet. Touching her chin, I lift her head and ask, "Believe me, Shanti. Secret. Not tell anyone. Help you."

She looks at me. Does she understand what I just told her?

"Who? Nick?" Dr. Nick Wilson is the first suspect, being the owner of the house. But Eliza stays at home all the time, and Nick is a busy man in his clinic.

"No. Good man."

There is no way a wonderful, caring man like Dr. Nick would do such a thing. I release a deep sigh. Nick is in the clear now.

"Soldier? Indian soldier?"

"No."

I am confused. This woman is working hard, accumulating savings so that one day she could go back and live her life in her village, holding her head high. But with this turn of events, she will be an outcast in her society. Although, she is still in the beginning of her pregnancy and has time to get rid of this. But how?

Sadhna comes to the room. "Knock. Door. Man." "Stay inside the room, Sadhna." I trudge to the main door.

An Indian guard is standing at the door. "Good afternoon, ma'am." He gives me a folded paper.

"Letter?"

"Yes, ma'am."

Impatience and curiosity haunt me. Who could have sent me a letter on this far-off island? That, too, inside an envelope? I open the letter and read it in one go while the man waits, watching me.

Only a few lines in quick but beautiful handwriting.

Dear madam Amelia, I am Rupen. Hope you recognise me. I came to know Sehnaz was with you in Sultanpur. Where is she now? You may write a line on this paper and send with Mahesh, the soldier, who is carrying this letter.

Mahesh is standing, expecting to carry my reply. I know Rupen, but I can't recognise his handwriting. And he is a prisoner—they aren't allowed to send letters. Is this a plan to extract information about Sehnaz?

"I am busy now and can't reply. You may please go."

"Do I come another time?"

No proper answer comes to my mind. Is Sehnaz in danger now? Do authorities already know the woman with me in the ship was the same Sehnaz who had stolen the sensitive map and helped the rebels in besieging The Residency?

My brain screams. Sweat pools under my arms. I slam the door in Mahesh's face and wobble to the kitchen. My throat is dry.

Am I also a suspect now?

CHAPTER TWENTY-FOUR

SEHNAZ, 4 JANUARY 1863, SOUTH COCO ISLANDS, MORNING

Sehnaz stood still in front of the door. Did Sheru babble again? It was almost ten in the morning, but he was still sleeping. How was his fever?

Sehnaz didn't dare to cross the door into Sheru's room. Since they moved from Jerry Island to their own cottage in South Coco, each of them had gotten separate rooms. No more chastity-stone as a barrier between the two. Sheru also did a day's penance for the sin he might have committed while sleeping in one room with Sehnaz. Who knew if he had unknowingly touched Sehnaz there?

Sehnaz had insisted that Sheru be a bit more careful about the fever, which might be malaria. He didn't listen to her and went to work for three days.

Sheru stopped working only when the fever didn't come down. He didn't even stop going to the pond for his daily bath. Wouldn't the cold pond water make him sicker?

Sheru's legs wobbled while walking, so she had been accompanying him to the pool.

"How could I worship my God when my body is not clean?" he would always reply when Sehnaz asked him not to take such a long bath in the cold water.

Sheru had never slept this long in the morning. When he babbled again, guilt twisted through Sehnaz. "I won't let you die, Sheru," she muttered.

She had seen her grandfather dying of untreated malaria and understood what happens if the fever goes up through the head.

Sheru had told her never to cross his doorframe, but this was an emergency! She entered and sat near his bed. His forehead was burning. She placed a wet cloth on his temple. The herbal juice the tribal people had given to him was not enough to cure malaria. Agatha ma'am had not come in the last two weeks; otherwise, she could have requested to bring some medicine from Coco.

After a while, Sheru opened his eyes. His high temperature had dropped.

"Sorry Sheru, I had to come to your room and even touch you. Your body was boiling hot."

Sheru smiled. "Thanks for putting the soaked cloth on my temple. Don't worry about the sin. I will do the penance when I am well."

A chuckle came out of her mouth. "Sure, you would. Should I bring some food for you? You must be starving."

"No, can't eat unless I bathe and worship Lord Shiva. My body is aching. Too tired now to go to the pond."

"Why don't you lie down and I give you a sponge bath? I'm sure you will feel better."

Sheru hesitated. "You? Bath?"

She realised his mind is saying yes, but his conscience is saying no. "Don't hesitate, Sheru. Lord Shiva is kind. You can do some more penance and wash away this sin, too. You have the method." She giggled.

Sheru stretched on the bed as Sehnaz got ready to give him a good sponge bath.

Sheru's fever spiked again in the evening. Sehnaz sat near him, lighting an oil lamp.

"This wet cloth on your forehead will bring the temperature down, Sheru. But this is not the solution. This herbal medicine is not working. I must go to Coco and bring proper medicine for you," she said as she massaged his head and neck.

"No, Sehnaz. Women aren't safe there. Don't you know what happened to Aung's wife? So many women are suffering there at the hands of the wealthy and powerful. Abduction of worker's wives is quite normal for them."

"I know, Sheru. But you know a shipload of women has just arrived from Rangoon. No shortage of women now."

"The women who came in the ship are all Burmese. Try to understand. None of them are as beautiful as you."

Fury moved through her. "Are the women goats or lambs, as if men are after tastier meat all the time?"

"For those demons, yes, women are like meat to be devoured. They don't have any mind or liking. Only white women are humans. Even though so many girls are now living in Coco, still—a beautiful and sexy woman like you should be extra careful."

Disappointment slammed Sehnaz, but she let out a laugh. "For the first time, you praised my beauty. But why do you care for me? I am not even your wife or lover. I understand last time, Rupen had requested you to take me safely to Varanasi, but you don't have any obligation now."

When Sheru didn't reply, Sehnaz stole a sideways glance at him. He was in a thoughtful mood. What was he thinking? They both had lost so much in their lives. Both were surviving so many hardships with only the positive hope of a better future and a free life.

Sehnaz was about to get up, but Sheru said, "Can you please sit here longer? I feel better when you are here. Please, Sehnaz."

She gazed at him. Tears were pooling in Sheru's eyes. The malaria fever could pull even the healthiest man down. She moved and sat closer to Sheru. His features had tensed, and his eyes grew dark.

Sheru glanced at her, and then, taking her palm, he cupped it inside his. She could hear his deep, shallow breaths. *What happened to Sheru today?* she wondered. But moments later, she heard her own shallow breaths. Sehnaz sat closer and crept her fingers across Sheru's muscular, hairy chest. His heart was beating with each move of her fingers. Heat aroused inside Sehnaz's groin when Sheru took her other palm and cupped it. She caressed Sheru's man nipples, and he tried containing his moan.

Her other palm slipped out of Sheru's grip and crawled to his waist. Sheru didn't resist. She realised he was hungry for love and affection. Only his religious conscience stopped him. It shouldn't. He was a devotee of Lord Shiva, the deity whose penis is worshipped and is always inside his consort's vagina. Scripture never demonised such association. Sex was a holy act. Divine. Meant to bring a man and woman together.

Sehnaz gently unbuttoned Sheru's pants and crept her fingers inside. Sheru's body shuddered, but he closed his eyes. He seemed to relish each movement of her. She fished out his long and hard shaft. Sheru leaned toward her, and a moan slipped out of her throat. Bringing his face near her, he planted a kiss on her cheeks. He slid his fingers inside her blouse and unhooked it with the other hand.

Sehnaz's heart quickened as her bubbies sprang out from her blouse and rolled inside Sheru's palms.

"Where were you for so many days?" Sheru murmured as he removed her skirt and pulled her onto his lap.

She didn't resist when Sheru deposited all her clothes on the bedside.

She was straddling his thighs, his love handle resting on her lady parts. Only moments to get united into one whole being. Like Lord Shiva and his consort Parvati.

She felt Sheru jerk. Something shook him.

"I am sorry, Sehnaz."

Sehnaz quietly got off from his lap.

"Sorry, Sehnaz. I have betrayed Rupen."

Sehnaz wasn't ready for that. Why would Rupen's name come up when she was about to receive the divine love from a man who could be a trustworthy husband forever?

"Rupen doesn't own me, Sheru. I didn't risk my life for the man I thought would end up marrying me. His patriotism and the sacrifice for the motherland are the qualities I worshipped. He had a wife, and I had never dreamt to be his spouse."

She picked up her skirt and top and put them on. "Time to cook dinner, Sheru." She got up and moved to the veranda. Jhumru was sitting near the hearth, waiting for Sehnaz to come and bring it to life with wood and fire.

As the fire of the hearth warmed the open veranda and Sehnaz put a pot of water above it to cook rice, Sheru came and sat near her. She gave him a long, measuring look. His features were apologetic. "You should never be pregnant from me, Sehnaz."

"The courtesan profession was never my choice, Sheru. The *kotha* was on one side of me and rotten hell on the other. I have never done business using my body. You can believe me or not."

"Your eyes can never tell lies, Sehnaz. We both are living stranded on this remote island and do not know if we can ever go back to the place we have come from. I trust you."

She added another piece of wood to the burning hearth. The flame rose to a new height around the earthen pot.

"So nice for the winter, Sehnaz. Reminds me of my days in my village. My wife and I both would sit near the fireside and relish the warmth."

"You are lucky to remember your married days, Sheru. Not like mine."

"Were you married?"

Sehnaz cast a pretend angry glance at him. "Do you think I was a courtesan since I came out of my mother's womb?"

Sheru didn't reply, but she felt the urge to bring out everything. Her past, which she had never said to anyone except Amelia. Not even to Rupen.

"My parents were poorest of the poor," she started, "married me off to an old man for money. A man fit to be my grandfather. I hadn't realised until I was in the groom's house alone and the wedding had finished without my parents' presence. While he was happy to sleep with me day and night, I was suffocating. I still had to rot in hell even after he died within a year, I was like a commodity. His first wife sold me to another man in Lucknow."

"Another old man?"

"Not sure. She got money for me. I didn't want to spend the rest of my life as someone's domestic animal, who could have kept or sold me at any time. A female neighbour showed me the light. She even organised my training in a *kotha* in Lucknow. I ran away when the first wife's son was driving me to the home of my next husband."

Sheru met her gaze with sympathy in his eyes. "So that's how you became a courtesan?"

She placed her palm on his forehead. "Better. Temperature has come down."

Sehnaz, 5 January 1863, Sunday Morning, South Coco Islands

When Sheru's fever spiked again in the morning, shock and fear slashed through Sehnaz. She would sacrifice anything to keep Sheru alive.

"I am going to Coco," she told Sheru.

Sheru got up from the bed. His eyes widened. "No, Sehnaz. It's not safe for you."

Sheru didn't know Sehnaz could use a pistol, but what was the point? She couldn't get one now.

"I would rather lose my respect, but I can't let you die, Sheru. I am also taking Bilu with me."

A faint smile curved Sheru's weak lips. "You have made that tribal boy your friend, huh?"

"He is a young man. Not that boy who owned Jhumru. And yes, a trusted tribal friend. He didn't even go to the forest today to collect food."

Sheru straightened his posture and gazed at her. "Okay. But remember, you can speak English like a memsahib. Anyone would wonder who you are and may even try to find out."

"I know. I will use broken English. Just like a worker's wife."

"Good. I will pray to Lord Shiva for your safety."

Sehnaz was about to go, but she stilled. "No Sheru, please pray that I can fight back. Demons will be demons, that can't change."

A trail from the carts' wheels led Sehnaz and Bilu toward the Coco market. "Looks like Agatha ma'am's horse cart has made impressions on the forest land," she said.

"Horse. Cart," Bilu said. He was Agatha's student and understood English but couldn't speak well.

After walking almost five long miles, Bilu and Sehnaz arrived at Coco's market. It was the same one she and Amelia had seen while the ship had stopped to load provisions from Coco.

"Do you know why the market is empty?"

"Market. Know."

Sehnaz let out a laugh at Bilu's single-syllable answer.

"You know nothing, stupid. Today is Sunday, and people have gone to the church. If we can meet a doctor before people get out of the congregation, we can go back soon."

She was not expecting any answer from Bilu, but she wanted to show the world that a tribal man with a bow and arrow was with her for her protection. Sehnaz knew Bilu could face the threat of guns without fear.

It wasn't difficult to find a doctor's clinic in the small place.

The doctor was sitting alone in the clinic. Covering her face with a scarf, she approached him. Bilu was awaiting her outside, sitting beneath a tree.

"Husband worker, sir. Malaria. Serious."

"Worker?" the doctor asked without raising his head from the book it was buried in. "Go away. No medicine for you."

"Serious sir, die if not." She pretended to weep.

"Nonsense." He got up and walked into another room.

"Sir, please. Money. I have. Pay you."

"Go back before people come from the church and find you, silly poor woman. How much money you can give me?"

The offence hit Sehnaz's heart hard . She had brought so much money from Sultanpur that she could buy out even a dozen doctors like this man. Could she show off her wealth now?

No. She needed only the medicine.

"Malaria medicine is always in short supply here in Coco," the doctor shouted from the other room. "I can't give it away. I don't know when the white people here will need it. The next shipment might come after a month. If more medicine arrives, I can think about giving you some."

"Month? Husband die, sir. Poor woman. Please," she wept.

The doctor didn't reply. She couldn't wait; she had to finish her job before people broke out of the church.

A Burmese man on the road guided Sehnaz and Bilu toward Agatha's house, which wasn't far.

"Bilu, you wait outside. Let me see if Agatha ma'am is available at home."

Making Bilu sit beneath a tree, Sehnaz knocked on Agatha's door.

A tall and ugly man opened the door.

"Good morning, sir. Agatha ma'am?"

The man's creepy stare pinched her guts, as if he had never seen a woman before.

"From south Coco, sir. She teaches. I, from there."

The man let out a faint smile and stepped back a little. "Agatha? Come inside."

Comfort washed through Sehnaz's chest, assuming she could see Agatha now. She stepped inside the drawing room, but the man vanished inside another room. An unease feathered into her.

"I must be anxious," she assured herself.

Sehnaz stood and glanced around. Agatha was smiling from her wedding photo that hung on the wall.

"Why are you here?" the man screamed from the back.

"I want to meet Agatha ma'am, sir." Sehnaz didn't use broken English as Agatha knew her well.

"She is not here. Has been with a friend. Might be here in the evening, or tomorrow."

Surprise and confusion hit Sehnaz. The township was so small there was no need to stay overnight with some friend. Urgency pricked her. She must be straightforward.

Sehnaz tried to remember his name. *Oh God, it's on the tip of my tongue.*

"Sir, I came to her with a request to get help. For malaria medicine for my husband. He has been sick for a week and won't survive if I don't get medicine today. I can't wait until Agatha ma'am comes back. You can ask her about Sanju. Wife of Sheru. I am not lying, sir."

Alfred. The memory clicked in Sehnaz's brain. Agatha had said her husband's name once.

Alfred ambled into the room and sat on the sofa. Sehnaz's gaze went to a pistol he placed on the adjacent table. Her heart raced. Didn't Sheru warn her crime was common in Coco township?

"Alfred sahib," she said, addressing him by name so that he would believe her closeness with his wife, "I have been to the doctor."

"And he said the medicine is only for the white people, right?" A sardonic smile curled his lips.

"Yes, sir. The next shipment might take a month. My husband can't wait that long, sir. I need help."

"Your English is so good," said Alfred. A confidence bloomed in Sehnaz's heart. "And you are a beautiful woman. Looks like you are from a decent family."

Sehnaz smiled inside with her praise, but she didn't know how to react.

"Here, you know, everything is in short supply. But anything comes for a price." Alfred lifted his face and gazed at her.

"Price? Yes, Alfred sir." Sehnaz unfastened the knot of her reticule. "I will pay, sir."

Alfred smirked and tapped his fingers on the side table, inches from the pistol. "What can an Indian woman like you pay to a senior English officer? By the way, Sanju is a nice name. I forgot to mention."

Sehnaz failed to understand what Alfred wanted. Sheru's fever might spike again. She would do anything to save his life.

She flicked a gaze at him. To her horror, Alfred's left hand continued tapping the side table, but his right hand fiddled with the buttons on his pants. A tent in his groin winked at Sehnaz.

A silent sigh escaped through Sehnaz's mouth thinking how Agatha was enduring this dirty pervert. She took a step back and looked at the main door. She couldn't shout for Bilu, but at least she could run to him. She was confident an English man would never harm a tribal. Angry tribals, when they decide to take revenge, never feared anything, not even death.

Conflict tightened in her stomach. Could she run away before getting the medicine?

She stared straight into Alfred's eyes. Getting out of the lion's den was tough. But she was no less than a *Nagin,* the Queen Cobra.

But tension rose in her gut. Would Sheru survive without the malaria drug? Would she surrender to this man to save Sheru?

Sehnaz glowered at him, her face reddening. Alfred's love handle had already jumped out through his unbuttoned pants and was taunting her.

Sehnaz had only minutes to decide whether to surrender or run away.

"You know, Sanju..." Alfred flashed a wry smile while massaging his shaft. "Here in the Coco Islands, the rule of the British government of Burma doesn't work. It's far away both from India and Burma. Officers like me, with guns, rule this place."

Sehnaz stole another glance at the main door. It was still open. She had the option to run away before he could lift the pistol. Why didn't she remember to borrow Amelia's firearm? She knew how to hit the goal with one bullet. *But the medicine...*

She had no time to ponder. *If Sheru dies from lack of medicine, I have no point in surviving.*

Sehnaz stepped forward, toward Alfred's chair. His legs rested against the tea table in front of him, and his fingers played with his own love handle. Bending her waist, she touched his erect shaft with her left hand. Alfred lifted his head and let out a flirtatious smile at her.

"Ahh," he moaned, "you came at the right time, Sanju. I will make sure you get the medicine today. I have kept some malaria tablets with me. You don't have to go to the doctor. Ahh, love it."

The main door was still open, and Sehnaz wondered how Alfred didn't care that someone could come in and see this.

Lifting his hand from the side table, Alfred touched Sehnaz's bubbies. "Your ripe fruits are lovely, Sanju. Huge. Agatha's are nothing."

Sehnaz had only seconds. Next, the man might remove her clothing. She allowed Alfred to squeeze her nipples from outside her top and bent a little more so that her lips would come closer to his.

"Love you, Sanju. Please kiss me."

"No, Alfred, now the bullet will kiss your head. And I would be away in the jungle before people come out from the church service." She had grabbed his pistol and pointed it at his skull.

Alfred's hand suddenly fell from Sehnaz's breasts.

"I need the medicine. Now." Her voice was low, but commanding.

"Don't have, here. With the doctor. I lied."

"I don't know. If you don't give it to me now, I will shoot you and then go to the doctor. Remember, I still have an hour left before people come out of the chapel."

"There!" He pointed at a cupboard, his mouth twisted with fright. "Please open and take."

"You stand up, motherfucker, and give the drug to me. Now. Get up."

Alfred stood, gazing at Sehnaz from the corners of his eyes. Sweat beaded on his forehead. Hadn't he ever seen a woman holding a pistol before? Opening a tiny box inside his cupboard, he brought a fistful of loose tablets and handed to Sehnaz.

Still clutching the pistol with one hand, Sehnaz pocketed the tablets. She noticed the word *malaria* on its cover. Sheru would survive. But could she indeed leave the place and reach her cottage?

Alfred could bring his force and capture her and Sheru in no time. Or even kill Sheru when he came for work. How long could they hide from this demon? Wasn't her victory only temporary? Should she finish this man and walk away with the pistol?

No. That wasn't the solution. The pistol was of no use unless she had enough bullets.

Think, Sehnaz, think.

"Sit down," she commanded again. "Sit on this chair. And listen to me."

Alfred sat, but not without noticing her previous hesitation. He smirked. "How long will you survive when you go from here? Even if you kill me, you and your husband wouldn't live long. I know where Agatha goes and can find you."

"Before I answer that, you answer my question," she spat forcefully.

His smirk dropped. "What?"

"How long will you rot on this island licking your so-called white skin?" She paused. As long as she held that pistol, she was safe. That, too, until the public poured back on the roads. "Are you from Burma? Rangoon? I know you English people rule over Burma."

"Yes." Alfred's eyes darted from the pistol to Sehnaz's face.

"And you don't know who I am? Do you know Nawab Wajid Ali of Awadh, in India? I am his daughter. Sez."

Nawab Wajid Ali's daughter? Sez?

Sehnaz didn't wait for his answer. She knew Alfred didn't know. Even she didn't know moments ago. "I have a plan. For you and me, both. Only if you cooperate."

Alfred gave a blank look.

"I am one of his daughters, Sez. That was my name. I became Sanju when I married a Hindu soldier. Do you know what happens when a Muslim girl marries a Hindu?"

"Yes. Society doesn't accept."

"Right." Sehnaz forced a smile. "Father didn't accept, and I had to leave home. That was before the war, the civil war in 1857. My father lost his kingdom to the British."

"So, you ran away and came to the Coco Islands?" Alfred's eyes were still wavering between the firearm and Sehnaz.

"That's not the point; I am here. My stepbrother was a cunning fellow. He knew the British would snatch our kingdom one day. He took away lots of gold and diamonds from the palace and hid them on an island near Calcutta."

The pistol was still in Sehnaz's hand, but no longer pointed at his head. Alfred's breathing had returned to normal. *Is he buying into my story?*

"My stepbrother died in the war, too. But my informer in the palace gave me the location where the booty is waiting. My husband and I came here as workers so that we could find the wealth and go back to Calcutta. Live there. Build our own palace."

Alfred smiled. He was a clever man, having guessed where the conversation was moving.

"Learning how to use a gun was compulsory for all princesses in the palace." *Is this more convincing that I am a princess?* "If you wish to be wealthy and get out of this godforsaken hell of a Coco, you can join hands with us. Get a share. Good for us both."

"Yes, your highness," Alfred said.

Isn't an intelligent brain stronger than a gun?

"And if you try to play with us, we know how to handle you."

"No, your highness. I will help find the treasure. Promise."

"And now keep your mouse inside your pants. My husband's is double the size and I am not interested in that tiny stick of yours."

Alfred buttoned up his pants. "Thanks, your highness." A smile of greed and satisfaction shone in his eyes. "Please don't tell this to Agatha. She would create trouble."

This man is really serious. Can I use this?

"I will never tell her. And I need your pistol. And some cartridges, too. My bodyguard is waiting for me outside."

If there was any doubt that Alfred didn't believe her, it disappeared when he beheld Bilu—her *bodyguard*—outside. His eyes widened, and he nodded eagerly at her. "Sure. And I can give you a horse cart, too."

Sehnaz thought for a while. "No, Agatha will question. She will see the cart with us. Let her still think I am a worker's wife and not a princess."

Bilu was waiting for her. They walked back—five miles to cover before Sehnaz could give the medicine to Sheru.

She would wonder where she could get Morticia's plunder later, after Sheru recovered. One problem at a time.

CHAPTER TWENTY-FIVE

AMELIA, 12 JANUARY 1863, ROSS ISLAND, AFTERNOON

It's been a long day of teaching on the island, while Nick was busy treating the sick. Nick sits opposite of me inside the vessel while the boatman starts the engine and we move towards the Ross Island through the North Bay. "Nick, is the name of the bay derived from the island's name or other way around?"

"I think first the island was named as North Bay Island, and then followed the bay's name."

We sail toward the south in the calm waters of the bay. I can see the gigantic waves of Andaman Sea, and in barely half a mile, we should touch it. To my west there is another island, but I've never known its name.

"If you don't mind, Nick, what is that island's name?" I ask, pointing my finger.

Nick thinks for a moment. Before he can reply, the boatman answers, "Ma'am, that is also North Bay Island. Three sides of this bay are North Bay Island."

"And what is the distance we will cover to arrive at Ross?" I ask.

"Three and a half miles from the point we started."

"Fantastic. Nick, can you believe that from the spot where you check the patients at North Bay, we can't see this sea even though it's less than a mile from it?"

He smiles. "Because of the snaking pathway, tall trees, and the hillocks in the way. They all have sheltered the island's villages from the natural calamities. Such is God's grace."

"We just pass through that pathway without bothering to look at them. Nick, one day if we can come early, I would love to spend some time there, looking at each hillock... We never bother to even notice each large tree that covers the sunrays when we touch North Bay shore where you have the makeshift clinic."

I steal a glance at Nick. He is smiling at me. I look away because I feel embarrassed. He has been good to me. I do not know what he is thinking. He did not talk much with me the whole time I was in the tribal village, as he was busy doing his medical work.

"Now I understand why the tribals had tied up the pregnant woman and left her to die," Nick says, surprising me.

"Why?" I ask.

"You gave her a name, but I forgot it. What is it?"

"Vanaja. Means 'born in a jungle.' Hindi."

"You know Hindi?" His appreciating smile mesmerises me.

"I learnt a little. I was teaching Indian children in school. Nick, please tell me why the islanders punished Vanaja."

"These people have a culture similar to ours. They believe in gods. They believe if a woman has a sexual relationship with another woman, that is a sin. Same for men."

"So, she had sex with another girl. And the other woman made Vanaja pregnant?" I chuckle at my own joke.

Nick laughs. "No. Not that way. They forced her to live with a man, of the tribal head's choice. And the man made her pregnant. They thought she would love the company of that man. But she still met the other woman, in secret. Her female lover had features of a male. I am sure I have seen her in the past. Plain chest and strong muscles. Like a man in a woman's body."

"Do people here think she is dead? And what about her female lover?

Nick narrowed his eyes. "I'm sure she also has been punished. Probably dead by now. Vanaja survived because we found her. She is lucky. But..."

"But what?"

"People here aren't that simple, Amelia. They are intelligent men and realise she has run away. They are looking for her. Be extra careful. Vanaja's life is in danger if they find her."

"You got a good deal of information in one day!" I spark a flirtatious smile, but my conscience haunts me—Nick is married and his wife Eliza is my friend.

"Your teaching is working. By mixing some English words with signals, I can now communicate better. You are an amazing teacher, Amelia. If you can teach their woman to cover their breasts..."

I laugh. "Too early, Nick."

"Our civilised men think if a woman is showing off her breasts, she is asking for sex."

"So wrong. But why should these women amend their way of living just because the so-called civilised men can't control their urge?"

Nick nods in agreement. "I'm worried about the day Morticia and Rave come back. What will happen to Vanaja?"

Morticia will love Vanaja's company. And Vanaja, too. They will love each other. I suppress my smile. *Does Nick know Morticia loves to sleep with women? No, I shouldn't tell him.* One thing I am sure of, Sadhna can no longer wear clothes once Morticia is back. I must teach her as quickly as possible to help her gain her independence.

I glance at the sky through the window. The clouds are building up. So far it has been a clear January sky. It is around nine in the evening, and I am about to retire to my bedroom after teaching Sadhna. She is a talented student and picking up the language quickly.

A knock sounds on the door. Who can be here at this moment?

Sadhna runs inside when I go to open the door. Shanti is standing there, sweating. Worry snaps through her eyes. Didn't her pregnancy end?

"Sahib..." She huffs. "Sahib, calling. Memsahib, urgent. Come. Please."

I wrap a shawl around me and rushed out. What happened to Eliza?

Nick opens the door. "Eliza is sick. Please come with me."

I follow him to his bedroom. Eliza is sleeping, covered with both a quilt and a blanket but still shivering. Seated on the bedside, I place my palm on her forehead. She shudders. Her temperature has spiked.

"I am afraid." Nick's helpless look scares me.

Isn't Nick a doctor?

"I am afraid she has malaria."

My stomach tightens. There have been many deaths here on Ross Island on account of malaria, even among the English. Sometimes even after medical treatment.

"Medicine! At your clinic. Do I come with you? You shouldn't wait until the morning."

"Karma..." Eliza's weak voice awakens something inside me.

I recollect this word from Mata Radhe. How does an English woman like Eliza know a Sanskrit word? Did I hear something wrong?

"Karma ... biting." She sobs. "Walker never ... cares for the Indian prisoners ... makes sure there is ... always a shortage of drugs ... so they die sooner. Hundreds have died ... wasn't enough medicine. Or treatment."

I glance at Dr. Nick. His gaze has fallen to his feet. He's standing like a guilty man, accepting each of her words as true.

"Nick?"

Eliza lifts her body on the bed with the help of her elbow. Shanti lopes forward and helps her sit. "Water, memsahib?"

"No, I am fine."

Eliza inhales a deep breath and then looks at me. "Why ask him? I know. When he asked for more medicine from Calcutta, Walker intervened. Slashed the quantity saying Indian prisoners do not need them. Somehow it was miscommunicated, and no malaria drug arrived in the last shipment. He never cares for any native, other than people like Rupen. Now even English people will not get medicine. Not even a doctor's wife."

A helpless doctor is standing before me like a culprit. He has no medication to treat his own wife. How can I help him?

"Tribal people have never come to me for treatment of malaria. I should have known which herbs they use. Much earlier."

Is Nick thinking of going to North Bay Island now and asking for herbs? At night? Dark clouds were building up since I came home. Wind is sighing through the trees outside. Can't this wait until tomorrow? Is Eliza that serious?

"Vanaja knows," Nick says. "Her pregnancy was in advanced stage, so she had to suffer, but she ended that with the herb."

My gaze goes to Shanti, who is standing nearby and listening. She moves her hand to her tummy, hearing about Vanaja from Nick. She has gotten rid of her unwanted pregnancy, too.

I stand up. Entering the forest at night is not possible.

"Tomorrow morning? I will ask Vanaja. But I don't know how to communicate with her about malaria."

"Try, please. And yes, she should go out early in the morning. Tribal men from North Bay come here for herbs that they don't get on their island. They shouldn't see her."

He sees me to the main door. I am almost halfway to my home when thunder claps and heavy rain assaults Ross Island.

I burst in my front door, clothes dripping wet. "Can Vanaja find herb for Eliza's treatment?" I call out, but am drown out by the ominous thunder.

Sehnaz, 12 January 1863, South Coco Islands, Evening

Sehnaz listened to the cold January breeze as it drifted through the woods. Jhumru walked onto her lap as she covered herself with a shawl, and a calm sense of security washed through her. Thank God, the medicine she had brought from Alfred worked. Sheru had recovered from malaria.

"Jhumru, tell Sheru he is weak and shouldn't go to work now."

Sheru was sitting on the bed. He let out a mild laugh. "Jhumru, tell your friend we wouldn't survive here eating tree leaves. Only Coco market has the groceries we need."

"Groceries? Jhumru, you have been to the kitchen. Did you see how many groceries I have bought from Coco market? Sheru thinks only he can buy them."

"Sorry, I didn't mean that Sehnaz."

"Sehnaz? No, Sanju."

"Oh, Sehnaz, my brain is not working with so many names. Sehnaz, then Sanju, and then Sez. This is confusing. Agatha knows you as Sanju. And you told her husband you are Sez. They are husband and wife and soon will find Sez and Sanju both are the same woman."

"I am sure she will never find out. She came here yesterday only for an hour, but I didn't tell her I had met her husband. I'm also sure Alfred wouldn't have told her. Even if Alfred asks, I can always say I made it Sanju to hide my identity that I am a princess."

"Princess? Who? You? When did you become a princess?"

Sehnaz chuckled. "Didn't my mother tell me I was a princess, when I was a child?"

"You shouldn't have told him about the booty in Jambu."

"I told whatever came to my mind at that moment. I was sure afterward he could bring some soldiers and finish us. Or even kill you when you go to Coco for work."

"You sure he won't kill me?"

"Never."

"Why?"

"Because you are the husband of a princess."

"This is no joke, Sehnaz. We have to look for a place to hide. You should have told me the day you came from Coco."

"You were sick. I didn't want to stress you out more. You would think being a man it is your duty to protect me. It's all right, Sheru. But you can't be with me all the time. When the time comes, I can fight." Sehnaz got up and brought a bag from the room. "Look at this."

"A pistol? Where did you steal it from?"

Sehnaz giggled again.

"Sehnaz! I am asking you."

"Shhhh. Do not question a princess."

"Please, Sehnaz. I must know."

"Alfred gave it to me."

"Alfred? But he was trying to rape you."

"And I put his own pistol to his head. Then... Do you know, these English are so paranoid when they hear the word 'royal.' He addressed me as 'your highness' when I told him I was a princess but my father lost his kingdom to the British. And he trusted me. Who else other than a nawab's daughter can snatch his gun and threaten him?"

"You convinced him!"

"Yes. And he said never to reveal anything to Agatha. So please..."

"You only talk to Agatha. But I'm not sure if we can find that plunder in Jambu. And what if Alfred cheats? He is a crook and would do anything to get it all for himself."

"We'll see when the occasion comes. Right now, I don't see any other way to get out of here. We ran away to escape the prison. But isn't this also a jail for us? Prison for life? With money, we can go back to Calcutta. Perhaps we go to Sultanpur, Shakti Ashram. I will live with the nuns, and you can work as a guard there."

"Guard? If we get so much money, why am I still working?"

"Okay, then. You settle in a place where no one knows you, with a new name. Spend money in a local Shiva temple for penance. For touching a woman who is not your wife, a Muslim and a courtesan."

Sheru didn't smile. "And you? Marry someone?"

"No, I have never had true love. Rupen had used me for his intelligence network. I thought it was my duty to help free a warrior who sacrificed his own family. But I don't know how to do it. Surely not remaining as a beggar. If we get the treasure, maybe we can buy a small ship of our own, sail to Andaman for trade. After changing names, of course. Once there, I can bribe guards."

Sheru gave a measuring look. "Do you think it will be that easy?"

"No, but with money, at least we can try harder."

Loud thunder startled both of them. Clouds had been building up since the afternoon. Another low pressure. Rain hammered on the thatched roof.

Sheru shifted and glanced up.

"What happened?"

"I should have repaired the roof earlier. Your side is good. But water is dripping here."

Sehnaz glanced at the roof. Within no time, it wasn't dripping through the roof—it was pouring.

"How will you sleep here tonight, Sheru?"

"Don't know."

"Please get up. Come to my room."

"Your room?"

"Yes. And note down in your penance list."

Both laughed as Sheru got up and lifted Sehnaz on his shoulder.

"What are you doing?"

"Checking if I am strong enough to work." He chortled but held her tight against his chest.

"Sheru. Put me down! Leave me." It was only her mouth that was resisting. A pleasant current passed through her soul.

"It is you who told me to sleep in your room at night." He chuckled and then, grabbing Sehnaz's face, started kissing her as he strode inside her room.

Sheru and love? Sehnaz let out a supressed giggle. "No, Sheru, don't please. Jhumru is here, what will she think?"

"But she is a cat. Why worry?"

She winked. "No, she is a young woman. Please, Sheru."

He placed Sehnaz on the floor and looked at Jhumru, who had followed them into the room.

"Jhumru, you are a nice girl. Can you please go out? I have something confidential to discuss with your friend."

"Mew." Jhumru, instead of going out, slithered alongside his legs. Sheru bent down and scooped her into his arms.

"It's cold and windy outside, Sheru. And your room is wet." Sehnaz had noticed the swelling in Sheru's groin. He was now ready for what she had wanted for a long time.

"Don't worry. She will be on the veranda, and I will cover her with the jute bag." He let out a coquettish smile at her.

She stood inside her room and awaited Sheru, breathing hard. A slow and smouldering desire built inside her as Sheru came back after closing the door.

Sehnaz's body trembled as Sheru brushed his lips softly over her cheeks.

"I love you, Sehnaz."

"I love you, too, Sheru."

She melted into his muscular chest.

CHAPTER TWENTY-SIX

AMELIA, 13 JANUARY 1863, ROSS ISLAND, EARLY MORNING

R ain lashed the entire night. By early morning it stops, but the sky is still cloudy. It might pour buckets again at any time. Last night after coming back from Nick's home, I tried my best to tell Vanaja that we needed to look for the herb in the morning.

Soon, we both leave for the forest. I have two important tasks at hand—finding the right herb for Eliza, and keeping Vanaja out of sight from the islander men. As Vanaja looks for the plant, my heart pounds inside the ribs.

We take almost two hours, but no success. Then Vanaja says the flower doesn't bloom in rain and we must wait until the sunrays warm up the island. My eyes wander between looking for the sun in the sky, and for any tribals in case I need to hide Vanaja. I should have covered her with a burqa I brought with me from Calcutta.

A sound of horse hooves approaches us. I stop looking at the sky. When a soldier comes near and salutes, I recognise him. He is Mahesh, the man who had come with Rupen's letter. Has he come with another letter from Rupen?

I force a smile. How did he find me here?

"Just saw you here, ma'am." He smiled. "Thought to have a talk with you."

What will this man have to say to me?

He gives me a letter. "Ma'am, I have been carrying this for the last few days. Thought this would be the right place to give it to you, when no one is around. As I have already been to your residence once, I didn't wish to go there again."

Unfolding the piece of paper, I read it in one breath.

Dear madam Amelia, I am Rupen again. I met someone here who had some information about Sehnaz. I also came to know that the British was hounding her for a so-called war crime. But I also found out a police officer in Sultanpur has reported this is not the same woman whom the authorities want to punish, because 'Sehnaz' is a popular Muslim name and any woman bearing that name can't be assumed to be a criminal. I'm happy. If you can just let me know where she is now, I would be ever grateful to you.

My gut says this letter must be from Rupen. None here knows I lived in Sultanpur.

Mahesh is still waiting, and I'm sure he is expecting a reply. Unfortunately, I don't have a pen and paper with me. Why would I carry it to the jungle? I tear the letter into pieces and throw it away. Any letter received from Rupen could ruin my plans for him. I am happy that there is no complaint against Sehnaz, but I am scared if my letter to Rupen falls in the wrong hands, it could be a disaster.

"Do you have a piece of paper?" I ask.

Mahesh's eyes dazzle in anticipation. He takes out a pocket notebook and pencil from his pocket. "Ma'am, please write on this notebook, I will tear and deliver."

I write a few words, *She is well, but not here.*

Mahesh pockets the notebook, salutes me and goes back.

Vanaja is nowhere near me. I scream her name over and over.

After running for almost half an hour, I cannot find her. Did I lose her forever? Did a tribal man find her and take her away? Many negative thoughts trouble me. I run to my house, but she is not there. At last, I scamper to Nick's house to tell him I not only am unsuccessful in finding the herbs but also lost Vanaja.

Dr. Nick is about to go to the medical centre and Eliza pleading with him not to go.

"Sorry, Nick. Please come with me. Vanaja—" my breath falters— "I can't find her. Please, don't go to your clinic."

I feel guilty for spending that time with Mahesh. He could have told me the same thing another day. Why now?

Nick and I run back into the forest and look for Vanaja. *God, please help me find Vanaja, and help her find the herb for Eliza.*

Nick stops abruptly and glances around, gasping for breath. "I have seen the place islanders harvest herbs. Don't know why I never took an interest in understanding them and depended only on western medicines."

Sweat drops from Nick's forehead. Surely he is under stress. Without proper medication, how would he treat Eliza?

Noticing a pistol hung to his belt, I ask, "Will you use this pistol to save Vanaja? In case?"

Hesitation reflects on Nick's face. "Against the islanders? No. Can't make them our enemy. Only a feeling of security, nothing else."

We arrive at the hill. "This is the place I've seen islanders collect herbs," Nick says.

I glance around. "I think I was very close to this place when I lost Vanaja. We should try to look for her here."

I am surprised. All those I think to be weeds are in fact different medications. But does Nick know which one he can use to treat malaria?

Nick slouches on a stone and gazes at the sky. "The shipment will take time to arrive, and I don't know if Eliza will survive until then."

For the first time, I notice fear in Nick's features. The same one when a doctor says to a patient that his chances of survival are zero. The thick tension in the air hits me, too. Anyone in Andaman could get malaria. Who knows if I am the next victim?

An idea strikes my mind. We can take a boat to North Bay and ask any tribal to come with us and find the flower. It should work. But what if that man finds Vanaja along with the medicine?

"Let's go back," Nick says. "I must go to North Bay and request help."

Can Nick read my mind? What about Vanaja? Where is she?

"I will come with you, Nick. I can communicate better with them and explain the same way I did to Vanaja this morning, a new sign language. But can we find Vanaja before that? She has already looked for the flower, but she said they won't bloom unless the sun is out."

"If we find Vanaja, there's no need to travel to the island."

Confusion consumes us, and we return home.

We are about to walk onto another hillock when a faint sound of a man's voice alerts me. I signal Nick to stop and whisper, "Did you hear that noise?"

We stand in silence. Nothing. When we are about to continue, another *"Huh"* stops us again.

That sound comes from the cave on our side. We tiptoe, Nick holding the pistol ready, and we peek inside the cave through the nature-made peephole. My God. What am I looking at?

Vanaja is there. Naked and sitting on a man's lap. An islander. Another man is standing nearby. With the faint sunlight, I can see the satisfaction on his face and hear the occasional moaning. Maybe the other man is waiting for his turn. I try to see Vanaja's face, but I can't.

"Is she also happy?" I whisper to Nick.

"I doubt it," Nick says when we tiptoe back to a safe distance. "Women with same sex tendency rarely enjoy sex with men."

"Then why has she surrendered herself? It appears she consented to this."

"You used the right word. Surrender. It is the duty of every tribal man to take her back to their leader and punish her again. She is bribing them to survive the death punishment. If I am right, we should wait here and see. The men should go back after finishing their job. And we may take Vanaja with us."

I try to stop the sardonic giggle coming out of my mouth but fail. "Who says the islanders are uncivilised? See, even their men know how to exploit women to their benefit. Like our men in England."

Nick smiles.

Nick's prediction proves right. The two men walk away after some time, and then we approach the cave. Vanaja comes out and meets me with a handful of weed flowers, a painful smile forming on her face, gaze dropping to her feet.

For the first time I see a faint smile on Nick's lips. "God, she has got those flowers," he says.

"And we also got Vanaja back. We are so lucky!"

The flowers must soak in water for a week. She explains this to me in words mixed with sign language.

One week? Dark thoughts smoke through my mind. I glance at Nick. Worry has etched into his features.

Eliza might not last a week.

CHAPTER TWENTY-SEVEN

AMELIA, 20 JANUARY 1863, ROSS ISLAND, MORNING

"When hope runs out, even a doctor depends upon the advice of an uneducated and half naked Aboriginal woman." These were the words from Nick last evening.

Nick's pale face kept me awake the whole night.

"You are the only doctor in Andaman, Dr. Wilson. The entire island will suffer if you become sick. Dr. Walker is no longer in touch with the medical practice after becoming the governor."

"What do I do, Amelia? Eliza is getting weaker day by day. I can't concentrate on my work."

He is right. Why did Dr. Walker never think of bringing more doctors here?

I keep checking the mantle brass English clock my father had given me as a wedding gift. When cockerels call it a day, all the hopes of stealing some sleep fades away, and I walk to Nick's house.

Shanti answers my knock. "Memsahib sleeping. Wake up, drink medicine."

Tension and lack of sleep have blurred my senses. I don't understand if she has already taken the medicine or will take it. "Nick sahib?" I ask.

"Go. Morning. Before."

"Clinic?"

"No. Ship. Coming. See. I see."

A ship has arrived. This must be the meaning if I'm connecting Shanti's single-word sentences correctly. And this is music to me.

There is a possibility that the ship has come from Calcutta with malaria drugs. And I am sure Eliza, being the only doctor's wife, would get the priority. Until then, Vanaja's herbal solution should keep her alive.

What would happen to the prisoners if, like in the past, only a small quantity comes? Malaria has become an epidemic on the island, and I fear the native inmates would be the worst sufferers.

Sehnaz, I will see that your Rupen gets treatment if he is sick. This herbal medicine must help him.

Squatting on the floor, I stir the pot, which is ready for Eliza to consume. I have great expectations from this liquid.

A sobbing breaks my attention. I didn't realise the six-year-old had come into the room. "Luke. Did you wake up early today?"

His sniffle hits my heart. I reach for Luke, scoop him up against my chest. "No, my boy, don't weep. Mummy will be all right. I am here." He weeps on my shoulder. The thick tension in the house has affected even a little boy.

I tread to Eliza's bedroom after collecting some herb-treated water in a cup and place it on the bedside table. Luke is standing next to me, and Shanti behind.

"Mum, wake up. Medicine for you. Mum, please." He sobs again.

His mother's sickness has made the little boy into almost a matured individual.

Eliza tries to open her eyes, but the weakness has crumpled even her eyelids. She is struggling to see and move her head. Shanti brings her to a sitting position, and I feed her the spoonful of herbal juice. But it comes out, dripping from her chin and wetting her clothing.

"No, memsahib. Please drink." Shanti lets out a painful wail. Tears streak down her cheeks.

I struggle to control mine. I have to. Resiliency is no more an option for me, but a necessity to meet the challenge. Didn't I promise myself that one day I would be a strong woman?

Eliza's forehead is hot, like a stone under the blistering summer sun. I must pour cold water on her head before the next attempt to feed her the medicine.

Will that be too late? Where is Dr. Nick?

"Eliza, I know you are weak. But please try to swallow this. You will feel better."

She blinks.

"Shanti, please hold memsahib a bit inclined, and I will try again."

The water still dribbles down her chin. But judging by the quantity, I guess she has consumed at least half a teaspoon. We fear she will choke if we feed her more, so Shanti puts her back to a sleeping position. I want to reassure both Luke and Shanti, but an unknown fear tightens my throat.

I run out and arrive at the seashore. Some fresh air might help me get some of my strength back. An anchored ship at a distance draws my attention. I shoot a prayer. *God, let the ship come to Andaman. God, please, it should be full of malaria drugs from Calcutta.*

I don't know how much time I spend standing there, watching the ship. The sight of ships sailing in the Bay of Bengal is normal, but only a few come to Ross Island. Is this just another ship passing by?

By noon, I am successful in feeding Eliza three more spoonfuls of herb water. Her temperature has also gone down. My head is reeling from the sleeplessness of last night and the tension since this morning. "Shanti, can you please look after both Luke and Eliza? Please call me if something is urgent."

I rush back home and collapse on my bed.

Incessant knocks wake me up. How long have I slept? Oh, my God. It's almost evening. Or do the dark clouds make it feel like evening?

I stagger to the door and throw it open. Shanti's pale face and tear-stricken eyes tell me more than she could speak.

"Memsahib not good, please come."

"Dr. Wilson? Did he come home?" I ask while trudging with her.

"Came and go."

"And medicine?"

"No."

Does this mean the ship I had seen was only a passing one? A chill crawls under my skin.

Shanti gazes at my tension ridden face. "Memsahib, all right?"

"All right." But the words are from my lips and not from my soul. My faith in Vanaja's herbal remedy also crumbles. She needs proper treatment. But that is impossible.

When I enter Eliza's bedroom, I find Luke sitting on her bedside. A dark chill of foreboding sinks into my chest.

"Not eat. Morning." Shanti points at Luke.

Guilt washes over me. Had I remained married, I could have a boy this age, almost. Shouldn't I have stayed here and looked after him? Why did I go back and sleep?

I run to the kitchen. Shanti must have cooked something for lunch. She follows me. All the utensils are empty. "Shanti, no cooking?"

She shakes her head. "Nothing at home. Sahib busy."

I can imagine the condition of the only doctor on the island struggling to distribute his time between a sick wife and hundreds of other patients. When would he find time to buy provisions? Why didn't I think of this before?

"Don't worry, Shanti. I will ask Sadhna to cook something." How can I see the hungry boy weeping all the time, sitting near his mother?

I am about to cross Nick's entrance door when Luke comes running and grabs my waist. "Don't go, please. Mummy, please come and see her."

Scooping Luke on my hip, I trudge to Eliza's bedroom. Liquid is leaking through her lips. I place Luke on the floor and touch her forehead. "No, temperature seems normal." But the leaking foam from her mouth makes me nervous.

I jump to my feet. "Shanti. I am going to call Dr. Wilson. Please take care of Luke."

I run back to my home and hop onto the horse's saddle, letting it loose on the road. The horse, which hardly sets its feet outside the compound nowadays, struggles to run. "Please don't disappoint me," I mutter at the horse. "I must reach the doctor's clinic, now."

"Doctor is not here. He has gone to the port to bring medicine," Dr. Wilson's compounder says.

"Port? Has a ship arrived?"

"Yes, ma'am."

Why did the doctor go by himself when he could have sent his compounder? I jump onto the horse's saddle again and run to the port.

Yes, a ship is there. And there is chaos—people shouting and hurling abuses at each other. I understand, as usual, less-than-required drugs have arrived and will go to white people on a priority basis. When I finally make some sort of sense of the chaos, I realize Indian guards are shouting at their English counterparts. I hear something like, "Our mates are sick, and you will kill them without giving medical treatment. Better to shoot them with bullets and kill them in one go."

My head tilts. This is their country. Andaman is part of India, even if it is eight hundred miles away from the mainland.

Eliza's deadly face drags me back. I must help her survive. A dozen English soldiers are guarding the entrance to the ship to stop people from rushing inside. I elbow my way to the front.

"Is Dr. Wilson inside?"

"Yes, ma'am," one soldier says, "he can't come out unless these people leave this place."

"I am the schoolteacher and Dr. Wilson's next-door neighbour. There is an emergency. Please let me in."

Within minutes, I am inside with Nick. He is walking back and forth, anxiety burning in his eyes. I notice the same tension on his face that I had this morning. He stands still and looks at me. "How is Eliza?"

"Can you please give me the tablets? Now? I need to give her them as soon as possible."

He calls me to come inside a small cabin and takes out a packet from his coat pocket. "Please hide this in your clothes."

"You are not coming home?"

Nick inhales a deep breath. "Me? You saw the angry crowd? There are more malaria patients than the quantity of drugs that have come. And yes, first powder the tablet and mix with water before giving to Eliza. She can't swallow. I'll try to come as soon as possible," Nick mutters.

Even this liquid might struggle to pass through Eliza's throat.

There is no time to argue. I run back to the horse and fly home, jumping off the horse's back at the gate.

"Luke, I have brought the tablets. Your mummy will be better." I plod into the house, holding the packet in my hand.

Luke is sitting on the floor, burying his head between the knees. Shanti is weeping, sitting near her.

"Memsahib," Shanti sobs, "nose not working."

I bend over Eliza and place my hand above her nose. She is not breathing. Desperation clutches me as I glance at the door. Dr. Wilson is standing there. He must have followed me after I left the port.

He checks Eliza's pulse. Tears roll down his cheeks. "My family is over, Amelia." He lets out a bellow. "She is dead."

CHAPTER TWENTY-EIGHT

AMELIA, 24 JANUARY 1863, ROSS ISLAND, AFTERNOON

It has been four days since Eliza's death. Sadhna is roaming naked when I come from Nick's home to collect my clothing. An unease feathers into me. *Why Sadhna, why?* What went wrong?

Morticia is, in fact, back. And she was in the market when I saw Sadhna.

"No English. Silent. I remember." Sadhna flashes a serious smile at me.

Thank God, she remembers my advice.

"Good girl, Sadhna. Stay mute when she is around."

"No, me going with you," she pleads like a child.

"No, I am going to stay in Nick's house only for a short period. You stay here. I will come back. And one day Morticia will also go back to Calcutta. Again. Like last time. Then you, Vanaja, and me. We will have fun."

Sadhna flashes another innocent smile. The smile that has always told me how much she trusts me.

I go to my bedroom, and she follows me. A drawing is staring at me from my bed.

I bend down to have a good look.

It is a picture of Morticia making love with tribal women in Jambu. Panic clutches at me. She would kill someone if she finds this.

Each character in this black and white picture seems alive with their expressions. In the art, Morticia is sitting on the top floor of the old palace of Jambu Island and fondling bubbies of tribal women. All, including Morticia, are naked. And one woman who is looking at Morticia is widening her thighs.

"Amazing. Looks like a photo. Who did this?"

"I." Sadhna smiles, expecting appreciation from me.

I find it difficult to imagine such an artist was hiding inside this girl. But fear of Morticia doesn't allow me to smile.

"Don't, Sadhna. She will kill you."

I think about tearing it up, but an idea flashes in my mind, and my fingers still. Folding the paper, I tuck it inside my clothing to hide at Nick's home. *Who knows if the woman would search my room when I am not here? She suspects almost everyone in this world,* I think.

Within moments, Morticia arrives. "How are you, Amelia?"

I try my best to compose myself and show how happy I am to see her. "At last, after so many days! You wouldn't believe, Mort darling, how my life was a vacuum when you left. I am in Nick's house as the boy is sick, and he needs help."

"I am sad to learn about Eliza's death. I will meet Nick soon and give my condolences. But I am tired after a long sail from Calcutta. And you know, we had to lift provisions from Coco Islands, too."

She must have stopped in Jambu, too, and added to her plunder there. The memory of Sehnaz in Jambu disturbs me. She must be hiding somewhere in Coco. I wonder how she is. But Morticia is not the right person to enquire about her.

"You know, Amelia, I had enquired about your friend, Sez. In Coco."

How did she know what I'm thinking?

"But it's not good news for you," she continues.

I flinch. Bad news? Did the British capture her? "What happened to Sez?"

"You know, there are only a few Indians there. Most workers are Burmese and then there are English. Easy to find her. I asked a man and gave her description. He had seen your friend. But he said she had died. From malaria."

My head starts reeling, and I inhale a deep breath. *I will never see Sehnaz again. Oh, no. God, why are you so cruel?*

"Are you all right, Amelia?" Concern reflects in her eyes. *I wonder, is she pretending? But she's has no personal enmity with Sehnaz. Why would she lie to me?*

An urge to flee from there to some isolated place and cry swells in my heart. "I will take your leave, Mort darling. Would have loved to stay here, but Nick and Luke need me, only a matter of days."

In fact, I am already suffocating with her. This is not the time nor place for grieving Sehnaz.

"Don't worry, you have gotten something for me, and I am happy with that. You are a wonderful woman, Amelia." She beams at me.

What do I have for her? I think. I try to smile without knowing what she is appreciating.

"This tribal woman you have gotten? She likes me." I can hear her heart dancing with joy.

The tribade knew at once which woman was like her? So quick! She has only arrived this morning. I held a sob inside my throat and plaster another smile. "The tribal people were punishing her to death, and I brought her here to hide her. She is all yours."

I know how much Vanaja loves women's company. And with her dark olive skin and large bubbies, she would be Morticia's favourite. She might even spare Sadhna from the painful love I am sure she never likes. And same with me. Didn't I just pretend that I loved her sexual sessions?

A feeling of sudden loneliness in this world after Sehnaz's death wrenches my guts, but I inhale deeply to maintain my composure.

"I have given her a name—Vanaja, meaning 'A girl born in the forest' in Hindi. And she will keep you happy, just keep it a secret. You can even take her to India. She looks like any other tribal woman in India, and you are safe. No hassle of keeping a slave." No sooner are the words out of my mouth than I wonder if I'd just put Vanaja in danger.

Amelia, 25 January 1863, Sunday, Ross Island, Afternoon

After a long time, I go to the church—that, too, with Nick. Eliza's death has rattled me. Luke has been ill, and I've shifted to Nick's house for a few days to take care of his son. With Nick's long hours in his clinic, who else can give a mother's attention to Luke? It will take time for him to come to the terms with life.

"God. Help me to keep my promise I made to Sehnaz." This is my only prayer at the church.

Luke has allowed me to share his room. Only a temporary arrangement. The little boy has matured years through his mother's sickness and subsequent death. Dr. Wilson stays away most of the time attending to his patients. Luke understands that, too. "My dad is helping fathers and mothers of other children to survive the sickness," he comments to me this afternoon. He clings to me, knowing that I will spend more days with him. After his mother's tragic death, I am trying to fill the void. How long can I stay here and be a mother?

Nick arrives home earlier than usual from the clinic.

"Thank God, at last you came home on a Sunday. No patients today?"

A relaxing smile engulfs Nick's face. "Patients are still in long queues. But another doctor has arrived from Calcutta, and now we can work in shifts." Nick says as we walk to his veranda and sip steaming tea while sitting there. Dusk is about to fall. The weather is just perfect—not freezing, as usual this time of year.

I glance at Nick. "Will you and Luke like to go to the beach with me? I want to spend some quality time with him."

"Would love to."

"What will you two doctors do if you don't have enough medicine? A prescription isn't enough to cure the patients."

Nick lets out a sigh and lowers his voice as if someone would hear him. "That day when you brought the medicine from the ship, I thought the quantity that had arrived was not enough. But later, I found so many boxes hidden in another cabin, all full of malaria doses. Enough for everyone—even the islanders. I don't understand why Dr. Walker wants to hoard them and not allow Indian prisoners and workers a fair treatment."

"Is he a sadist?"

Nick doesn't reply for a while. He has drifted to a thoughtful mode.

"Amelia, confidential news. Will you keep this a secret?" His eyes wander around to check that Shanti is not listening, as she sometimes meets maids of other officers and gossips with them. "I hope this situation will change."

"You can count on me, Nick." My heart jumps inside my ribs. Is it good news or bad?

"Another administrator is going to replace Walker. Robert Christopher Tytler. There were complaints against Walker about the way he was handling Andaman administration. But there's no official declaration so far. Walker will be given some position in Calcutta. Until then, this is confidential."

"Smoke! Look, Dad, smoke." Luke comes over and holds Nick's arm.

We roll our eyes to the right, where thick smoke is curling above the forest. It is not unusual for people to burn timbers in January cold.

"Must be some Indian workers. Sometimes they get together in their village and make a bonfire, to get warmth in the winter. And Sundays, most of them get a half-day off. Must be celebrating."

He might be right; I've also been here for months and have seen smoke arising sometimes. But not this thick. Within minutes, we notice dense smoke rising high in the jungle, and the sky is bright orange—like fire has engulfed the entire north side of the island.

I jump out of my chair. "Nick, that side is the encampment. The prisoners are in danger!"

"I have to go. I don't know if we can treat patients with burn injuries." Urgency radiates from his eyes.

Nick is about to hop onto his horse when an English guard rushes through the gate. "Sir," he huffs as he gets off, "another revolt."

Nick stops dead in his tracks. "Again? Prisoners?"

"No, Indian guards. They have started. They are complaining several of their people are dying of malaria. Not getting medical treatment. And they have let loose the inmates of the camp. Maybe the prisoners have already joined them. Or will join soon."

His hands go to his head. "And this fire?"

"They are responsible, sir—knowing well that a bunch of English soldiers won't be able to control all three in a row. Fire, guards' revolt, and also..."

"No time to talk, soldier. I am coming with you."

Then, looking at me, Nick says, "Take care, Amelia. Tonight will be tough. Don't know how many will suffer injury."

I stand like a statue as both leave the premises in a hurry. Luke also stands there, wrapping his arms around my waist.

"Dad never stays at home." Luke's voice is full of sadness.

How do I tell a little boy the repercussions of the fire in the encampment?

My breath catches, and fear consumes me as I watch the fire and smoke. Will Rupen help Walker contain this chaos, too? I want to shout and let Sehnaz's soul know her Rupen has changed and we should never think of his freedom from the prison.

CHAPTER TWENTY-NINE

AMELIA, 26 JANUARY 1863, PAST MIDNIGHT, ROSS ISLAND

It's past midnight and still I can't sleep. Yesterday was the worst day of my life which I need to write in my diary, but I can't. First learning about my best friend Sehnaz's death and then this inferno caused by the rebels. Most of the time I keep the doors and windows closed to prevent the ashes trespassing into the home, but the smell of the burning woods still sneaks through and clouds my mind with depressing thoughts. So many scenarios crossed my mind.

"You look so weak, Amelia. Did you take too much stress in Andaman? See, we are back now in Sultanpur." Sehnaz hugs me. Her sweet, attar perfume engulfs my whole being. But thunder roars, and I wake up on the bed. Did I get a few moments of sleep?

I run to the front veranda to watch the inferno, but within moments, I find Luke with me. "Luke, baby, please go inside and sleep. I am joining you soon."

He doesn't reply, but stands close to me. The trauma in the air is so heavy that even a kid loses his slumber. Another lightning and a huge thunder rattle my bones. "Luke, let's go inside and sleep."

He follows me into the bedroom.

Downpour begins, bringing the hope that it will soon douse the inferno. Seated at Luke's bedside in Nick's room, I try to lull him to sleep. My eyes wander around in the dim lantern light as I pat Luke's back. Eliza's wedding photo watches me from the frame on the wall. Guilt whispers through me as I wonder if the care I've given her son is enough. Not being a mother is making it hard for me to manage a six-year-old.

I try to hide my face from Eliza's photo. But then my gaze lands on another photo. The smiling face of Nick gazes at me from inside the frame. I smile back at him, but then lower my gaze. Am I blushing?

When the morning sunrays fall on me through slits of the timber windowpanes, I realise I shouldn't have slept on his cot.

But the night is over, and I am awake now. I don't feel like getting up for a while. Nick's scents tingle my conscious from his pillow, and a sense of familiarity keeps me on the bed.

The sound of the horse's bray tears through the walls of the house. Anxiety makes me jump out of bed and lope through the door. I am sure Eliza is rebuking me from her photo. Guilt runs over me, and I scurry to open the main gate.

An exhausted Nick hobbles inside. Shanti is still sleeping inside her room.

"Awake so early?" Nick's sleep-starving eyes gaze at me with a guilty smile. "Sorry I am troubling you so much, Amelia."

"No, please." Stepping forward, I place my finger on his lips and mutter, "He didn't fall asleep until the early morning. Don't worry about us, we are all good. Tell me what happened."

Realisation strikes me. I have taken too much liberty—standing so close, touching him. What would Eliza think from the heavens? I am here to help her little son come to terms, not to replace her. I quickly drop my hand and step back.

"Sad news, Amelia."

Fear of hearing something terrible makes me a statue.

"At midnight, the Indian guards surrendered. But by then the prisoners had revolted, too. You know the encampment is so easy to break out of. When Indian guards didn't cooperate to contain them, English soldiers shot at them in the dark, without breaking. I could only hear the gun sound. The report is that many prisoners jumped into the sea to save their lives but died there. So sad."

I have seen blood before. The Indian rebels had ambushed a ferry load of British soldiers in the Gomti River when I was sailing with Sehnaz and Sheru. That was years ago, in May 1857. During the peak of the Sepoy Mutiny. The blue waters of the Gomti River had turned pink.

A rude shock passes through my nerves. Closing my eyes, I visualise ex-soldiers-turned-prisoners running and jumping into the Andaman Sea to survive the bullets of the English soldiers. Within minutes, the surrounding water turning pink. But only for moments, until the waves wash them away. Would their family members in India ever see their bodies one last time?

I don't think so. They are lesser humans because of their dark skin. My white skin teases me. My anger is now after Walker's blood. "And Walker?"

"This morning Tytler took over for him. That was the government's direction from Calcutta. He should have taken over the charge yesterday morning. As soon as he took charge, he went to the Indian soldiers and assured them..."

Nick's sleepy eyes discourage me from asking further questions. He needs some rest. But my anxious brain doesn't allow me to stop.

"What assurance?"

He rubs his drooping eyelids. "That the Indian guards would get equal medical treatment like the English. And those who have spent three or more years in Andaman would get preference to go back to the mainland."

"He sounds like a sane man. Not cruel, like Walker."

"Yes." Nick coughs.

"And Rupen?" I repent within moments of asking. No one here knows my sole purpose of requesting Andaman posting was to help Rupen achieve his freedom.

He tilts his head in surprise. "You know him?"

"Who doesn't? He was the army chief of Awadh kingdom and was the key man behind The Residency siege." *Thank God I had an immediate answer.*

"He is also missing. Don't know if he is alive or not."

My jaw stills. What reply would I give to Sehnaz's soul? But my gaze goes to Nick and his weak features.

"Are you all right, Nick?"

"Yes, maybe bit cold."

"Cold?" I move over to him again and touch his forehead. "Nick, your body is boiling."

"Don't worry about me, Amelia. I'll be all right. You should go home. You are also suffering with both of us, father and son. Today is Monday, your school."

"You are forgetting, Nick. I'm taking a few days off from the school. And I am not going home. This is my home for some time, and I will take care of you both."

Nick swings back and smiles at me—a special smile I think I can never forget.

Asking Nick to change his clothes and lie down on his bed, I sit near him with a pot of cold water and a piece of cloth. His fever must come down before evening or I'll have to call for the doctor. *Doctor? But Nick himself is a doctor!*

As I spread the wet cloth on Nick's forehead, my mind goes to Rupen. Which side did he support last night? Is he also alive, or is his body floating somewhere in the Andaman Sea?

Mustering courage to ask Nick about Rupen, I dip the cloth again in the water. But Nick has started snoring.

So many thoughts cross my mind. Why am I here if Rupen is dead? And if he is alive, where is he? And there is no one on this god-forsaken island that I can ask.

CHAPTER THIRTY
SEHNAZ, 26 JANUARY 1863, EVENING, SOUTH COCO ISLANDS

"Jhumru, come and sit on my lap, girl. I am so alone today." Sehnaz scooped Jhumru from the floor and settled her on her knees. As she massaged her fur, she said, "Why is Amelia coming to my mind so often today? How happy would I be if I were with her in Andaman?

Boredom was another term of this quiet afternoon. Agatha was seldom coming to south Coco nowadays. She was even planning to go back to Rangoon, leaving her husband Alfred alone in the Coco Islands. How could Sehnaz keep herself busy with no company around? The only dream that kept her alive was getting Morticia's treasure and going back to India, rich and independent. But day by day, her determination gave way to frustration.

"Mew." Jhumru jumped down and walked away from Sehnaz. She didn't stop her, just observed. Jhumru ambled to a small bush in front of her cottage and circled around it, watching. *Looking for prey?*

"Come back, Jhumru. Are you hungry? Didn't I give you enough rice and vegetables at lunch? One day that I can't give you fish, and you are looking for a mouse. You are a princess, Jhumru. Don't eat those dirty foods."

Jhumru looked like she understood. She came back and slept on the floor in front of Sehnaz. Seated cross-legged on the floor, Sehnaz again ruffled her fur.

"We will not be here forever, Jhumru. Once I get the treasure, I will go back to India. Not to Sultanpur or even Lucknow. At those places, people recognise me and might inform the rogue English officers. I will go to a faraway place and buy a bungalow. A big one, with a separate room for you near my bedroom. With servants, a horse cart, and a large garden in front of the house."

Jhumru threw her legs onto Sehnaz's lap.

"You want to hear more? I see. Why else would you come here onto my thighs? And this is a confidential talk, Jhumru. Promise me you will never tell anyone." She giggled. "I will, you know..." Raising the cat to her ear's height, she muttered, "I'll find a suitable match for you. A boy. And you both will sleep in your bedroom. And produce lots of kittens. No, I am wrong. Children. Both boy and girl cats. I will play with them like I would with my own children."

Heat flowed inside her groin. Her other hand crawled inside her blouse and titillated her nipples. A daydream made her smile but soon moved in the reverse direction.

"Sheru will never love me, Jhumru. He slept with me once as he knew he could get rid of his sin. I am a Muslim and that, too, a courtesan. Once we are in India and away from these Coco Islands, I'm sure he will stay away from me. Miles away, where I would never hear from him. He might even marry a brahmin girl and set up his own family. With all the money I'll have, will I ever find a nice husband who would love me? I mean true love? But you don't worry, Jhumru. You will find a nice boy cat and marry. I am sure."

A shadow of a man made Sehnaz jump off the ground. Sheru was standing before her. *So soon today? Did he hear what I was saying about him?*

"Finished early, Sehnaz."

Sehnaz stared into his eyes. As calm as the pond water. It was difficult to guess his mood.

Will he confront her with what she just said to Jhumru? Did she just reveal her feelings for this man, which she had kept secure behind her heart, in a closed compartment?

"I got some news, Sehnaz. Something happened when I was lying here sick and couldn't go to Coco for work."

Sehnaz's brain made a sudden jump from her own secret feelings to an unknown and dark foreboding. Sheru would never have come from work early otherwise. Did something go seriously wrong?

"Rave and Morticia. Their ship had passed through Coco when I was sick," Sheru said.

"What is news about that? They always buy provisions for Andaman from Coco on their way from Calcutta."

"That's not the point, Sehnaz." Sheru wrapped his arm around Sehnaz's waist and guided her to the tree branch lying next to their hutment. Both sat on it. "Any idea what Rave's principal business is?"

"What?"

"Not transporting goods and men between mainland and Andaman. That's just something to cover up what the couple is up to. Amassing wealth by illegal means. One Indian guard had told me he used them for piracy."

"Let them do it, Sheru. Why are we concerned about how they got so much money? The fact is that I know where they are hiding the loot and how we lay our hands on it. And flee. She would never, ever find out we did that. Maybe the islanders would report that I had come there. They have seen me before. But where in India would she look for me? In such a vast country? And she can't even report the theft to the police. They are illegal, anyway."

Sheru sat in silence for a while. Jhumru again came to Sehnaz and jumped onto her thighs. "Jhumru, can you tell Uncle Sheru not to worry too much?"

"I'm not worried about that, Sehnaz. I am thinking, what if..."

"What if...what, Sheru? Do we have any other way?"

"Not that. See, from where will Alfred organise a ship? What we are planning to do is secret and illegal, too. Can he arrange a vessel? And wouldn't they inform the authorities?" He paused for a moment, but then continued. "What if Alfred hires the ship from Rave? And the couple would know that we both are trying to steal what they have hidden."

"No. Not possible." Sehnaz placed Jhumru on the ground and came closer to Sheru. "He was here."

"Who?"

"Alfred. He came to meet me."

"Today? He came all the way here? And saw how the princess is living in a dirty hutment?"

"Don't utter the word 'dirty.' Hutment is right. But I spend most of the day trying to keep our home clean. And it also surprised him we have a bed, tables and chairs here. I didn't say his wife arranged these for us. For free."

Sheru laughed. "But why did he come? Has he found a ship for us?"

"Not yet. He is trying. It's not that easy. But he is serious, otherwise he wouldn't have come. But I got other news from him."

"News?"

"About Morticia. And her husband, Rave Hunt."

"You already knew they had come to Coco?"

"Even more." Sehnaz chuckled and planted a kiss on Sheru's cheeks. A tribal man was passing through at a distance and watching them.

"Careful, Sehnaz." He moved away a little. "That man is watching."

"Let him." Sehnaz giggled again. "They also do this with their women. And in broad daylight."

"Daylight?"

"Yes. You are not here the entire day. And I have been around. When they make love, they don't even care who is watching them. This is a natural act between a man and a woman, and they do it whenever and wherever they get the urge."

"You are changing the topic, Sehnaz. Why did he come to see you? And why, when I am not here?" Sheru grabbed Sehnaz's waist and pulled her into his chest. "I am afraid of that man, Sehnaz. He is a characterless fellow."

Sehnaz leaned her head against his chest and grinned. "But I haven't told you what he said to me about Morticia."

Sheru inhaled a deep breath that Sehnaz could feel.

"Morticia was asking about me."

"What?"

"She was trying to extract information about me, telling him I am a princess and ran away last time when her ship was in Coco."

"Then?"

"Then? Alfred sensed conspiracy and said he has seen me, but I have died of malaria."

Sheru's gaze brightened. "Even Morticia said you are a princess?"

Sehnaz let out a laugh. "Amelia must have told her. But look at the facts. If Alfred would have trusted Morticia, he wouldn't have lied to her. And don't worry about his wrong intentions. I can defend myself. And do you think an honest officer would help us steal the wealth which is ill-gotten in the first place?"

Suspicion floated in Sheru's eyes. "We are just two. And he must take some people with him. What if he betrays us after getting the treasure and doesn't share with us?"

"This life we are living here is no better than a prisoner's life. Jambu is only four miles away from Sagar Island. Only one side of Sagar touches the Bay of Bengal. The other three sides sit along the Hooghly River. The worst-case scenario—assume he runs away with the money. We can at least go to Sagar Island, and from there we can find our freedom."

"Freedom?"

Sehnaz winked. "Yes. More valuable than Morticia's treasure."

"Police wouldn't pick me up again?"

She let out a confident smile. "Police? Why? You know what Rave reports when prisoners' count decreases? He must have reported that you died on the way and he threw your body into the ocean. In the records of the government, you are dead. You can take a new name and settle far away from your village. A sort of rebirth for you. Same for me."

Sheru smiled and got up. "You are such an intelligent woman, Sehnaz. Rupen was right in making you manage his network. You can fish out so much information!"

"I've not finished yet, Sheru. There's more news to share."

"More?"

"Yes. But not from Alfred, though."

Sheru turned and stared into Sehnaz's eyes.

She loved the way her capability surprised Sheru.

"Agatha is leaving this man."

"Agatha ma'am?"

"Please don't address her as 'ma'am' anymore in front of Alfred. Don't forget that now you are the husband of a princess. Alfred addresses me as 'your highness.'"

"Yes, your highness." Sheru chuckled and bowed his head.

"Agatha knows her husband is a womaniser and an idiot. She is planning to go back to Rangoon in the next available ship, and she will never come back here again."

"And we are planning everything with that man."

"Yes. Honest men are of no use in this case."

Sheru went to the pond to bathe before his evening prayers.

Sehnaz glanced at the sky. Messy clouds started teasing her. For the first time, both freedom and wealth looked so real. What then, was pinching her mind?

Amelia's memory began haunting her again. Morticia must have told her Sehnaz was dead. How would she take that news? Would she go back to Sultanpur? What about Rupen's freedom?

CHAPTER THIRTY-ONE

RUPEN, 1 MARCH 1863, MORNING, RUTLAND ISLAND, NEAR PORTMAN BAY (PART OF ANDAMAN ISLANDS GROUP)

Rupen glanced at the sea while sitting on the veranda on the makeshift chair the tribal men had built for him. Within a short time, they had erected a cottage with close fences on all sides. Built on a small hillock, he could even keep watch on the ten Indian prisoners (ex-soldiers) who had escaped with him the night the second uprising broke out.

Rupen felt his own grim smile. Clever brain of Dr. Walker, to plan such chaos.

The advice of the monk in the prison sounded in his ears as he took a sip of *mahua* from the stone glass. "*Swamiji*, I respect your advice that I should escape from the prison at any cost. But why is the price so high? How can I forget the dead bodies floating in the sea? Why did they have to face the bullets from the English guards? Please tell me *Swamiji*, why? Why did they sacrifice their lives so that Dr. Walker could help me flee?"

He got over the guilt when he finished two glasses of *mahua*. Didn't ordinary soldiers always sacrifice their lives for the kings? As the ex-army chief of Awadh, was he any less than a royal himself?

"My dear friends, my heart goes with you," Rupen addressed the dead soldiers when he poured a third glass from the earthen pot. "I will let the world see the inhuman treatment the British are giving to its prisoners of war in these remote Andaman Islands."

There was no more *mahua* in the pot.

Rupen got to his feet and staggered into the small courtyard outside his fence overlooking Portman Bay. Rave should have arrived days before. He feared his prolonged stay here would attract danger for him. Would the new administrator, Robert Tytler, find his hiding place?

During his last secret meeting, Rave had assured him his knowledge about Andaman Islands was better than any other British official. He had spent months exploring and found this—the safest location. Seventeen miles from Port Blair through Andaman Sea and then inside the Portman Bay, Rutland Island was another of five hundred islands the English might not set foot on for the next five years. And the location near the Portman Bay would keep him beyond the sights of any English ship sailing in Andaman Sea.

This last month seemed like ages to Rupen. Could he trust Rave's network? What if one of his men opens his mouth to the authorities, and all his plans fail?

"Good morning, sir."

Rupen glanced down the hillock at the hutments where his soldiers lived until he saw the owner of the voice. A smile came out of his throat.

"Morning, Shyam."

"Sir, we all are taking turns watching for Mr. Rave Hunt coming with the ship."

"Good. Remember, it wouldn't be the same one he uses to loot. So, be careful, and watch for the enemy ship, too. Mr. Hunt will wave a saffron flag with Lord Hanuman's picture on it."

Rupen himself was the last hope of these ten soldiers. What if Mr. Hunt couldn't come?

Shyam gave a shout as soon as Rupen stepped inside his cottage. "Sir, a boat."

He strode back out. Sure enough, a boat was entering the bay. Rupen's heart sank. Rave should have come on a ship. Did some incident happen meanwhile? Did the authorities find out he was hiding here?

"Shyam, call your mates and be ready with your rifles."

Within minutes, all his soldiers appeared and took their positions. The stolen guns from the Ross Island barracks were ready to roar, waiting only for Rupen's command.

The ferry came closer. A fat man was waving a saffron flag from the cockpit of the boat. *He must be Mr. Hunt.* Confidence bloomed inside Rupen. But why did he come in a boat instead of a ship?

"You have made a beautiful cottage in such a short time, Mr. Naik." Rave smiled as he entered Rupen's house.

Rupen flashed a grin. "Hmm, it wasn't possible to build a bungalow on this desolate island. What else could I have done?"

Rupen had met Mr. Hunt only a few times at Dr. Walker's house. But with his years' long diplomatic experience, he was sure this was the man he could depend on for his life beyond the prison.

Didn't he ask his followers to help Rave in the piracy expeditions?

"This is not a miserable island, Mr. Naik. Rather, the safest place you can hide until we can all sail back to India."

Impatience was feasting on Rupen's peace. He was about to ask when Rave would bring his ship.

"I had been checking into this place while Morticia was busy enjoying her life with women."

After they settled on the porch overlooking the Portman Bay, two tribal girls entered and bowed to Rave. Rupen followed Rave's gaze at them, from their tiny cloths covering their groins to the breastbands which could hardly cover their bubbies.

"Strange. I have never seen any islander woman covering her breasts. These two are exceptions," Rave said.

Rupen smirked as he glanced at the girls.

Rave batted an eyelid. "Mr. Naik, for God's sake, please control your mind. Behave like a saint as long as you are here. Islanders will kill you if you stare at their women. I had already warned you beforehand."

Rupen beamed back. "I understand. Already told my soldiers. They are all meditating to control their minds, day and night. And also helping each other to relieve their energy. I said to them, 'once you are back at your home, marry girls of your choice and enjoy life.'"

The girls came holding two stone glasses and handed them off them to Rupen and Rave.

"*Mahua* drink. Please enjoy," Rupen said.

He noticed another bolt of surprise in Rave's eyes.

"Who are these girls?"

"You know I understand their language. They also think I am a king from India. They are daughters of the tribal chief of North Bay

Island. He is the head of Rutland, too. His wife was the daughter of an ex-Indian king from a tribal woman. He offered his daughters' hands to me."

"And you said yes." Rave let out a loud laugh. "Clever man. Good way to spend time while you are here."

Rupen didn't find it funny, but still managed to smile. "Mr. Hunt, I am a devotee of goddess Kali. I never harm women. These two girls have accepted me as their husband. I will take care of them, even at the cost of my life. And you probably don't have knowledge of how your British government murdered my wife in the name of winning a war. Don't I need a new life partner?"

Rave sipped *mahua* from the glass. "Right. At least they're women. Not like mine." He chortled.

"I don't understand how you married Morticia. Did she possess any womanly quality at all?"

Rave looked apologetic. "She was not this fat before. I also got to work as a captain because of her father's contact. And how would I know there are women who love to sleep with other women only? But one good thing about her, she never minds if I sleep with another woman. A mutual arrangement between us. As long as I go on finding new treasures for her, she is happy."

"You must be happy, Mr. Hunt. She wouldn't see any of those treasures." Rupen cackled. "But my worry is, when are you arranging the ship?"

"Trying, Mr. Naik. I am doing my best. One ship was available only a day before the uprising. I had to let it go. I wasn't sure if you and your men would escape and that, too, avoiding the bullets. Now we have to wait. Enjoy *mahua* drink and your new beautiful wives until then," Rave said with a twinkle in his eyes.

An uneasy feeling sank into Rupen's stomach. He had already waited over five years, hoping he would see freedom again. He also understood he was depending upon two unscrupulous men who would go to any extent for money. But did he have another choice?

"But Mr. Hunt, you can bring your own ship."

"My ship?" Rave gazed through the rim of the glass. "Then Morticia will find out what I am doing. What makes you think she would allow me?"

"Unnecessary worry, Mr. Hunt. Once we are in Jambu, my men can chop her into pieces and throw her into the Bay of Bengal. Sharks will feast. What do you think?"

"You don't know her. She can smell things from a distance. And she understands how to play games. The best player. She alone can fight a dozen armed men with her brain only. I don't want to awaken the poisonous snake. Rather, I will take my share in the treasure and settle in a small town of Burma."

So much fear toward a woman! "Your wife, Mr. Hunt, you know how to handle."

A wry smile twisted Rave's mouth. "My snake and I know how to make her dance." Rave chortled again. Finishing the last sip from the glass, he stood up. "I will take your leave, Mr. Naik. Time to go."

Rupen stood up. "One last question, Mr. Hunt. Will Dr. Walker also join us?" he asked while walking with him.

Rave stopped and swung around. He held Rupen's gaze for a few moments. "Dr. Walker—" he swallowed— "I am not sure. He might maintain distance."

Rupen shrugged his shoulders. "How would he get his share? Would you come back to Andaman for him?"

"Morticia would be waiting for me. I am at a loss, Mr. Naik. He is not leaving Ross Island. I know he is not going back to Calcutta, either, as he would join our venture. But Morticia has eyes on me when I go to meet anyone in Ross, especially Walker. All she knows is my arrangement with Walker was that he would provide soldiers for our operation in the ocean. Let me see what I can do."

Rave got into his boat and left. Rupen glanced at the sky. A dark cloud was building up. Four of his soldiers were fishing along the waterside of the bay using a cloth as a fishing net.

The pleasant chitchat between those men stabbed Rupen's heart. How happy these men looked thinking that he could reward them with freedom. They would see their loved ones.

"Oh, God. Is it possible? I have no family in Lucknow and would go to a place where nobody knows me. But if these men go to their villages, wouldn't someone inform the British?"

CHAPTER THIRTY-TWO

AMELIA, 1 MARCH 1863, SUNDAY, NORTH BAY ISLAND (PART OF ANDAMAN ISLANDS GROUP)

E ach Sunday, people go to church and pray. But Nick and I come to North Bay Island. Didn't Jesus say, *Service to humanity is service to God*?

Nick was feeling guilty leaving Luke alone at home after Eliza's death. Nowadays, he also accompanies us. But today he will play with his friends instead. So here we are, Nick and I. He will treat patients, and I will teach English to men and women here. For me, this is a two-way education. I have also learnt some local language, and it makes my work easier in teaching them English.

Nick's patients are already waiting for him, and he jumps into action as soon as we arrive at North Bay, roughly a three-and-half-mile boat journey from Ross. But my students would take time to arrive.

"Nick, I am going for a stroll. I'll be back in about half an hour."

"Sure." He smiles and then talks to his first patient.

I walk down almost a furlong, where a *Gulmohar*–a Royal Peacock Flower tree—takes my breath away. There is a similar tree in my garden in Sultanpur. Sehnaz's favourite.

Memories of Sehnaz jump out of the flowers and into my heart. The tropical flowering tree is in full bloom. The orange-red petals have blanketed the entire tree, with days-old petals scattered on the ground like a scarlet carpet.

"I will travel back to Calcutta, Sehnaz." Sitting on the grass, I hold a bunch of Gulmohar and assume Sehnaz is gazing at me. "The promise I had given to you is meaningless now. I am sure Rupen has died during the indiscriminate firing on the twenty-sixth of January, along with other prisoners who jumped into the sea. And you are dead, too. What would I do here?"

She was a brave woman. She would have said to me, "Why delay, Amelia? Morticia and Rave both are sailing to and from Calcutta regularly. Jump onto her ship and come back to Sultanpur. We'll meet there and talk an entire day."

"No, Sehnaz. I am scared to travel with that woman. She would halt in Coco, I am sure. That would bring a dark memory. Didn't I lose you at the Coco Islands? Forever? With you, I almost lost everything. Do you know, Sehnaz, I met one Indian soldier here. He brought me a letter from Rupen, something about you. You know what it was?"

I glance at the flower in my hand, expecting Sehnaz to respond. But I can sense her in my heart and sense what she would like to say.

"What was in that letter, Amelia?"

I let out a laugh, then glance around as if there's anyone nearby. Islanders shouldn't think I've become mad and am talking to myself.

"A police officer in Sultanpur has reported that 'Sehnaz' is a popular female name, and that means any woman with that name is not a war criminal. According to his report, you have a clean background. Why didn't I get this information before? You would have been with me, now."

Tears streak down my cheeks. Let them. No need to wipe them here.

"That's all right, Amelia. I'm always with you. Whenever you are alone, remind me and we both can talk for hours. Now, my dear girl, can you please smile?"

"Yes, I will." A giggle comes out of my throat. "But I also don't want to leave Luke alone. The boy needs time to adjust to life without a mother. Nick is also thinking of going back to Calcutta. I am thinking we all can go back together in one ship. I would love to spend more time with Luke. The little boy has gotten a special place in my heart. I would miss him in Sultanpur."

"Is that Luke, or Nick? You are in love with Nick, do you know?"

Sehnaz's remark stuns me as if she is really with me now. "No, Sehnaz. I am thinking only of the little boy."

"But I can bet, you are falling in love with Nick."

"Come on, Sehnaz. You are bringing topics from the air. I haven't even thought about it. Believe me. And yes, I will be late for teaching.

Talk to you again. Bye."

I get up and walk to where my tribal students are waiting for me. I don't know why I am in no mood to teach anything. Nick is busy with his patients in another shed. Women have surrounded me and are gossiping among themselves. Civilised or uncivilised, all women love to talk with other women.

When can I go back to Sultanpur? Or should I go back to my parents in London and tell my mother she was right? That like every other woman, I should have also strived to become a better wife and a better mother. The dream I had since my childhood to become a special woman—was that wrong? An illusion? Is it true that a woman should never think outside the four boundary walls of her husband's house and do something on her own?

Desperation fogs my mind. I glance above. The sky is full of dark clouds. Slow breeze blows my hair across my face. The scent of sea water tingles my nose, but I am deep inside my thoughts. The tribal women are all looking at me, and some of them are pointing at the sky. Without focusing, I can't understand their conversation. After months of my teachings, they are mixing their words with some English.

"Storm. Sky. Cloud."

Do I hear them correctly? Are they warning me or just teasing me with the words I have taught them?

No. They don't sound funny. I get up from the timber log bench and approach them.

They repeat— "Storm. Sky. Cloud."

The afternoon sun is hiding behind the black clouds. Oh, no. It's not another patch of rain. The islanders must be right, and I notice the fear of a dangerous storm in their eyes. I rush to Nick. He is talking to his patients with his sign language.

"Nick, a storm is building up. We must go."

"Only few more patients."

Few more? A dozen men and women are lining up for him. And more are coming. Should he stop treating his patients and run with me?

I don't want to get stuck on the island during the storm. We must arrive at Ross before evening.

"Nick, hurry. Please. I am afraid of this storm."

"I will," he says, focussing on the next patient.

I stand there gazing at him and the patients. Maybe my presence will encourage him to go.

The women—heading home in order to miss the storm, as well—come to me and hug me, one after another. This is their routine when I leave the island and prepare to go on the boat. Why are they doing this now, when Nick has many more patients to look after?

One by one, the women leave. Wind off the Andaman Sea has buffeted the trees and branches, swishing them violently. I glance at Nick. Seated on a mound, he is checking the pulse of his patients and handing them the tablets from his bag. Referring to the drawings of morning sun, noon, and evening stars on a piece of paper, he is instructing them when to consume the tablets. Helplessness freezes in my veins. When would he finish?

The men in the queue are pointing fingers at the sky and deciding to leave, as well. The last man whom Nick is checking with his stethoscope is also looking above, and there is an urgency in his features.

I trudge closer to Nick and grab his bag. "Nick, look, everyone here has left. We must go. NOW."

Nick hurriedly gives some medicine to his last patient and follows me. We lope toward the shore through the snaking pathway, wind howling like a ghost and tree branches blocking our way. My hair is whipping about my face, impeding my vision. When I stop and try to contain my unruly hair, Nick pulls me along by the hand.

"We must reach the boat before the rain lashes," he shrieks into my ear.

We arrive at the makeshift jetty to find the boat yawing violently and waves slapping over the lip of the deck. Where is the boatman?

"He might have taken shelter somewhere," I shout to compete with the groaning sea.

"We shouldn't have come here at all. It's dangerous to sail in this storm. Should've thought before. Can we go back and ask islanders to give us shelter in their home?" Nick sounds as if he is pleading with me for help.

I know islanders don't like any English males inside their homes. They think their women would be in danger. Can I approach them instead?

This is a benefit of being a woman—the first time I appreciate my womanhood. People trust women more than men.

"Yes, Nick. Let's go back."

Large drops of water beat down on my skin.

"But where do we go?" Nick asks while running. "Same spot I check patients? But that is open from all sides."

"Yes, but there is a roof. If it hasn't already blown away. We will see if we can go to the village." Urgency and panic are shaking my voice.

We approach the turn where we have to climb through steps. A fallen branch blocks our way. Rain is pummelling us. We must find a shelter, at least to save our heads from falling branches. I cast a quick glance around to find another way. We spot a hill that throws a glim of hope. We dart through the trees and arrive at the base of the hill, taking shelter beneath a rock in hopes to prevent the rain from whipping us.

"God has provided us a stone bench with a roof made of rock," Nick titters as he helps me climb on it—it's almost a foot taller than what a normal wooden bench would be.

I realise I'm sitting so close to Nick, his back nearly pressed against my chest. My conscience fights me against the need to get some warmth. He is also shivering from the cold. But at least we can spend an hour or two here until the storm calms down. Right?

When something crawls beneath my dangling feet, my gaze goes down. Rainwater is flowing beneath us.

"Looks like the place has become a temporary stream," Nick says. "It should clear the moment the rain stops."

Only the rain continues to lash at everything around us.

"Nick, see, the water level is rising."

Until now, our ankles were inside the water. But the speed at which the water level is rising—soon it will touch our knees.

Nick snakes his neck out and scans around. "Amelia," he says, fear sprouting through his voice, "seems like we are sitting on a riverbed."

A narrow and dry river has sprung into life because of the heavy rain. The Andaman Sea is not far away. The current is growing at a rapid pace and dragging our feet. If the water comes to our buttocks, it might yank us away and into the sea.

"We must go to higher grounds, Amelia. Now. Right away."

"How? The water beneath this rock might go above our waist, and the current is strong." I grab his waist tighter against me, as if he is a solid rock fighting against the strong current.

"Another step higher on this hill." Nick gets up and climbs on a stone.

"Where do we go?"

"With me. Higher on this hill."

We have to, if we want to see Ross Island again. After climbing a few more steps, we find another spot, a higher one. The place we were sitting is now underwater. It could have taken us away already, if not for Nick's foresight.

We squeeze through a small stone. I am almost sitting on Nick's lap. His hot breath touches my head, tearing through the coldness.

I lift my head and gaze at him. His smiling face warms me up. "We will survive, Amelia. Here. This place is better. More secure."

A giggle escapes my mouth. "We will, Nick. Because you are with me."

A man protecting his female friend!

Realising I have kept his waist inside my arms, I loosen them. But another gale force wind shakes me, and I grab his neck, bringing my face closer to his. His curly chest hairs tease me through his wet, white, now semi-transparent shirt. A vibration passes through my cold skin, warming it up.

Another thunder growls after a sudden and massive lightning. I cling tighter against Nick. *Does he mind my behaviour? Does he feel guilty that his dead wife might be watching from above?*

I steal a glance at his face through the rain. His gaze is roaming over me—my shoulders and chest. Oh, my! I am wearing a summer top and skirt, as it was warm this morning. The thin fabric is clinging to my breasts, and my nipples are poking through it without shame. Is he crazy? No. Didn't I just admire his shirt a minute ago?

I bend forward a little, grab his face, and plant a kiss on his cheek. Nick responds, bringing his lips to mine. And soon we both are in a lip lock. More lightning and another loud thunder. Nick wraps one of his arms around my waist. His fingers crawl inside my top, fiddling with my bubbies. "Love you, Amelia," he moans inside my lips.

"Love you, too." My fingers explore his hairy chest, unbuttoning his shirt. When I feel something warm swelling beneath my buttocks, I realise I am sitting on his lap with his love handle warming up. He removes my top over my head and deposits it behind him, secure against the rock wall. My bubbies are now in the open as he caresses them.

I move from his lap and unbutton his pants. Within seconds, his love handle springs up, poking fun at me. Another giggle comes out of me as he lifts my skirt.

"Still time for the rain to stop, please come above."

Before I understand what he meant by 'come above,' he lifts me on his lap and guides his hard member inside me. The pleasure is too much to say no. Still mustering courage, I say, "Nick, don't make me pregnant. Please."

"Don't worry. Vanaja has remedies. Drink her herbal water tomorrow. You will be all right."

Vanaja's herbs are my safety drug. I again lock his lips with mine as we two humans become one for the next few moments.

Almost an hour later, the boat starts for Ross Island. Dark clouds are clearing away, and dusk is creeping in. The helmsman's stealing glances unnerve me. I shift my torso and put my right shoulder toward him, Nick sitting to my left.

"Doctor sahib," the helmsman says, "your chest is bleeding."

I gaze at Nick's torn shirt, which is exposing his chest. A shock wave passes through me. They are my nail marks. Was I so crazy in love that I couldn't control myself? We exchange a few quick glances, a mild smile brightening his lips.

I clear my throat. "That twig..."

"Twig?"

"No, the tree branch that fell in front of us. It had some thorns." Did I say it with conviction?

I glance at the sailor and find his face has split into a smile.

Shame washes over me as I sit with guilt written all over my body. I fervently glance at the sky. Why are there still some sunrays? When would the darkness of the evening protect me from my humiliation?

I cast a sideways glance at Nick. He is sitting in a relaxed pose as if nothing has happened.

When the man anchors the boat after arriving at Ross, I jump out without replying to his "Goodnight" and pretend to be in a hurry for home. I ride on Nick's horse, clasping him from the back. It's Sunday evening, so we don't see anyone on the road.

"Aunt Amelia, Shanti is cooking curry for us tonight. Yeah," Luke lopes toward me even before I step down from the saddle.

The aroma of chicken curry hangs in the air, and my stomach craves the food. Shanti comes out of the kitchen holding a spatula. "Memsahib, fresh up. Serve dinner."

"Thanks, Shanti," I respond and vanish into the bedroom to change into my night clothing.

When I come out, Nick and Luke are waiting for me at the dining table. Shanti is serving rice and curry. I sit on the chair next to Luke.

"Tytler has said he will relieve me when another doctor arrives," Nick says over dinner. "Will you also go back?"

"Yes, forever. I came on my own and don't need anyone to relieve me." I feel a confident smile beaming from my lips. "Will you stay in Calcutta?"

"Maybe. And you?"

"Sultanpur. I have an island mansion in the Gomti River."

"Island mansion?" Nick drops his fork.

Luke stops eating and is staring at me.

"Yes, I bought from a businessperson very cheap when the rebellion finished in 1857. It's connected to Gomti's banks by a small bridge. A namesake island, but exquisite."

"Lovely." Nick smiles.

"Why don't you request a transfer to Sultanpur? You will love the place. And I have more than a dozen rooms you can stay in, if you'd like."

Luke's eyes widen. "Dad, we'll go to Sultanpur. Dad, please."

"Did your husband buy that when he was alive?" Nick asks, narrowing his eyes.

I swallow. "No. He paid me a penalty for hitting me, and I used that money to buy the place."

Nick stares at me, his eyebrows shooting up. "Penalty?"

"In fact, I used his estate. He died. Long story, Nick. Another time."

CHAPTER THIRTY-THREE

SEHNAZ, 10 MARCH 1863, EARLY MORNING 3 AM, COCO ISLAND

Tension was reflecting on Sheru's oily skin, dazzling in the moonlight. Seated near him in the boat, with Alfred and Agatha in her peripheral, Sehnaz watched his muscles jumping with the movement of the paddle. They were embarking on the first phase of their journey—taking this paddle boat from Coco to a much more inconspicuous one—Table Island, which was almost three miles north of Coco. Alfred didn't want to wake Coco's sleeping residents at the beginning of their adventure to Jambu Island, which Sheru and Sehnaz had whole-heartedly agreed. Too many prying eyes on Coco Island. So the ship Alfred had arranged would wait for them at Table Island to take them away before anyone could wake up and notice.

Sheru's heavy breathing disturbed Sehnaz. "Are you tired, Sheru?" she whispered.

Alfred had warned not to talk in a loud voice, as the ferry was sailing along the coast and houses were not far away. They were also careful to make sure nobody would see them. Not even a lantern was illuminating the craft.

Sheru cast a glance around. "I don't understand. Why is he asking to go this way? We are headed east."

"What's wrong?" Sehnaz muttered back.

"The jetty is not this way. A ship can't anchor anywhere. We should be headed north. Sounds fishy."

"Fishy?"

"What else could it be?" He tossed his head toward Agatha. "Didn't you say his wife wanted to go back to Rangoon? Why she is with us?"

Sehnaz looked at Alfred who was sitting toward the stern of the vessel. Agatha was dozing, sitting near him.

"They're a couple, they might have compromised. He is staring at us, Sheru. Didn't he say we shouldn't wake up residents?"

Sheru grumbled unintelligibly but fell quiet. After paddling for almost a half hour, they arrived at a small bay hidden behind large trees on the Coco Island side.

"Never seen this before. This still looks like Coco Island." Sehnaz followed Sheru's gaze. A tiny hut was waiting for them inside the large trees, and an anchored steamboat in the bay.

Sheru and Alfred transferred the metal trunks to the steamboat.

"Why didn't the ship come here?" Agatha asked.

"It is waiting near another island, only two miles away. They would've charged me more money to come here." Impatience sounded in Alfred's voice.

Sheru's eyes lit up, and Sehnaz realised he just came to the same conclusion she did—Alfred had made their initial voyage more detailed than simply a straight shot to Table Island, all to confuse anyone who may see them. Sending them on a *wild goose chase*, as Amelia would've said.

Sehnaz and Sheru gave each other relieved, knowing smiles. But then Sheru's eyes slipped briefly toward Agatha, and Sehnaz's followed. While one mystery was solved, they still didn't know why Agatha was accompanying them—nor why she kept casting furtive glances at them. What was she doing? Did Agatha know of their plans?

Sehnaz planned not to discuss anything with Agatha before knowing if she was aware of the mission. But Agatha hadn't come to the south of Coco in the past six weeks, so Sehnaz couldn't talk to her. So while Agatha's presence on this journey was a surprise, she may have simply made up with her husband for greed of the treasure. Who on the earth doesn't love money?

"Sail north along the coast and then turn left until we arrive at the northern tip of Coco. From there, you will notice another island. Just two miles away," Alfred said in a low voice once they had successfully boarded the waiting steamboat.

Sheru nodded confidently, and within an hour, they reached the other island.

"This is Table Island. And nobody lives here," Sheru said.

"Why didn't you tell me before? I could have set up a kingdom here." Sehnaz chuckled.

The ship was waiting there. Confidence bloomed in Sehnaz. So far, her plans seemed to be working. She wondered if she could also buy a ship like this once the treasures had fallen into her hand.

The sun was just rising in the Bay of Bengal. Only four other sailors were on the ship. Alfred shook hands with each of them and said, "Meet Princess Sez."

"Princess?" Agatha's eyes brightened. "You never told me you are a princess!"

Sehnaz didn't know how to tackle this confusion. Agatha's eyes lasered into her.

"What princess? The British have already taken over my father's kingdom. He is no longer a king. That means I am no longer a princess. I am an ordinary woman now."

Was this enough to convince Agatha? She was now sure Alfred had never spoken to his wife about Sehnaz; however, it did explain why Agatha kept giving them funny looks. But more importantly, she still didn't know why they were going together. Would she ever find a secluded place? She needed to ask Alfred what he had said to his wife.

The steamship was, in fact, a large ferry. Sehnaz saw there were only two cabins. Before she realised it, Agatha and Alfred had already occupied one toward the stern. The other cabin was near the deck. She asked Sheru to put her belongings inside.

Sheru returned from the cuddy door. "But these men are occupying it."

Shock washed over Sehnaz. She stumped to the cuddy and peeked in its door. The man sitting inside gazed at her.

"The ship has only two cabins?" she asked.

"Correct," the man said without raising his head. "And this is our ship."

"And you expect a woman—a *princess* to sleep on the deck. Perfect. Do you guys have any sense?"

Another man standing on the deck trudged toward them. "We are sorry, ma'am. We can't give you a room."

Indignity slammed Sehnaz. Her image in the eyes of Alfred was that of a princess. The moment her true identity exposed itself, the mistrust would destroy her partnership with Alfred. She must establish her identity to avoid casualty in mid-ocean. "That's all right. Move the ship back. Now. I will go back to Coco. You guys go on your own."

The man who standing on the deck hinted for the other to come out. They walked away and talked among themselves in a low tone. Sehnaz prayed they didn't call her bluff.

Soon, the man came back. "Alfred had said he wanted a ship with at least two cabins. And we got this one that has only two rooms."

"Right. He said two cabins for us. One for Alfred and his wife and the other for me and my husband. Not for you. You take your belongings outside and sleep in the corridor."

The men sulked at first but then took their belongings and vacated the cuddy.

Sehnaz nodded satisfactorily, her arms crossed. "Don't worry. I will pay you more once we arrive at our destination."

That was their first night of the new and dangerous venture. Several questions swirled in Sehnaz's mind as she sat idly in her cuddy. They had almost nothing other than the knowledge of where Morticia had hidden the treasure. That was the only hope for freedom —to lead another life away from the suspicious gaze of the British. She knew she couldn't go back to either Sultanpur or Lucknow. Would Rangoon be a better choice?

Sheru shut the door and climbed on the bed. "You told them you will pay when you arrive at the destination. Will you pay them in gold coins? Do they understand where we are going and why?"

Sehnaz flipped a hand. "Those men don't own the ship. Didn't you notice that they all look like bandits? These people rent ships for their dirty missions in the high sea."

"And now we have become a part of that." Sheru's voice sounded tense and grief.

"Listen, Sheru." Sehnaz got up from the bed and sat. "I would rather die trying to escape, but I can't spend my life inside the Coco Islands."

Sheru put his finger on her lips. "People are outside. They will hear us."

Sehnaz focussed her ears. "We are talking in Hindi," she whispered, "so don't worry."

She opened the cabin's door and stepped outside. Two of the four men were near the rudder. Agatha was standing there, holding a siderail.

She came near Agatha. "Not getting sleep, ma'am?"

"You also haven't slept?" Agatha swung around and asked.

"First night on the ship, even though the water is calm."

"Sez—" Agatha paused— "how do I address you? Your highness?"

"Just Sez. As I said, I'm no longer a princess. You can continue calling me Sanju or Sez, whichever you like. We are friends."

An awkward pause stood between them for a few moments.

"Where is your cat?"

A pain began inside Sehnaz's ribs. "Jhumru? A tribal boy owned her before she came to me. He asked me if he could keep the cat. I couldn't say no." Sehnaz's heart sank. Not only Jhumru, but she also had left Bilu behind, her only tribal friend.

Something was troubling Agatha. Sehnaz could feel the heat but didn't know what it was. Had she not compromised with Alfred? Did Alfred threaten her to agree to his terms, the way Colin had done with Amelia?

"I hope you haven't told Alfred about my plans," Agatha muttered, her eyes pooling.

"Alfred? No. Never."

"That's good to know. As soon as I arrive at Rangoon, I will leave this man." She paused. Sehnaz could hear a heart beating against ribs, but not her heart. That was why Agatha had joined them—she was fulfilling her plans to leave her husband. But they were going to Rangoon, not Jambu.

"This man," Agatha said again, "he is a criminal. He has a relationship with pirates. The men on this ship must be thugs, and they must have some sinister plans. Be careful, Sez."

Bitterness filled Sehnaz's mouth. Was Alfred playing games with her? Did she make a bad decision in planning to find treasure in Jambu with him?

"Goodnight, Agatha ma'am." She trudged back to her cabin before Agatha could wish her goodnight.

"The ship is going to Rangoon," she said after closing cabin door. "I don't know what the plans of this man are."

Still seated on the bed Sheru said, "It might have been a last-minute decision, as his wife knew he was planning to sail. And he had to tell her lies."

Sehnaz opened her bag and unfolded the map.

Sheru lit up the lantern. "What do you want to check, Sehnaz?"

"Just checking. See, Jambu is here. And Burma? Far away. Right?"

Sheru bent over the map. "Right."

"First, we will go to Rangoon. May be one week less than the time to Jambu. And then?"

"I understand." Sheru sat up straight. "This is, in fact, a ferry. Dangerous to sail longer in deep sea if the weather turns violent. It's possible that, after arriving at Rangoon, he has plans to sail along the coast."

"Coast?"

"Yes, look here." Sheru placed his finger beneath Rangoon on the map. "From Rangoon, we will come along the coast here. This is Assam. And from here, all the way to Sagar Island. Jambu is only miles away. No danger if we're caught in a storm. The ship can take shelter anytime on the coast."

She flicked a glance at him. "Sheru, you said you were in Rangoon, correct?"

"Yes. How else did I learn Burmese?"

"I have an idea, Sheru." She peeked out the door to make sure no one was eavesdropping, then turned back and stepped closer to Sheru. "I think Alfred will first take the ship to Rangoon." She could feel Sheru's hot breath on her mouth. "And we both will escape."

"Escape?" Sheru's eyes widened.

"I mean... I mean, just run away. And hide. Away from the port. And pretend to work as daily labourers."

"You mean I will carry out as a daily labourer."

She let out a giggle. "Yes. I am your wife. Pretending, like we are doing now. And we should think of alternative names, both of us. Then we come to Bengal by road. Maybe to Calcutta. From there we buy a boat and sail to Sagar Island."

"Sagar Island?"

They both looked at the map again.

"We will sail along the coastline of Sagar to check if any ships are anchoring near Jambu. If not, we are free. Find the treasure and we are all set."

Sheru thought for a while. "And what if the police get me in Calcutta? The British will send me to Andaman prison."

Sehnaz snickered. "You are not so famous like Rupen that your photo will be there. Didn't I tell you Rave must have reported that you died on the way, and he had to throw your body into the sea? Would he ever admit the security failed and a convict ran away?"

Sheru pulled Sehnaz onto his lap and started kissing her. "You are so intelligent, Sehnaz."

Sehnaz placed a mild slap on his cheeks. "Again! Again, you touched a woman who is not your wife. Please write this on paper, or else you will forget how many times you need to do penance."

Sheru laughed.

A noise flew into their cabin—a man and a woman fighting. The only other woman on the ship was Agatha. Was she shouting at Alfred?

"Sheru, this is not English."

"And not even Burmese, either."

"Then what is their language? Are they both not English?"

CHAPTER THIRTY-FOUR

AMELIA, 15 MARCH 1863, SUNDAY MORNING, NICK'S HOUSE ON ROSS ISLAND (PART OF ANDAMAN ISLANDS GROUP)

Storm, flash flood, and me sitting on Nick's lap. These three events have occupied my conscience. Embarrassment stopped me from accompanying Nick last Sunday to North Bay Island, but we plan to go there again this Sunday.

My own bare body winks at me when I stand in front of the mirror in the bathroom. Did that Indian sailor see me naked? Why didn't I think twice before making love with Nick? Shouldn't we have waited and done it inside a closed room instead?

Shanti has left a half bucket of hot water for me in the bathroom. I can stay in Nick's house until we all leave Andaman. Forever. It's possible he might propose to me before that. Goosebumps chase down my spine. Taking water in a jug, I pour it on me and watch how it flows down my neck, then breasts, and then to my belly. A drop of water is still hanging on my nipple, and I bend my head to check when it will fall.

Nick is so understanding. He realised why I didn't accompany him to North Bay. This time, he could get another sailor for the boat.

Still, I'm not comfortable going with him to that island. Am I already the main character of a juicy story circulating among the Indian guards in Andaman? Has the Indian sailor already spread among his friends that he found me and Nick making love sitting on a rock? They can't bring their families and are craving for women's love. And here, a doctor—he is getting a woman within months of his wife's death. Benefits of being white!

Luke's angry voice smashes into my daydream. I stop pouring warm water on me and stand still in the bathroom. My ears perk up.

"You don't love my mother," Luke screams, "you never did."

"Calm down, my boy. Tell me why you are angry?"

"No. You never stay with me on Sundays. Not even when Mum was alive."

"Try to understand, Luke. I am the only doctor volunteering to go to the North Bay Island. Who else will take care of those men and women on that island? There are children there, too. Like you."

"Why didn't you take me before when Mum was alive? You are always going with that woman."

"Quiet, Luke. She is here and will mind."

"Let her mind. I love my Mum."

It's not just a child's tantrum. Truth has come from Luke's mouth. But I'm confused. I was sure Luke liked me. Is it me or his anger on his father and I am a casualty?

I wipe myself with a dry towel, slip into my dress, and exit the bathroom. Nick and Luke both are standing face to face in the living room, Shanti watching in silence. My feet freeze. Should I bend and scoop Luke onto my lap?

Before I can do anything, Luke notices me and stomps inside his room, growling.

"I don't wish to see anybody. Nobody," he yells before breaking down into sobbing.

Nick gazes at me, trying to hide his guilt. "We'll be late Amelia. Let's go."

I try to stay calm. "No. We are going there almost every Sunday. And I'm sure after you leave for Calcutta no other doctor will go there. But you should also give some time to your boy. He is alone."

"But, Amelia..."

"No *ifs, ands, or buts,* Nick. He needs you. You can't ignore your own blood. Do you want to lose your only child?"

Nick hands the medicine box to Shanti, who until now has been a mute witness.

"Sahib, baba not happy," Shanti says of Luke. "Stay him. With. Sahib."

"See, Shanti also agrees with me." I force a smile.

"All right then." Nick brings a grin to his face. "We will go to the market. And also have lunch outside."

He walks into the bedroom to cajole Luke. I walk to the front garden, because father and son should get some privacy. He is definitely a good man. But after Eliza's death, he grieved by burying himself in his work. But he must learn how to balance his tremendous work pressure with fatherhood, because Luke is grieving, too. And I must accept we have yet to formalise our relationship and am not sure of our future together.

Within minutes, a beaming Luke walks out with his father, a bright smile unfurling on his lips. I yearn to capture the moment in a camera. But where do I find one?

"I asked Shanti not to cook for us," Nick says, "we three will eat outside."

"Three?" I glance at Luke, who is holding his father's hand. His smile has vanished. Another spurt of disappointment gushes through me. Who am I to spoil his day?

"No, Nick. Just remembered there are some tasks to finish. I must stay home to set the question paper for tomorrow's examination in the school," I lie.

Nick's face falls. My heart sinks, too. Not for missing the lunch in a restaurant, but for suddenly losing Luke's trust. I may not become his stepmother, but he is the first child to whom I have ever given my affection.

"Let's go, Dad." Luke drags his father by the fingers.

"You are delaying, Nick. And Luke, have a wonderful time. Bye. See you."

"Bye." Luke throws the word without looking at me.

Father and son leave, and I step back into the house. Shanti's curious gaze unsettles me.

"Baba angry. No worry. He happy on you, again."

Has Shanti also noticed I've become closer to Nick these days? He has never come inside my bedroom, even after that stormy day when we slept together on the hill.

Depression claws down my throat. I slap on a grin and walk past Shanti. Time for me to hide inside the room.

I open my diary and start writing. Since when have I not entered my life's events there? Should I also write how I slept with Nick? No. Don't I imagine one day my diary will serve as evidence of India's history? How would the culture-conscious people of this country judge me if they knew this woman could sleep with a man who hasn't even proposed to her?

Tears roll down my cheeks. Why am I even thinking I could lead a life with Nick? Why would he marry me, when after that first incident he has never even said *I love you* to me?

That was a weak moment for both of us. I made a mistake in offering my body to him. After all, he is a man. It's only me who had to boil Vanaja's herb and drink its water to avoid pregnancy. What will happen to me if that herb doesn't work?

I am here to take care of Luke, and I shouldn't have crossed that boundary. Have I lost Luke's trust forever?

I will never marry Nick, even if he asks. Not unless Luke accepts me as his mother.

Memories of Sultanpur knock into my mind. I must go back as soon as possible. But how do I live without Sehnaz, my best friend?

My conscience still cannot accept Sehnaz is dead. The whole idea of coming to Andaman was to free Rupen, and now even Rupen is dead. I have overestimated my determination. I have gone far away from the reality that two women could never fight against the mightiest power of the world.

Has the time come to make a decision?

"Memsahib, tea." Shanti flashes a smile at me.

"Tea?"

"Memsahib, you worry. Tea. Mood good."

A chuckle escapes from my mouth. "You are so understanding, Shanti. You brought the tea at the right time. Did you make one for you, also?"

"Yes, memsahib."

I settle down on a chair, and Shanti sits near me, holding her teacup.

"Your parents?"

I gaze at Shanti. Why is she asking about my parents?

"They are in England. I haven't seen them since I came to India in 1856."

"Memsahib, go and see, parents. They like. Blessings."

Indian culture values blessings of seniors, especially parents. Shanti is right. I should go to England first and see them.

"You reminded me at the perfect time, Shanti. But I will come back. Now India is my country, and I will spend the rest of my life in

Sultanpur. Maybe I will open a girls-only school. People who don't want their daughters to mingle with boys will send them to my school. And that will be the first girls' school in India's history."

Shanti smiles and nods at me.

I look at my diary. A wave of peace engulfs me. Why do I need others to make me happy? Didn't I once daydream to be an empowered woman and enable others, too? Isn't this God's wish to keep me unmarried so that I can devote my full time to girls' education in India? Even though I used teachership as an excuse to come to Andaman Islands, I've always been sincere while teaching at school here. Rupen's rescue plan didn't interfere when I decided to teach the islanders.

A knock on the door brings me out from my reverie. Nick can't be back so soon from the market. Who then has come?

I lope to the main door of the house before Shanti reacts. Morticia smiles at me, and she has Sadhna with her. I startle—how did the slave girl come out? That too, not naked—she is wearing the dress I had bought for her! Hadn't Morticia warned her never to cross the confines of her house?

"I am here to hand over Sadhna to you," Morticia says, "and look, she is wearing clothes. Didn't you always say she shouldn't remain naked?"

Sadhna's beautiful smile cools down my nerves. This is like her day of freedom from slavery. Am I daydreaming now?

Morticia continues. "I don't need her, as I have Vanaja. And I am also going to Port Blair. Rave has no news. He has spent too many days there. And I also want to see how the construction of the new prison and township is going."

Morticia will never be worried for Rave's whereabouts unless it is for her own interest. And I'm also no more interested in the jail construction in Port Blair as Rupen's rescue is no more a goal for me. But I'm thankful to her for giving freedom to Sadhna.

"I always knew you were a goodhearted person, Mort. Thank you. Will you like to have a cup of tea here?"

"No Amelia, I'm truly in a hurry. Bye." And she leaves.

I turn to Sadhna, and we burst into laughter and embrace.

That afternoon, the soft beating of the horse's hooves alerts me. Father and son have arrived back from the market. I stand near the main entrance with lots of apprehension when a cheerful Luke returns with Nick.

"How was your day, Luke?" I manage a grin.

"Yeh," Luke replies with a million-pound smile. I long to bend over him and scoop him into my lap, but an unknown fear stops me. Now I am a *nobody* for this family.

"Now, this is my turn to run to the market," I announce and walk toward the gate.

"What for? You could have told me, and I would've brought it for you." Nick looks at me with surprised eyes.

"Something I should find myself." I plaster a sneer on my face.

Confusion blurs across Nick's features, and he stares at me. Suddenly, the surrounding air becomes thick.

"I'm looking for a house of my own. You know I came to your place only for a few days, and the other one belongs to Morticia." I try to lighten the atmosphere as rain begins pattering.

Nick stands in front of me with the most compassionate looks in his eyes. "Getting another accommodation is not only difficult on Ross Island, but impossible. You know everything will move over to Port Blair. And you aren't planning to stay here much longer, so why look for a house?"

Nick is right. But I want to stay outside this house, and I also don't wish to move back with Morticia.

"Memsahib, I clean outhouse. You live. I, veranda." Shanti is a matured woman. She understands my thoughts even if I have never discussed them with her.

"Why, Shanti? Isn't the room big enough to accommodate three of us?"

"Three?" Nick's eyes widened.

Before I can say anything, Sadhna comes out of my room.

"She is here?" Nick fumbles. "And Morticia allowed that?"

"She has Vanaja. She is happy with her and allowed me to keep this girl. And we three will sleep in the outhouse, with Shanti," I announce, as if I have some sort of authority.

"Memsahib..." Concern glints in Shanti's eyes. "I maid. You, memsahib."

"You are also daughter of a brahmin," I protest, "and brahmins don't touch food when a Christian woman cooks it."

Shanti laughs.

"Morticia is clever," Nick says. "What explanation will you give in Calcutta for having a slave girl?"

"Slave? Who is a slave? We rescued her from the pirates."

He smiles. "We will talk about your accommodation, Amelia."

"Sure." But I have already decided.

CHAPTER THIRTY-FIVE

RUPEN, 17 MARCH 1863, AFTERNOON, RUTLAND ISLAND (PART OF ANDAMAN ISLANDS GROUP)

Something was wrong with Rave—Rupen's guts warned him.

"Is everything all right with you, Mr. Hunt?" Rupen asked as he and Rave walked inside his hutment on the hillock of Rutland Island. His two wives welcomed Rave in a *namaste* pose. "Please sit here." Rupen showed him one of the two wooden chairs and asked his wives to go to the next room.

"Mr. Naik, you should be happy that I was able to organise a ship and have your men prepare for the last journey out of Andaman." Rave flashed a warm smile.

Even though Rupen tried to reciprocate with another smile, he couldn't. "Last time you said it might take another week to arrange a ship. And now a ship is available? Should we just hire anyone before checking them out first? Mr. Hunt, you seem like you're in a hurry."

Rave gave a measuring glance. "I was in Port Blair and got information that Morticia is coming. I had told her I am making another business deal with a contractor to build houses in Port Blair. And soon she will find they are all lies."

"So?"

Rave throws his hands up. "So what? She will know I am planning something different than what I told her. All our plans will bust. We must go to Jambu before she arrives in Port Blair."

Rupen didn't find Rave's explanation convincing. "I am asking again. Take her along with us. In your ship. And my people will finish her in Jambu."

"But..."

"Okay, okay, got it. People in Jambu respect her like a queen and they will outnumber us. I understand. What about mid-ocean? Finish her before arriving in Jambu and throw her into the sea?"

A *you-don't-understand-women* look flashed in Rave's eyes. "She will smell fish when she sees you and the Indian soldiers. News has spread in Ross that you are dead. And now when she finds you boarding the ship, your life, your freedom, and everything will end. She has already developed a friendship with the new administrator, Tytler. Walker helped us only this much. He is an average person now, like any other person in Andaman."

Urgency prickled at Rupen. It was a blunder to underestimate Morticia. He had never thought of staying long in Rutland. He had even told his father-in-law that he was planning to go to India with his daughters. And he must ask his soldiers to remain prepared.

"Is Dr. Walker coming with us?"

"I've sent him a message and asked him to wait at a point in Port Blair. Our ship will anchor in the sea, and I will send a boat to fetch him. He has already given his resignation from the job, so no one will ask why he left without informing."

Rupen's wives entered to serve fruits to Rave. "Mr. Hunt, you need some rest. Please stay here. I will ask my soldiers to plan for the journey." He stomped out and cast an eye to the ship Rave had hired and anchored in the Portman Bay. Shyam and other soldiers were already there and waiting for him.

"Time to go back, Sir?" A massive smile widened Shyam's eyes.

"This is the *freedom vessel*, Sir," another soldier commented, also with a broad grin on his face. "Sir, I think the crew is all Thai. Is that all right?"

Rupen nodded. He didn't know if this ship would give them freedom from the prison, or freedom from life itself. The soldiers trusted him so much that he didn't wish to dampen their mood.

"I have no authority to choose which ships he should use," Rupen muttered to himself. "I also can't hide any longer in Rutland. It's a matter of time until the British find our hideout and throw us back into prison."

Shyam, who was standing close to him, whispered, "Sir, these people have so much hope in your leadership."

Rupen swung toward his army of ten soldiers. "Friends, if we need to opt between prison and death, what do you choose?"

"Death," replied the chorus.

"Happy to learn that. This evening will be our last evening in Andaman. Either we will enjoy freedom or die fighting. Remember what Lord Krishna has said in the holy Geeta. *Those who embrace death while fighting against the injustice, go to the heaven.* So your next destination will be heaven or mainland India. Never the prison of the Ross Island."

Morticia, 17 March 1863, Morning until Evening, Port Blair (Part of Andaman Islands Group)

Morticia could smell something in the air. She had always relied on her own gut feelings. Her fears were perhaps right.

This might be a decisive stage of her life...

Including doom.

"You are doomed, Morticia. Trust nobody." She didn't waste time on Ross Island and rushed to Port Blair, where Rave had said he would be partnering with a construction business.

Morticia cursed her own brain. Why did she believe what Rave said?

"If we take out the treasures from Jambu and live like wealthy people, people will suspect us," Rave had said. "We should invest in another business and show we are earning a handsome profit."

What a brilliant idea! Was it to dupe the public, or your own wife?

Yes, Rave was right that they both had created enough enemies while undertaking the piracy activities in the ocean. And what would happen to them if the owner of the ship removed Rave from his job?

"Rave, you have never appreciated how much my brain has saved your job." Morticia felt as if Rave were arguing with her. "Whose idea was it to part with a portion of our plunder and give it to the ship's owner as extra profit?"

Ross Island to Port Blair, hardly six miles, but Morticia felt the boat was taking ages to arrive.

As the boat moved ahead in the Andaman Sea toward Port Blair, a new thought clicked in Morticia's brain. She had made a mistake in not following up with Rave. How much money had he invested? What about the profits?

Just her luck, she didn't find Rave's whereabouts upon arriving in Port Blair. She even met the engineers who were supervising the construction of the massive prison building. They didn't even know who Rave was. Was he going to other islands of Andaman and working on something outside her knowledge?

Andaman was comprised of over five hundred islands, and if she spent just a day and a half on each, she would take two years—and even after that, she still might not find Rave.

But she understood that Dr. Walker was living in Port Blair after handing over charge to Tytler, and now he had been spending most of his free time collecting shells in Andaman. Did he know anything about Rave?

The daylight blurred into evening as she went to meet Walker. The man who had always welcomed her wore a surprised look when she arrived at his place. 'Surprised' might be the wrong word; rather, he looked disturbed. He made the eye contact with Mrs. Walker and then looked away slowly, and that didn't go unnoticed by Morticia.

Something was going on. Three big boxes were sitting in his front room.

"Are you going somewhere, Dr. Walker?" she asked.

"Me? No. No, not now," Walker replied.

"And these boxes?"

Mrs. Walker had just returned to the front room. "These boxes, yes, we will spend some time in the beachfront cottage."

Dr. Walker wiped his hands on his pants and nodded eagerly. "In fact, we are going there now. Not with these boxes, though. They are for our next and final trip to Calcutta. And from there to London. And sorry, we are in a hurry. We should have been there before darkness. Anything I can help you with, Mrs. Hunt?"

Dr. Walker had always addressed her as Morticia, never as Mrs. Hunt. What was wrong with him?

She narrowed her eyes at him. "I just came here to ask where Rave is living."

He blinked rapidly. "I, I, no idea."

"That's all right. I will ask somebody else. He must be busy in his construction business."

"Construction? Rave?"

"Yes. He told me about partnering with some construction contractor."

Mrs. Walker elbowed Dr. Walker, but Morticia watched that through a sideways glance.

"Oh, yes. Yes. I forgot," Walker said.

Two Indian men came and carried those boxes outside.

"I won't waste your time, Dr. Walker. I hope before you go back to Calcutta, Rave and I both can meet you again. If not, we will see you in Calcutta. Goodnight."

"Goodnight, Morticia." Walker released a breath when Morticia left.

Coming out from his house, she saw those two men were loading the large boxes into a horse cart. Didn't Mrs. Walker say they were going to the beachfront cottage for a few days? And didn't Mr. Walker confirm these boxes are for moving back to Calcutta?

"Good evening, memsahib." Both the men greeted her one after another as she was about to get into her own cart. A known face among the men triggered a plan.

Morticia swung back. "Gopal, can I talk to you?"

Gopal ran to her. "Yes, memsahib."

"How is your family in Calcutta, Gopal? Any news?"

"Last letter I had received a fortnight ago, memsahib. My father was not well."

"Oh, that is sad, Gopal. You come to my place tomorrow, and I will note down where they live. When I go back to Calcutta, I will send some money to your family there. All right?"

She noticed Gopal's eyes brightening even in the evening's darkness.

"When are you going back to Calcutta, memsahib?"

"In about a week's time. And can you do me a favour?"

"Favour?" He tilted his head. "Memsahib, I am just a poor worker. A servant."

"Don't worry. I will pay you even more money." She whispered to him, "Tomorrow morning, come to me and tell me what Dr. Walker is going to do after arriving in that *beachfront cottage*."

"Yes, memsahib. I will."

"And yes, do not tell him what I asked you." She took some money out of her bag. "Here are your tips."

Gopal's eyes glinted as he took the money from her. "You can rely on me, memsahib."

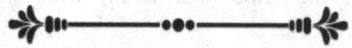

Rupen Naik, 17 March 1863, Evening, Andaman Sea

Evening provided the much-needed cover to the ship Rupen and Rave were sailing in the Andaman Sea. The boat carrying Dr. Walker arrived, and Walker climbed the rope ladder with his wife. Rupen's men carried three large boxes from the boat.

Walker extended his hand to him with an enormous smile on his face. "I have brought exclusive toys for your boys, Mr. Naik."

"Toys?" Rupen asked.

"Yes. In those boxes." He opened one box and handed a gun to Rupen.

A thrill chased up Rupen's arms. It was over five years since he had touched such a gun.

"Thanks, Dr. Walker. I hope no one has seen you coming here."

"A servant." A confident smile unfurled on Walker's mouth. "He brought me in a horse cart. I said I am going to another island in the boat and will come back in a week. I had built a small house there as a holiday accommodation, so that no one doubts when I visit the place."

"So clever of you, Dr. Walker. I must appreciate your foresight." Rupen understood how cunning Walker was. Didn't he also plan the uprising so that Rupen could escape with his men? And he was the one who made the deal between him and Rave.

"Now we are all set!" A laugh came out of Rupen's throat.

"But there is a minor hindrance." Walker turned to Rave. "Just before I left for here, Morticia met me. What business have you told her you are doing here?"

"Partnership with a builder."

"I didn't know. But she asked me, and I had to give some vague answer. Sorry, Mr. Hunt."

Rupen noticed a dark cloud covering Rave's features.

"That means tonight or tomorrow she will find out I had lied to her. And tomorrow she might come to meet you again. And soon will understand we all have fled."

"That's all right, Mr. Hunt." Dr. Walker flashed an assuring smile. "What can she do? She can't take your ship and sail alone to Jambu. Can she?"

Rave burst into a laughter. "Dr. Walker, you have met her so many times but still miscalculate her capability. We have sailors, and all they need is instruction to start. Believe me, she is the queen of Jambu Island, and fighting with her there is the same as fighting with a shark in the water."

Rupen had to intervene. "This tense discussion has no meaning to us, Mr. Hunt. Whatever she can do, she will. Now no one can stop her. So, please retire to your cabins. We have ample time to plan."

"Are you not worried about your life?" Rave squinted his eyes.

"I am afraid of the jail. But if I have to die fighting someone, that is more than welcome. In fact, if you don't know, when the British caught me in Lucknow, I had begged for death punishment, instead of life in prison." He plodded to his cabin. He must finish his evening prayer before dinner.

His wives were waiting for him. Rupen sat cross-legged on a mat.

"Om Namah Shivay," he chanted the prayer.

But his mind refused to focus. After over five years, he was on his way to freedom again. But anything could still come between him and freedom. All he had was ten dedicated soldiers. If Morticia alerted the English, he could soon face hundreds of British soldiers in Jambu or even before arriving there. In the middle of the ocean. But he was determined this time. He wouldn't allow the enemy to capture him alive.

Rupen folded his hands and thanked both Goddess Kali and Lord Shiva for the achievements so far.

Both tribal girls sat on his sides in prayer position as they had learnt from him.

"Om Namah Shivay," Rupen chanted again.

Halfway through the prayer, a knock sounded on the door. A current of dissatisfaction passed through his nerves. Rupen hated any disturbance during his ritual.

Another knock.

"Who is that?" He opened his eyes and went to the door, holding the gun he had just received from Dr. Walker.

One of his boys was standing at the door with questions in his gaze. "Sir, we shouldn't have boarded this ship without knowing who these sailors are," the man whispered.

This was his exact fear, which was why he had asked Rave before coming. Had Morticia not interfered, they could have waited until they found a ship with harmless sailors.

"Did you see anything?"

"These men look rogue. And one of our friends saw them hiding firearms. They must be pirates. And we are using them to find treasure for us. It's like asking a vulture to treat a patient."

Rupen gasped. "Did you guys listen to what they were discussing among them?"

"How could we, Sir? We don't even know their language." He furrowed his brow.

Rupen rubbed his hands together. "Right. And they don't know Hindi, either. That is our strength. And don't expect that rewards will come to us on a silver platter. At least you guys have a chance now. Either we will win and see better lives, or we will die and go to heaven. Were we safe in Rutland? Sooner or later, the British would have found us and threw us into the prison again. Better to fight the enemies and die."

The man nodded and smiled. "Right, Sir. We are all ready to combat anytime."

"Yes, anytime. If we win, the reward I give you will be enough to lead a comfortable life. Settle somewhere as anonymous persons in India, and never visit your native place. The British will never doubt you are the escaped prisoners. In their records, you guys are already dead."

"And if Rave and Walker betray you? I mean, if they take the sailors and attack you?"

"Lower your voice, man. They might understand some Hindi. And yes, I have seen betrayal once and will never let that happen again. You guys remain alert all the time. Some of you must remain awake when others take rest. Got me?"

"Yes, sir."

"Goodnight. And don't forget to pray to God." Rupen closed the door. The girls came to him, probably having sensed something was not right.

"Listen to me. Carefully. You both." Rupen pulled them close to him. "If anyone puts a knife on your neck, never wait for me to save you. Grab the man's balls and keep on squeezing until he dies. Even if his knife cuts through your neck. Got me?"

The girls nodded with a smile on their lips.

"And never remove your clothes. Not even while sleeping with me. From now on, until we arrive safe in India, no more lovemaking."

CHAPTER THIRTY-SIX

MORTICIA, 18 MARCH 1863, MORNING, PORT BLAIR AND THEN ROSS ISLAND (PART OF ANDAMAN ISLANDS GROUP)

Since this morning, Morticia had been pacing from the house to the front gate of her host, Mr. and Mrs. William—a family friend. Did Gopal forget to come and meet her?

Patches of clouds passing through the sky taunted her. Her thoughts morphed, twisting and turning around Rave and his sinister plans.

Did Walker catch Gopal when she paid him? Or did Gopal avoid her?

No. She had paid him money. And she had also promised to send more money to his family in Calcutta.

Many possibilities tightened her guts. Morticia hasn't even told Mr. Williams she was looking for her husband. Did Rave plan something against her and she didn't even get a glimpse of it?

All throughout her marriage with Rave, she had kept him under her tight control. How dare the pet cat behave like a tiger now?

She noticed a man approaching the gate and trudged forward to meet him. Her host shouldn't hear what she was about to discuss with Gopal.

"Walker sahib arrived at that cottage, but didn't stay there, memsahib." Gopal's eyes dazzled when he saw the money Morticia was holding in full view.

Morticia glanced around. She must finish the business before anyone noticed. "Then?"

"A boat was waiting for sahib. He asked us to load the boxes on the boat. And he also ordered me to go back. Before, I would stay there to cook for him. But..."

"Did you watch where the boat sailed?"

"It was evening, memsahib. Moonlight." Gopal thought for a while then said, "I saw a ship. In the sea. The boat stopped near the ship, and sahib climbed into it. Both sahib and memsahib."

"Good. And the boxes?"

"People took the boxes to the ship."

"What was in the boxes?"

Gopal looked frightened.

"Don't worry, Gopal. Trust me. I wouldn't tell anyone."

"Guns, memsahib. Guns."

This didn't surprise Morticia. Walker had always provided her with guns and men from the prison to undertake piracy. Did he partner with another man? Walker had never been on her ship when they had been looting other ships. Why did he board the ship and even take his wife with him?

"Did you see anybody on the ship?"

"Memsahib, I couldn't recognise. But he was talking something about Rupen sahib when he was sitting in the carriage. And yes, something else. An... Jambu, not clear memsahib. But I couldn't hear everything."

Jambu! Rupen! Didn't he die during the uprising? Now I understand. The uprising just a night before Walker handed over authority to Tytler was a drama. Rave has met Rupen many times, and his men had always helped them in looting. I must find Rupen. And where I find Rupen, I shall find Rave.

"Memsahib?" Gopal was waiting for instruction.

"You go back, Gopal. I will send money to your family. Have you brought the address?"

Gopal gave her a folded paper.

After heading back to Ross Island, Morticia sent a slip with her coachman to Tytler with just one sentence: *Rupen is still alive, can we talk at my home?*

He sent back that he would arrive the next morning.

Morticia had never imagined Tytler would stop everything and come to her house on such short notice. But she understood that

Walker's darling boy was Tytler's eyesore. How could Tytler forego such a chance to expose what Walker had done?

The next morning, before Tytler came to her house, Sadhna came to meet Vanaja. Sadhna flashed a smile at her and walked inside.

Morticia's heart fluttered when Tytler finally came and sat in her front room. The man must be serious in his business. But how would she use him to save her treasure? Rupen, dead or alive, had no meaning to her, unless she could use his name to her own benefit.

"You know something about Rupen, Mrs. Hunt?"

"You may call me Morticia, Mr. Tytler."

"Okay, Morticia. How can I help you?"

"Help? Me? No. In fact, I am here to help you. And the reason I didn't go to your office is serious." She pretended to wipe away tears, at the same time watching Tytler's reaction from the corner of her eyes.

Tytler sat straight on the sofa. "I'm sorry, Morticia. I'm sure you are undergoing tremendous stress."

Morticia stopped crying. "Yes, Mr. Tytler. All my life, I have been a loyal British citizen. And the only reason the British are controlling such a large country like India is because of hundreds of thousands of loyal citizens like me. We are the empire's backbone. And I understand you are one of those who can give life for the cause of the British."

Tytler's mouth widened with a smile at her praise. "That's right, Morticia. But you have knowledge of Rupen's whereabouts?"

She faked sobbing again. "My husband..."

"What happened to your husband? Is he all right? And did Rupen do something?"

Meat cooks well only when its marination is perfect, Morticia thought. Now was the time she would apply her plans.

"I am so sad to say my dearest husband has joined the enemies of the British. And if you try to see things—well, you will realise the uprising that happened on the last night of Walker as head of Andaman... I fear he staged it to help Rupen free."

Tytler's hesitation was clear on his face. "I don't know about that. Is that correct? I have heard Rupen had helped in containing another uprising, and Walker was even inviting him to his home. But..."

"He is alive. Rupen is alive. People have seen him. And my husband..." she sobbed harder.

Sadhna entered the room with a tray of two teacups and placed it on the table.

Tytler froze and stared with wide eyes. "This... She..."

"She is a negro woman. Amelia had found her somewhere and has kept her as her maid."

"Amelia?"

"She is the schoolteacher."

"Yes, I have heard. The only female teacher here."

"Yes."

"But the woman is still standing here and listening to us," Tytler whispered when Sadhna didn't leave.

"Don't worry, Mr. Tytler. She doesn't understand English. And you see, negros are uncivilised, never learnt the etiquette. Let her stand."

"Morticia, you were saying about your husband." Tytler leaned forward in interest.

"Mr. Rave Hunt, that's my husband. He and Rupen had been together. They are planning something. I understand they have hired a ship and left Port Blair last night."

Tytler's gaze went briefly to Sadhna who was cleaning the windowpane with a cloth. He took another sip of tea and looked at Morticia. "Where will they go? Calcutta? I will send a letter to Calcutta when the next ship goes from here. Calcutta police will remain alert and capture Rupen Naik. Don't worry."

Morticia rubbed her palms. My *plans are going in the wrong direction.*

"You think Rupen doesn't understand authorities will nab him again if he goes to India? He must have planned something better. And my husband is an accomplice. I wouldn't mind if he also gets punishments. I don't want a traitor as my husband."

She stole a glance at Tytler. It was difficult to know what was going on inside his mind. Was he serious? Had she disclosed too much while asking for his help?

Sadhna took the empty cups and placed them on another table in the room. Morticia wanted to tell her to go to the kitchen, but she directed her attention at Tytler instead.

"We don't have a ship ready now," Tytler said, "and I don't know how to handle this. Anyway, Rupen is dead as per our records."

Disquiet trickled through Morticia. She would lose everything if Tytler didn't agree to an immediate action. "Mr. Tytler, will your men update the record when he starts another war against the British? And do you think when that happens, I will not shout that one day I had given confidential information to you?"

Tytler straightened his back and stared at her. "You are misunderstanding me, Morticia. The fact is, I don't have a ship here to send my soldiers."

Morticia let out a smile. "Ship? I can give ours. Our ship undertakes only government duties. So what if Rave is not here? I'm sailing with him all the time, I know captaincy. The sailors are ready; just send some soldiers, and I will get them to you." Excitement and tension pushed her from her seat.

Does Tytler believe a woman can be a captain?

"I can send them, but..." Tytler put his hands over his ears.

Sadhna was again busy in cleaning the windowpanes. Morticia's voice went up. "You don't have a choice, Mr. Tytler. If you have doubt, you may nominate a man as captain, and I will guide him. If you think a woman can't be a captain."

"Where do they find Rupen and your husband?"

"Jambu. An island just near the estuary of the Hooghly River."

"But how are you so sure Rave will go to Jambu Island?"

Her own fear stabbed her like a sharp knife. Sadhna stopped her work and swung around, but only for a moment before she continued her work. *Silly girl!*

How could she admit Rave and she had hidden the entire loot on Jambu Island? Where else could Rave go without his wife, though, unless he had plans to deprive Morticia of the treasure?

She scratched her head. Only some urgent idea could save her hidden wealth.

"There is an old, rejected palace there. We had stayed there many times while on our way to and from Andaman. The tribal people living there are friendly to us and take care of the building in our absence. I am sure Rave would use Jambu as a base before sending Rupen to some safe place. And he must get an enormous amount from Rupen for this."

Tytler got up. "All right then, I will soon inform you. See you soon."

Sadhna was still standing there like a statue when Tytler left. Morticia pinched her and signalled her to go back. *Dumb girl. No, an animal in a woman's features.* Morticia cast a funny look at her and went inside her bedroom.

I must thwart Rave's plan to get all the treasure for himself. They are all mine. Mine only.

Amelia, 19 March 1863, Afternoon, Ross Island (Part of Andaman Islands Group)

I have moved to Shanti's room since I found out Luke wasn't happy with me. All three of us, Shanti, Sadhna, and I, are sharing the servant's quarters. It also has a toilet, so I don't have to go inside Nick's house. Nick was worried for some time, but I explained to him, this is only a temporary arrangement. He would leave Andaman as soon as Tytler relieves him. And I am also all set to go back in the next available ship.

I have never tried to become Luke's caretaker since I moved with Shanti. And he loves when Shanti bathes him and feeds him because she is not a threat to take his mother's place with his dad. But he goes to school with me and comes back, too.

Today, when we come back from school, I find Sadhna waiting for me outside the gate, wearing a winner's look. Why is Sadhna so happy?

I signal her to come inside the outhouse. She shouldn't talk to me in front of the gate. That is an understanding between her and me. Morticia should never find out Sadhna knows English. For her, she is the same dumb woman as before.

"Rupen." Sadhna giggled once I shut the door of the servant's quarters.

"What, Rupen, did his ghost tell you a joke? In your dream?"

"Dead. No. No dead."

One needs a great deal of patience to understand her language. No doubt, Rupen is dead. I ignore her and move to change clothes. As I take the top above my head, Sadhna stands in front of me, her breath massaging my breasts.

"What happened, Sadhna?"

"He came. Meet, memsahib, big."

Someone came to meet Morticia? "Rupen?"

"No. He." She raised her hand to show a tall man.

"Name? You know?"

"Tyt."

I have to scratch my head now. But it doesn't take long. "Tytler? The man with the bald head?"

"Ya." She smiles again.

"Did they say that Rupen is alive?"

"Rupen, Rave, Walker. Go to Jambu."

This is important news. Morticia is going to Jambu to find Rupen and Rave. Does it mean Rave revolted against his wife? And Rupen is also alive? I take Sadhna into a solid hug. "Good news, Sadhna. Keep it up. And never, ever speak English outside this room."

"More." She continues to stand before me.

A sound of someone opening the gate alerts me. Nick? I crane my neck out the door and notice Morticia is coming.

"Sadhna. No more talking." I stomp out, slapping a smile on my face.

"I am going back to Calcutta. Today or tomorrow." She smiles at me.

I glance around to check if Sadhna is poking her head out. "Mr. Hunt is back from Port Blair?"

"Rave? Rave, um..." She glances around. "No. I'm going alone."

Surprise darts through me, and I swallow.

"Rave went away with someone. Urgent work. He will wait for me in Jambu. I will pick him up there and leave. Do you want to come with me? You said you want to go back."

Joy leaks through my lips. I can't hide my smile. "Go back? You are so kind, Mort darling! I love you."

"Okay then. I will let you know when I leave." With a wink, she turns and marches toward the gate.

I stare at her until she crosses the gate. Finally, my Andaman venture will end. Though I have done nothing to free Rupen, at least he has fled, and this is significant news for Sehnaz.

Sehnaz! But she is dead. A sob gathers in the back of my throat.

The soft beating of the horse's hooves meets my ears. Nick enters the fence, wearing a smile. He is earlier than usual.

"Grand news, Amelia. Pack your bags." he says as he gets off the horse.

How does he know I am about to pack my bags?

"Tytler just gave me some good news. I can leave now." Nick comes where I am standing. "He said a ship is going to Calcutta. Within a day or two."

"Good to know, Nick. I am dying to leave Andaman."

"Yes, we both can go. But the ship may make a brief stopover on the way."

"Stopover? Coco island?"

"No, an island called Jambu. I have never heard of that."

Now the complete picture comes together. I inhale a deep breath. And that woman has some plans for Rave. She must. Nick goes inside his house, leaving me standing there, engrossed in my thoughts.

Sadhna has brought the right news. Rave has planned to leave Morticia forever after striking a deal with Rupen.

I glance at the sky. A clear, blue sky. One small, white cloud smiles at me. Time to pack. I must lodge all these in my diary this evening. We may have to leave at any time.

Eliza's memory knocks at my mind. Will Nick leave his wife alone on this island? Forever?

"Can I come inside?" I say, standing at the open door of Nick's house.

"Door is open, Amelia. You don't have to get permission to come in."

"Thanks." I amble inside, and Luke is gazing at me standing near him. "No, Nick. This is basic courtesy I teach all the children in school. One must knock on the door and get permission before entering another person's home." My eyes dart to Luke for his approval.

Luke's gaze slides down to his feet. From the day Luke fought with his father, accusing him of giving his mum's place to me, I am careful about my dealings with Nick. And I am sure he is still feeling bad about that. I still have the same soft feelings toward him, but I'm not sure how it would go to the next level. Will Luke ever accept me? Where would Nick like to live after leaving Andaman? I'm sure I can't leave Sultanpur, so until these questions are answered, I must tread carefully in this relationship.

Nick turns his face to Luke. Before he could reprimand him, I speak up. "Can we now go to the graveyard and lay flowers on Eliza's grave, for the last time? "

Luke's face brightens up. "Yes, Dad. We will go to see Mum."

Shanti plucks some flowers from the garden and makes a small bouquet for us. Then we three walk to the graveyard, which is only fifteen minutes from the home.

It is an emotional scene I will never forget and must write in my diary. I may never see Nick and Luke after this. Father and son offer flowers to Eliza's grave, and tears roll down their cheeks. My heart flutters.

"I came to Andaman with you, but leaving you alone here, my dear," Nick mutters, kneeling near the grave, "but you will be in my heart forever. You are still my love."

They need some privacy. I walk some distance and pluck more flowers. Someone else is awaiting my offerings.

I lay flowers near a tree, and kneel on the grass, closing my eyes. "Miss you, Sehnaz. You would have loved to get this news. Your dearest Rupen is a lion, and the British can't cage him forever. He is now out, and I hope he is safe. I'm sorry I couldn't do anything to fulfill my promise to you, but the goal is complete, even without me. We could have both gone back to Sultanpur together. Your name is also clear from the wanted list. The confirmation was from a reliable man who was working in Sultanpur cantonment." I hug the tree with a tear streaming down my cheek.

A lovely touch on my shoulder awakens me. Luke is there, tears glistening in his eyes. He comes forward and wraps his arms around my neck. "I'm sorry, Aunt Amelia." Tears streak down his cheeks. "I won't be angry at you."

"Thanks, Luke. You are a good boy." I take him into a tight hug. Soft affection fills my chest.

"Will you come and stay inside our home?" Luke's soft breath warms my face.

I think to say we are all set to leave Andaman. But my heart stops me from hurting the little boy's emotion. "I will. Promise. Are you happy?"

His face splits into a smile.

"Is she the same Sehnaz from Lucknow?" Nick's question gets me up on my heels, and I swing back. Why did I think he wouldn't be near me?

"You know her?"

"I was a personal doctor to Nawab Wajid Ali, and Rupen was close to me."

Surprise dances through me. An invisible bond bridges both of us in an instant, as if two close friends are recounting some sweet, old memories.

"Rupen was a kind person. He helped me a lot. And he had even assured me during The Residency siege that his soldiers would never harm women and children. Or even English civilians."

Nick had heard everything I was muttering to Sehnaz a while ago, so Rupen's escape is no longer a secret to him. "Authorities will punish him again if they find out about his escape," I warn.

"I am the one who has helped him in escaping." Nick glances around and whispers, "and don't worry. He knows how to keep his freedom intact."

CHAPTER THIRTY-SEVEN

SEHNAZ, 26 MARCH 1863, MORNING, SHIP IN BAY OF BENGAL

Standing in front of her cuddy, Sehnaz kept her eyes on the crews as the ship sailed through the waves of the Bay of Bengal. The messy, dark clouds made her head heavy, like she was sick.

"Sheru, can you guess the direction the ship is heading?"

"I woke up early this morning, but I still couldn't see the sun. Cloudy sky. Why don't you ask Alfred?"

Sehnaz inched closer to Sheru and stood with her arm wrapped around his shoulder. "Don't say his name in a loud voice. I have asked, and he avoided every time. Even the crews have sealed their lips for us."

"Maybe he is afraid his wife would find out where we are going. He might have told her the ship is heading to Rangoon when in fact, we're going to Jambu. I have the best idea how to find out."

She cast a flirtatious glance at him. "What?"

"I have some experience sailing a ship. I'm sure the crews are tired, and they will never say no, if I offer my service."

"Always thinking like a worker or a junior rank soldier, Sheru. You are the husband of a princess. Maintain your dignity."

Sheru let out a mild laugh. "Princess! Husband!"

"Did you watch me laughing when I said that? We have nothing to protect us except two strengths—that I'm a princess, and I can lead us to the place where the plunder is sitting."

"What do I do, then?"

"Just watch the blue water of the ocean sitting in front of the cabin."

"I love your confident smile, Sehnaz."

Only Sehnaz learnt how much pain she had hidden underneath that smile.

So many thoughts revolved around her. What if she found Morticia when they arrive at Jambu? Should she ask Alfred to keep the ship waiting in the sea until Rave and Morticia's ship leaves? What reply would she give if he asks whom she is fearing?

Her gaze fell on Agatha standing on the deck and watching the ocean through a binocular.

"She can see nothing. Poor woman."

Sheru didn't reply.

"Sheru, what if Morticia and Rave arrive while we are in Jambu distributing the treasure? She always had armed guards on the ship because of her carrying convicts to Andaman. Will she attack us?"

"Sehnaz, you know that woman. I can't predict anything."

She would jump into the sea and die in case any untoward incident happened. But what about Sheru? Why did she persuade him to come along when she herself was not sure about the future?

Agatha walked toward the sailors. She had always stayed inside her cabin, except for the occasional chat with Sehnaz. Sehnaz was sure she was counting the days to be a free woman once the ship arrived in Rangoon. *If...*

She tried to eavesdrop on the chat between Agatha and the sailors, but couldn't. But within minutes, Agatha's voice shot up.

"I need an answer. Rangoon is only two hundred and fifty miles from Coco, why is the ship taking so long?"

"Ma'am, again I am requesting you," one of the sailors tried to pacify her, "please ask Mr. Alfred."

"These men are so stupid," she muttered to Sheru, "they could've said the wind slowed the ship and avoided the argument."

"You are so sympathetic to her as she is a woman, and now you are planning on keeping her in dark?"

"I am not. Rather, I would be happy if the ship goes to Rangoon. But it looks like Alfred has decided to go to Jambu first. That means we are going back to plan A."

"We don't have a choice, Sehnaz."

Sehnaz saw Alfred coming out of the cabin when Agatha shouted at the sailors. She walked up to him. "Alfred, if Agatha wants to go to Rangoon first, let that be. We can go to our place after that."

Before Alfred could say anything, Agatha charged up. "Where is your place, Sez? I have helped you so much, but you are also hiding things from me?"

Sehnaz felt as if someone stabbed her conscience. She shot a gaze at Alfred. His eyes were burning. Was he drunk?

She never expected Alfred to come to her rescue. But why was he not trying to convince his wife that he would take her to Rangoon?

Sheru was watching without a word.

"Sorry, Agatha ma'am." Sehnaz stepped closer to her and tried her best to sound genuine. "I had told you the first time we met that we are from Calcutta. But during the last around two weeks, we have hardly spoken to each other. I didn't get a chance to say where we were going. And I also thought you knew your husband had given kind assurance to drop us in Calcutta." She tried to signal Alfred, but he was looking elsewhere. "And I thought this ship would sail to Calcutta after Rangoon."

"My husband?" Agatha's voice pitched up, as if she had decided to explode that day. "And you believe this man? He is a fraud. Traitor. He is capable of doing anything."

Alfred jumped between like a wounded lion and grabbed Agatha's arm. "You damn whore, didn't I ask you not to open your mouth?"

He dragged her away into his cabin.

The next morning, surprise rippled through Sehnaz when she woke up and saw the crew anchoring the ship near an island. She tried to figure out—was this Jambu? It was—Sehnaz recognized the various landmarks.

"Yes, Sehnaz," Sheru said. "Mr. Hunt had kept us on this side of the island when his ship had halted in Jambu. Look at those hutments. They don't belong to the tribal people. I think Rave Hunt's men had built them."

The morning sun was smiling at her when she came to the deck. Would her dream of getting a share of Morticia's hidden treasure finally come true?

"Good morning, Princess," Alfred sounded from behind.

Sehnaz swung back to face him, but his sneer disturbed her. His palm was resting on the pistol at his waist. Her worry edged into an anxiety.

The crew climbed down and readied the rope ladder for them. Sehnaz, holding Sheru's hand, stepped on the ladder before the crew even asked her to, as if she would run away from the penetrating and dreaded gaze of Alfred. There was a day she was daring enough to face anything. But something was holding up today.

Alfred followed them.

Sehnaz was surprised that she didn't hear Agatha screaming after realising the place was neither Rangoon nor Calcutta. Then she realised Agatha was not there at all. An alarm sounded in her head. "Agatha? Where is Agatha?"

Alfred didn't even look at her. The crew was gathering the ladder into a knot. Jumping onto the ladder again, she climbed onto the ship and arrived at Agatha's cabin.

An empty cuddy mocked her. Something was wrong.

"Sez, please come back," Sheru was shouting from the jetty.

An impatient Alfred was pacing near him, shooting fire from his eyes.

Sehnaz dragged her feet to the shore, Agatha's absence haunting her.

"We must finish the job soon and go back. I got no time, and why don't you take that seriously?" Alfred growled.

"But where is Agatha?" Sehnaz had decided not to move without her.

"She is not here." Alfred looked away as if he had never had a wife.

"No, Alfred. Do not play with me. I am a princess and not your maid. I must know about Agatha before I move."

The crew stood like passive spectators. Sheru's hands were making tight fists, his teeth grinding.

Alfred came near. "She jumped into the sea last night. I was sleeping."

"You were sleeping—" Sehnaz brought a taunt to her voice— "then how did you know she jumped?"

Alfred's gaze fell to his feet. Sehnaz let out a sardonic smile.

"Before dawn when I didn't find her, I went out and asked the crew. They said they heard a sound. But they were not sure. We all believe the sound came when Agatha jumped. Where do I find her now in this vast sea?"

Sehnaz cursed herself. Alfred must have planned this well before starting from Great Coco Islands. Agatha's secret plans to leave him after arriving at Rangoon weren't unknown to him.

Her mood at once morphed from anger to concern for Agatha. Agatha was adept at swimming. She, along with Agatha, had already swum in the ocean many times before. And she also doubted a woman who was dreaming of independence only a day ago would commit suicide. Could she swim back to Jambu if the ship was already near the island?

Five sets of vulture eyes lasered her as she walked from the shore to the narrow path connecting the makeshift jetty to the mainland.

Sehnaz, 27 March 1863, Morning, Ship in Bay of Bengal

"I need to find that old palace Morticia had accommodated Amelia and me. And if this is Jambu Island, where are the tribal men?"

"I doubt this man will share any of the booty with us," Sheru muttered in Hindi as he tried to walk closer to her. "They all look rogue to me."

"Forget that now. The man who can kill his wife can do anything. Even if he drops both of us in Rangoon, that would be great. At least we can go back to India and live with a changed identity somewhere."

"You think so?"

"Freedom is our only aim now, Sheru, I'm no longer concerned with money. But if you think we should get a share, let me talk to him."

Sehnaz stilled. All five men, including Alfred, stopped behind her.

"Look, Mr. Alfred, I need to talk to you. Now. In private."

Alfred cast a glance around. He wore a storm on his face.

"Let's go to that side." She pointed at a tree less than a furlong away. Gesturing for Sheru to come along, she walked up to the tree. Sehnaz had no time to study the crew's questioning looks as they waited.

Show confidence, Sehnaz. That's your only weapon now. Your confidence and intelligence.

She inhaled a deep breath and met Alfred's gaze. A tiger also thinks twice before attacking if a person stares into its eyes.

"Mr. Alfred…" She paused for a few beats and saw three tribal men with their bow and arrows walking past. A narrow path near the tree wall led to the water. Recognition shot through her, and she yelled, "*Bhaya!* Brother!" The men glanced at her and smiled back. Did they remember her from months ago?

"I must make it clear before we even arrive at the cave." Sehnaz cast another glance at the tribal men, who were untying the canoes on the shore, about to descend into the water. "The treasure my brother has kept is my property. And thank you for helping me in coming here. I can't give over twenty-five percent of the amount we get from there. You must understand these islander men have been guarding the cave in the absence of my family, and I must give them a sizeable amount."

Alfred glared at her, but soon it blurred into a sneer. "All right. I'm into it. Please don't waste time, we must leave today."

"Sure." Sehnaz flashed a confident smile, having successfully negotiated like a real princess. "And where do you drop us both off? Calcutta?"

Sheru elbowed her and whispered, "Not Calcutta, Sagar Island." But Sehnaz elbowed him back and winked.

"Calcutta will be tough, your highness, the police there might check the ferry."

"I have an alternative, Alfred. Sagar Island will suit you and us, too. Only four miles from here," she said as if she had visited the place many times.

He agreed, and Sehnaz and Sheru continued taking the lead while Alfred and the crew followed.

"He agreed without arguing!" Sheru muttered.

"Yes, but you shouldn't have asked me about Sagar Island. I could've asked him again before leaving."

"But I said it in Hindi."

"Hindi? The name of the island you said is the same in both languages. He would understand."

Sehnaz badly wished she could see all the men following her. Check their expressions. But she had to lead the way, and she was struggling to locate the cave. The only thing she knew was they had anchored on the north side of the island, and the old palace was on the south. The cave was only two to three furlongs away from the palace.

The sun had turned up its intensity, and she glared at the sky. Must be around ten in the morning. Sheru was sweating, and she was also thirsty.

"Where's that place, Princess?" Impatience emitted from Alfred's voice.

"Shouldn't be far. Paths have changed since my last visit. When people stop using a trail, weeds take over."

She heard the crew and Alfred talking among themselves. Not in English, though. She already knew Alfred was not English when the couple were talking on the ship. Did he bring his own countrymen on a purpose?

Her feet didn't move when she saw a stream of water. She must drink or she couldn't walk farther.

As she descended along with Sheru, she glanced backward. All the men followed her and bent over the water.

River. A memory stabbed at her.

She must locate the river the English man had jumped into before the islanders' arrow snatched away his life. Where was it? Was this stream a tributary to that river?

"Sheru, if we follow this water, we should come across a river. A narrow one. We must cross it to go to the other side where the cave is," she said in English so Alfred would know she was genuinely trying to find the cave.

"Let's get along with this," Alfred said.

Sehnaz got her feet moving. She had thought Jambu was a tiny island which she could walk across in hours.

But where is that river? And where are the men living here?

"You sure it was near the river?" Tension sounded in Sheru's voice.

"Not near the river. I might find the old palace on the other border of it. Where are the islanders?"

"Didn't they enter the sea?"

"Only a few. Where are the others?"

"Will they guide us to the cave?"

"No, Sheru. I don't... I..."

The men behind her started talking again. She didn't understand a single word, but the heat from their words radiated and pinched her chest.

Within no time, the voices rose to heated arguments. Sehnaz stopped and swung back. She was sure they were talking about her and Sheru. She decided to interfere with the altercation. "We must find the river. And the cave is on the other side," she announced, as if she was sure of the location.

"Find the river," Alfred shouted, "and find the cave. Who is stopping you? I need the cave. Now. And they also need it. More urgently than I do."

Alfred must have promised these people a large stake of the hidden money. Sehnaz forced her feet to move faster, the intense sunrays needling every bit of her exhausted body. She wondered if she could run in case the event didn't go as planned, which was becoming more and more likely.

Why can't I see the tribal men? And where is the river? Are we really in Jambu? Uncertainty streamed through her, weakening her feet further.

A whoop escaped from her mouth when at last, she saw the narrow river. And it was dry. "See, I found it!"

The memory of the floating, slain English soldier blurred her vision. Would she also find more islanders after this?

After crossing the waterway, she recollected the way to the ancient palace and the path leading to Morticia's secret cave. The treasure was not far now. More confidence bloomed inside her as she cast a satisfactory glance at Sheru. "Sheru, time to get rich or..." She didn't wish to bring up the contingency she hated. Or even feared.

After walking a few furlongs, she noticed the old palace where Morticia used to live while staying on the island. Amelia's sweet face appeared in Sehnaz's mind's eye as she led the team through winding pathways through the woods. For a moment she longed to go inside the palace and visit the room she and Amelia had shared months ago. Her scent might be still lingering.

"Now I know how I can go to the cave," she said in Hindi.

"You remember?" Sheru asked.

"Yes, Amelia and I had followed that woman and saw the cave from outside. We didn't enter it until next day when we saw the large boxes she had hidden. Don't utter her name, this man knows her."

The same mango and tamarind trees stood along the winding pathway above the hillock; Sehnaz closed her eyes and imagined the day last August when she and Amelia were exploring this place. Ripe mangoes hung on every tree, their aroma sweet and inviting. The sight of the green hills rolling down to the seashore and the sparkling blue ocean was breathtaking. She could see Amelia standing beside her, holding a big stick with a bunch of flowers tied to it.

"Sez..." Sheru touched her arm.

"Oh, yes, sorry, I went into the past." She glanced around. The mangoes on the trees were raw and green, and their aroma was intoxicating. "I will never forget the day Amelia and I went into that cave."

In almost fifteen minutes, they arrived near the cave. The front had been covered with tall weeds. "Looks like that woman hasn't come here for a long time," she commented.

"Are you sure this is that cave?" Sheru asked.

"There was only one cave here. This is the one, I'm certain."

Sheru cleared the weeds, and Sehnaz grabbed his arm and trudged inside the cave, as if she could separate her part before Alfred and his thugs even got a glimpse.

"Is there a door to go inside?" Sheru asked, standing in an empty cave.

Sehnaz's mouth tightened. She ran outside to check if it was the same cave. She tried to recollect when she and Amelia had come here. All they had seen was that Morticia and Rave had locked boxes with thorny weeds blocking the entrance. Where were those boxes? She hadn't known if there was another entry leading to another secret cave behind this. Why didn't she enter the cave the first time she saw it?

Was the hidden treasure too good to be true?

She had read stories. How people lose their lives when their greed pulls them in quest of mysterious fortune. She had always laughed at their foolishness. All those dumb characters came out from the pages of the story books and stood before her. *Greed takes lives.*

She understood now that the same greed would take her and Sheru's lives. Could she survive these four thugs?

Sehnaz, think of something. Quick. You have no time Forget about running away. Alfred and his gang are watching.

She started laughing.

Sheru stared at her, sweat dripping from his torso and a ghost appearing in his eyes.

"Sheru, that woman is clever. She has taken away everything," she said to him in Hindi. Then turning around, she faced Alfred. "This is my fault."

Alfred pulled out the pistol from his waistband and pointed it at Sehnaz.

She stood holding Sheru's arm, then closed her eyes and muttered a prayer. "Oh God, I asked for freedom, and you gave me freedom from life. I accept the fate. But please keep Amelia safe, wherever she is."

The gun hadn't fired. She opened her eyes.

The scene before her had gotten complicated.

The four crewmen had raised their guns at Alfred. Not only Sehnaz and Sheru, but Alfred would also die with them.

"You don't understand, Alfred." She let out another loud laugh. "I am so forgetful. I was too excited. And now I remember." Then she looked at the men and said, "Lower your guns. If hot heads could find treasures, all the angry men on this earth would be wealthy. Don't behave like stupids." Her self-confidence was taking a dive, and she was the only person who could stop that.

"So does the booty exist or not? Be clear," Alfred growled.

"It's here, but in a safer place." *God, please come inside my brain and show me the way out of this mess.*

"I don't have patience, pr—"

"Tribal!" She clasped her hands. "Yes, I must see the chief. I had told him last time to move it to another cave. This is so close to the sea and I... I told... I told him to shift it."

"Are you sure?" Alfred's voice was shaking as he glanced around.

The tension in the cave was intensifying.

"Then go to the tribal chief," Alfred said.

"Did he get the news that the princess is arriving?" She remembered to use the word *princess* as that was the only weapon against four rifles and one pistol. "They will come back home after a days' work and gather. Near their village. And I must see him and ask where the new cave is. Impatience won't help."

One man stepped forward and growled, pointing his gun at her, "Don't care if you are a princess."

Sehnaz's heart was in her throat. Sheru moved closer and wrapped his arm around her waist. She met his gaze; his eyes were glowering. "We will die together. I am not leaving you," he said in Hindi again.

Another crewman charged forward. "What? What did he say in his bloody language?"

"He said—" Sehnaz swallowed— "he said, we must wait until the evening and meet the chief."

"Are you sure?"

Sheru took the man by surprise and grabbed the tip of his gun. "You in a hurry? Are you? Then fire the gun and walk away if you think you can find all the money by yourself. We haven't come all this way to go back empty-handed. The princess has waited years for this day, and you people lost hope after only hours?"

Alfred held up his hands in an attempt to pacify everyone. "We must meet the chief and follow the advice of the princess."

Then he said something to the crewmen in his language.

Sehnaz pulled Sheru out of the cave. She could prolong her life by a few more hours. But what after that?

Only she knew the tribal leader didn't have a clue about the plunder. Morticia had already taken it away. Or even moved it to another secured place.

They must wait until evening.

Three men kept Alfred under their watch while the fourth had gone to the ship to bring food for them. On the other hand, Alfred also kept Sehnaz and Sheru under his supervision.

Sehnaz and Sheru were his lifeline until evening.

Sheru got a few raw coconuts for his and Sehnaz's lunch. Sehnaz sat in silence when Sheru knifed through the coconuts. "*Om Namah Shivay,*" he murmured.

A giggle slipped out of her mouth, to her own surprise. "Sheru, are you trying to ask for forgiveness? You know you don't have time for the penance for sleeping with me."

Sheru stilled and gazed at her. A long pause stood between them.

"Sehnaz, will you marry me?"

She chuckled again. Sheru was finally proposing? Alfred and his men's glares and the threat of the gun had no meaning now. She was ready for death. "Are you sure? Yes! Yes from me, Sheru. We couldn't live together, but now we can die at the same time." Her eyes moistened.

A sigh escaped his mouth as the knife cut into his finger.

"What did you do, Sheru?" Sehnaz grabbed his bleeding finger.

"Don't worry." Sheru yanked his finger from her clutch and touched Sehnaz's forehead. Warm blood dripped onto her head.

"I have coloured your forehead with my blood, Sehnaz. This is a symbolic red dot of a Vedic wedding, and from now on you are my wife."

Sehnaz couldn't believe this. She knew as per Hindu customs applying vermilion on a woman's forehead amounted to a quick wedding. With this, she became Sheru's wife. Until this evening, when even death couldn't separate them. Their souls would fly to heaven together.

Grabbing Sheru's neck and pulling him toward her, she kissed her fervently. "I am no longer afraid, Sheru. I can face everything as long as you are with me." She felt the saltiness of her own tears on her tongue. "And I am sure Lord Shiva will forgive you for bedding down with me. He knew you would have no time to sleep with your wife after this short wedding, so he granted you those months before."

Sheru laughed. Sehnaz giggled into his chest.

Sehnaz glanced around. Alfred was the only one who wasn't eating. He was alone in this game, and fear accompanied his every move.

"Sheru, we must invite this poor soul to our wedding feast."

Sheru got up and gave him the white flesh of the coconut.

When the sun was slipping down behind the peak, Alfred rose from the ground. "Time to move."

This might be the final evening. The last evening of Sehnaz's and Sheru's life. But she must strive until the end.

Sehnaz remembered the way the tribal men one day had guided her and Amelia back to the old mansion. Their village was the only hope for her.

"Come on, Sheru. We should meet our fellow villagers and party with them for our wedding. I am so happy now."

"But Sehnaz, what after that? The villagers know nothing about the treasure," Sheru whispered.

"That's better, Sheru. They would've killed us by now had I found the money for them. We are alive only because they still have hope. And this will be our last effort."

Dusk was creeping in. She scanned the sky. A large moon smiled at her from the blue heavens. Is the moon welcoming the couple to heaven? How many people could embrace death with a smile?

Full moon night.

Most tribals of India celebrate the full moon nights. The villagers gathered in the enormous field in the village. A large lamb was roasting, hanging above a firepit, radiating a delicious aroma into the spring air. Dozens of women naked above the waist were dancing around it to the tune of drumbeats.

Sehnaz cast a sideways glance at the rogue crewmen. All of them were licking their lips. She came to them and said, "I can meet the chief only after this dance. Here on this island, there are more women than men. And women love to have white babies."

The men gazed at her, lust reflecting from each of their eyes.

"You people are double lucky," Sehnaz said. "Treasure, and before that, women. You have guns. And there are bushes nearby."

She walked away from them and stood near Sheru. "Don't get too much into the dance, Sheru. Watch me, and act when I hint."

He winked at her.

Friendly glances welcomed her to the party. Three women came to serve *mahua* to her. She signalled for the women to serve drinks to Alfred and the four men. As the women approached them, Sehnaz shouted, "Nice drinks. Have fun."

The dance went on for some time. Suddenly, she heard gunshots and swung around. Three of the men had grabbed one woman each and the fourth man had fired at the sky, threatening the villagers.

"Sheru, inside the crowd of villagers. Now. With me."

She ran to the tribal chief, who was sitting on a large stone. As she looked back, all the village men had raised their bows and arrows, pointing at the crew. Alfred was yelling at them, "You fools, you ruined everything!"

"I will kill everybody here," the crewman waving the gun in the air screamed.

Sheru laughed. "He is stupid! That gun can hold only one bullet inside. He has already fired the only shot it had, and before he loads another, he will die from the arrows."

The men stepped back, trying to escape while still grabbing the women with one hand and their guns with the other. But in no time, arrows from behind pierced their necks. Sehnaz closed her eyes in fear. But she couldn't close her ears. The whizzing of angry arrows hung in the air. The splat as they pierced into the flesh of the rogue men and their yowl cooled down her nerves.

"Sez, you all right?"

She opened her eyes to the cries of joy of the tribal women and villagers dragging the bodies.

"One, two, three, four, and five. Five bodies. Sheru, we survived!" She hugged him.

"I can't believe it, Sehnaz." He held her tight. "And no more Sez. No more Sanju. You are my dear Sehnaz."

After the feast, the tribal men guided them to the old palace.

"It's our first night after the real wedding between us, Sheru. Let's spend time inside the palace. Until Morticia comes back here."

"And if she comes?"

"We have the ship. We will see."

CHAPTER THIRTY-EIGHT

RUPEN NAIK, 7 APRIL 1863, AFTERNOON, JAMBU ISLAND

Rupen had never thought everything would be so easy for him. He had prepared his men for so many contingencies. But not a single bullet had left the guns so far.

"Rupen, sir, isn't this too good to be true?" Shyam, Rupen's trusted soldier, asked.

Rupen let out a mild laugh. "No, Shyam, I pinched my skin. Not only once, but a few times. It wasn't a dream."

Rupen smiled at the clear, blue sky. One of his tribal wives was plucking Jambu Island's wild spring flowers, and the other was playing with shells near the water.

"Sir, can I say something to you?" Shyam asked.

"Please."

"The society in Lucknow might not accept your marriage to the tribal girls. But they have brought luck to your life. Otherwise, who would have thought two months ago you would get away from the dreaded prison?"

"And get so much treasure?" He returned a grin.

"Right, sir. Not only you. By your kindness, we all got something. Look at your soldiers, sir. They are planning a picnic. Free from jail and a share in the booty. What else do we need?"

Rupen's eyes darted between the soldiers and his wives. His chest vibrated. Could all this treasure he earned today bring back his happy family? He was just a breath away from sobbing.

"You know, Shyam. These girls are only three or four years older than my two slain daughters."

Shyam moved closer and held Rupen's hands. "Sir, I read the holy Gita every day. Those who die fighting in a war deserve heaven. Who said women can't join an army? Your wife and daughters were all behind-the-scenes warriors in the Sepoy Mutiny. You should celebrate their sacrifice."

"I will try. But it's difficult."

His gaze fell on Rave Hunt and Dr. Walker. Both were coming out of the old palace and walking toward him.

"Any plans, Mr. Naik?" Dr. Walker said with a wide grin. "I didn't congratulate you when you escaped the prison. I had doubts earlier. But today, congratulations."

"Thanks, Dr. Walker. Grateful for your help." Rupen knew his escape still wasn't over until he arrived somewhere he could live anonymously and away from the British scrutiny. He tried to suppress it, but his gut said trouble could still be at large for him and his team.

"Anything for a true patriot. You could have slaughtered many civilians, women, and children. Like the Bibighar Massacre. This is your reward. Unofficially." He laughed and cast a bright glance at Mrs. Walker at his side. She reciprocated with a silent chortle.

Rave joined the laughter. "Dr. Walker knows the British government would take a century to decide that you were never a criminal. Where do you aim to live?" He shot a gaze at Rupen's wives who were chatting among themselves.

"Anywhere in the world is better than Andaman's Black Waters prison. Even this old palace here, on this island." Rupen kicked a grin toward the house said, "And with Mr. Hunt's blessings, I also got a share in the treasure."

"You and Dr. Walker both have contributed to amass this wealth, Mr. Naik. I am always an honest man with those who partner with me, and I give them their due share always. And yes, do not even dream to stay in this old palace. This is a haunted place. A witch lived here." He laughed.

"Where is the witch? This is our last night here, and we have seen nothing," Dr. Walker said as his wife put her arms around his shoulders, giggling at their witch jokes.

"The witch comes here sometimes, with me of course," Rave sneered. "And I was afraid she might have been here when we arrived. She could smell things. Last time when we were here, she asked me to move the treasure to another location, fearing someone might loot them. Clearly she had gut feeling her wealth was going to vanish."

"I am sure she hasn't." Confidence bloomed in Dr. Walker's eyes. "She came to me just before we were about to leave Port Blair. And the diplomatic way I replied to her, I am sure she wouldn't even think her husband had made such an elaborate plan."

Mrs. Walker intervened. "No way. She is a clever woman and must have planned something. Doesn't she realise it's been almost three weeks, and Mr. Hunt has not returned home? She must have started with Mr. Hunt's ship and may arrive here anytime. We should stop all these parties and think of leaving this place. Soon." Then, turning toward Rave, she said, "Mr. Hunt, you should recognise your wife better than others. How are you so passive?"

"Because I know her well." Rave flashed a victory smile. "I'm sure she has started with the ship the same night she met Dr. Walker. You can't underestimate her. And she was here. Must have been days ago. Didn't you all notice that the house was so clean? As if someone had cleaned with a broom just before we arrived. After checking that her treasure has remained intact, she has left. She must have thought I had gone on another piracy venture without taking her."

"So where do you think she might be?" Walker asked.

"She must be on the way to Andaman again." Rave flashed a funny smile. "Somehow we didn't notice. It's possible her ship crossed ours during the night we arrived here. So, just relax and enjoy."

"We must plan to leave this place before anything happens," Walker said, and then, turning to Rupen, he asked, "Where do you plan to go from here, Mr. Naik?"

"Not sure, but definitely not to Lucknow. Should be some other place where your government is not very active. Maybe Orissa."

Rave grinned. "Careful, Mr. Naik. I have seen many places of India, and with two tribal wives, the society there may not accept you. Anyway, I am planning to drop you on Sagar Island."

"Sagar Island?" Rupen wondered why he hadn't thought of how he would go back to India. Calcutta was never an option.

"That island, you can see from here." Rave pointed toward the northeast. "A quiet place in Bengal province, and no English man would ever have stepped foot there. Only about four miles from here. The island's other sides are banks of the Hooghly River, and you can ferry to the other side in a short time. After dropping you there, we all will go to Rangoon."

Relief washed over Rupen. Rave's knowledge of India's geography was much better than his. "You wouldn't go to England?"

"No way." Rave laughed. "That bitch will find me anywhere in India, and even England. I must hide somewhere outside these two countries. Forever. Yes, Dr. Walker will take the next ship to England."

Dr. Walker inched forward with an enormous grin. "I have retired, and no one will ever think that I've got a share of Morticia's treasure. I will go back to London and settle there."

Mrs. Walker nodded and smiled at Mr. Walker's answer.

Rupen tried to focus his eyes on Sagar Island. The gateway to his motherland. He thought about suggesting that his sepoys settle there with their share of the booty. They could buy agricultural lands and do farming. They could even marry again. But he must advise them not to contact their families. That would be disastrous. English dogs could smell and fish them out. Should he also settle in Sagar? No way. He must go to some remote place and live in disguise—without even trying to contact anyone in Lucknow. Rupen Naik would die forever, and a fresh man would take birth. Shouldn't he think of a new name?

"Sir, sir."

Rupen's gaze flicked toward a sepoy who was running toward him.

"Sir, ship. Ship coming."

Rupen noticed the shade of a ghost in the sepoy's eyes.

Both Dr. Walker and Rave swung toward the south. Mrs. Walker clung to her husband. The ship was almost there. Why didn't they see that before?

Rupen chuckled. "The ship is coming for me, Mr. Hunt. You don't have to drop me on Sagar Island. I will hire it and will take wherever I like."

Rave's gaze was fixed on the ship. "Mort... Morticia," he fumbled, "she is coming. This is our ship."

Rupen noticed the blood had drained from Rave's face. His fingers clenched into a fist. "Don't worry, Mr. Hunt. My men will take care of everything. They haven't fired a single shot from the guns Dr. Walker has gifted us. When will they test if the firearms are working?"

"Not a time for jokes, Mr. Naik." Rave was sweating. "Now we must rush, get away. Or else..."

"Or else what, Mr. Hunt?" Rupen removed his pistol from his waistband. "How many sailors are there in your ship? Can they fight with my men?"

"You don't know her." Rave said. "She is like a queen on this island. She could mobilise the islanders. And your ten guns are no match to a thousand bows and arrows. They don't care how many people you gun down."

Dr. Walker came forward. "We have no time, Mr. Hunt. We must face them. And don't be afraid. This is the opportunity to get rid of that witch in your life. Let Mr. Naik and his sepoys do their job."

"Kill his wife? This is what you advised to your friend?" Mrs. Walker spat fire at her husband.

Mr. Walker turned to his wife. "We all will be in trouble if that woman leaves from here alive. Not only Mr. Hunt. She will spread the news, and the entire British government machinery will unleash hunting dogs behind us. This is rather an opportunity if you wish to live in peace after today."

Mrs. Walker let out a sigh.

"My men are ready, Dr. Walker." A hunger for war was boiling in Rupen.

His sepoys stood in position near him. "Don't fire until I say. There must be only some sailors and one woman on that side. So, relax. This should be the easiest fight of your life."

"Sir, we know Rave sahib's sailors," one sepoy chuckled. "They can't even hold a gun right. Haven't we gone so many times in his ship together to find treasure in the ocean?"

A loud laugh from the other soldiers startled a few birds in the bushes, and they fluttered away. This must be the last war they fight. Rupen noticed thirst for human blood dazzling in their eyes.

But Rave was standing like a statue. As if he could see his death approaching. Why was this man so worried about his woman?

When a small army platoon along with an officer got off the ship, Rupen's calculation changed.

"Mr. Hunt was right, Mr. Naik," Dr. Walker muttered, coming near him. "With just ten soldiers, you are no comparison to so many sepoys."

"I see." Rupen swallowed. "I was wrong. But my men and I will give them the toughest fight of their life. For them this might be another war. For all of us ex-prisoners it's a matter of life and death."

Then he swung toward his sepoys. "Friends, now we have to decide. Do we go back to the Black Waters prison, or die fighting here?"

"Die fighting!" the sepoys said in a chorus.

Walker was about to leave the place with his wife, when the officer from the other side—nearly a hundred gauges from them—shouted, "Dr. Walker, we see you have joined a convict and helped him flee. Mr. Tytler has given me orders to shoot you and even your wife. You are a traitor. Still, I am giving you one last opportunity. Please surrender. I will spare your life." Mrs. Walker muttered something to her husband, but Rupen couldn't hear.

He cast a quick glance around. Rave was sitting on the ground, sweating. Morticia was standing behind the soldiers with a sneer on her lips. Would he allow the bitch to win?

"Dr. Walker," Rupen said, "please don't surrender. You will rot in the prison, mostly in Andaman. I will save you at the cost of my own life. Believe me."

Walker threw a desperate glance at the sky while he and his wife were holding each other, his pistol in his hand.

"Officer," Rupen growled, "none of us will surrender. And we have enough ammunitions to kill each one of you. If you want to go back alive from here, just go back. And tell Tytler you didn't see any of us here. And leave this bitch of a woman with us. We'll take care of her."

"Wait, Mr. Naik," Morticia shouted from behind, "I am not involved in this war. I am with you. Please believe me. I am with you." She moved past the English team and came to Rupen's side, standing close to his wives.

Rave was right. No one could predict Morticia's motives. Rupen narrowed his eyes. Why would she bring English soldiers with her then?

Rupen glanced at the enemy. The most influential individual from that side allegedly changed sides already. There are only three English including the officer, and all others are Indians. Morticia quietly slipped away from the place. He decided to deal with the platoon first.

"Stop, officer," he yelled again. "What do you want to achieve? My sepoys and I do not care if we survive or die. But I will make sure all of you die here. In today's war, there will be no survivor."

A gun roared like thunder.

Rupen jumped to his side. Mrs. Walker's blood ridden body was shivering on the ground, while Dr. Walker stared at her, the pistol at his side smoking.

"Wait, Dr. Walker," he hollered, "what did you do?"

"Thanks, Mr. Naik. For everything." Another shot from Walker's pistol pierced his own skull, scattering pieces of flesh, bones, and blood—and some blood on Rupen's face and body.

Wiping the blood to clear his vision, Rupen swung back to face the government soldiers. His victory seemed to slip away from him when he noticed two Indian soldiers carrying a cannon from the ship.

"Last chance, Mr. Naik," the official shouted. "You still have time to surrender. I wouldn't kill anyone. Dr. Walker was a traitor and killed himself. You were spending life in prison, anyway. You and your sepoys. Just come back inside the prison. I guarantee life for you and your men. Remember, no death punishment if you come back."

Rupen stilled. The sight of the massive cannon had reduced his confidence by half. Sure, he was ready to die. But his wives? Didn't he promise them a better life? Shouldn't he at least make a last effort before succumbing to death?

His wives were standing behind them, even after Morticia had vanished from the scene. Rupen thought for a moment to ask them to hide somewhere, but time was not on his side.

"Your last chance is finished, Mr. Naik." The officer standing above a mound commanded as if he had already won. Then, looking at the two Indian sepoys near the cannon he said, "Be prepared and fire when I say. Understood?"

The men took position near the cannon. Rupen's sepoys also took their positions. "We are ready to kill or die, sir. Do not surrender. We wouldn't go back to that prison again," one sepoy yelled.

"Mr. Naik, I am counting. One. Two...and now three. Fire."

The silence of the massive cannon was deafening. The officer screamed, "I said, fire, now!"

The sepoys stood still.

"You bloody Indian dogs," he squealed. "Soldiers!" He gazed at his two English soldiers and commanded, "Finish those two traitors!"

Rupen didn't waste time. "My dear friends," he addressed the Indian sepoys standing idly by the English cannon, "I am Rupen Naik, chief of the army of Awadh kingdom. You saw with your own eyes how this English officer is treating you. Now is the time to save the honour of your motherland. Remember, you are saving your mother's honour."

The guns pointed at him bent down.

"No way," the officer thundered. "I will never allow this! I will send all of you to jail, remember. Raise your guns. And fire! Now!"

Guns behind Rupen fired. Before he could realise, the officer and two English soldiers succumbed to the ground.

Rupen's soldiers shouted in a chorus, "Hail, Mother India." The Indian soldiers on the British side also joined the slogan, "*Jai ho*, Mother India."

Rupen cast a victory glance at his wives, both were smiling. But where was Morticia? Rave was still looking tense.

"Thanks, brothers on both my sides—those who were with me and those who just joined me. I have already shared some of the treasure I had obtained. And everyone who joined me will also receive the same. I know the British will punish you if you go back to the barracks. None of you will go back. I will see that you all enjoy lives of abundance."

He turned back at Rave. "Cheers, my friend! Now we have won. Now all that's left is your wife."

"We won?" Questions flickered from Rave's eyes.

"You still don't believe?"

"You don't understand Morticia, Mr. Naik. Careful."

"Careful of what? All the English soldiers are dead. Do you think another shipload of English soldiers will arrive?"

"No, but she is the—"

"Queen." A harsh female voice made Rupen jump on his heels and look up.

Almost a hundred islanders were standing on the hillock, with arrows ready to jump from their angry bows.

The tribals were less than fifty gauges away. Rupen knew he must handle this with care.

"Please do not ask your men to fire, Mr. Naik." Rave's voice was low but commanding. "Hundreds of others must be behind them, and they wouldn't stop even if your guns killed half of them."

Victory came for Rupen, but disappeared in a moment, like lightning. He inhaled a deep breath to keep his calm, as he used to do during the wars. But this dilemma haunted him. He had never thought of this situation. He must find a way. Where else would his diplomacy skills work?

"Hold on Mrs. Hunt," he shouted toward the hill. "We must talk."

"Talk about what? After taking all my treasure and distributing among yourselves?"

"We will—"

"Wait, Mr. Naik? And Morticia, please stop. No more bloodshed, please."

Rupen swung around to find Amelia and Nick approaching. Rupen was sure both had come with Morticia in the same ship. Amelia came and stood between the tribals and Rupen's soldiers.

"Amelia," Morticia yelled, "please come to my side, I can't leave these people alive."

She climbed the hill, holding a leather-bound book. "I am coming to you, Mort darling," she yelled. "Please stop your men. I know you will win, but so many tribal men will also die. Nobody wins this war. And I promise, you will get your treasure back."

Rupen's jaw dropped in shock as he beheld all this, causing him to startle when Dr. Wilson stopped quietly at his side.

"Who told you about that?" Morticia yelled.

"You, hours ago. About your treasure." Amelia went atop the hill and mingled with the tribals while Nick continued standing like a statue.

"Dr. Wilson," Morticia shouted, "please come onto the hill. These tribal men here are dumb. They will kill everybody on that side. I will first finish my eunuch husband and then take care of the Indians. Please come, quick."

Rupen didn't know what to do. He couldn't command his men to kill the islanders; they were all innocent. And killing Morticia meant certain death to him and his men from the islanders. He was at a loss as to how this woman mobilised them all against his troop. *Ma Kali, please guide me. Help me. I don't want to kill any innocent tribal.*

His gaze went to Amelia. She had opened a notebook and was showing something to an elderly islander who, with his feather cap, looked like their chief—*sardar*.

Suddenly, he got an idea. He turned to his sepoys. "Friends, please deposit your guns on the ground and stand armless," Rupen commanded in Hindi. "We wouldn't want to harm any tribal brother."

All the guns kissed the ground in an instant.

Rupen cast a quick glance at his soldiers and winked, then he tried to meet the *sardar's* gaze. Could he signal him for a ceasefire?

Morticia roared again, ordering the tribal men to attack Rupen and his troop.

"*Sardar!*" Rupen didn't know if his Hindi word for the tribal head would reach him, but he kept going anyway. "Please do not attack. I am surrendering to you. I respect you." He raised both hands in the air.

He knew all these words had no meaning. Neither the *sardar* nor his men would understand those words.

Rupen's gaze fell on Amelia, who was still trying to communicate with the chief. Did she know their language? What was in her notebook?

One of the tribal men raised his bow and fixed an arrow on it.

"Good, now fire!" Morticia screamed again.

"Sir, please allow us to raise our guns, sir, please," one sepoy requested, "or else he will kill us."

"Ma Kali will save you." Rupen closed his eyes and muttered a prayer. Maybe the arrow will pierce his chest first as he was the leader on this side.

He kept his eyes closed, ready to face his death.

The arrow left the bow. Rupen braced for the impact and shot a prayer to goddess Kali. Within seconds a death roar pounds in his ears, and he opened his eyes to find Morticia in her own blood puddle. He folded his hands for goddess Kali who could do wonders for his devotees and gave him a much-deserved victory

The *sardar* screamed, raising his hand. Rupen's soldiers cheered loudly, raising their guns above their heads and dancing.

The soldiers who had deserted the British officer sprinted toward the Indian sepoys and joined in their dancing. "Jai ho, Mother India."

Amelia marched down the hill, joining Nick, and stood near Rupen. "You are now safe, Mr. Naik."

"Thank you, Mrs. Lawrence. I owe my and my people's lives to you. You changed everything. How did you manage this?"

She flashed a smile at him. "Another time, Mr. Naik. And yes, I have rejected my ex-husband's surname. My name is now Amelia Elliott Spencer. My husband had betrayed you and killed your family. I had promised Sehnaz to save you."

Dr. Nick Wilson smiled at them both. "You deserve this, Mr. Naik. Amelia has told me everything. Now you are a free man again."

Rave came to Rupen and hugged him. "We've won, Mr. Naik. Finally, we have won. I'm so happy."

"Yes, Mr. Hunt, this's Independence Day for you." Rupen burst into a loud laugh.

"Mr. Naik. You were right in not attacking the islanders. You are a genuine leader. Thank you." He gazed at Amelia with moist eyes. "You had a magic notebook. How did you convince the chief?"

She flashed another mysterious smile. "Another time, Mr. Hunt."

"You are a wonderful lady."

"If only Sehnaz were alive today," Amelia said, her eyes pooling.

The gun fell from Rupen's hand. "Sehnaz dead? How do you know?"

"Morticia had visited Coco before coming to Andaman. There was someone who knew Sehnaz. She has died of malaria. In fact, we both had planned to come together to Andaman to free you. You are free now, but I lost my best friend."

Amelia's words filled Rupen's ears. Could he shake them out and make Sehnaz alive again?

Grief ran through Rupen's nerves. He had two tribal wives. But Sehnaz? She had done so much for him. Lifting his heavy head, he gazed at the tribal men. They were leaving one after another. The sun had already gone behind the peak, and darkness was almost there.

Rupen's gaze flicked on two familiar faces coming down the hill.

Was he dreaming? A woman and a man were coming toward them. She looked like Sehnaz. And the man, like Sheru. How did Sheru get there?

The Sehnaz-looking woman began running down the hill, her arms open wide. "Amelia!"

Amelia turned and beheld the woman, her knees buckling and a joyful shriek erupting from her throat. "Oh my God, Sehnaz, you're alive? Thank God!" The women fell into each other in a messy, tearful hug.

Rupen, standing frozen, was watching them both. He, too, wished to gather Sehnaz in his arms, his love. But somehow Sheru's presence near her built a mental wall between. Why? Wasn't Sheru also his trusted man?

His two tribal wives came and stood near him. Rupen thought about how he would introduce them to Sehnaz. The girls deserved his respect, irrespective of his past with Sehnaz.

Sheru proceeded toward Rupen, pushing through the crowd of Indian soldiers. Rupen met his gaze—just as loyal and trusted as he was before. But he also noticed a loyalty and love for Sehnaz in his eyes as Sheru exchanged a smiling glance with her. Sheru approached and saluted Rupen.

Rupen let out a smile of recognition at Sheru and said, "How are you, Sheru? I appreciate you are still guarding Sehnaz with the same zeal as when I had entrusted you with the job. Well done."

Then he turned to Sehnaz without waiting for Sheru's reply. "I didn't get the opportunity to meet you since the mutiny began against the British. Without you, I could never have fought the British. Glad to see you after so many years, at last. But I never expected to see you here, on this island." Rupen still wanted to move forward and hug Sehnaz, but his gut said to wait. "How did you arrive here? I'm still confused. Am I in a dream?"

Sehnaz giggled. "It's true. I was hiding in Coco Islands along with Sheru. I tricked an English officer to help us come to Jambu. But that is a long story. I will tell you everything afterwards. Sheru and I both were living in this old palace for the past ten days, as the ship we planned to take had some fault and Sheru couldn't fix it. Yesterday when we saw a ship approaching, we thought Morticia was coming, and we both escaped into the forest for the night. We were watching the drama from a distance and came to meet you when the fight ended."

"Yes, the fight ended. This fight." Rupen made a few firm and precise movements, looking at his soldiers and the dead bodies of the English soldiers.

Rave spoke to Sehnaz for the first time and said, "Now I understand why the old palace looked like someone had cleaned it with a broom. I feared it was Morticia."

"Yes, it was me, Mr. Hunt," Sehnaz said.

Amelia came close to Sehnaz and stood by her side.

"Rupen, do you know what Amelia has written in her diary? That the war against the invaders had just begun, so it's not right to say the British won the war of 1857."

Rupen cast an appreciative glance at Amelia. His heart bubbled with gratitude, but no words came to his mind about how to express the same.

"Mata Radhe has given a prediction—that India will be free on 15 August 1947," Amelia said with a broad smile on her face. "None of us will survive to witness that day, but there will be a prolonged war. And finally the end will be ours. Sorry, I'm talking like an Indian. I've become one practically." She giggled.

Rave burst into a loud laugh. "1947? I love it. But today I got my freedom, and I don't mind if the English finally leave this country one day."

A chorus of laughter followed Rave's comment.

"True, Mr. Hunt," Rupen said, turning to him. His voice was that of a concerned leader. "We must not forget to give a proper and respectful burial to Dr. and Mrs. Walker. And to the slain British soldiers. And even to your wife, Morticia."

Rave let out a half-smile. "Burial to Dr. and Mrs. Walker is understood. Even dead English soldiers. But why Morticia? She had no quality to become even a woman, forget becoming a wife."

One soldier came forward and said, "Sir, we all are planning a daylong celebration. Why would we bury the English soldiers? Weren't they our enemy? We should throw their bodies in the water, like the way they treat our dead."

Rupen walked to the nearest mound and stood on it. "My friends, in our culture, we never disrespect the dead. And taking revenge on the dead is a fool's dream. If we do the same, the way the English treat us, in what way do we differ from them? I would even like to send off the dead English soldiers with due respect, because they were soldiers and died fighting a war. Yes, we all must celebrate the victory, but after burying the dead. Did I say anything wrong, Sehnaz?"

Sehnaz smiled at him.

"Sehnaz, I just want to know—why did you hide in Coco Islands? Why did you leave India in the first place?"

Sehnaz met his gaze and said, "Amelia and I were coming to Andaman Islands with a plan to free you. But once we left Calcutta, we got the information that the British might capture me for a war crime. I had to escape when the ship was at Coco, and Amelia travelled to Andaman alone. At last, Amelia and I are successful. You are free from prison."

Rupen returned with a grin. "Yes. Thank you so much. You are a genuine friend. But I have done something without your knowledge. I hope you will forgive me. It was essential in my game plan to save my life and my freedom."

"What?" Sehnaz bit her lip, her eyes dancing with unspoken words.

"I have married these two tribal girls. They are the daughters of the *sardar* in an Andaman Island. And I have promised them a respectful life."

"Wonderful!" Sehnaz said as she stood near Sheru. "I also have married. Sheru is my husband now."

Amelia shrieked as if something fell from the heaven. "Oh, my God! I am so thrilled, Sehnaz! You are a married woman now. You are a lucky man, Sheru."

"And what about you, Amelia?" Sehnaz asked.

Amelia laughed. "Me? Another time."

CHAPTER THIRTY-NINE

AMELIA, 15 AUGUST 1863, AFTERNOON, SULTANPUR, INDIA

Seated on the balcony overlooking the River Gomti, I open my diary—Amelia Elliott Spencer's diary. I have named this *The Black Waters*.

Isn't it unusual to name a diary?

Yes. But I hope one day, long after my death, someone will publish my story, and the name of the book will be *The Black Waters*. And my previous diary's name is *The Pink Mutiny*.

These diaries, if the authorities find them, could send hundreds of people, including me, behind bars. Some people might even face death punishments.

This is my story. I was Mrs. Amelia Lawrence after my wedding to Brigadier Colin Lawrence. I have written in *The Pink Mutiny* how I became Amelia Elliott Spencer.

After leaving Jambu Island, Mr. Rave Hunt's ship sailed to Sagar Island, which is just west of mainland Bengal. Rupen, along with his two tribal wives and his sepoys, all got off there. Rupen advised his sepoys never to visit their native villages, even though they might think the sepoys were still in Andaman prison or dead. They must have settled there. The treasure Rupen had given them should have been enough to buy farmlands.

Sehnaz comes to the balcony and leans against the siderail, watching the river.

"Sehnaz, do you know what is going on with Rupen and his wives these days?"

Sehnaz turns to me and chortles. "I thought madam was preparing an exam paper, and you are writing in your diary? Show me!"

I let out a giggle. Whatever I write is always an open book for her. Especially if I intend for the public to see this book a century later, even more.

"I had been to the garden to supervise the workers who are clearing the weeds. One of them had worked as a servant of Rupen when I was in Varanasi. He said to me Rupen is now living in Orissa state. On an island inside Chilika Lake. I don't know how much of this is true. I also don't know if he has taken a new name. But news moves through word of mouth. He must be careful of the British spies."

"All right, let me write two lines for him. And Mr. Rave Hunt?"

"I do not know where Mr. Rave Hunt has gone. I remember he had told you he would settle in Rangoon."

"Yes, but that was when Morticia was alive. But he has no danger from her now. All right dear, you want to see what I wrote? See here. Starts with you and Sheru."

Sehnaz reaches up to tuck her dark hair behind her ear and takes my book.

"Sehnaz, Sheru, and I came back to Sultanpur. Sadhna and Vanaja, also—they are living with me. Before we both had left Sultanpur for Andaman, she was living with me under the same roof. But now that she has married Sheru Pandey, I gifted her a part of the land I am living on now. She has built a house and is living with her new husband. Sheru's name was on the dead prisoners' list when Mr. Rave Hunt lost him in the Great Coco Islands. Here, he is identifying himself as a brahmin-turned-business owner from Orissa (he was, in fact, from Bihar). Sehnaz has changed her name to

> Sanju. In the conservative society of India, a Hindu and
> a Muslim living as a couple is taboo. But for me, she is
> still Sehnaz."

She hands the diary back to me. "Amelia, can you add another line for Sheru?"

"What?"

"That Sheru has a steamboat in the Gomti River, and he is transporting goods between Lucknow and Sultanpur. He is an entrepreneur in his own right."

"And what about your pregnancy?" I chuckle as I take the book and begin her additions.

> "Either a little Sheru or baby Sehnaz is awaiting our
> welcome in a few months from now."

Sehnaz blushes. "Wait, Amelia. First, let us find out if it is a boy or girl. What would you love?"

"Me? We are all girls living on this little island, other than Sheru. Don't you think Sheru is surrounded by enough females? A boy would be good for him. And you can think of a girl in the next round."

We both laugh. "It is in God's hands, if I will get a boy or a girl. Do you know what the doctor said?"

"Doctor? Can he know the sex of the child even before the birth?"

"No, he can't. But he said I might get twins."

I jump up and hug her. "Oh, that is lovely! I will play with them. Can't wait until they come to this world. I love you, Sehnaz."

Sehnaz rolls her eyes and deadpans, "Ha, ha, ha. I will bear all the extra pain to deliver two babies at one time, and you are thinking of how to play with them?"

"What should I do? I will be their aunt." I laugh.

"Don't show your teeth. Please show me what you are writing."

I read out loud.

"My application to the government for a girls-only
school got approved. I have been appointed as the
headteacher. Sehnaz will also join the school as a Hindi
teacher. Besides, she is also writing poems in her spare
time. Mr. Rave Hunt and Rupen Naik were kind
enough to donate a portion of Morticia's treasure to us.
We use that fund to build and maintain a girl's hostel in
Sultanpur."

"Fantastic. How many pages are left in this book?"

"Only two. I must finish The Black Waters now. No more writing
for some time after I finish this one. You got me?"

"Yes, but shouldn't you write about how you convinced Jambu's
tribal chief to attack Morticia? Without her death, we all would have
died there."

"Right. Let me put in few lines."

I read out loud as I pen the lines.

"You must want to know—what did I show the tribal
head from my diary in Jambu Island that caused his
men to revolt against Morticia and kill her? Was the
chief an educated man?

No.

Do you remember Sadhna had drawn a picture of
Morticia forcing the tribal women into sexual acts?
Tribals protect their women at all costs—just like they
did with the English soldier when we were on Jambu

Island while going to Andaman. The chief ordered to
kill Morticia for the same reason they had eliminated the
English soldier."

I look up from the book. "Did I cover everything?"

"No, Amelia madam. What about your love story?"

"Love story? Sehnaz, I am single and don't think I will ever marry."

"But you have written some detail about Eliza and Dr. Nick
Wilson. Where are they now? Why did you refuse his wedding
proposal? Please write."

I add a paragraph.

"Yes, for the second time in my life, I had fallen in love
with a man. But our paths are different. He wanted to
go back to London and settle there. But my life is here,
in Sultanpur. I didn't even plan to visit my parents in
London. Until now I am communicating through
letters, and they are happy with the decisions I have
made with my life."

I set my pen down and look up at Sehnaz. "God has created
circumstances to keep me single, so that I can be useful for women's
emancipation in this country."

"You are right, Amelia. But God has also kept Harry single so far, so
that he could finance our schools."

I blink a smile of approval. "Yes, he also loves to take part in the
girls' education. I forgot to tell you. He has sent a letter."

"Letter?"

"Yes, he is coming next month for some business work and will be
with us for a month. He would love to see how much we have
progressed in female education here."

"Female education? Or he wants to see the beautiful female behind
the education?"

We laugh together. Yes, I still adore Harry, my forever first love, even after he declined to marry at the last minute.

If you are reading this a hundred years or more after the year 1863, I hope your society is much different from the society I am in. Although I know there will always be different beliefs and opinions in any generation, just like there will always be good people and bad people. But I pray that good may always triumph, regardless of societies or the centuries that span between them. Good must always win.

Lots of water has flowed in the Gomti River since I left Lucknow in 1857. I had one very close friend there, Nancy.

I still remember that evening in May of 1857, when I had packed my bags and was about to flee from Colin's home in The Residency. But at the last moment, I hesitated.

"What are you afraid of, Amelia?" Nancy had asked me.

"What if Colin gets hold of me? Will I survive his anger? And what will happen to you?"

I can never forget the painful smile Nancy had on her face. "The rebel war might continue for several months; my husband told me. I am sure your brigadier husband can never leave the barracks to come home."

"The horse cart is ready?" I asked her.

"Yes. Also, the house I have arranged for you. On the outskirts of Lucknow. You will be there only for a night and leave the next morning. Another cart will pick you up tomorrow morning, so that there will be no trace of where you have gone."

I took a long pause.

"What are you thinking, Amelia?"

"Rebel soldiers. I mean Indian sepoys."

She came and wrapped her arm around my shoulder. "Believe me, I have been in India for over ten years. I can guarantee, no Indian soldier will harm you—even if they count each single English as an enemy."

"How so?"

"Because you are a woman. This is in their culture. It would be a sin for them to harm a woman. I mean any woman, including us whites."

Without Nancy's advice and courage, I could have never left the hell I was in. And now, she has come here to meet me after so many years—to Sultanpur. Alone.

Nancy plans to spend a month with me.

"Do you still write a diary?" she asked me when we were sitting on the balcony of my mansion sipping tea.

"You still remember my habit?" I flash a smile at her wonderful memory. "I even gave names to them."

"You diary has a name?"

"Nancy, my diaries are in fact books for the future century. It was not my idea. Rather, Sehnaz's."

"Sehnaz's?"

"Yes, it was the fifteenth of August, in 1860. The book I was writing was on its last page. Sehnaz knew how I loved the pink colour and had preserved the pink clothing I was wearing when I became a dancer. Pink is also a masculine colour, it denotes strength. She also said that even though the Indian rebels lost the mutiny, I won the mutiny against my abusive husband. She wrote *The Pink Mutiny* on the cover page and made another register for me."

"You got the idea of the book, then?"

"Yes. And I have a plan." I wink at Nancy.

"What plan?"

"If Harry helps, I will open a museum in Sultanpur. My two books will be in sealed envelopes there. I will write notes on them, then after more than a century, someone should publish them as books. People will see a horrible part of the history of this country."

Nancy lets out a smile. "Lovely."

"Let's now talk about you."

"What?"

"I had come here to perform a dance for Harry in 1857, when I heard about The Residency siege. My heart was crying for you and everyone else I knew when I was living in Lucknow."

"Those days were horrible, Amelia. After the Bibighar Massacre, we were living each moment, fearing how long we would survive. It's difficult to believe that the man who had besieged the fort was Sehnaz's lover."

Why didn't I talk to Sehnaz when I first saw she had the map?

"I had seen the map with Sehnaz, long before the siege happened. But in those days, she was a different Sehnaz. She had fire in her blood against the British occupiers. It took time for me to find out beneath that fire there is a soft and loving heart."

"We survived, Amelia."

"If you are okay, can you please tell me what happened after I left?"

"I will. And I will let you read the diary I've written."

"I can read your diary?"

"Why not? If you are ready to allow me to read yours. I have not only written about the siege, but much more. Starting with how your husband had made me his sex slave and incidents that happened after you left."

"Can I suggest something, Nancy?"

"What?"

"Please give it a name. And let's also keep your book in the museum with a similar note. Only if you approve. You will be the hero of that story when people read it after a hundred years."

"I would love it. But what about the name, can you suggest something?"

"The Residency Siege."

FROM THE AUTHOR

Thank you so much for reading The Black Waters. I hope Amelia, Sehnaz and Sheru's story appealed you.

If you enjoyed this book, Please leave a review now. They can be as long or as short as you'd like. Even a star rating is amazing and appreciated. Thanks in advance. I love getting the feedback, and your review will help other readers discover the book. You may also leave a review on Goodreads.

Please sign up below for my newsletter, I will send links to many FREE Books and discounted books.

Email Sign Up

https://blisspublishing.com.au/sign-up/

You will never receive emails unless there's a new book to share, and I will never share your email with anyone else. You can unsubscribe any time by simply clicking the "Unsubscribe" link in the newsletters.

Please connect with me on Twitter (https://mobile.twitter.com/AESpencer4) and Goodreads (https://www.goodreads.com/author/show/21306969.A_E_Spencer)